# THE WAR BETWEEN US

## *Friends and Enemies*

BOOK 1
UNCIVIL WAR SERIES

Rosie Bosse lives and writes on a small ranch in Northeast Kansas with her sweetheart and husband of many years. She has always been fascinated with American history, and her novels allow her to combine that interest with her love of storytelling. "The War Between Us" is the first novel in her *Uncivil War Series*.

*Home on the Range* was her first series, and it includes eleven novels. That series is set in the American West between 1868 and 1888. Rosie also writes children's books about farm animals and anything else that comes to her mind.

May her books pull you in and hold you until the last line, and may her "friends" become your "friends."

*Sampler featuring the design of Order # 11 Civil War Quilt*

# THE WAR BETWEEN US

## *Friends and Enemies*

**ROSIE BOSSE**

**COVER ILLUSTRATED BY CYNTHIA MARTIN**

POST ROCK
PUBLISHING

ISBN: Softcover - 978-1-958227-47-3
ISBN: eBook - 978-1-958227-48-0

**POST ROCK PUBLISHING**

Post Rock Publishing
17055 Day Rd.
Onaga, KS 66521

www.rosiebosse.com

I dedicate this book to our American Civil
War soldiers on both sides of that terrible
war. May they never be forgotten.

# DIVISION OF STATES DURING THE AMERICAN CIVIL WAR

Officially fought from April 12, 1861, through April 9, 1865

| Confederate/ Southern States | Union/ Northern States | Border States |
|---|---|---|
| Pro-Slavery States that Seceded<br><br>Pro-State's Rights | Anti-Slavery States<br><br>Pro-Federal Government | Slave-holding States that Remained in the Union |
| North Carolina | Maine | Missouri |
| South Carolina | New York | Delaware (Northern State) |
| Virginia | New Hampshire | Maryland (Northern State) |
| Mississippi | Vermont | Kentucky |
| Florida | Massachusetts | |
| Alabama | Connecticut | |
| Tennessee | Rhode Island | |
| Georgia | Pennsylvania | |
| Louisiana | New Jersey | |
| Texas | Ohio | |
| Arkansas | Indiana | |
| | Iowa | |
| | Illinois | |
| | Michigan | |
| | Wisconsin | |
| | Minnesota | |
| | Nevada | |
| | California | |
| | Oregon | |
| | Kansas | |

# MISCELLANEOUS INFORMATION

- CSA: Confederate States of America

- Distance from Chattanooga, Tennessee, to Chickamauga, Georgia: 15 miles

- Distance from Chattanooga, Tennessee, to Atlanta, Georgia: 118 miles

- Confederate Trains: Speed dropped from 25 miles per hour to less than 10 miles per hour by 1863 due to lack of repairs and shortage of fuel.

- Georgia: Most self-sufficient of all Southern states because they did not export their cotton—all produce was marketed within the state. Union blockades did not affect them as much financially in the early days of the war.

- As the war continued, food and feed supplies as well as processing plants were destroyed. Hunger and deprivation became rampant throughout all the Southern states.

- While the Civil War divided the North and the South, the slavery issue was not cut and dried. In fact, slave ownership was accepted in some of the Northern states. Not all in the South believed in slavery either, but most were strong proponents of state's rights. There was and still is wide debate over whether the Civil War was fought for state's rights or slavery.

# CONFEDERATES

Other names used by the Confederates for the American Civil War: The War Between the States, The War for Southern Independence, The War Against Northern Aggression, and The Second War of Independence

## CHARACTER LIST

### CONFEDERATES, CONFEDERATE SYMPATHIZERS, SOUTHERN SYMPATHIZERS, REBELS, REBS, JOHNNY REB, BUSHWHACKERS

## *Fictional Characters*

**Bates County, Missouri/Kansas Border**

Avaline Marie Olivia Bowman: Also known as Ava Bowman, Ella Bowman, and Ella Bradley

Deuce: Ava's stud horse

Lieutenant Charlie Bowman: Ava's brother and a Confederate soldier

Daniel Bowman: Ava's father—Barrel maker who worked for the Union Army. Also raised and sold horses

Mary Bowman: Ava's mother—Southern Sympathizer

Granny Bowman: Ava's grandmother and Daniel's mother—Olivia Eleanora Avaline Bradley Bowman—known as Libby—Southern Sympathizer and despised Yankees

Alfred Bowman: Granny's deceased husband

**Battle of Chickamauga, Northwest Georgia**

Captain Eberle

Sergeant Marley

Private Weatherby

Private "Johnny Luck" Caston

Doctor Reuben Williams: Surgeon—also known as Dr. Jones

Captain Stegall

Private Andy Andrews

Private Wes Leiker

Private Paneer

Private Timpkins

"One Shot": Famous sniper but never identified

**Chattanooga, Tennessee, and St. Louis, Missouri**

Sister Marie Christi and her nuns: Treated and cared for civilians and soldiers on both sides of the war—answerable only to the Good Lord

# Historical Characters

General Braxton Bragg: Field Commander during Battle of Chickamauga

General Joseph Wheeler: Army of Tennessee—captured Gordon House during Battle of Chickamauga

Missouri State Guard: Fierce guerilla fighters

Quantrill's Raiders: Led by William Quantrill—continued to be active after Quantrill's death in June 1865

Bushwhackers: Were active after the War Against Northern Aggression ended

# UNIONISTS

Other names used by the Union for the American Civil War: The War of the Rebellion, The War of the Southern Rebellion, War of Secession, and The Civil War

## CHARACTER LIST

### UNION, UNION SYMPATHIZERS, YANKEES, FEDERALS, UNIONISTS, BLUEBELLIES, JAYHAWKERS

## Fictional Characters

**Kansas Red Legs:** *Historical fighting unit but these soldiers are fictional*
Sergeant Nielson
Privates Mitchell and Jack "Slug" Cotter
Private Billy Goat: From Indian Territory—service unknown

**Merrill's Horse:** *Historical military force but these soldiers are fictional*
Captain Noble Headrick
Lieutenant Noah Lampkin
Corporal Boston Blake
Private Hanson
Private Peter Headrick: Captain Headrick's little brother

**St. Louis and Benton Barracks**
Huck (Walter) Layton: Mailman and driver
Evie Smith: Volunteer nurse
Major Lew Minsky: Judge Advocate
Lucy Weatherby Sneed: Older widow and friend to all Union officers
Will Tillman: Young soldier in Benton Barracks Hospital
Major John Reynolds: Judge Advocate
Miss Jessie Reynolds: Major Reynolds' little sister
Henry "Badger" McCune: Raised, trained, and sold mules

**Fulton County Jail, Atlanta, Georgia**

Private Jackson Lampkin: Nephew of Lieutenant Noah Lampkin
Private Feathers
Privates Bixby and Sutter
Privates Balt and Clement
Lieutenant John Hermann and Private Karl Hermann: Brothers
Private Mert Dixon

**Battle of Chickamauga, Northwest Georgia**

Major Burke: Red Leg surgeon
Sergeant John Wilsey: 11th Kansas Cavalry. Also stationed at Benton
  Barracks

**Chattanooga, Tennessee**

Doctors Watt and McCay
Private James Espy
Private Pack O'Neill
Private James Reid
Oscar Quick: Hostler and handyman

**Centralia, Missouri, in the Heart of "Little Dixie"**

Major Johnson
Corporal Barnes
Sergeant English
Private Trainer Freeman: Freed Slave
Private Fastly Walker: Freed Slave
Private Goodly Tinker: Freed Slave

**Various Other Locations**

Claudia "Chloe" Moore: Volunteer nurse from Lawrence, Kansas
Owen Weatherby: Orphan Train in Louisville, Kentucky
General Ault: Temporary Commander, Fort Leavenworth, Kansas

# Historical Characters

General Thomas Ewing, Jr.: Commander of District of the Border (Between Kansas and Missouri)

Captain Hartwig: Commanding Officer of Harrisonville, Missouri, in 1863

Nurse Emily Parsons: Supervisor of Nurses, Benton Barracks Hospital, St. Louis, Missouri

Nurse Belle Coddington: Matron in Charge of Measles Unit, Benton Barracks Hospital, St. Louis, Missouri

Colonel Benjamin Bonneville: Commander of Benton Barracks, St. Louis, Missouri

General William S. Rosecrans: Field Commander, Battle of Chickamauga

Doctor Mary Edwards Walker: Contract Acting Assistant Surgeon, Battle of Chickamauga

Solon Hyde: Hospital Steward, 17th Regiment Ohio Volunteer Infantry, Battle of Chickamauga. He wrote *A Captive of the War* documenting his experiences in the Civil War.

Private Thomas Gallagher: Company G, 29th Regiment of Massachusetts Infantry Volunteers. Thomas is the great-grandfather of the author. He lost his right leg below the knee due to a rifled musket ball injury. A copy of his discharge certificate is included in this book.

Mother Bickerdyke: Nurse in multiple locations and field hospitals

Colonel and Brigadier General Lewis Merrill: Organized Merrill's Horse and was Colonel of Volunteers. Promoted twice to Brigadier General

Major General Henry Halleck: Commander of the Western Department

# DISCHARGE CERTIFICATE.

## To all Whom it May Concern:

Know ye, That *Thomas Gallagher* , a *Private* of Company *G,* *Twenty-ninth* Regiment of *Massachusetts Infantry* VOLUNTEERS, who was *enrolled* on the *eleventh* day of *January* , one thousand eight hundred and *sixty-two* , to serve *three years* , was Discharged from the service of the United States on the *twelfth* day of *March* , one thousand eight hundred and *sixty-three* , by reason of *disability* .

This Certificate is given under the provisions of the Act of Congress approved July 1, 1902, "to authorize the Secretary of War to furnish certificates in lieu of lost or destroyed discharges," to honorably discharged officers or enlisted men or their widows, upon evidence that the original discharge certificate has been lost or destroyed, and upon the condition imposed by said Act that this certificate "shall not be accepted as a voucher for the payment of any claim against the United States for pay, bounty, or other allowances, or as evidence in any other case."

Given at the War Department, Washington, D. C., this *twenty-eighth* day of *July* , one thousand nine hundred and *thirteen* .

By authority of the Secretary of War:

F. J. Korsten
Adjutant General.

(A. G. O. 150)

1025068

General Order No. 11,

Headquarters District of the Border,
Kansas City, August 25, 1863.

1. All persons living in Jackson, Cass, and Bates counties, Missouri, and in that part of Vernon included in this district, except those living within one mile of the limits of Independence, Hickman's Mills, Pleasant Hill, and Harrisonville, and except those in that part of Kaw Township, Jackson County, north of Brush Creek and west of Big Blue, are hereby ordered to remove from their present places of residence within fifteen days from the date hereof.

Those who within that time establish their loyalty to the satisfaction of the commanding officer of the military station near their present place of residence will receive from him a certificate stating the fact of their loyalty, and the names of the witnesses by whom it can be shown. All who receive such certificates will be permitted to remove to any military station in this district, or to any part of the State of Kansas, except the counties of the eastern border of the State. All others shall remove out of the district. Officers commanding companies and detachments serving in the counties named will see that this paragraph is promptly obeyed.

2. All grain and hay in the field or under shelter, in the district from which inhabitants are required to remove, within reach of military stations after the 9th day of September next, will be taken to such stations and turned over to the proper officers there and report of the amount so turned over made to district headquarters, specifying the names of all loyal owners and amount of such product taken from them. All grain and hay found in such district after the 9th day of September next, not convenient to such stations, will be destroyed.

3. The provisions of General Order No. 10 from these headquarters will be at once vigorously executed by officers commanding in the parts of the district and at the station not subject to the operations of paragraph 1 of this order, and especially the towns of Independence, Westport and Kansas City.

4. Paragraph 3, General Order No. 10 is revoked as to all who have borne arms against the Government in the district since the 20th day of August, 1863.

By order of Brigadier General Ewing.

H. Hannahs, Adjt.-Gen'l.

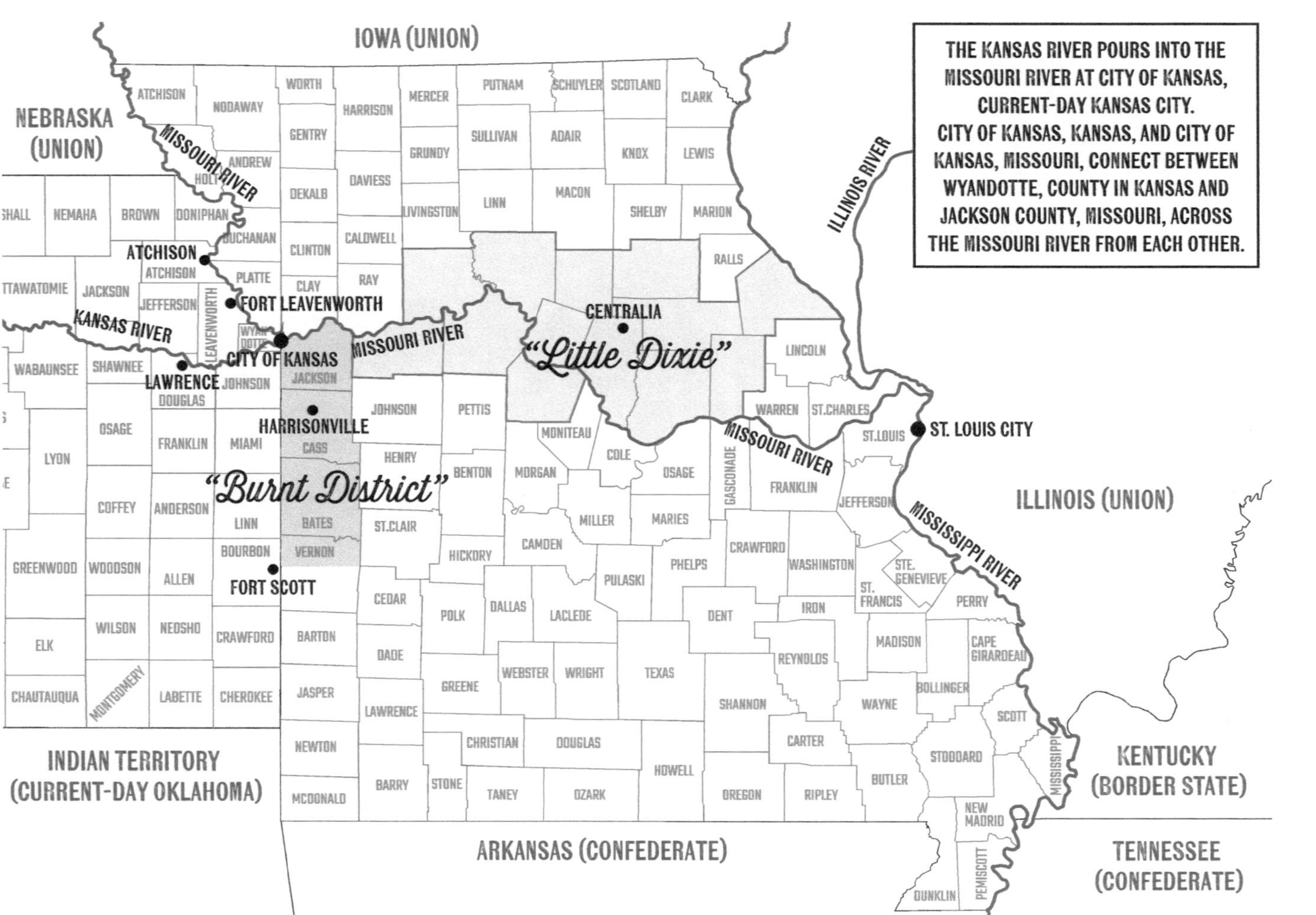

THE KANSAS RIVER POURS INTO THE MISSOURI RIVER AT CITY OF KANSAS, CURRENT-DAY KANSAS CITY. CITY OF KANSAS, KANSAS, AND CITY OF KANSAS, MISSOURI, CONNECT BETWEEN WYANDOTTE, COUNTY IN KANSAS AND JACKSON COUNTY, MISSOURI, ACROSS THE MISSOURI RIVER FROM EACH OTHER.
IOWA (UNION)
NEBRASKA (UNION)
ILLINOIS (UNION)
KENTUCKY (BORDER STATE)
TENNESSEE (CONFEDERATE)
ARKANSAS (CONFEDERATE)
INDIAN TERRITORY (CURRENT-DAY OKLAHOMA)
ILLINOIS RIVER
MISSISSIPPI RIVER
MISSOURI RIVER
KANSAS RIVER
"Little Dixie"
"Burnt District"
ST. LOUIS CITY
CENTRALIA
CITY OF KANSAS
FORT LEAVENWORTH
LEAVENWORTH
ATCHISON
LAWRENCE
HARRISONVILLE
FORT SCOTT
MARSHALL
NEMAHA
BROWN
DONIPHAN
ATCHISON
OTTAWATOMIE
JACKSON
JEFFERSON
WABAUNSEE
SHAWNEE
DOUGLAS
OSAGE
FRANKLIN
MIAMI
LYON
COFFEY
ANDERSON
LINN
BOURBON
GREENWOOD
WOODSON
ALLEN
ELK
WILSON
NEOSHO
CRAWFORD
CHAUTAUQUA
MONTGOMERY
LABETTE
CHEROKEE
ATCHISON
NODAWAY
WORTH
HARRISON
MERCER
PUTNAM
SCHUYLER
SCOTLAND
CLARK
GENTRY
ANDREW
HOLT
SULLIVAN
ADAIR
KNOX
LEWIS
DEKALB
DAVIESS
GRUNDY
BUCHANAN
LIVINGSTON
LINN
MACON
SHELBY
MARION
CLINTON
CALDWELL
PLATTE
CLAY
RAY
RALLS
WYANDOTTE
JACKSON
CASS
BATES
VERNON
JOHNSON
PETTIS
LINCOLN
WARREN
ST. CHARLES
ST. LOUIS
MONITEAU
COLE
HENRY
BENTON
MORGAN
OSAGE
GASCONADE
FRANKLIN
JEFFERSON
ST. CLAIR
MILLER
MARIES
CRAWFORD
WASHINGTON
STE. GENEVIEVE
PERRY
HICKORY
CAMDEN
PULASKI
PHELPS
ST. FRANCIS
CEDAR
POLK
DALLAS
LACLEDE
DENT
IRON
MADISON
CAPE GIRARDEAU
BARTON
DADE
REYNOLDS
BOLLINGER
SCOTT
JASPER
GREENE
WEBSTER
WRIGHT
TEXAS
SHANNON
WAYNE
LAWRENCE
CARTER
STODDARD
NEWTON
CHRISTIAN
DOUGLAS
HOWELL
BUTLER
MCDONALD
BARRY
STONE
TANEY
OZARK
OREGON
RIPLEY
NEW MADRID
DUNKLIN
PEMISCOTT
MISSISSIPPI

# PROLOGUE

The American Civil War officially began on April 12, 1861. It brought four long years of bloody fighting between the Northern Unionists and the Southern Confederates. However, on the border of Kansas and Missouri, sporadic fighting was commonplace for over nine years before the official war began.

The Missouri Compromise was passed in 1820. It allowed Missouri to be part of the Union as a "slave" state but prohibited slavery above the 36°30' latitude line for the remainder of the Louisiana Territory.

When the Kansas-Nebraska Act became law on May 30, 1854, it nullified the Missouri Compromise and allowed the new states to determine if they were slave or free states. Nebraska was always assumed to be a free state. However, Kansas, on the western border of Missouri, was sought by both the Northern Free Staters who opposed slavery and the Proslavery South. Border violence was commonplace.

In 1863, three events took place that escalated the War in the West to new levels: the collapse of the temporary jail that held young family members of some of the most active Bushwhackers, the sacking of Lawrence, Kansas, and General Order 11 which evacuated four Missouri counties on the Kansas-Missouri border. This story begins shortly after those connected events.

Enjoy my first novel set during the American Civil War, *The War Between Us, Friends and Enemies.*

## JAYHAWKERS, RED LEGS, AND BUSHWHACKERS

Jayhawkers, Red Legs, and Bushwhackers were all terms that were used during the Civil War. In the beginning, each had its own meaning. However, as time went on, some of those definitions became blurred.

C.M. Chase, a newspaper editor for the *True Republican and Sentinel* in Sycamore, Illinois, passed through the border region. In an article written for his paper on August 10, 1863, he attempted to define the different groups. "A Jayhawker is a Unionist who professes to rob, burn out, and murder only rebels in arms against the government. A Redleg is a Jayhawker originally distinguished by the uniform of red leggings. A Redleg, however, is regarded as more purely an indiscriminate thief and murderer then the Jayhawker or Bushwhacker. A Bushwhacker is a rebel Jayhawker, or a rebel who bands with others for the purpose of preying upon the lives and property of Union citizens. They are all lawless and indiscriminate in their iniquities…"

Captain Charles "Doc" Jennison arrived in Kansas City on June 19, 1861, with one hundred Mound City Sharps Rifle Guards. He claimed they were there to support Captain Edgar Prince in occupying the town but there is no record of any such orders. Against Prince's orders, Jennison soon began raiding in Missouri. His men were known as "Jennison's Jayhawkers" or the "Southern Kansas, Jay-Hawkers."

In July of 1861, James Lane, a new United States senator for Kansas and a brigadier general in the Indiana militia, with permission from President Lincoln, began forming the "Lane Brigade." Many of the men he picked were experienced thieves and known marauders. Jennison and his men became Company H and were the most notorious unit in Lane's brigade of ruffians.

While it was not mustered into service until October 28, 1861, this new unit eventually became the Seventh Kansas Volunteer Cavalry. Lieutenant Colonel Daniel Anthony (brother to Susan B. Anthony) and Major James D. Snoddy were the officers in charge while their commander, General Lane, mostly played poker in a nearby town. From November that year and continuing for four more months, Daniel Anthony's Seventh Kansas Cavalry plundered and stole in Cass and Jackson Counties in Missouri.

Kansas governor, Charles Robinson, predicted that the continued Jayhawker raids and forays into Missouri would lead to revenge and retaliation. In late 1861, a guerrilla movement exploded in Missouri fulfilling Robinson's prediction. Its retaliatory purpose was to protect Missouri citizens as well as to seek revenge for the years of depredations in their state.

By mid-1862, the Seventh Cavalry and their officers, Colonel Anthony and Lieutenant George H. Hoyt, also a staunch follower of Jennison, had been moved to Mississippi. Lane spent his time as a senator and his brigade left Missouri. However, a new marauding unit was formed with Charles Jennison as the leader. Hoyt, now a captain, soon became commander, and the new paramilitary unit was called the "Red Legs" or the "Red Legged Scouts." Their stated purpose was to serve as scouts and spies for the Union Army. Although no one wanted to officially claim them, Generals Thomas Ewing Jr. and James G. Blunt are credited with their creation "for desperate service along the border."

George W. Martin, secretary of the Kansas State Historical Society stated in his 1910 writings, "During the war on the border there was a legitimate organization of Union scouts called the "Red Legs." There were never less than 50 of them, nor more than 100…They were employed by the generals in command, and were carried on the pay rolls at seven dollars each per day…"

Because the Red Legs were never officially mustered into the army, there are no definitive unit records or history. However, their actions made them notorious. Membership was fluid but some of the men did go on to serve in the 7th Kansas Cavalry or other sanctioned military units. The Red Legs liked to distinguish themselves as a unit and usually wore tan or red leggings of some kind. Multiple sources claim to know how this attachment to red came to be, but nothing is formally documented.

They often made forays into Missouri where they stole livestock and committed other atrocities. The stolen loot was then taken back to Lawerence, Kansas, and sold at public auction. While not all Lawrence residents agreed with the blatant and illegal thievery, no one dared or tried to interfere. Later, loot was also fenced in Leavenworth, Kansas.

Even though the Red Legs were considered thugs and killers by the people of Missouri, they were respected by some in the United States Government. They had more freedom than soldiers and were unsupervised. According to Albert Greene, a soldier in the Ninth Kansas Cavalry, they were hand-picked men who could act on their own without orders from their superiors nor were they encumbered by military etiquette. Two of those who served in this capacity are names many know—Willaim F. "Buffalo Bill" Cody and James Butler "Wild Bill" Hickok. Buffalo Bill is quoted as saying, "We were the biggest gang of thieves on record."

While the activities of the Red Legs ceased with the end of the Civil War, the memories of the Bushwhackers were long. Some, such as Jesse James and Cole Younger, were active for many more years. By that time, the term "jayhawking" was a common, generic term for stealing or generally bad behavior. Quantrill's Raiders and other Bushwhackers continued jayhawking after the war ended.

If you tour the No. 10 Saloon in Deadwood, South Dakota (originally called Nuttal & Mann's Saloon), where Wild Bill Hickok was killed, you will see "scout" listed as one of his services to the United States Government. No mention is made that he was a Red Leg.

# THE THOMAS BUILDING, TEMPORARY WOMEN'S PRISON

In late July 1863, Brigadier General Thomas Ewing, as Commander of the District of the Border, appropriated the Thomas building near 1425 Grand Avenue in Kansas City, Kansas, for use as a temporary women's prison. The three-story building belonged to the wife of George Caleb Bingham, a prominent Kansas City Unionist. The three-story building, known by locals as The Longhorn Tavern, was six years old at the time and was solidly built.

In addition to the Thomas building, Ewing also took control of the older Cockerel building. The two buildings shared a common wall, and Ewing planned to use the Cockerel building as a guardhouse.

By Ewing's orders, family members of known Rebel guerrillas were to be imprisoned. Spying or aiding the enemy was the charge, and without corroborating evidence, these women were to be arrested—no trial, no bail, and no legal recourse.

The first women were arrested in mid-July and were held in the Union Hotel in Kansas City. When that hotel became overcrowded, they were moved to the Mechanics Bank at Delaware and Commercial. The building was infested with rats and was unfit for human habitation of any kind. However, the women were held there until the guards complained about the rodents and the stench. From there, the female prisoners were moved to the Thomas building. They were to be held there until they could be moved to the notorious Gratiot Military Prison in St. Louis where they would be tried as spies.

Shortly after the transfer of the prisoners to the Thomas building, it began to shake and sway. Plaster often fell from the ceilings terrifying the women imprisoned there. The shaking was known to be caused by a weakened foundation. Even after multiple warnings, federal officials ignored this. In some instances, they were accused of *hoping* the building would collapse since some of the women were relatives to well-known Bushwhackers. On August 13, 1863, the building did fall.

It is not known how many prisoners were held there because recorded numbers range from nine to twenty-seven. However, the identified Southern prisoners were all under twenty years of age, and the youngest was ten. As the building began to collapse, one young woman jumped from the window. A second girl tried to follow her. However, the twelve-pound weight attached to her leg as punishment prevented her, and she went down with the building. Four women died in the collapse, a fifth was fatally injured, and one was permanently crippled. The others suffered varying degrees of injuries.

Rumors began to rage immediately. Some believed that Ewing had commanded his soldiers to sabotage the building. This was supposedly substantiated by the claim that a merchant who stored his goods on the first floor frantically removed them with some of the soldiers' help. This was said to have taken place shortly before the collapse giving further "proof" that the collapse was planned. Others claimed the Southern girls themselves had weakened the walls by trying to tunnel out through the cellar—even though they were held on the second floor and third floors. One story suggested that hogs had rooted along the walls, undermining the foundation while another stated that Ewing's soldiers had cut the supporting girders in the basement to give themselves more office space.

According to an article written by George Bingham and published in the Washington Sentinel on March 9, 1878, "While their prison walls were trembling, its doors remained closed, and they were allowed no hope for release except through the portals of a horrible death…" Bingham believed the women were deliberately killed, especially since General Ewing did not order an investigation. Excuses were made but no blame was placed on General Ewing or his soldiers.

Doctor Joshua Thorne testified nearly eleven years after the collapse that women "of bad character and diseased" were held in the cellar of the Thomas building. He stated that soldiers had tunneled through the walls of the guardhouse to gain access to them. The guards as well as other soldiers were often in the cellar, and intoxication was common. Doctor Thorne, who was in charge of the health of the Southern women, even claimed when he went to the basement that he "found many of the female prisoners intoxicated—one of the women was cutting with an axe at one of the posts in the basement—which supported a girder and upon which girder the joists of the floor above rested—[and I] reported to the officer on duty the fact of the drunken condition of the women and the danger in cutting away the supports of the building…"

The doctor reported what he had seen to General Ewing the next morning, the same morning both buildings collapsed. According to witnesses, the Cockerel building collapsed first followed by the Thomas building. No reason is recorded as to why the doctor's testimony was given eleven years after the collapse.

History makes no mention of prostitutes housed in the Thomas building's basement nor is there any military record of tunnels in the connecting wall between the two buildings. However, no officer with advancement or political aspirations would want it to be known that prostitution was taking place in one of his prisons.

While there is no definitive proof that General Ewing wanted the building to collapse or the Southern women to die, the foundation was certainly faulty. Ewing did nothing to remove the women from a dangerous situation. Instead, he left them locked inside with no escape except through the windows. Even if not directly guilty for all the deaths, he was undeniably complicit. And if there were prostitutes in the basement, they most certainly died in the collapse eliminating an embarrassing problem. Perhaps those unlucky women are the reason for confusion over the number of women imprisoned there.

Of course, the Confederate family members of the dead and injured women were furious. They demanded Yankee blood, and Lawrence, Kansas, was sacked eight days later.

# THE SECOND SACKING OF LAWRENCE OR THE LAWRENCE MASSACRE

Quantrill had long wanted to raid Lawrence, Kansas. The town was despised by all Missourians because it was a hotbed of abolitionism and the home of the Red Legs. Quantrill believed it would be a strike at the heart of the forces who were constantly invading his state. In addition, he believed the plunder stolen in Missouri would be found there.

He gathered his officers and chieftains together on August 10, 1863. Most of the guerrillas wanted to strike Lawrence, and Quantrill's spies told him that the town was ripe for picking. Still, it would be a dangerous undertaking that would require planning and secrecy. Some of the raiders were not convinced they would have the element of surprise on their side. They knew Lawrence was well-armed and protected. The citizens of Lawrence had even bragged they could resist and defeat any Missouri force with just fifteen to thirty minutes of notice.

Besides the collapse of the Thomas building, General Ewing's Orders No. 9 and No. 10 were also triggering factors for the attack. In Order No. 9, Ewing dictated that slaves would be taken from Missourians, and those freed slaves would be conscripted into the Kansas Colored Infantry units to fight for the North. Interestingly, the Emancipation Proclamation that freed slaves did not apply in Missouri since it was only directed at those slave-holding states who left the Union. Missouri never seceded. Therefore, Missourians saw this as an act of war.

Order No. 10 was put in place on August 18, 1863, just four days after the collapse of the Thomas building. It mandated that identified sons and daughters of those who aided guerrillas leave the district along with the wives and children of specified guerrillas. If they did not leave immediately, they were to be escorted to Kansas City for shipment south with only their clothes and what was deemed necessary or worth removing by the arresting parties. While Ewing's order forbade depredations by his forces against the Missourians, those orders were not strictly obeyed. He even allowed units of Red Legs and Jayhawkers to enforce the order. The Bushwhackers saw Orders 9 and 10 for what they were—a ratcheting up of the fighting on the border.

Quantrill and his raiders began their ride to Kansas on August 18. Spies were an ongoing problem, and the men were told that Lawrence was the target of their planned raid after the ride began. Men were given the option to walk away. Even knowing that they could all be killed, only a few chose not to go. The raiders numbered nearly four hundred and fifty.

The night was dark, and Quantrill was concerned about losing his way. However, his chosen route was populated, and the settlers who lived there were familiar with the area. As farmsteads were encountered, they were surrounded, and the man of the house was called out. If he was German, he was shot immediately because Germans were typically Unionists. The man was also immediately shot if he was a recognized abolitionist or Jayhawker. The prisoner was then forced to guide them. He was shot when the next farmstead came into view. Ten men were killed that night in an eight-mile stretch. The last man captured was clubbed to death near Lawrence since a shot could have alerted the town.

Quantrill recognized some of the landmarks, but a small boy from the last household was still taken in case they needed directions. The boy was kept with the band the entire morning. He was released with a new suit of clothes stolen in Lawrence when the raiders began their retreat.

It was daylight on August 21 when the Bushwhackers reached a bluff overlooking Lawrence. They could see the soldier encampments, and some of the raiders wanted to turn back. Quantrill refused and charged his horse toward town. The rest of his men followed. The killing began before they reached the outskirts.

A young woman was captured and forced to lead small groups of raiders to the houses of the men on Quantrill's death list. Even though she pleaded for men's lives and property, she was later jailed for aiding the Bushwhackers. After the raid, she was taken to Fort Leavenworth for trial where the charges were dismissed.

While they did have a list of names they wanted to kill, the guerrillas were soon shooting at every man and teenage boy old enough to carry a gun. As the looting continued, the Bushwhackers raided the liquor stores. Drunkenness made them even more reckless and angry. Before the morning was finished, one hundred fifty men and teenage boys were dead. The downtown area was burned along with many of the houses. The town was caught off guard, and the devastation was overwhelming. A citizen was later quoted as saying, "…The calamity had burst upon all with such sudden and unconceived force and flashed with such terror that the will was subdued and the emotions paralyzed." The town leaders had posted no guards, and Lawrence's response to the attack was unorganized shock.

The sacking and destruction of Lawrence took place eight days after the collapse of the temporary jail that held the Southern women and four days after Order No. 10 was decreed. The building's collapse especially helped convince those who were hesitant to join the attack and likely added to the viciousness once the invasion began. Lawrence was considered a "fence house" for property stolen from Missouri, and the raiders were vengeful.

While the town was decimated and many men died, no women were raped or killed. In the Bushwhackers' eyes, they had shown more mercy to Lawrence than had been shown to their border counties for years.

## GENERAL ORDER NO. 11

On August 25, 1863, Brigadier General Thomas Ewing, Jr., issued Order No. 11 which depopulated four Missouri counties. The order was issued four days after the August 21 Sacking of Lawrence. Government leaders believed that the Missouri Bushwhackers drew their support from the local population, primarily the rural areas of four counties south of the Missouri River on the eastern border of Kansas: Jackson, Cass, Bates, and northern Vernon Counties. Ewing was not only concerned with border violence. He was also concerned about repercussions from Unionist Jayhawkers such as Senator James Lane following Quantrill's raid on Lawrence. Lane is quoted as saying, "You are a dead dog if you fail to issue that order as agreed between us."

President Lincoln approved Ewing's order. However, he warned that the military should take care not to permit vigilante enforcement. That warning was ignored. While agreeing that the order was legal, General Henry Hallack suggested that all Missouri and Kansas troops be removed from the border. Troops from other states should be used to carry out enforcement. That suggestion was also ignored.

It was General Ewing's decision that Kansas troops be used to carry out the enforcement—men who often had agendas of their own. While Order No. 11 was already in the works, Lane's threat may have affected how the order was enforced.

George Caleb Bingham, a well-known artist and Missouri's provisional state treasurer, had no lost love for General Ewing. Still angry over the collapse of the Thomas building and the loss of life there, he described the results of General Order 11. Some "were shot down in the very act of obeying the order; one in which their wagons and effects were seized by the murderers…Large trains of wagons, extending over the prairies, and moving Kansasward were freighted with every description of household furniture and wearing apparel belonging to the exiled inhabitants." He said the raid put "an end to predatory raids of Kansas Red-Legs and Jayhawkers by surrendering to them all they coveted and leaving nothing that could further excite their cupidity."

The affected area was twenty-eight miles wide by ninety miles long. Accurate figures don't exist, but it is estimated that around twenty thousand people—women, children, and elderly—were forced from their homes by Order No. 11. Bates County was a vacant wilderness and only six hundred people were allowed to remain in Cass County.

Ewing's order to take only grain and hay spiraled out of control because the men knew that force was acceptable. By the time the Red Legs and Kansas troops finished, most of the four counties were pillaged and burned. That area became known as the "Burnt District."

Order No. 11 stood until November 20 of that year when General Ewing was pressured to issue Order No. 20. That order allowed limited resettlement by those who could pass a strict test of loyalty—loyalty that was nearly impossible to prove.

The raids against Kansas greatly decreased in 1864. While some in the military claimed it was because the "cleansing of the border" was successful, others said it was because the guerrillas were now "scouting" for the Confederate army—they were conducting diversionary missions and destroying railroads. Regardless, Quantrill's forces were not weakened by the event, and many neutral residents of those counties became hardened Confederate sympathizers.

## MERRILL'S HORSE (2ND MISSOURI VOLUNTEER CAVALRY)

Merrill's Horse was an elite Union cavalry regiment that served during the American Civil War. It was raised by Major General John C. Fremont at Benton Barracks in St. Louis, Missouri, in 1861. Fremont was commander of the United States Army's Western Department and was headquartered in St. Louis.

Captain Lewis Merrill, army officer and veteran of the U.S. 2nd Dragoons, organized the regiment. At a time when recruitment was slow, Merrill was able to recruit and enlist nearly eight hundred men in less than a month. Merrill was promoted to Colonel of Volunteers, and as such, he was working with men who were not used to military regimen. Still, he demanded strong professionalism and discipline, something that was not always present in volunteer companies. Merrill organized two additional companies in 1863.

Colonel Merrill wanted his men to be distinguished from other companies, and he requisitioned a special uniform. Horsehead panels trimmed in cavalry yellow covered the fronts of their tunics, and they wore sky-blue forage caps with orange welts. These uniforms were chosen to honor Merrill's service in the 2nd Dragoons, and he allowed no deviations or additions.

Merrill's Horse was originally assigned to fight guerrillas and irregular Confederate cavalry in Missouri. Their missions changed throughout the war, but they were often called on when guerrilla fighting was necessary. That included efforts in Arkansas, Tennessee, Georgia, and Alabama. The regiment was sent to Chattanooga, Tennessee, in the winter of 1865. They fought guerrillas and escorted trains from Chattanooga to Atlanta until September of 1865. Merrill's Horse became known for its aggressiveness towards guerrillas as well as its effectiveness in fighting them.

When Major General Henry Halleck replaced General Fremont as Commander of the Western Department, Merrill's Horse received a second official designation. This was the result of legal issues. General Fremont personally signed officers' commissions during his tenure. However, only the president, state governors, or designated representatives had the authority to do that. Halleck worked around this problem when he took charge by asking Provisional Governor of Missouri, Hamilton Gamble, to provide retroactive new commissions for all his officers as part of the Missouri Volunteer troops. They were then called the 2nd Missouri Volunteer Cavalry. However, in most records and reports, they were still referred to as Merrill's Horse.

The original members mustered out as their terms of service expired. Those veterans and recruits left were retained in service until September 19, 1865, when the regiment was mustered out at Nashville, Tennessee.

Three officers and fifty-three enlisted men were killed or mortally wounded while the regiment was enlisted to fight. In addition, disease took one officer and two hundred five enlisted men. Considering the type of fighting they did, the number killed in combat was low. Unfortunately, disease caused the death of many soldiers on both sides during the Civil War.

Colonel Merrill was breveted Brigadier General, U.S. Volunteers from March 13, 1865, until he mustered out of volunteer service on December 14, 1865. He was again breveted Brigadier General, U.S. Army on February 27, 1890.

I did take some liberty with the dates that Merrill's Horse would have been deployed in Tennessee and Georgia, nor were they present at the Battle of Chattanooga. However, I wanted to include some of their storied history in this novel. I also set back the date of Colonel Merrill's promotion to Brigadier General to make it fit my timeline.

## CIVIL WAR QUILTS

Rachel Short McKim was a quilt designer from Independence, Missouri. The quilt she made in 1929 was based on a story told by young Fannie Kreeger Haller. The child was ten when she saw her mother's quilt "jayhawked" from their bed by raiders in 1863 after Order No. 11 was issued. The pattern the young girl remembered was an old applique design popular in the 1830s and 1840s. The design has been called Hickory Leaf, Orange Peel, and The Reel. McKim showed hers as two colors with nine pieces. She named it Order No. 11.

Florence Peto, a quilt historian, used the same pattern name in her *Historic Quilts* book published in 1939. According to her story, a quilt was found buried with other family treasures somewhere near Chattanooga after the War Between the States. The pattern was not one familiar to Southern quilt makers and was the object of study and admiration. Peto's version was likely a fabrication, but it did make a great story to sell quilt patterns and books!

Quilts were a sought-after commodity during the Civil War. Most soldiers slept on the ground in all kinds of weather, so quilts were a treat. Women during that time were frequently visited by soldiers and raiders from both sides looking for food and supplies. The ladies of the house often kept large tubs of water by their doors. When soldiers were spotted, the women dunked their quilts in the tubs. Water-soaked quilts were too heavy to carry and were not taken!

The design of the quilt sampler pictured in the front of this novel is Order No. 11 . When you read this story, I hope you visualize that quilt in your mind, the same quilt pattern that was "jayhawked" from my character, Ava Bowman.

# BENTON BARRACKS HOSPITAL

While Major General John C. Fremont was Union Commander of the Western Department, he ordered a training barracks to be built at the site of the St. Louis Fairgrounds in St. Louis, Missouri. In 1861, the original barracks consisted of five buildings. Each building was seven hundred forty feet in length and forty feet wide. A two-story building was constructed as headquarters for the barracks commander. The barracks accommodated up to thirty thousand soldiers and was primarily for those attached to the Western Division.

The ongoing Civil War required even more facilities. By 1863, Benton Barracks extended over a mile in length with warehouses, cavalry stables, and parade grounds.

A large military hospital was constructed from the fairgrounds' amphitheater after the Battle of Lexington. The hospital treated the hundreds of incoming wounded and offered services for up to three thousand soldiers. During the Civil War, Benton Barracks Hospital was the largest in the West.

St. Louis was under Union control all during the Civil War due to the huge military presence there as well as many freedom-loving German immigrants. Most area volunteers did serve in the Union Army. However, there was a contingency of Southern sympathizers who assisted

Confederate soldiers with smuggled medicine and supplies. No major battles were fought in the city but the area outside St. Louis was still dangerous with the presence of spies and rebel fighters.

Always a major port and commercial center, St. Louis is located at the junction of three rivers: the Missouri, the Illinois, and the Mississippi. Population reached one hundred sixty thousand in 1860 with many German and Irish American immigrants.

When the war ended, Benton Barracks was dismantled. The land was returned to its pre-war use as a fairground and racetrack. No trace of Benton Barracks remains.

## NOTABLE CIVIL WAR NURSES

Over twenty-one thousand women served as volunteer nurses in Union military hospitals during the Civil War. A similar number is estimated in the South. However, many Southern soldiers were treated in homes and churches. Those records were optional and were often destroyed.

Before the war, military nursing was dominated by men. However, the massive numbers of sick and wounded brought women to the forefront. They volunteered in droves and the patients appreciated them. The female nurses provided mental care as well as physical. They read to the wounded. They prayed and talked with the soldiers and wrote letters for them.

The nurses worked long hours, and their jobs required more than just wound treatment. They were expected to clean the facilities and change the bedding as well as feed the patients, administer medication, and change bandages. One nurse stated that after the Battle of Fredericksburg, in one day she had cooked and served nine hundred twenty-six rations of soup, farina, tea, and coffee—by herself. For some of the nurses, their first days were traumatizing. Amputated limbs, gangrenous wounds, and severe injuries were the order of the day. Crying was not tolerated.

Nursing was also dangerous. The women were exposed to the same infections and diseases as the sick they attended. In addition, germs were not fully understood, so cleanliness and sanitization were not necessarily prerequisites to wound treatment. In fact, contracting a disease in a hospital was a common concern. Work assignments for the nurses were sometimes determined by race and class depending on who was in charge.

## Dorothea Dix

Miss Dix was appointed Superintendent of Nurses for the Union Army in June of 1861. The sixty-year-old woman was not trained in nursing. However, she was fearless in her battles with political and social forces. She was also very disciplined and extremely organized. Miss Dix set stringent requirements for women entering her new nursing corps. They included an age range between thirty-five and fifty.

Dix preferred matronly women of experience and good character. Her nurses also had to be in good health. Applicants committed to three months or more of service and agreed to take orders. Dress requirements stated no hoops in skirts and black or brown dresses. In addition, the women were to wear no jewelry or cosmetics. Compensation was set at $.40 per day. The age requirement must not have been enforced during the Civil War because many younger women did serve as nurses.

## Emily Elizabeth Parsons

Miss Parsons was born in Massachusetts in 1824, the oldest of seven children. A childhood injury left her blind in her right eye and damaged her vision in the left. She then contracted scarlet fever at seven, and it permanently damaged her hearing. An ankle injury as a young woman also made walking difficult.

Emily's father tried to deter her from nursing. He believed with all her disabilities that she would not be an effective nurse.

Nurse Parson's health did fail early in her nursing career due partly to her sixteen-hour workdays. Much to her dismay, she had to temporarily leave nursing to recuperate. While convalescing, she met Jesse Benton Fremont who offered her a job in St. Louis. Miss Parsons accepted. She hoped her health would improve in the West.

She worked first at Lawson Hospital in St. Louis. A month later she was appointed head nurse on a hospital transport ship on the Mississippi River carrying sick and wounded soldiers to hospitals in Memphis.

Nurse Parsons wrote many letters home. She talked about the filthy conditions on the ship and the men who were treated there. While on the steamship, she contracted malaria. When she recovered enough to work again, she was sent to St. Louis where she was assigned supervisor of nurses at the newly established Benton Barracks Hospital—one of the most prestigious appointments given to a woman during the Civil War.

The hospital cared for both Black and White soldiers, and Nurse Parsons accepted volunteers of all colors and nationalities. Under her management, the hospital's death rate was significantly reduced.

Nurse Parsons was a dedicated nurse despite her physical impairments. I made no mention of her handicaps in this novel because she did not let them affect her work. She died in 1880 of apoplexy or stroke as it is called today.

## Belle Coddington

Mrs. Belle Graham Tannehill was a schoolteacher in Iowa when her husband, Ninnian H. Tannehill, died of typhoid fever in 1863 at a military hospital in Louisianna. The twenty-year-old widow soon applied for the Army Nurses' Corp. She was assigned to Benton Barracks as a ward matron working with Nurse Emily Parsons in early 1864 where she ran the measles ward.

Mrs. Tannehill contracted measles from the soldiers she treated. She suffered from long-term health issues as a result. Her pension as a war widow was increased by Congress in 1888 due to the continuing complications of that disease.

Belle married a second time after the war ended in 1866 to Eli Helmick Coddington. He was a disabled veteran and minister from Iowa. The couple had four children. Two died in infancy and Mr. Coddington died in 1877. Belle died in 1920, outliving both of her remaining children. She is remembered in history as Belle Coddington.

## Mother Bickerdyke

Mary Ann Ball was born into a farm family in 1817 in Knox County, Ohio. Her mother died when Mary Ann was less than two years old. She and her sister were sent to live with her grandparents. After the grandparents died, an uncle cared for her. She is believed to have enrolled at Oberlin College in Ohio at age sixteen. However, no records confirm that since she did not graduate.

In 1847, she married Robert Bickerdyke. The couple had two boys. In 1856, they moved to Galesburg, Illinois, where a daughter was born. Her husband died in 1858, and their two-year-old daughter died a year later. Emily became the sole provider for her two sons.

Mrs. Bickerdyke began her medical career as a botanic physician. She treated patients with herbs and plants, remedies she learned as a child and possibly in college. That knowledge led her to use wet compresses, herbal teas, healthy soups, and steam as part of her healing processes. She also stressed fresh water and overall cleanliness.

In 1861, she arranged for someone to care for her sons and answered a plea for help in treating Union soldiers in Cairo, Illinois. The town of Galesburg had collected medical supplies valued at $500, and Mary Ann was asked to deliver them. Upon arriving in Cairo, she used the supplies to establish a hospital there for Union soldiers.

Mrs. Bickerdyke charged through the dirty army camp. Tents were cleaned and sanitized, field kitchens were set up, and laundries were put in place. She focused on cleanliness and fresh air—barrels were even cut in half for makeshift bathtubs. She was unafraid of offending anyone and often angered male physicians, staff, and officers because she would not back down when it came to patient care…and she won most of her fights. Once when asked by a surgeon on whose authority she was acting, she replied, "On the authority of Lord God Almighty. Have you anything that outranks that?"

By the end of the war, Mother Bickerdyke as she was known, had helped build three hundred hospitals and served the wounded on nineteen battlefields. When the fighting ended, she helped soldiers and nurses secure pensions even though she did not receive hers until 1880.

After the war, Mother Bickerdyke moved to Kansas where she obtained a $10,000 donation from a banker there to help Civil War veterans settle in Kansas. General Sherman even authorized the use of government wagons and teams to help transport them—possibly because of Mother Bickerdyke's tenacity and his awareness of how long she would persist. After working for a time in New York and San Franscisco, Mother Bickerdyke made Kansas her final home.

Bickerdyke Elementary School in Russell, Kansas, where her son was the first superintendent of schools, was dedicated in her memory in 1962. Two other memorials are located near Ellsworth, Kansas. In addition, the Barton County Courthouse in Great Bend, Kansas, contains records of the two hundred train cars of donations she organized during the Grasshopper Plague of 1874.

Mother Bickerdyke died of a stroke in 1901 in Bunker Hill, Kansas, a small community just east of Russell. She was eighty-four years old. Her body was returned to Galesburg, Illinois, to be buried beside her husband. A statue of her holding a wounded soldier and offering him a drink was erected in front of the courthouse there in 1906.

I found no definitive information of Mother Bickerdyke running a hospital in Chattanooga. However, she was near there in various field hospitals. I loved her story as well as her Kansas connections and decided to put her in charge of the Chattanooga hospital in this novel.

# DR. MARY EDWARDS WALKER: SURGEON AND SUFFRAGIST

Mary Walker was born in Oswego, New York, on November 26, 1832, the youngest of seven children. She often helped outside on their family farm and typically wore the more-functional men's britches. She became a teacher and saved her money to enroll in Syracuse Medical College. She graduated in 1855 with honors, the only woman in her class. Dr. Walker married one of her classmates, Albert Miller, shortly after graduation. However, she did not take his last name since hers was "as dear to her as his was to him." She wore trousers with a dress coat to her wedding and refused to say "obey" in her vows. Neither their marriage nor their practice was successful, and Mary filed for divorce.

When the Civil War began in 1861, Dr. Walker traveled to Washington D.C. to join the United States Army as a surgeon. She was denied a commission because she was a woman. She then volunteered as an unpaid surgeon in various hospitals and served on the front lines.

After volunteering for many months, Dr. Walker received a commission as a "Contract Acting Assistant Surgeon," a civilian role. She served with the 52$^{nd}$ Ohio Infantry and was at the Battle of Chickamauga in September of 1863.

In November 1865, President Andrew Johnson awarded Dr. Walker the Medal of Honor. It was for her work with sick and wounded soldiers as well as for the four months she spent in prison. Dr. Walker wore her medal proudly. When it was rescinded fifty-two years later because she had not engaged in "actual combat with the enemy," she refused to relinquish it. (The honor was restored posthumously in 1977.)

Throughout her lifetime, Dr. Walker adamantly refused to change the way she dressed and was arrested numerous times for wearing men's clothing. At a trial where she was charged for impersonating a man, Dr. Walker declared that she had the right "to dress as I please in free America on whose tented fields I have served for four years in the cause of human freedom." The judge dismissed the case and ordered the police to never arrest her again on such charges.

Even with failing health, Dr. Mary Edwards Walker remained involved in medicine and women's rights. She died in her home in Oswego, New York, on February 21, 1919. She was eighty-six years old and was buried in britches.

# THE BATTLE OF CHICKAMAUGA

The Battle of Chickamauga was fought from September 18 through September 20, 1863. Crawfish Spring was the first name given to the area around what is now Chickamauga, Georgia. It was named by the Cherokee Indians. When the three-day battle ended, there were 16,170 Union and 18,454 Confederate casualties (dead and wounded). The battle was the deadliest fought in the West and the third deadliest battle during the entire war.

Chickamauga Creek roughly translated from Cherokee means "River of Death." It was a deep, tree-lined creek with rocky banks. The surrounding area was full of trees and thickets with bristling stickers, and the ground beneath was swampy. Because of the terrain, clearly drawn battle lines were impossible. Commanding officers and often the soldiers themselves could not see the enemy. The fluid battle lines and dense woods led to close and vicious combat.

After the South's victory on September 20, Confederate Generals Longstreet and Forrest wanted to pursue the Federal troops. They hoped to destroy Rosecrans' army before it could reorganize after its retreat north. However, General Braxton Bragg had lost over twenty percent of his men. Ten generals had been killed or wounded along with severe losses of junior officers. He refused.

Two months later, the reinforced Union Army defeated the Confederates and routed them from their attempted siege of Chattanooga. The North took control of the city, opening the southern door to Atlanta, Georgia. Bragg's costly win at Chickamauga became a hollow victory.

In September of 1889, thousands of veterans from both the North and the South met in a large tent at Chattanooga to make plans for a memorial park at Chickamauga. The next day, they traveled to Crawfish Spring for what was said to be the largest barbeque ever held. Four hundred twenty-eight hogs, cattle, goats, and sheep were butchered to provide the twelve thousand pounds of meat that was served.

A ceremonial peace smoke followed the meal. The men were provided pipes made of wood harvested from Snodgrass Hill. The stems were made from river cane that was cut from the banks of West Chickamauga Creek, and eighty-five pounds of tobacco were smoked. While members of the Park Association discussed their plans, the rest of the veterans wandered around the battlefield. At first it was small groups who fought together, but soon, soldiers from both sides were discussing battles and tactics. By the end of the day, the Chickamauga Memorial Association was formed. A bill establishing the park moved quickly through Congress, and the nation's first National Military Park was designated.

Great soldiers fought in the Battle of Chickamauga. They met twenty-four years later to forgive the past and heal old wounds.

## THE GORDON HOMESTEAD AT CRAWFISH SPRING (CHICKAMAUGA, GEORGIA)

The Gordon home, owned by James Gordon, took seven years to build since each brick was crafted on-site. It was to be the grandest house in the Crawfish Spring area and was completed in 1847. One of the first Confederate units was organized there. James Clark Gordon was elected captain and commander of the company. He stood on a large rock to accept his command, and that rock still rests by the entrance of the drive leading to the house.

On September 16, 1863, Union General Willaim S. Rosecrans appropriated the house to serve as his headquarters. The family members living there were relegated to one of the brick structures that housed the slaves.

When the Battle of Chickamauga began on September 18, Rosecrans moved his headquarters north to a different house, and the Gordon house was taken over as a field hospital. Every room and outbuilding soon held wounded Union soldiers. When the house and outbuildings were full, the available trees provided shelter. Many wounded laid outside.

The bloodstains that soaked into the floorboards of the mansion were so large and so dark that rugs had to be used to hide them. Those stains are still visible today. Wounded and dying men also carved desperate messages into the walls for loved ones they would likely never see again. The Gordon women copied every message with the hope that they could be passed on to the soldiers' families.

The library is located on the first floor to the right of the front door. It was used for surgeries and amputations. Those amputated limbs were tossed out the side window and dropped into a wagon. When the wagon was full, the limbs were hauled away to be buried or burned.

The cover of this book features the Gordon home as it would have looked in 1863. The house is now known as the Gordon-Lee Mansion and is available for tours.

## CRAWFISH SPRING, NORTHWEST GEORGIA

The summer of 1863 had been particularly dry, and Crawfish Spring was the most reliable source of water in the area. Thousands of soldiers filled their canteens there. Because of the water, Crawfish Spring was also chosen as the main Federal hospital depot during the Battle of Chickamauga. Seven division hospitals were set up there.

Lieutenant John W. Andes, Company K, described the spring in his reports. "…We occupied the ground at Crawfish Spring, a large spring, the basin of which is about 100 yards in circumference, and deep enough to swim a horse. A large creek ran off from it, to the banks of which our wounded, a large portion of them, were carried during the day, several hundred tents having been put up there. Before night the tents were filled with wounded and dying soldiers. Hundreds were laid out on the leaves and the sedge grass of an old field just by, and hardly out of range of the enemy's guns…" When the wounded kept arriving, they were arranged in rows, and lines of campfires were built at their feet to help keep them warm.

The battle lines kept shifting and the hospital was ordered to evacuate on September 20. Once all the available ambulances and wagons had been loaded, some soldiers dismounted and placed wounded comrades on their horses. When the commanding officer saw this, he ordered the wounded to be returned to the hospital. Some could barely sit a horse, and he wanted his able-bodied soldiers ready to fight.

Lieutenant Andes also described the state of the wounded who were abandoned as his regiment retreated. "…I shall never forget the piteous cries of hundreds of our men as we would ride by. Some with an arm off, some with a leg and others seriously or mortally wounded. When they realized that they were about to fall into the hands of the enemy, their appeals were heart-rending…" In addition, the exploding shells set fire to the leaves, grass, and underbrush. Some of the wounded left by the spring as well as those still in the field were in danger of being burned to death.

By Sunday evening, September 20, the Confederates, led by General Joseph Wheeler's Cavalry, had captured the hospital along with twenty wagons of medicine and miscellaneous supplies. Over one thousand wounded soldiers were taken prisoner. At that point, the mansion became a Confederate hospital. When the Confederate soldiers began to pull blankets off beds and loot the hospital, one of the Yankee doctors protested. General Wheeler ordered his men to leave the wounded alone.

The Gordon house and the field hospitals around Crawfish Spring remained in use until the end of September. Between September 29 and October 1, a prisoner exchange took place between the two armies.

Crawfish Spring is located down the hill and east of the Gordon-Lee Mansion. It is the main water source for the town of Chickamauga today. However, with the water development and piping, Crawfish Spring looks much different now than it did in 1863.

## THE RIFLED MUSKET, THE MINIÉ BALL, AND REPEATING RIFLES

The rifled musket was the most common weapon of the Civil War infantry. It was fired from the shoulder and had grooves cut inside the barrel. When the powder exploded, it shot the bullet forward and the rifled grooves made it spin. Rifled muskets were more accurate and had a longer range than the older, smoothbore guns.

The Minié ball was a new type of bullet invented by French army officer Claude-Etienne Minié in 1849. The bullet was cylindrical with a conical point. Its hollow base contained an iron plug that expanded when fired and made it more accurate at longer distances. The bullet was also smaller than the diameter of the rifle barrel which allowed it to be loaded easily and fired even when the rifle was dirty.

In the early 1850s, James Burton, an employee of the United States Armory at Harper's Ferry, Virginia, improved the bullet further by eliminating the need for the iron plug. This made it easier and cheaper to produce. Throughout the Civil War, both sides used this bullet in their rifled muskets. The long-range accuracy of the minnie ball, as the soldiers called the bullet, changed how war was fought. Bayonets became nearly obsolete. The role of cavalry and artillery was changed as well.

The Spencer Repeating Rifle changed the war even more. It was not issued until late 1863 and quickly became a popular firearm. The new carbine had a magazine that could hold seven metallic rimfire cartridges.

They were fed into the breech by a compressed spring in the magazine which was loaded through the butt of the rifle. When the trigger guard was lowered, the breech block dropped down and the empty cartridge was ejected. As the trigger guard returned to its normal position, the breech block moved up. This caught a new cartridge and inserted it into the breech.

A Blakeslee quick-loading box was designed to work with the Spencer carbine, and it held several loaded magazines that could be pushed quickly into the butt. Ninety-five thousand Spencer carbines were purchased during the Civil War by the United States Government.

Union Colonel John T. Wilder's "Lightning Brigade" of mounted infantry was the first brigade on either side to be armed with Spencer repeating rifles. Those rifles allowed the shooter to fire fourteen rounds per minute instead of the typical two to three shots per minute which was standard for a Civil War rifle. The carnage shocked even the Union soldiers. After the Battle of Horseshoe Ridge, Colonel Wilder wrote, "It actually seemed a pity to kill men so. They fell in heaps; and I had it in my heart to order the firing to cease, to end the awful sight."

## PONTOON BRIDGE

A pontoon bridge is a floating bridge and is usually a temporary way to cross a river. It uses floats or shallow-draft boats such as river barges to support the deck. This method of crossing rivers has been used since ancient times, typically in wartimes or during emergencies. Pontoon bridges moved larger numbers of soldiers much faster than ferries.

William Wiley of the 77th Illinois Infantry wrote in detail in his war diary about driving mules across one of these bridges. He said they hitched one mule that was saddle-broken to the wagon and then used whatever mules were available for the rest of the four- or six-mule teams. (During the war, mules were often purchased or "acquired" in the countryside, and some of the Reb-sympathizing farmers prided themselves on selling the Yankees their meanest mules.) Once the mules were hitched, a teamster would mount the rideable three-bell mule. Then the wild trip would begin.

The bridge Wiley crossed was constructed of large skiff-like boats anchored in the river about twelve feet apart. Timbers were laid from one boat to the other with two-inch planks spiked onto the timbers. The bridge was twelve to fourteen feet wide with no side railings. It swayed sideways as well as up and down. The mule teams were forced onto the moving bridge with great difficulty. Once on, all the mules pushed as hard as they could toward the center of the bridge because none wanted to go over the side. Unlike horses that panic and run, mules typically avoid hurting themselves.

The unbroken teams were driven around until they were tired enough to be unhitched safely. The harnesses were not taken off until they were broken to pull.

Teamsters could identify what tasks mules were broken to do by looking at their tails. One bell or a chunk of cut-out hair meant they were broken to carry a pack saddle. Two bells meant they could pack and pull a wagon. A third bell meant the mule could be ridden as well.

## CIVIL WAR MULES AND HORSES

Over a million horses and mules died during the Civil War. Union Captain Charles Francis Adams, Jr. wrote about the hard and dangerous lives of war horses. "You have no idea of the sufferings…I do the best I can for my horses and am sorry for them; but all war is cruel…a horse must go until he can't be spurred any further and then the rider must get another horse as soon as he can seize one."

Horses were a primary means of transportation until the invention of the automobile in the early 1900s. During the Civil War, they were ridden in battle. They were also used to transport artillery and supplies which exposed them to gunfire and cannon balls. Once the battle ended, they were required to carry the cavalrymen hundreds of miles, often with little rest or food. While many died in battle, thousands more died from starvation and neglect. Part of this was due to poor animal care and wound treatment. However, battle locations and logistics determined livestock health as well.

Early in the war, the United States War Department recognized this problem. Orders were given for each cavalry regiment to have a "Veterinary Sergeant." Unfortunately, few formally educated veterinarians applied. When they were hired, they ordered sick or lame horses and mules out of commission, orders that were often ignored. That meant disease and other ailments often went untreated or were treated incorrectly.

Because of their importance, horses were also targeted in battle. One Union officer, when requisitioning more horses, claimed the Rebels had slain ten times as many of his horses. Often the fastest way to end a skirmish was to kill the other side's horses.

When the war first began, Confederate horses fared better. That was because Southern cavalrymen rode their own horses—horses they usually had a bond with. As the war continued, basic care became more difficult. Horses in wartime needed twenty-five pounds of grain and hay per day. During continued fighting, more horses were placed on starvation diets. Adequate fresh water was also a common problem.

Southern soldiers were responsible for supplying and caring for their own animals. They were also expected to find replacements should their horses die. Men could be gone for weeks as they "searched" for mounts. Others just went home because a cavalry soldier was unable to fight if he had no horse…and most men in the cavalry refused to join the infantry.

In the early days of the war, Southern soldiers received a token amount to help with the cost of feeding their horses. As the war progressed though, both money and feed became scarce. Some horses received a pound of corn each day. Other days, they received nothing.

Some historians claim that horses helped the North to win the war. The Union began with over three million horses while the South had just over one and one-half million. Even though the Southern cavalry horses were better trained, the number of available horses certainly benefited the North.

## GALVANIZED SOLDIERS

Galvanized Yankees were Confederate prisoners who won their freedom by swearing allegiance to the Union. They were enlisted in the Union Army but were usually sent West for frontier duty. Not only was their loyalty in question, there was also no way to effectively test it outside of battle. Around six thousand men made up the six regiments of these "volunteers" during 1864 and 1865.

Samuel Bowles, a newspaper reporter from Massachusetts, is credited with coining the term "Galvanized Yankees" in an article he wrote in 1865. He compared the prisoners to galvanized metal. The process of galvanization coats the gray surface of steel with a thin layer of bluish zinc while the underlying metal remains the same. However, the released prisoners' Confederate peers were the first to use the term "Galvanized Yankees," and the name was meant as an insult.

In the first years of the Civil War, prisoner exchanges were common and were typically done between the officers in command at the battles. Those exchanges broke down when Black soldiers were recruited. In addition, many freed soldiers returned to the battlefields.

When the prisoner exchanges ended, the prisons on both sides quickly became overcrowded. In the South, food was in short supply for everyone, so the prisoners starved along with the men who guarded them. In the North, Confederate soldiers were starved in retaliation for the treatment of Yankees prisoners. Fresh, uncontaminated water was also a problem due to massive overcrowding. Soldiers were usually forced into areas too small to accommodate the number imprisoned there, often with little room to lie down. Minimal or no shelter was provided and sick soldiers usually died. The prisoners arrived with the clothing they wore and little else was provided for them. In some cases, the food and clothing that was sent to them was confiscated by the guards.

Some Southern soldiers saw enlistment in the Union Army as a way out. Many of them had been starving before they were captured, and to stay in prison often meant certain death. While some did desert, the overall desertion rate was similar to other enlisted soldiers during that time.

The South also enlisted Yankee soldiers from its prisons. However, those men were immediately sent into battle, and in some cases, against their former comrades. Records show that more than sixteen hundred Yankee prisoners were recruited to fight for the South in the last months of the war, many foreign-born. Once on the battlefield, many of those men deserted or surrendered. Galvanized soldiers on both sides were usually considered traitors by their comrades.

In 1866, the last of all Galvanized regiments were disbanded and the soldiers were discharged. Some stayed in the West or migrated there to avoid poverty and possible ostracization in their home communities.

## FORT LEAVENWORTH, KANSAS

Fort Leavenworth is the oldest active army post west of the Mississippi River and has been in service since it was established in 1827. Located twenty-six miles northwest of Kansas City, Missouri, the old post is also the location of the first federal military prison. Until the federal prison was built, military prisoners were housed in twenty-one different army stockades as well as in nearly a dozen civilian prisons.

A bill was submitted to congress on January 16, 1872, for approval of a federal military prison. The original location was supposed to be Rock Island, Illinois. However, the Ordinance Department and the Secretary of War protested. They were concerned about the location of a prison near the munitions factory already in operation at Rock Island. On May 21, 1874, the original bill was amended to locate the prison at Fort Leavenworth, Kansas. The prison opened on May 21, 1875, one year later, and was the first penal institution in the Federal system. The old prison was decommissioned in 2002 when a new state-of-the-art facility was completed.

# PRIVATE THOMAS GALLAGHER, COMPANY G, 29TH REGIMENT OF MASSACHUSETTS INFANTRY VOLUNTEERS

The soldiers of the first seven companies that composed the 29th Regiment of Massachusetts Infantry Volunteers were among the first volunteers to enlist. They mustered in between December 13 and 17, 1861, in Newport News, Virginia. Companies F, G, and H were added in January of 1862. Those three companies enlisted for three years of service and completed the regiment.

In June of 1862, the 29th Regiment of Massachusetts Infantry Volunteers was attached to the "Irish Brigade." The 63rd, 69th, and 88th New York Infantry Regiments that composed the Irish Brigade were mostly Irish Catholic immigrants. There are questions as to why the 29th Massachusetts was chosen since many of the men were said to be "protestants from Plymouth County." They were from proud old Yankee stock, and religious frictions at the time were strong. (Special note: The officers of the 29th Regiment of Massachusetts Infantry Volunteers were predominantly English, but there are many names on the regimental manifest that show Irish ethnicity.)

Regardless of religious and political differences, the 29th Regiment of Massachusetts Infantry Volunteers and the Irish Brigade were a fighting force on the field. They fought together through December of 1862 when the 29th Massachusetts Infantry was replaced by the "more Irish" 28th Massachusetts Infantry.

Thomas C. Gallagher, a coal miner by trade, enlisted on January 11, 1862, in Rhode Island with the rest of the newly organized G Company. Private Gallagher was discharged on March 12, 1863, after losing his right leg below the knee. Unfortunately, his name is not listed on the regimental manifest, and we have no information on the battle where that injury occurred. However, the 29th Massachusetts did fight at Fredericksburg from December 12 through 15, 1862.

After being discharged, Gallagher married. He and his wife moved to Jewell County, Kansas, where they homesteaded and farmed. Mary Gallagher was passionate about farming and helped her husband adjust to his new life. She also did most of the fieldwork since it meant walking behind a horse.

While the 29th Regiment of Massachusetts Infantry Volunteers did not fight at Chickamauga, I made my great-grandfather part of that battle in this story.

---

Thank you for choosing to read the first novel in my *Uncivil War Series*, "The War Between Us, Friends and Enemies." My novels and children's books are available through your local bookstore, your library, and various online providers. They are also available on my website listed below. May you enjoy this dip into Civil War history and the fictional story that ties it together.

Rosie Bosse, Author
Living and Writing in the Middle of Nowhere
rosiebosse.com

# BATES COUNTY, MISSOURI
## BORDER OF KANSAS AND MISSOURI
### SEPTEMBER 1, 1863

# Chapter 1

# RED LEGS!

A LARGE SORREL HORSE CHARGED INTO THE FARMYARD and slid to stop. The young woman who dropped to the ground had a smile on her face. Her reddish-brown hair hung in a long braid down her back and her green eyes sparkled.

"That was a fine ride, Deuce. You love to run, and I love to ride fast!" She hugged the horse's neck as she turned toward the barn. He nickered and pushed against her back as he followed her. She stopped with a laugh and hugged him again.

"Fine. I will get you an apple but only if you behave." She turned toward the house where a tall, middle-aged woman stood in the doorway.

"Ava, how many times do I have to tell you that young ladies of eighteen should ride more respectably? Goodness. What would your father say if he saw you riding astraddle like that, and in britches too?"

Before Ava could answer, an old woman with bright eyes that snapped and danced stepped through the door. She laughed.

"Ah, Mary. She reminds me of myself when I was her age. I too wore pants. Of course, we were so poor when we first married that I couldn't afford any dresses." The old lady shrugged and added, "So, Ava's grandfather let me wear his." Her eyes sparkled and her wrinkled face broke into a grin as she whispered to her daughter-in-law, "Alfred said he liked to watch me get in his britches."

Mary stared at her mother-in-law in horror. The old lady laughed and winked before she turned back to Ava.

"Come, Ava. Bring Deuce up here and I will share my apple with him. My, how I love that horse. He is a picture of the first stud raised on this farm. Jewel was his name. He was your grandfather's favorite, you know."

Ava ran toward the house and hugged her grandmother.

"Oh, Granny. I do wish you would go riding with me again. There are so many places you have told me about, and I just can't find them all."

All three women turned to look down the lane as a young boy raced his horse toward them. Ava grabbed Deuce's reins when the horse tried to shy and run.

"Red Legs! About fifteen of 'em a couple a miles behind me. They're evictin' ever'body in their path an' burnin' down houses! My pa said to warn folks within fifteen miles, an' yore place is the next one on this road." His face turned slightly red as he looked at Ava. "Pa said to tell the young women to hide. He said ya won't be safe. Y'all need to get out now."

Both Ava and Mary stared at the young man, but Granny reacted quickly.

"Ava! You grab that pillowcase I showed you last week. Take that small ham on the table and run up to your room in the loft. You pack every piece of clothing you own in my valise and climb out your window. You need to get as high as you can in that big oak tree. Now go!"

Mary's face blanched white and she put her hand over her heart. Ava thrust Deuce's reins toward the young man.

"George, take Deuce. Ride him but don't turn him loose until you are several farms away. I don't want him to be taken, and he will come home on his own. Your horse is already tired, and you will be able to go faster if you have two horses to trade between.

"Go! Get out of here before they see you!"

She rushed into the house and grabbed the pillowcase from under Granny's bed. She didn't look inside as she shoved the ham inside. Even though it wasn't even half full, the pillowcase was heavy. As Ava raced up the ladder to the loft, she heard her mother cry, "Ride, George! I can see soldiers on the road!"

Ava's clothes were in her bag, and she was just climbing out of the window when she heard her grandmother's voice calling up the stairway, "Ava, no matter what happens—no matter what you hear—you do not come back to this house. Understand?" When Ava sobbed, her grandmother added softly, "We love you, Ava. Now be a good girl and hide in your tree."

A long tree branch was close to the west window and Ava ran across it quickly. She had been hiding in that tree since she was a small child. She climbed as high as she could and settled on a high branch. Her heart was beating quickly, and she took deep breaths to slow her breathing.

She had barely settled in the tree when she heard riders racing up the lane.

# Chapter 2

# A NOT SO FRIENDLY VISIT

**T**HE SOLDIER IN FRONT THREW ONE LEG OVER HIS horse's neck and grinned insolently at the two women. "Mornin', ladies. It's a right nice day fer a visit, ain't it?"

Mary's voice was firm when she answered.

"Well, I guess that depends on who the guests are, doesn't it?" She stared from face to face before she added, "Why are you here? You Red Legs have no business on this farm. My husband is a farmer and a cooper. We have no part in whatever war you are fighting."

The man who had been talking pulled a piece of paper from his pocket.

"Order 11 by Brigadier General Ewing says you *are* part of this war.

"Daniel an' Mary Bowman. Ages fifty-two an' forty-eight. Libby Bowman, age seventy. Two children, Ava Marie, age eighteen, an' Charlie John, age nineteen." He studied the list for a moment before he looked at the two women standing in the doorway. He tapped the paper before he spoke.

"It says here that Charlie enlisted to fight fer the Rebs. That makes y'all collaborators with the enemy. We have the right to run ya off an' burn ya out."

Mary's face became even paler, but Granny stepped forward. She held a double-barreled shotgun in her hands.

"The first one of you boys who tries to come into this house gets the first barrel. I'll save the second for those who follow." Granny's old blue eyes were hard as she stared at the men in front of her.

"The man of this house is Daniel Bowman. He has a contract with the Union army to provide horses and lumber. In fact, he left this morning with a load of barrels. He was to deliver them to Fort Scott in Kansas, and he's to take some horses down there next week.

"Now you men get out of here. You aren't welcome and you sure aren't wanted."

The group of men sat on their horses. Some were uneasy while others were laughing.

"I tell ya what. Ya let us come in an' look around. If we don't find no men here, we'll let ya be fer fifteen days. That'll be 'nough time fer yur man to git back. If he cin prove he's true to the Union, mebbie he cin talk General Ewing into lettin' y'all stay."

Granny pointed at a boy in the back who appeared to be much younger than the rest of the men.

"You send that boy up here. I'll let him in and no one else.

"Get up here, Boy. And drop your guns on the ground when you get off that nag of a horse."

The young man slid off his horse. He left his rifle in the boot of his saddle, but he didn't remove the large Colt from inside his loose shirt. He didn't think anyone could see it anyway. He walked slowly forward and stopped in front of the man who had been talking.

"Sergeant? You want me to go on in?"

"You look around in there good. There's a loft in that house. You get up in there. I want to know what ya see, right down to women's bloomers."

Mary's face blushed and Granny's old face became harder.

"And you had better not steal anything, Boy. My Mary is going to keep an eye on you so be smart." She thrust a revolver into her daughter-in-law's hands.

"You watch him, Mary, and you call out if he tries to start a fire."

The young man stared at Granny and shook his head as he stuttered, "I—I wouldn't do that, ma'am. I'll just look around. You have my word."

Granny peered at him and then motioned with her gun.

"Get then. You have five minutes."

The boy hurried into the house. He looked around downstairs before he poked his head out the door.

"Nothing so far, Sergeant. I'm headed up to the loft now."

The young man climbed the ladder quickly. He leaned out the far window and stared from side to side. The soldiers were scattered around the front of the house. They were lounging on their horses, but all had their guns ready. Some were talking crudely about what they would do to the young woman when they found her.

The young soldier hurried across the room and leaned out over the big limb as he stared into the tree. A flash of white showed, and he looked closer.

"Miss," he whispered softly, "I can see you up in that tree. Now I'm gonna pretend like y'all have snakes in this room. When you hear me start shootin', y'all start to climb down. I'll try to put all their attention on the far side of the house.

"You shimmy down that tree and find someplace to hide in that brush yonder. And you'd better be quick. This here group don't have good things in mind for you folks."

The young man began to throw things around and yell. Finally, he began shooting.

"You dad blame snake! I hate snakes! And rats too! You keep crawling—I'll get you if I have to shoot this floor plumb full of holes!"

He shot three times, firing as he banged his way to the far window. He threw a box out the window and continued to shoot, narrowly missing a man who rushed around the house.

As the soldiers rushed their horses to the east side of the house, Ava slid down the tree. She raced for the brush and rolled inside just as men appeared on the west side. She crawled as far as she could into the prickly thicket and held still.

The sergeant rode his horse around the house slowly and looked up the big tree.

"Slug! Git up here. I want ya to climb up in that tree an' make sure no one is up there. It would be right easy fer somebody to ease out that window an' hide up there."

The young man who had been shooting came down the ladder from the loft carrying a large quilt. He blushed slightly as he stopped in front of the women. His voice was soft when he spoke.

"I'm sorry to take this, ladies. I'll try real hard to keep it nice." He turned his back slightly toward the door and whispered, "Yore gal got away. She made it to the brush."

Mary stared at the young man a moment and tears filled her eyes.

"Thank you," she whispered, "thank you for letting our daughter go." Then she backed away as she yelled, "Thieves! Thieves and thugs, you all are. Get out of my home!"

Granny thrust an apple in the young soldier's pocket as he rushed by. She shoved him and shouted, "And don't you ever come back!"

The sergeant sat on his horse and looked down at the two angry women.

"Fifteen days. We'll be back in fifteen days an' yore man had better be here." The sergeant waved his hand, and the men rode away. Two of the soldiers were protesting but the sergeant ignored them. When they were around a bend in the road, Nielson pulled his horse to a stop. Two men rode up beside him and he pushed his horse close to them as he spoke quietly.

"Slug, I want you an' Mitchell to go back tonight. Don't make no noise when ya leave camp. Ya burn those women out if they don't give up that gal. Don't kill 'em right off though. I want 'em to know what we're goin' to do to 'er once we catch 'er. Then kill all the livestock ya cin find. I know they have a milk cow hid somewhere. Shoot, I'll go with ya."

Nielson turned toward another man and hollered, "Henry, take five boys an' round up those hosses. No point in lettin' good hossflesh like that go to waste. Catch those chickens too, an' bring 'em back to camp. We'll have us some fresh meat tonight."

One of the men pulled his horse in front of the sergeant's mount.

"Sir, you can't take their horses. You gave them fifteen days. Their man is on our side!"

"General Ewing said to burn out all Reb collaborators who didn't swear allegiance to the Union. Do those two gals act like they'd swear allegiance to anyone but the South? Not in a pig's eye.

"'Sides, he said we could use our discretion. Now my discretion don't give no exceptions. We don't have to give 'em fifteen days. Mebbie we will an' mebbie we won't. Besides, they was hidin' someone an' I want to know who. Slug said there was scrape marks in that tree where someone was likely hidin'."

"Shoot, Sarge. That tree was so close to that window that ever' little kid around ran down that limb at some point in time. That don't give us a call to—"

"Those are my orders, Corporal Blake. Ya don't have to like 'em, but ya damn shore will follow 'em."

"Then send me back instead of Slug. You know Slug can't be trusted around women!"

Sergeant Nielson stared at Blake and laughed.

"Those women be the enemy. You know that old lady woulda shot all of us, an' the other one—who knows. She ain't a bad lookin' woman, but I'm guessin' she's jist as mean as the old gal."

"Now y'all fall in line or I'll have ya thrown in the brig.

"Move out!"

Blake's face showed his disgust. He rode away shaking his head. He muttered under his breath, "I am going to talk to Captain Headrick. I'm pretty sure he wouldn't approve of this.

"If this is what they have been doing for the last week, I don't want to be any part of it. Captain Headrick said nothing about burning farms and houses when he sent me out to find his brother. We just happened on these fellows. They said they were riding toward our camp, so we joined them."

Sergeant Nielson grinned as he watched Blake ride away. He bumped the man riding next to him and laughed wickedly.

"Slug'll find out who they was hidin'. I'll bet it was that daughter. The spy we have in this area give me the rundown on their family. He said she was a looker too. I told Slug if he found her to send Mitchell to get me. Ya cin come too if ya want. We'll have our fun an' then Slug'll kill 'em all an' burn down the whole works.

"An' as far as their man—he was killed on his way to Fort Scott. Word is the Bushwhackers got 'im." Sergeant Nielson laughed mockingly. "Bushwhackers killed 'im 'cause he was workin' with the Yankees. Now Yankees kill his family 'cause the son is fightin' fer the Rebs. Ain't that a pickle?

"We'll kill the whole lot of 'em an' move on up the road. Likely no one will miss 'em. Shoot, there won't be no one left to miss 'em by the time we finish with these four counties. An' if anyone raises a ruckus, we'll be in the right 'cause of General Ewing's Order 11.

"I love this war. It gives a man freedoms he jist don't always have."

# NIGHT MARAUDERS

WHEN IT WAS ALMOST DARK, GRANNY CARRIED A basket out to the clothesline. She hung up a pair of men's britches. Then she hung a second pair. She looked toward the lane and slowly walked back to the house.

Ava watched from the bushes. Her heart clutched and her breath came quickly. It was Granny's signal for her to hide.

She crawled out the brush and ran for the caves on the back side of their land. Granny had shown her many caves as a small child.

"Ava," Granny always said, "Pay attention. Someday, you may need to hide in here, and you have to know all the ways to get out."

The cave was dark, and Ava didn't dare light a fire. She looked toward the direction of their farm and listened closely. Around ten that night, she fell asleep. She awoke to the sound of gunfire. From the opening in the cave, she could see their farm burning.

Ava sank to her knees and began to sob.

"Granny and Mother, please don't die." Before long, she heard horses coming toward the cave. She slipped deeper into the shadows.

A man called, "I know yore in there, girlie. We was told 'bout this here cave. Yore folks down there told us you was hidin' up here. They said fer ya to come out.

"Come on out now. We won't do nothin' to ya. We jist want to talk a little." The man waited but Ava didn't answer.

The man's voice was harder when he spoke again. "'Course, if ya don't come out, we'll close off this here openin' an' ya won't never get out."

When there was still no answer, the man slid off his horse and laughed.

"Last chance, girlie. We'll close this here hole up an' you'll rot in there!" The man waited for a short time again before he cursed loudly.

"Yore womenfolk ain't 'round to talk no more, so no one 'ill know where to find ya." He laughed harshly and added, "This is yore last chance. Ya cin join 'em if ya want or ya cin be friendly-like."

Ava covered her mouth to hide the sobs that were trying to leak out before she hurried toward the back of the cave. She felt for the torch that Granny kept beside a large opening. She lit it and ran as fast as she could.

She could hear the men rolling rocks into the cave. There was a stir from above and then a crash as rocks slid down over the opening.

Ava ran faster. As she wove through the crooked tunnels, she thought of her grandmother. "You prepared me for this, Granny. You said, 'When you see me hang two pairs of britches on the clothesline and walk away, you run for the caves.' Mother just shook her head.

"'Your grandmother overreacts to everything. I'm sure you will never have to hide in those caves. Besides, they are dark and dangerous. I don't even like for you to be in them during the day let alone go there with Granny at night.'"

Still, Ava and Granny went often. After Granny was bucked off her horse and broke her leg two years ago though, she didn't go riding as much. Walking was even harder for her. Since then, all of her teaching had been from the front porch.

"Oh, Granny," Ava whispered, "what am I going to do if something happens to you or Mother?"

Ava climbed through a back opening to the cave and slipped between the rocks. The caves curled around the west side of their farm and brought her out on the north side. She was less than one hundred yards from her house. She could see both the barn and the house burning.

The three men rode back into the yard. One of them shot down at someone on the ground. Then he kicked a second still form.

"Sarge won't be happy we didn't find that gal. Neither of those women would say a thing. Never saw the like. That old lady especially. She was one tough old gal."

"Well, come on. Stick that note Sarge wrote over this nail. Bushwhackers'll get blamed fer this."

The three men rode slowly down the lane and Ava slipped out of her hiding place. She ran toward the two women.

Her mother was the one the Red Leg had shot before he left. Ava reached for her and stared in horror at the huge hole in her mother's once-pretty face. Her mother's body was limp. Either gunshot wound would have been fatal.

Ava sobbed as she rushed toward the little form that was her grandmother. A slight moan came from the woman and Ava turned her over.

"Granny? Oh, Granny!"

Granny opened her eyes and tried to smile.

"They didn't find you, did they? I knew those caves would save our family someday." Granny gasped and struggled to breathe. "Your mother?"

Ava's breath caught in her throat, and she shook her head. Granny squeezed her hand.

"Sweetheart, I'm not going to make it. Now there is some Yankee money in the bottom of that pillowcase. You take that and you leave here. You can't tell anyone who you are. Folks will think you died today, and we will let them think it. From now on, your name is Ella Bradley. Bradley was my maiden name, but few around here know that. You use that name until you are a long ways from here—you might even have to use it forever.

"You were always interested in nursing. Here is your chance. You find a military unit and you sign on to be a nurse

"Your horse will be back here before long. I heard him snort not long ago. You ride him to Harrisonville up in Cass County. That is only about thirty-five miles from here. You tell the Yankee commander there that Bushwhackers burned your place out across the border in Kansas. You tell him you are a nurse and you want to help with the war efforts.

"Shoot, you have more training than most nurses do anyway.

"Harrisonville was just burned and sacked by those Bluebellies. Those blasted Yankees are in charge now. It won't be long before our boys take that town back, but you have to get along until that happens. Of course, if you see lots of gray uniforms, that means our Rebs are already there. If they are, you tell them it was the Red Legs who burned you out."

Ava listened to her grandmother and then started crying.

"I can't just leave you, Granny! Who will bury you and Mother?"

"Oh, those Yankees will be back. I heard one of those fellows say he left a note saying the Bushwhackers did this. The officer in charge will be here by dawn, no doubt. I'd have you take that note but then those soldier boys would know someone survived."

Ava stubbornly shook her head.

"I'm not leaving you, Granny. Maybe you aren't hurt as bad as you think. We can both ride. Let me look at you."

Granny's blue eyes were dim as she smiled up at her granddaughter in the moonlight.

"Ava Marie, you always made me proud. I'll be passing on before too long, and as soon as I go, I want you to ride out. Just know that I will always be around to keep an eye on you. If the Good Lord won't let me be an angel, then I'll be a ghost." Granny's grin was fleeting before the pain returned to her face.

"Now you be strong, Ava, and you make our name proud. We Bradleys and Bowmans came from good stock. Someday, you'll marry a good man and you can tell him—" Granny gasped and gripped Ava's hand hard. "When you meet a man who you can trust, you tell him the truth. Don't ever lie to those you love."

Granny smiled and squeezed Ava's hand again. "I love you, Ava." Her grip relaxed and Granny's eyes closed. The last smile she gave Ava was still on her face.

Ava stared at her grandmother and then hugged her tightly.

"Oh, Granny. I love you and mother so much." She stretched her grandmother's hand over to her mother and left the two of them lying close together on the ground with their hands touching.

She heard stirring behind her and Deuce nickered softly. Ava turned to him.

"Deuce, it's just you and me now. You stand still while I tie this valise and pillowcase on you. The two of us are riding north."

# Chapter 4

# CAPTAIN HEADRICK'S PROBLEM

CORPORAL BLAKE WAS ANGRY. "I DON'T LIKE IT, Captain. Nielson was up to no good yesterday. And Slug and Mitchell are just downright bad men." Blake swore and added, "And why do all Nielson's men wear those red leather leggings? They look and act like a bunch of hooligans.

"I heard Nielson talking quiet-like to Slug and Mitchell before he ordered them to steal the horses and chickens. I think they all went back last night. Nielson was mighty mad he didn't find out who was climbing around in that tree."

Captain Headrick listened closely as he frowned.

"You believe Nielson sent them back, but you heard no gunfire. They couldn't have done much in the short time you say they were gone. According to the men, Slug and Mitchell were with Nielson when he arrived yesterday afternoon." Captain Headrick frowned deeper and added, "Unless they slipped out of camp. The sentry should have caught them though if they tried to slip out. If not when they left, for sure when they came back. He said nothing to me.

"As far as Order 11, Nielson was correct. He does have orders to evict folks and burn out those who aren't loyal to the United States Government. He takes those orders directly from General Ewing, so I can't stop him. The fact that the majority of folks they are displacing are women and kids is of little concern to Ewing. He considers family members of Rebs to be collaborators." Captain Headrick frowned and shook his head. "I'm guessing if those families weren't sympathizers before, they will be after getting burned out.

"So no, I don't approve of that order. However, General Ewing issued it, and he has more rank than me. I'm just glad they didn't call on me to help implement it." Captain Headrick drummed his fingers on his desk and then looked up. "We'll ride out first thing this morning.

"Was Peter with Nielson? I sent him to Harrisonville to deliver a message, and he was to join up with any company he ran into on the way back here. I was out on patrol and didn't get back until late last night, so I haven't talked to him."

"He was there. He's the one that went into the house first. He was supposed to see if anyone was hiding in there. He said he ran into some snakes in the loft. He did a bunch of shooting and finally threw a box out the window." Corporal Blake frowned before he continued. "I didn't see any snakes or rats either so I'm not sure what Peter saw. Nielson sent Slug up a tree that was close to the other window. Slug said he could tell it had been climbed around in.

"I didn't put much stake in that tree business though," Blake added disgustingly. "A branch that close to a window would have been used by every kid who was ever in that house. It was just too handy not to climb out and play in that tree.

"Nielson said there were two kids. Well, not kids really. The girl is eighteen and her brother is nineteen. The young man is supposedly off fighting for the Rebs. It was the girl they couldn't find.

"Their pa was gone. He works with us and that's what struck me as wrong. Why would any of these folks help us Yankees if we burn out their kinfolk while they're gone?" Corporal Blake's face showed his anger as he spoke.

Captain Headrick stood.

"Send Peter in to see me. I want to know what he saw.

"And, Corporal, thanks for your report. I will keep that in mind when we ride out there this morning."

Corporal Blake saluted and left the tent with a frown on his face. He saw Peter walking toward the mess tent and caught up with him.

"Your brother wants to see you right away." He grinned at the young man and wrapped a big arm around his neck. "Good to have you back, Pete."

Peter tapped on the captain's tent.

"Private Headrick reporting, sir."

Captain Headrick looked up with a smile.

"Come in, Private."

When the tent flap opened, Peter saluted and then grinned.

"Morning, Noble. Blake said you wanted to see me."

"Yes, I did. You delivered the message I gave you to General Hartwig at Harrisonville?"

"Yes, sir."

The captain smiled at his younger brother.

"Sit down, Peter, and tell me what took place out at the Bowman farm yesterday afternoon."

Peter frowned and looked away before he finally answered.

"There was a gal hiding in a tree by the house. I pretended there were snakes and rats in the loft. I shot several times and got Nielson's men to go around the east side so she could get away." He blushed slightly and added, "I didn't think Sergeant Nielson's intentions were honorable. He seemed mighty determined to find her."

Captain Headrick drummed his fingers on the table in front of him for a moment before he looked up.

"Do you know who she was? And did she get away?"

"I think she was kin to the two women who were there, but I never saw her. She was gone when I looked up the tree after I did all the shooting." His face blushed a deeper red. "I took her quilt. I was sorry to do it, but I was afraid it would be stolen by one of the other men if I didn't."

"Were there any other quilts taken?"

Peter grinned and shook his head. "Naw, those ladies had tubs of water by the door, and they were plumb full of wet, soggy quilts. Besides, the old lady wouldn't let any other men in but me.

"I would like to take that quilt back with me when we go out there this morning. If the Red Legs are going to run those women out, they might appreciate their quilt."

"Did Sergeant Nielson set anything on fire while you were there?"

"No, but he sent Slug and Mitchell back for their horses and chickens as we were leaving. They weren't gone long so I'm not sure if they did then or not."

"The women were all right when you left?"

"Yes, but Sarge was talking quiet-like to some of his men after we left. I think he had some plans for last night."

The captain looked at him sharply.

"You think someone sneaked out of this camp?"

"I know they did. I put an extra loop on the hobbles of Slug's and Mitchell's horses. That loop wasn't there when I gathered the horses this morning. I didn't do that to Sergeant Nielson's horse, but he looked like he had been put away wet. I purposely rubbed that horse down after we returned yesterday afternoon."

Captain Headrick cursed under his breath. Peter stood and fidgeted before he asked, "May I go now, sir?"

"Peter, I wish you would go home. You are too young to be involved in this war. Shoot, you're not even thirteen. It's dangerous every day, and situations like this are making things more dangerous."

Peter grinned at his brother.

"We both know I don't have a home anymore. Besides, I'd rather be here with you."

Captain Noble Headrick wrapped his little brother up in a hug and tousled his hair.

"Get on out of here then. And keep your head low. I want to ride out to the Bowman place as soon as chow is over so have the horses ready. You can come with me." He winked and grinned at his brother as he added, "And don't forget that quilt.

"Dismissed."

Peter laughed as he ducked out of the tent opening. Captain Noble Headrick sat for a moment staring straight ahead. *Peter is right. We have nothing left at home. When the war broke out, our plantation in Georgia was one of the first ones to be destroyed. We were Union supporters, and in the eyes of our neighbors, we were traitors.*

*It didn't matter that I graduated from West Point with high scores. Of course, after that altercation I was in with that arrogant junior cadet, I killed my career path in the army. The commander told me I had lots of potential and as much or more leadership abilities than that cadet had. However, his gal had connections to some bigwig in the military.*

"The commander said, 'Headrick, you just shot down your opportunity to move up through the ranks. You will be commissioned second lieutenant when you graduate, but you will never get past the rank of captain.'

"He was right too. I have been in the army for seven years, and I have made it as high as I will ever go. I'm all right with that though. I've decided I like cattle and horses better than most folks.

"I'll serve through the end of this war and then I'm moving west. I'll buy me a little ranch out in the Dakota Territory and settle down with a bunch of cows in the middle of nowhere. Or maybe farther north along the Missouri River. There is some fine land there too." Captain Headrick frowned and shook his head.

"Pa and Ma died years ago, and Peter has been in my care since he was seven. Well, my care and Indigo's. Old Indigo was more like a mother to us than a cook, but she is gone now too. And even though it is nice for me to see Peter every day, I don't like having him here."

Captain Headrick cursed again and jerked on his hat. "Well, I'd better check on those women. They may need a ride somewhere if Nielson gave the order to burn them out.

"Dang Red Legs. They aren't accountable to anyone but Ewing."

# Chapter 5

# "BRUSH WAKERS DUN IT"

CAPTAIN HEADRICK SAT ON HIS HORSE AND STARED at the women's bodies. The younger woman had been shot twice, and the second shot was in the face at close range. She was fully clothed, but her dress was torn. The older woman had been shot once in the abdomen. He could tell by the wound that her death had been lingering and painful. Fury almost leaked from the captain as he looked from their bodies to the burned farmstead.

"Sergeant Nielson! Did you order these women's deaths?"

"Naw. Private Cotter an' Private Mitchell said they was alive when they left yesterday afternoon."

"And they didn't burn the house or the barn?"

"Naw, both was still standin' when they left."

Captain Headrick's eyes were hard as he looked at the sergeant.

"Why exactly did you target this homestead?"

"They was on our list. I knew those two women was hidin' someone. I believed it to be a woman we been lookin' fer. She is on my list as a spy, an' I was given orders to find 'er.

"Those two women wouldn't tell us nothin'. They wouldn't even let us in the house so she mighta been hidin' there. Private Headrick was the onliest one they let in so mebbie talk to him."

About that time, one of the other soldiers rode up.

"This was nailed to a corral post." He handed a blackened piece of paper to Captain Headrick.

### BRUSH WAKERS DUN IT

Captain Headrick stared at the letter. *Bushwhackers my eye. This is all Nielson and his men.*

He looked up and Nielson laughed. The sergeant took a metal toothpick from his pocket and began to pick his teeth.

"Too bad they shot the missus in the face. She was a good-lookin' woman 'fore that happened."

Captain Headrick's voice was angry when he spoke.

"Sergeant, I want you, Mitchell, and Cotter to dig two holes. I want them deep and long enough to bury those women. Corporal Blake, you and Private Headrick carve some markers. The rest of you, make sure those fires are out."

Sergeant Nielson paused from picking his teeth. He stared at Captain Headrick and finally shook his head.

"I don't have to take no orders from you, Captain. My orders come from General Ewing."

Captain Headrick wheeled his horse around and slammed it into Nielson's.

"Sergeant Nielson, you dig those holes, or you find another troop to bunk with. I won't have a soldier in my command who refuses to take orders from me." The captain's face was drawn down in hard lines as he waited for a response.

The sergeant shook his head. "We jist as well part ways now then. I didn't leave nothin' back to yur camp I cain't live without. We'll mosey on outa here an' report back to General Ewing in Kansas City." Nielson swung his horse around and the Red Legs who were with him followed.

Captain Headrick spoke softly, "And you make sure you stay out of this part of Missouri, Sergeant. You aren't welcome here. Your actions make you mighty hard to distinguish from a Bushwhacker."

Nielson pulled his horse to a stop. His eyes were cold when he looked back over his shoulder.

"You cain't threaten me, Captain. I'm actin' on orders from General Ewing."

"That wasn't a threat, Sergeant. It was a promise and one you had better remember." Captain Headrick wheeled his horse around.

"Corporal Blake! Pick two men and start digging those graves."

Peter stared from his brother to the departing backs of the laughing men. His eyes narrowed down, and he cursed softly as he dropped from his horse.

"Ladies, I'll hang onto this quilt. Maybe one of these days, we'll find your girl and I can give it back to her."

# Chapter 6

# TEARS AND ANGER

IT WAS NEARLY THREE IN THE MORNING WHEN AVA rode Deuce toward the caves. She walked him slowly down the small creek until she came to an opening in the wall of rock. She rode him inside the hidden cave and pulled his saddle off.

"We both need to get some rest, old fellow. These next few days are going to be long ones." She turned Deuce loose and he crossed the water to graze on the thick grass above the creekbank.

When Ava awakened, the morning sun was up. She dug in the pillowcase that Granny had sent with her. Besides the ham, there were some hard biscuits and apples. There was also a knife in a sheath. After she had cut off several slices of ham, she returned it to the pillowcase and tied the top shut. The money she put in the bottom of her saddlebag. She wrapped the silver candlesticks in her dresses, folding and pushing until she had everything back in the valise. Once she was packed, she whistled for Deuce. She soon had him saddled and was riding toward the main road that led north to Harrisonville.

When she reached the road, Ava stopped and stared. Women and children of all ages and health were walking on the rough road. All were slowly plodding north. Only a few were on horseback, but there were no wagons or buggies. She rode Deuce toward the road.

A pregnant mother was struggling to walk. She held the hand of a small girl who was crying. A boy who was just a little older was tripping with exhaustion. Ava slid off Deuce and led him toward the mother.

"Here, ride my horse for a little while. I will lead him so you can put both of your children on with you."

The young woman's face was pale with fear and exhaustion.

"I can't thank you enough. We are so tired. The children need to rest, but I am terrified to be on this road by myself. I was praying we would be able to make it to Harrisonville. My parents live north of there. I am hoping they will start down this way to look for us when they hear the news." She smiled tiredly as she pulled herself up on Deuce's back. She reached her arms down and Ava handed her the children.

"My name is Penny Winters. My son's name is James, and we call this little one Sissy." She placed both children in front of her and they were soon slipping from side to side as they slept.

"Have you been on the road long?"

"Since yesterday morning. The Red Legs burned us out three days ago. I hid the children, but we had to leave. We had nothing to eat." Her voice was bitter as she added, "They rode their horses through my garden and killed our milk cow. They didn't even butcher her. They took our milk source and wasted all that meat. They threw the eggs at each other and then killed all the chickens they could catch. A few got away but they won't make it. There are too many varmints around.

"I despise them, every one of them. If this is the Union's way of bringing us over to their side, it certainly isn't working with me.

"My husband would tell me not to talk like that if he were here. He's not around though. I haven't seen him in over six months. They were passing through and he stopped in for a visit." She laughed and patted her stomach. "That's all it took and now we have another little one who will be arriving in three months. I haven't heard from him since." A sob slipped out of Penny's throat, and she became quiet.

Ava said nothing. She was angry and bitter as well, but she had no intention of sharing her feelings with a stranger.

Deuce was moving along smartly, and they were nearly at the front of the slow-moving column. After two hours, Ava was tired.

"Let's stop for a time, Penny. We are small enough that we can both ride after we eat. I have a little ham and some biscuits as well as apples."

Ava led Deuce off to the side of the road and lifted the pillowcase off his back. She lifted the large knife out of a saddlebag and dropped down on the ground.

Penny eased back against the tree and sighed. She blushed slightly as she turned toward Ava.

"I'm so sorry. I didn't even ask you your name!"

"I'm Ella Bradley from Kansas. We were burned out too. Luckily, they didn't catch Deuce here or we'd all be on foot." She sliced off some ham and passed out her biscuits. Several people looked at their food longingly. They said nothing as they slowly trudged by. Finally, a small boy walked over to where they were eating and stood watching them.

Ava offered him a slice of ham as well as a biscuit and an apple. He smiled shyly and rushed back to catch up with his family. She almost cried when she saw him share his meager food with a younger brother. *We have so little. I can't feed everyone but at least those two little boys will have something.*

The end of the caravan was just passing them when they finished. Ava quickly packed the rest of the food. It all now fit in the saddle bags. Penny mounted and slid back behind the saddle. Ava handed her James and then set Sissy in front of the saddle. She tied the valise to the saddle horn and mounted before she pulled Sissy into the saddle in front of her. Deuce looked around and snorted.

"I know there are a lot of people on you, Deuce, but we are all small. Together, we weigh little more than Father."

# Chapter 7

# A CROWDED TOWN

THE BLUE UNIFORMS OF THE UNION ARMY WERE everywhere when they arrived at Harrisonville just before dark. They had been on the road over twelve hours and everyone was tired.

Ava guided Deuce toward the main part of town and almost staggered with exhaustion as she stepped down. She lifted the kids down and then helped Penny off. The two women stared around the crowded town. Women and children were everywhere.

"Let's see if there is room for Deuce in the stable. I am guessing we will be sleeping with him tonight."

They both turned around at the sound of a woman's cry. A middle-aged woman was running toward them. A man was following her, and they both had tears in their eyes.

"Penny, oh Penny! Your father and I were so worried. We heard about what was going on and we rushed here to find you. We arrived just an hour ago.

"There is absolutely no place to stay here so Father wants to leave tonight. We will go to your Aunt Bea's and spend the night there."

She held her daughter away and looked down at her round belly. Then she pulled her close again. She cried softly as she kissed her. The man had lifted the two small children, and he hugged them as he smiled. They were staring at him somberly but when he pulled a sandwich out of his pocket, they ate hungrily. He cleared his throat and pecked Penny on the cheek as he spoke huskily.

"Come along now. We have a ten-mile drive in a buggy, and there is little moon tonight."

Penny paused as she pulled Ava up beside her.

"Mother, Father—this is Ella. She is the reason we were able to make this difficult trip. May we take her with us?" Her parents smiled and Penny's mother reached out her hand.

"Of course! Please join us, Ella. We don't have much, but we'd be pleased to make a place for you."

Ava paused briefly but shook her head.

"No, I am going to see if I can find work as a nurse. My family is gone, and I have no husband. I don't care where they send me as long as I can help men on both sides of this terrible war." She smiled and hugged Penny.

"Thank you though." She hugged James and Sissy as well. "Now you two have fun with your grandparents." She gave each of them one of the broken cookies she had been hoarding and quickly turned away. As she led Deuce toward the stable, she looked down at the dirty britches she was wearing and almost laughed. *Mother, you would be horrified if you saw me right now. I'm filthy dirty and wearing britches in public as well!*

A man in uniform with lots of bars on his chest nearly knocked her down. Ava staggered and struggled to regain her balance.

The officer caught her and then looked at her closely.

"Miss, you shouldn't be out on the streets this late. There are lots of strangers in this town right now. I hope you have family here. There are no open rooms here whatsoever."

Ava shook her head and pointed at Deuce. "I am going to sleep in the barn with my horse—and my pistol too." She paused and asked cautiously, "I'd like to volunteer as a nurse once I get some rest and get cleaned up. Can you tell me whom I need to talk to about that?"

The man studied her closer and slowly nodded.

"I do but that train is leaving at six tomorrow morning." He paused and added carefully, "There are skirmishes going on all over and they are begging for field nurses. You do realize that field nurses work in tents, and often without all the amenities of a real hospital."

Ava nodded. Tears filled her eyes, but she looked at him directly.

"I understand. I want to help but I won't leave a man die with no treatment just because his uniform is a different color. I intend to treat all of the wounded, not just the Union soldiers."

General Hartwig studied at the determined young woman in front of him. He nodded slowly.

"You can treat any man who shows up, but our soldiers come first.

"Follow me. I will take you to the nurse's quarters so you can clean up." He barked at a young soldier standing behind him.

"Private, untie that valise and grab those saddlebags. Then take that horse down to the livery. Put him with our horses and give him a bait of grain." He paused before he asked, "I'm guessing you will be leaving him?"

"No, I want to take Deuce with me. He can be hitched to a wagon if necessary. Besides, he would break loose and chase the train. He goes where I go." Ava's chin lifted as she spoke and General Hartwig chuckled.

He offered her his arm.

"Tell me your name, miss. I think you will do just fine as a field nurse."

# Chapter 8

# A NEW FRIEND

AVA DIDN'T FEEL NEARLY AS BRAVE AS SHE PRETENDED to be. In addition, many of the young women stared at her dirty face and britches without speaking. She found an empty bunk and sat down heavily. She looked around for a tub and a bucket to carry water. Just as she pushed herself off the bunk, a young woman with a friendly smile rushed over to her.

"I can show you where to draw the water. There is a small room in the back where you can take a bath as well. It will give you a little privacy.

"My name is Chlolea but my friends call me Chloe. Chloe Moore. Did you just arrive? So many women and children have arrived in the last few days. It is terrible what is happening around us."

Ava nodded. "Yes, I just rode in. There was a large group of us on the road. I am thankful we made it before it became too dark." She put out her hand and then stared at it before she pulled it back. Her fingernails were broken and black. Grit and grime were in every crease of her hand.

"I'm sorry. I am so dirty. We were burned out two days ago, and I have been on the move ever since. My name is Ella. Ella Bradley.

"And thank you for your help. I have barely slept in three days. That cot almost won out over a bath."

Chloe grabbed two buckets and led Ava out the door.

"Don't mind the rest of those girls. Some of them want to become nurses because they think it sounds romantic. They have no idea the horrors we will see."

Ava was quiet a moment as she looked over at Chloe.

"You have worked as a field nurse before?"

"No, but I was in Lawrence when it was sacked. It was terrifying. So much death and destruction. That was when I volunteered to be a nurse. I thought maybe they would keep me there, but General Ewing ordered all volunteers to come here. He knew General Hartwig was putting a group of nurses together to send East. We are leaving by train first thing in the morning.

"Do you have any family? My father passed away several years ago." Chloe laughed softly and added, "My mother was hysterical when I told her I was volunteering."

"No, my mother and grandmother both died when our farm was burned." A sob caught in Ava's throat and she almost tripped.

"I have always enjoyed medicine. My father and grandmother were both known as healers. Father took care of the animals and Granny took care of the people. I learned a lot from both of them.

"Maybe when this terrible war is over, I will try to go to medical school. I think I would enjoy being a doctor—if they let women in. Granny was quite accomplished although she had no formal training." Ava was quiet as they walked quickly toward the pump. She choked back another sob when she thought of her mother and grandmother.

Chloe stared at her new friend and laughed softly.

"Oh, if my mother only knew that my first friend in this wild town was a girl who wore britches and talked of becoming a doctor! She would probably hire someone to drive out here and 'rescue' me!" She squeezed Ava's arm.

"I'm so glad you came here. It will be nice to have a friend to travel and work with."

# Chapter 9

# A LONG TRAIN RIDE

AVA STARED OUT THE TRAIN'S DIRTY WINDOW. SHE tucked a reddish-brown curl back under her hat and sighed.

She hadn't seen many soldiers on the train, but Chloe told her before they left that the enlisted men often rode on top of the cars.

Chloe chose the window seat, and her voice was animated when she gestured toward the top of the train.

"I'll bet there are men all over the top of this train. They probably boarded after us and that's why we didn't see them. There are so many soldiers moving around all the time. They feel lucky to have a seat at all. Why they are just marched everywhere," Her eyes were serious as she continued, "We won't take this train all the way east though. Those Rebs would like nothing better than to blow up an entire train of Yankees and Yankee sympathizers."

When Ava stared at her, Chloe nodded. "Oh yes. That is what we are called. According to the Rebs, anyone who helps the north is a Yankee sympathizer even if that person is just trying to survive.

"I've even heard that some of those captured Reb soldiers don't want a Yankee nurse working on them."

Chloe twisted her fingers together and added softly, "We all hate each other. It's sad because in a different time and place, we would probably get along. Our sweethearts could even be Rebs. Maybe things will be different when this war ends." She giggled and added, "Still, Mother would have a heart attack if I brought home a Reb husband!"

Ava laughed in spite of herself. She spoke softly, "My Granny was an independent woman. I never met my grandfather. He died before I was born. Granny lived by herself in central Missouri for a time, but Father kept begging her to move west and live with us.

"She finally did when I was about four." Ava smiled wistfully. "I adored my granny. She was so spunky and fearless. Wise too. She taught me all the time, even when we were playing.

"And she always made plans for what might happen. It used to irritate my mother. One day I heard her tell Granny, 'Don't be so morbid, Livvy. You will frighten that girl out of her wits.'

"Granny just smiled. She said, 'Ava's not afraid. She is going to be fearless when she grows up, and I am going to help her. Besides, it never hurts to be prepared.'

"I so miss her."

Chloe listened closely. Her brow puckered and she asked, "So your grandmother called you Ava? Was that a nickname?"

Ava frowned as she remembered her slip. Then she tried to cover up her use of her real name.

"Yes, that was what she called me." She smiled at Chloe. "Olivia Eleanora Aveline Bradley was Granny's name, but most folks called her Livvy. I was named after her. I think I spent more time with her growing up than I did with my own mother.

"They were so different. Mother was very proper. She was a perfect lady in every way and my father was smitten with her.

"She always wanted me to ride sidesaddle. I refused and Father just laughed. He said, 'Let the girl alone, Mary. She takes after her granny. They are a happy pair.'

"Still, I learned a lot from my mother. She was a wonderfully kind person. She demonstrated how to love unconditionally."

"She was a true Southern lady who lived on a small farm on the border of Kansas and Missouri. I think she would have been more comfortable in town, but she loved my father. She gave up all that she had to marry him.

"Granny, on the other hand, was wild. She loved going on adventures and she tried to teach me everything she knew. I adored her. Somehow, even baking was more interesting when Granny taught me." Ava laughed and the two girls visited a while longer before Chloe dozed off. Her friend was leaning against the window, and Ava shifted in her seat to stretch out her legs.

She enjoyed her new friend, but she appreciated the quiet too. Still, when it was quiet, she thought about her family. *Maybe noise is better. I don't want to cry on this train.*

A tall man in a blue uniform stopped beside her seat. He looked down at her. He looked away and shifted his feet before he finally spoke.

"Excuse me, ma'am. Would you mind if I take this seat? I'm sure you appreciate the extra room, but this train is full. I've walked through all three passenger cars, and this is the only open seat I found."

Ava looked up when the man spoke. He was tall with dark, curly hair and brilliant blue eyes. He had laugh wrinkles in the corners of his eyes and his mouth was turned up in a smile. Still, she could see a little sadness behind his eyes. That and complete exhaustion.

She nodded. "Do sit down. My friend is asleep, but I know she won't mind."

"I am Captain Headrick, Captain Noble Headrick. And who do I have the pleasure of sitting beside?"

"Av—Ella Bradley. My friend and I volunteered to be field nurses." She gave him a quick smile and then turned her face away. There was something disconcerting about having a man she didn't know this close to her, especially one in the blue uniform of a Yankee.

Captain Headrick was quiet as he studied the side of the woman's face beside him. *Now why would she lie about her name? Is she running away?* He faced forward as he stretched out his long legs and leaned back in the seat with a sigh. *Probably. I guess we are all running from memories of some kind.* He was soon asleep.

Ava stole a sideways look at him.

The soldier's uniform was clean and freshly pressed. He had been talking just moments before and now was snoring softly. *He acts even more tired than me.* His snoring brought Ava back to the present and she sighed deeply.

She whispered to herself, "Now they are all gone. Well, I'm not sure about my brother. He is with the Rebs, but we haven't heard from him in over a year. I don't know where he is or even if he is still alive. And now that our home is gone, he might not be able to find me even if he comes back."

The seats were hard, and Ava shifted her body in her seat. Her shoulder bumped the sleeping man beside her and he sat up.

"I'm sorry. I didn't mean to wake you. These seats are so confining." Ava's face was light pink as she apologized.

Captain Headrick laughed, and Ava looked away quickly. She glanced toward him again and asked, "So you are moving your men to a new location? My friend was telling me that you often march instead of going by train."

"We are cavalry, so we travel on horseback. The infantry march on foot. We all take trains when we can through Union-held ground though.

"We'll ride as far as we can and make the rest of the journey on horseback. Train rides allow the men to rest up a little even if most of them do ride on top. They aren't usually comfortable, but they are faster.

"This ride will give our mounts a little time to rest as well." Captain Headrick shifted in his seat and added, "Trains always make me a little nervous though. Too easy of a target for some eager Rebs."

Ava pointed to Chloe who was asleep.

"My friend said we are to go to St. Louis—maybe even farther. Are you going to St. Louis as well?"

The soldier stared at Ava a moment before he answered. His voice was guarded when he spoke.

"You know, Miss Bradley, that is not an answer I can give as an officer. For all I know, you could be a spy using your charm to ply me for information." His eyes were twinkling but Ava recognized an undertone of seriousness.

Her face blushed a deep red and she turned away.

"I—I'm sorry. I didn't mean to pry." She clenched her hands tightly on her lap and looked straight ahead. Just then, they heard the sound of an explosion and the train's brake system locked the wheels. The screech of metal on metal filled the train.

# Chapter 10

# REBEL ATTACK!

CHLOE AWOKE WITH A START AND BOTH WOMEN stared out the window as loud Rebel yells filled the air. A young man with curly, blond hair raced toward the train giving orders to the men who appeared in the trees.

Ava gasped and stood in her seat.

Captain Headrick shouted, "Get on the floor, both of you. Get on the floor *now!*"

Chloe dropped to the floor, but Ava continued to stare out the window. The captain wrapped a large arm around her waist and jerked her to the floor. He rolled to put his body under hers and she landed heavily on top of him as two bullets cut through the air where she had been standing.

"Sharpshooters fire at targets on a train. They don't stop to ask if they are men or women. You could have been killed!" The officer's face was angry as he barked the words at Ava.

She rolled away from him and said nothing.

Captain Headrick pointed at the two women. "Stay down. You are safer on the floor. And don't come out of this car until one of my men comes to get you."

He rushed out hollering, "Get the horses! Don't let those Rebs steal our mounts!"

The gunfire outside the car was loud and close. Several more bullets smashed through the wall of the train car and ricocheted out the other side. The bullets bounced wildly through the train car before they finally found their way out.

Slowly, the shooting subsided and the shouting became more distant. A young soldier appeared behind them.

"Here, let me help you up. The captain said to come and get you ladies. We are leaving here on horseback." He looked over at Ava.

"We think we have your horse saddled, Miss Bradley. It was with our horses and didn't have a military brand." He gave Ava a quick grin and added, "That's why Cap assumed it was yours.

"Miss Moore can ride one of our mounts." He blushed slightly and added, "I'm Private Headrick. Captain Headrick is my brother. He said you might want to change. I am to watch the door for you if you do." He grinned and added, "My name is Peter."

Ava smiled at Peter.

"That would be wonderful, Peter. Yes, if you would do that, we will change quickly."

The two women slid down between the seats and changed quickly. Ava had on her britches and a loose blouse while Chloe had brought a riding skirt.

Chloe stared at Ava for a moment and laughed.

"Another thing my mother would never approve of. Heaven forbid I should keep company with a woman who *prefers* to ride in britches!"

Ava laughed. "Nor did my mother like it but my granny approved." The two women called to Peter and then hurried out of the car. Ava stopped to stare at the soldiers who were gathered around the train. They seemed to be working to repair the tracks.

Chloe pointed at them. "Those are Galvanized Yankees. They were Reb prisoners who were granted their freedom provided they joined the Yankee cause. However, no one is too sure about their loyalties.

"They will be left behind to fix the track, and then they will probably be moved to the West. That way they won't have to fight their old comrades, and their officers won't have to worry about them defecting or leaking troop movements to the other side."

Captain Headrick turned their way when he heard Chloe speaking. He looked at Ava's britches in surprise and then his eyes moved up to her defiant face.

"Is there something you would like to say to me, Captain Headrick?" Ava's voice was even but her body was tensed for a fight.

The captain grinned and shook his head.

"I reckon not. I told the men to leave your pistol in your saddlebag. I'm guessing you know how to use it."

Ava pointed at his shoulder. A bullet had cut a groove through the top of his arm.

"That should have a clean wrap around it. Do you want me to treat it before we leave?"

"No, you can wrap it this evening. Right now, we need to keep moving."

The women were placed toward the center and the column moved out.

# Chapter 11

# A PRETTY LITTLE LIAR

**AVA STUDIED THE SOLDIERS RIDING CLOSE TO HER.**
Each wore a sky-blue forage cap with an orange welt. The front of their uniforms featured a horsehead panel trimmed in cavalry yellow. She turned to look at the soldiers behind her. All wore the same uniform.

*This must be some kind of elite riding force. I certainly have never seen this type of uniform before.*

Captain Headrick soon dropped back to ride beside them.

Ava looked from his uniform to his face and asked, "Why do you all have horses on your shirts and caps? I am not familiar with that uniform."

Captain Headrick pointed at his hat and nodded.

"We were organized by Captain Lewis Merrill. He was a veteran of the United States Second Dragoons. Our hats are done in the colors of his pre-war Dragoon regiment. Of course, he's a general now." He waved his hand toward the men. "Our regiment is known as Merrill's Horse although our official name is the Second Missouri Volunteer Cavalry."

"Have you always been stationed in this area?"

"We were mostly in northern Missouri at the beginning of the war. Now we are moved all over. Still, guerrilla warfare is our specialty. We are sent where help is needed."

"Where all have you fought?"

"Arkansas, Georgia, Alabama—wherever there is guerrilla fighting." Captain Headrick grinned at Ava and added, "There you go asking lots of questions again. I think it's my turn.

"Why didn't you drop to the floor when shots were fired on the train? You were almost killed—and I got my best hat notched."

Ava stared at him for a moment and then her eyes went to his cavalry hat. A bullet hole showed in the crown of the hat, cutting diagonally from front to back. Her eyes opened wide.

"You could have been killed!"

Captain Headrick grinned and drawled, "Well, I am all about saving pretty ladies. You haven't answered my question though."

Ava's face became pale, and she faced straight ahead.

"I—I was afraid, that's all."

Captain Headrick stared at Ava and his eyes narrowed. *She's lying again. I need to keep an eye on this gal. She's pretty and she's smart. Just the kind who would be recruited to spy. And I doubt she was afraid. I think she grew up handling a gun. I'm guessing she's as good a shot as most of the men in this company. Maybe better.*

His voice was soft when he answered.

"When you are ready to talk about those fears, I'll be ready to listen." He pulled his horse out of formation and rode back to the front.

Ava stared after him and real fear churned up through her chest. *He knows I am lying and he is suspicious of me!*

Chloe had been listening and she looked over at her friend.

"That captain is a handsome man, but he is downright cranky. Why he barely smiles. And just now, he almost threatened you!"

Ava was silent as she watched Captain Headrick's rigid back. She almost snorted.

"He is suspicious of everyone and that makes him grouchy. He doesn't trust outsiders and we are outsiders. And I don't think he is all that good-looking. It takes more than muscles and a nice smile to impress me."

Chloe began laughing softly. "But you did notice his smile *and* his muscles. I don't think you are as cold as you pretend to be."

Ava blushed slightly before she laughed with her friend.

"Let's talk about something else. He's probably arrogant too, and if he hears us discussing him, he will be even more full of himself."

The captain did not ride with them the rest of the day. In fact, they didn't talk to him again until that evening.

"We put up a tent for you ladies so you will have a little privacy. However, several of the men have some minor wounds if you would look at them." Captain Headrick turned around and barked orders at the men as he walked away.

Chloe whispered, "Very cranky and all business. I doubt he has ever even kissed a woman."

Ava blushed furiously.

"Good grief, Chloe! Why do you say things like that? One of his men could hear you!"

# Chapter 12

# A REB WOMAN IN A UNION CAMP

**O**VER HALF OF CAPTAIN HEADRICK'S TROOP LINED UP to have their various ailments treated. The complaints from the fifty-plus men ranged from sore throats to three men with bullet wounds. Some of the soldiers couldn't even think of a thing that was ailing them. They just wanted to talk to the pretty young nurses.

Chloe enjoyed herself but Ava wasn't taken in by all of the men's attempts at charm. When they were down to the last three, she picked up her medicine bag and walked over to the captain's tent. She asked the young soldier who was standing in front to tell the captain that she needed to see him.

When the Captain barked, "Come in," Ava just stood in the opening of the tent.

"I want to look at your arm, but I won't do it in your tent since you will need to remove your shirt."

The captain looked at her in surprise and slowly nodded. He stood and strode toward Ava. She stepped aside and he led the way to a large rock about a hundred yards from the encampment.

"It's just a scratch. In fact, it barely bled."

Ava didn't answer as she applied some horse liniment to the open wound. When she finished binding it, she looked up and commented softly, "Many men have died in this war because of illness and infections. There is no point in taking a chance."

Captain Headrick studied her face before he asked quietly, "Who did you recognize when those Rebs attacked?"

Ava's breath caught in her throat and her face became pale. She shook her head and reached to pick up her bag.

The captain grabbed her arm and looked up at her.

"Ella, I know you recognized someone. Your husband perhaps?"

Surprise registered in Ava's eyes, and she let out a small laugh.

"Nothing so romantic. I—I thought I saw my brother, but I could have been mistaken."

Captain Headrick continued to probe her face with his eyes before he finally spoke.

"When did you last hear from him?"

"Over a year ago. I wasn't sure if he was even alive and then that young man came racing toward the train. He looked so much like Charlie that I just couldn't move. I wanted him to look up so I could see his eyes. He didn't though and then you jerked me down."

"So why is a Confederate woman using her nursing skills on Union forces?"

Ava's voice was bitter as she pulled her arm away.

"Your government didn't give me much choice. Yankee soldiers stole our horses and destroyed our feed. If Deuce hadn't gotten away, I wouldn't even have him." Her bottom lip trembled as she added, "And then your Red Legs burned our farm and killed all the livestock they could find. They killed my mother and my grandmother. One of them shot my mother in her face. My grandmother was shot in the stomach and suffered terribly." A large tear leaked from Ava's eye as she whispered, "I hated all Yankees by the time I arrived in Harrisonville."

Captain Headrick frowned as he listened. His neck slowly turned red, and he looked down to keep Ella from seeing the emotions that were racing across his face.

Ava continued, her words dripping with quiet anger.

"That trip north was terrible. So many women and children. They had no food for the entire journey, and no way to buy any once they arrived at Harrisonville. Your government inflicted pain and suffering on people who were barely surviving. On *defenseless* people!

"And now what? Swear allegiance to *your* Union? Why would any of us do that after the way we were treated? Besides, there aren't enough jobs for the thousands of women whose homes and farms were destroyed. How are they going to support their families?" Ava glared at Captain Headrick as her bottom lip quivered.

"I asked an officer in Harrisonville if I could become a field nurse. I helped my grandmother doctor people, and I helped my father treat animals. I told him I would help as long as I could treat all men, not just those in blue uniforms." She stomped her foot as she added, "And look at you. You can't even look me in the eyes when I speak to you!"

Ava was nearly hissing her words when she finished. Her eyes were full of tears, but she was angry. Angry and fearless.

Captain Headrick looked up. He reached for her arm again.

"Ella—" he began.

Ava jerked her arm away.

"My name is Ava. Ava Bowman. I am a Rebel sympathizer so go ahead and arrest me if you want."

The captain stood. His voice was soft when he spoke.

"Ava, you are an excellent nurse. If you give me your word that you will treat Union soldiers with care and gentleness, that is good enough for me."

"I already gave my word that I would never harm a wounded man unless he was trying to hurt me or someone in my charge. I don't have to repeat that pledge to you." Tears were flowing freely from Ava's eyes as she backed away from Captain Headrick.

"Just leave me alone and let me hate you. I don't want you to be nice to me." She spun around and ran toward the trees.

Chloe stood. She looked from Captain Headrick to Ava's disappearing back and then hurried after her.

Captain Headrick watched them go.

"Peter, keep an eye on our nurses. Make sure they get something warm to eat tonight."

He cursed softly as he walked toward his tent.

"Red Legs. I feel the same way you do about them, Ava, but I doubt you would ever believe that. And now that I know your name, I know exactly who your mother and grandmother were. Your father was in our employment—your family should never have been bothered." He frowned as he thought of the quilt Peter had taken.

"I can't get that quilt from Pete unless I tell him who Ava is, and I won't do that. I'll just make sure he keeps it as clean as possible."

# Chapter 13

# TIME TO TELL THE TRUTH

AVA WAS SLUMPED AGAINST A TREE WHEN CHLOE found her. Her sobs were almost silent and came from deep in her chest.

"Ella, please don't cry. I'm sure the captain didn't mean to make you cry."

Ava stared at Chloe. She wiped her face and sat up.

"I haven't been honest with you, Chloe. In fact, I haven't been honest with anyone but the officer who gave me this job.

"My name is Ava—Ava Bowman. Red Legs killed my mother and grandmother. They burned us out and left me with nothing. That's why I signed on to become a military nurse." Tears filled her eyes again and she whispered, "When I arrived in Harrisonville, I hated all Yankees for what those men did to my family.

"These soldiers have been so kind though. Peter is just the sweetest boy around. When I think about wishing they were all dead, I start to make exceptions.

"Then I think of my brother fighting on the other side and it terrifies me."

Chloe listened with large eyes. She hugged Ava.

"I like the name Ava. It suits you better than Ella." She sat down beside Ava.

"You thought you saw your brother when our train was attacked, didn't you? I wasn't sure if you were too terrified to move or if you saw someone you knew." She giggled and poked Ava with her elbow.

"You are too fearless to be immobilized by fear though, so I guessed you saw someone you knew." Chloe became more serious and asked cautiously, "Did Captain Headrick scold you?"

Ava shook her head. She buried her face in her knees when she started to cry again. She finally took a deep breath and looked over at Chloe.

"No, he was very kind. I want to hate him, but I just can't. I told him that too when I told him about my brother. He wanted me to pledge that I would treat the Yankees properly and I refused. I already promised that officer who offered me the job that I would. I didn't need to give my word twice.

"I am guessing I will be dropped at the next post we reach and be relieved of my position."

Chloe turned to face Ava, and her face was serious. She squatted in front of her and took her by the shoulders as she looked into her eyes.

"Ava, you would never refuse to treat someone because of the color of his uniform, or the color of his skin either for that matter. I watched how gentle you were with the men when you treated their injuries, even the silly things they complained about just so they could talk to you.

"You are efficient too. Why, you treated two men in the time it took me to treat one. You are a wonderful nurse, and this cavalry troop is lucky to have you.

"No, I don't think you will be released. Captain Headrick is a fair man. He would never do that." She pointed toward the east.

"We are moving quickly though. I'm certain we are heading for St. Louis since that is one of the best places to cross the Mississippi River. The men are whispering some. I have heard Tennessee mentioned, so I'm not sure how long we will be in St. Louis.

"I think the hospitals are short on nurses around battleground areas the farther to the east . We will probably end up in one of the hospitals that treats the wounded brought in from the battlefront."

Ava stared at Chloe and then looked away. When she looked back, her eyes had tears in them.

"When I signed on, I promised myself that I would make no friends. I wanted to hate everyone," she whispered. "And now, look at me. A Yankee nurse is my friend."

Chloe laughed and hugged Ava again.

"I guess we both had to make some compromises. When the other girls in Harrisonville were whispering about your britches, I just about didn't talk to you. You are so different from my friends back in Lawrence." She pulled Ava up. "I'm glad I did though.

"Let's go back to camp. My stomach is growling so it must be about supper time."

# Chapter 14

# A SUSPICIOUS LIEUTENANT

**S**ECOND LIEUTENANT NOAH LAMPKIN WATCHED THE two women from where he was hiding in the brush. He frowned as he listened to Ava speak. He couldn't hear everything she said, but he heard enough to know she was sympathetic to the Southern cause. Captain Headrick was walking toward the mess area when the lieutenant caught him.

"Permission to speak candidly, sir. An' in private."

Captain Headrick stopped when his lieutenant asked for a private meeting. He pointed back toward his tent.

"Let's talk in there. We don't have much for privacy around here."

Once they were inside, Lieutenant Lampkin took a deep breath. He pulled his hat off and cursed once before he spoke.

"We have a spy in camp. I was suspicious after that attack on the train, so I have been prowlin' 'round at night. I found tracks where he met with someone down by the little creek that flows west of here."

Captain Headrick's eyes became hard.

"Do you know who it is?"

"Not yet. I ain't been able to single out his tracks on bare enough ground to be able to tell what condition his boots are in. The only folks he could meet with 'round here are Rebs though."

Captain Headrick drummed his fingers on the crate he used as a desk.

"How many men do you think are involved?"

"I ain't sure. Somebody has to know of his leavin', but no one's reported 'im. I been sleepin' down by the hosses at night to keep an eye out for Bushwhackers. They're short on mounts, an' we don't want to lose any hosses.

"Ain't nobody come by me, but somebody is fer shore slippin' out." Lampkin paused and then cleared his throat as he watched Captain Headrick.

The captain frowned. His frown became deeper as he watched his lieutenant.

"Is there something else?"

"It's that quiet nurse. She has a brother who's a Reb. I think she's a Reb through an' through. I ain't sure she's trustworthy." His hands shook slightly as he turned his hat, and he cursed again. "An' I hate to say that. She's a fine nurse but I heard those two women talkin' after they went into the trees. Miss Bradley was a cryin' an' seemed to be mighty upset. Miss Moore was comfortin' her. Miss Moore is a Yankee but Miss Bradley, she's fer shore a Reb." He paused and his eyes were hard as he added, "I heard her say she hates Yankees."

Captain Headrick took a deep breath. He pushed his hand through his damp hair and nodded.

"I have been wondering about her too. I know she recognized one of those Rebs who attacked the train.

"I'm not sure what to do with her. She's a fine nurse. Both of them are. I have orders to deliver them St. Louis and then they will go on to a hospital in Tennessee. They are short on nurses in Chattanooga. We were to take the train, so I didn't plan to travel all the way across

Missouri on horseback with two women." Captain Headrick studied the man in front of him.

Lieutenant Lampkin was a loyal Yankee. His father, Ezekiel, migrated to Missouri from Georgia after Noah's mother died. They settled in the central part of the state. Noah was ten.

Ezekiel told Noah, "I like the green trees and the black soil. The temperate climate suits my bones and the farms here are small. No big plantations to push out the little man." Once they arrived in Missouri, the two of them spent their free time in the forest and hills near their farm.

Ezekiel Lampkin was a woodsman and a fierce teacher, and his son was an eager learner. By the time Noah was fifteen, he could track better than most of the men they knew. He was also a dead shot with his Henry rifle. He enlisted at seventeen and was assigned to Captain Headrick. Shortly after that, he was approached about becoming a sniper. He declined because he wanted to remain part of Merrill's Horse. He also respected Captain Headrick, and Lieutenant Noah Lampkin didn't respect too many officers.

"Are you thinking Miss Bradley might be compromised?"

Lampkin nodded slowly.

"I fear she could become a target if she ain't already. It would be mighty handy to have a purty nurse gatherin' information 'bout our weaknesses an' where we are a goin'—things she could hear from the men as she treats 'em. She could feed that information to the durn spy, an' he could pass it on."

Captain Headrick nodded.

"We'll keep an officer with them when we ride. We could even bring them closer to the front, so they aren't surrounded by the enlisted men." He looked toward the front of the tent and cursed under his breath. A *nurse who has a Reb brother and a spy in camp too. Yes, she bears watching.* He finally grinned as he looked at his second in command.

"Maybe you could ride beside them."

Lampkin shook his head and blushed slightly.

"Not ever' day. I'd run outa stuff to talk 'bout. Put Peterson with 'em. He could talk the ear off an elephant. You could ride some there too." He blushed again and cleared his throat as he looked at Captain Headrick uncomfortably.

"I ain't sayin' that gal is a bad woman. I'm jist a sayin' she's give us cause to have someone keep an eye on 'er." He rolled his blue eyes as he grinned and added, "Not me though. I want to be free to ride alongside the men. I want to know who that spy is."

Supper was quiet. Ava avoided Captain Headrick. She ate quickly and hurried back to her tent. Although she listened, she didn't appear when Private Fitzgerald took out his fiddle.

Chloe visited easily with the men. She sat by Lieutenant Lampkin for a time. He smiled at her from time to time but barely spoke. Finally, he just disappeared. Still, Chloe enjoyed the music.

The men were mostly young, and many were homesick. They talked about their families and friends back home. A few had sweethearts and ten men told Chloe they had wives. She shivered as she thought about sending a husband or sweetheart away to fight in a war. *Or a brother. Poor Ava.* She finally excused herself and went back to their tent.

Ava was already asleep. Chloe could see she had been sewing. She picked up the white apron and stared at it. The stitching was small and neat. The embroidery on the front was done in red and it was neat as well.

Chloe looked over at her sleeping friend and laughed softly.

"Ava, you are just full of surprises."

# Chapter 15

# TO CATCH A SPY

**T**HE CAVALRY MOVED FASTER THE NEXT DAY. CAPTAIN Headrick alternated between a trot and a walk. He wanted to average eight miles per hour. By evening, he estimated they had covered over fifty miles. He was avoiding the main roads though, and that made the trip a little slower.

"I sure wish we could have gone a little farther by train. We made seventy-five miles in three hours on that train plus another twenty on horseback. Today we went another fifty miles or so. If all goes well, we should make St. Louis by Sunday night. Of course, it could be Monday or later if we run into trouble. Two hundred sixty miles isn't bad if you are on roads, but traveling the way we are is a little slower," he commented softly to himself.

The men wanted to visit while they ate that evening, but Captain Headrick ordered them to remain as quiet as possible. He put out extra sentries and stopped all music that night. The men grumbled some, but they understood. The camp was quiet by eight except for the stamping and grazing of the horses and mules.

Ava awoke around three in the morning to the sound of scratching on the back of her tent. She quietly pulled the pistol from her valise and pointed it toward the noise.

"My finger is on the trigger of this pistol, and I won't miss at this distance." Her voice was quiet when she spoke but the gun she held didn't waver. There was silence and then a man laughed softly.

"Sis, I knew you was in there. I thought I saw ya on that train with these here Yanks but I figgered I must be dreamin'. Come on out here an' talk to yore brother!"

Ava gasped before looking quickly toward Chloe's bunk. Her friend was asleep. She grabbed a lantern and hurried out of her tent. When the sentry stopped her, she whispered, "I need to relieve myself. I will just be over there." She pointed at the trees behind her tent. He nodded and turned away.

As she hurried by a grove of trees, a strong arm grabbed her. The man's hand was over her mouth, and she struggled furiously to get away.

"Calm down, Sis. It's me. Now don't holler. Someone will hear us."

Charlie let go and Ava wrapped her arms around his neck.

"I was so worried about you!" Her smile slowly disappeared. She could see Charlie's face in the moonlight, and she added sadly, "Mother and Granny are dead. The Red Legs killed them."

Charlie nodded. "Pop is gone too. Word is the Bushwhackers took him out for helpin' the Yankees. I ain't so sure though. I think mebbie those Red Legs had somethin' to do with that too. Either way, it's jist you an' me now." He pulled a letter from his pocket and thrust it into her hands.

"I want ya to send this here letter fer me. I don't have any way to post it. It's to my gal in St. Louis. She lives with our aunt." Charlie backed away quickly and faded into the night. Ava heard a soft "I love ya, Sis," before he disappeared.

Ava squatted quickly when she heard the sentry call, "Are you all right, Miss Bradley? The captain doesn't want anyone out in the woods for too long. Too many Rebs around." He stepped into the clearing and then backed away quickly.

"I'm sorry, Miss Bradley. I thought I heard somethin' and I wanted to make sure you was all right."

Ava finished quickly and shook out her nightgown. As she hurried back toward her tent, she smiled at the sentry.

"Thank you for checking on me, Jed. I'm not used to all this protection, but I do appreciate it."

She set the lamp down on the floor and removed her robe. She was about to snuff out the lamp when Charlie's letter fell out of her drawers. She looked at it and started to lay it down. It had been sealed but the seal was partially broken. Ava stared at the letter a moment longer and then broke the seal. As she scanned the contents, she frowned in confusion. Then she realized what she held.

"Charlie is asking me to post a letter for him that gives information about this camp!" She reread the letter quickly. She covered her mouth with her hand as she read the last line.

tell pax to take out that captain with his first shot. that feller is already suspicious. besides, his men will foller him thru hell and back. get that lieutenant who rides back and forth by the men next. he's the one who's been tracking me. lay low after ya pass this on. there are too many men in camp who are starting to take notice.

nightrider

Ava stared at the letter in horror. If she posted it as Charlie asked, she would be responsible for the death of Captain Headrick and Lieutenant Lampkin. If she didn't, she would betray Charlie's trust.

She slid the letter back into the envelope and stared at the front again. It was addressed to Charlotte Bowman in St. Louis, Missouri.

"What am I going to do? Charlie knew what was in the letter. He is using our last name!"

Just then, the silence of the camp exploded with sounds of shooting and horses neighing. Men were shouting as they rushed from their tents.

Captain Headrick was shouting orders in his long handles. They were cut off at the knees and were unbuttoned nearly to his waist. Ava stared a moment before she looked at the chaos in the camp.

Fires were lit and the camp was as bright as daylight. Men were soon mounted, and Lieutenant Lampkin led the riders out of camp on the run.

Captain Headrick strode toward Ava's tent.

"Pack up. We are leaving as soon as it's daylight. Make sure your canteen is filled. It's going to be a long day." He paused and then smiled at her.

"Ava, you almost look like an angel with the moon shining behind you like that. Your face looks like it's glowing."

Ava's eyes opened wide, and she backed into her tent. Her breath was coming in short gasps and the letter felt like it was burning her. She dressed quickly. When she thought no one was watching, she dropped the letter into the closest fire. It burned quickly and she stirred the sticks to make sure nothing was left. When she looked up, she looked right into Captain Headrick's eyes. She pointed at the fire and then waved her hand toward the rest of the fires.

"Do you want me to put these fires out? We surely aren't going to let them burn."

"We are going to let them burn. I doubt they will fool those Rebs, but we can try. Besides, they are in pits. They should burn out without catching anything else on fire." He paused a moment and Ava looked up at him.

Captain Headrick's eyes were sad. Ava could almost feel her betrayal emanating from the hurt way he was looking at her. He glanced at the fire and looked at Ava one more time before he turned back to his tent.

Ava rushed into her tent. Chloe was already up. She had changed and was packing her bag.

"Let's pull this tent down. That will save the men some time."

Peter was smiling when he arrived with their horses. He slid off to give them a hand up.

"It is nearly sixty miles to St. Louis. I'm hoping we can rest there a day but I'm not sure. Cap is mighty angry today. He doesn't like it when Rebs sneak up on us." His smile faded as he added, "One of the horses that was stolen was yours, Miss Bradley. Lieutenant Lampkin is going to try to steal them back though."

Captain Headrick let off at a trot. He brought the two women up front to ride beside him. He was so angry and abrupt that even Chloe quit talking and the three of them rode in silence.

Lieutenant Lampkin and his men caught them at noon.

"We got all the hosses back but three. We didn't see Miss Bradley's hoss. The other two was lame, so we left 'em." He looked up to see Ava staring at him and he blushed slightly.

"Sorry, Miss Bradley. Yore hoss wasn't with the rest of the mounts. One of those Rebs musta claimed 'im already."

Ava laughed softly.

"He won't claim him for long. Deuce will dump him and find me. He doesn't like strangers, especially men."

When both the lieutenant and Captain Headrick stared at her without speaking, Ava blushed and looked away. *They both think I am a traitor! Maybe I am. I just don't know what I am anymore.*

# Chapter 16

# YOUR ENEMY, MY BROTHER

**THEY BARELY STOPPED FOR DINNER AND THERE WERE** no fires. The men ate what they carried in their saddlebags. Captain Headrick barked orders again and the men moved out. However, instead of moving out with his men, he and Lieutenant Lampkin stayed behind.

When Ava and Chloe started to join the column, the captain stopped them.

"Miss Bradley, you sit down there beside Lieutenant Lampkin. I want to talk to Miss Moore by herself."

Ava stared from her friend to the captain and then sat down slowly. She clenched her hands together as she waited.

Chloe's face was pale when she returned. She hugged Ava and whispered, "Tell the truth. He already knows anyway." She followed the quiet lieutenant toward the column of men and horses.

When they were out of hearing distance, Captain Headrick turned toward Ava. His voice was hard and angry when he spoke, but his face was sad.

"Ava, tell me about last night and don't lie to me. I'm quite certain I know everything, but I want to hear your version."

When Ava stared at him, he added, "We caught a spy last night. We know he was supposed to receive a letter from someone in our camp. That person received it from a Reb he or she met last night." His voice was soft and deadly when he added, "And I saw you burn a letter last night when you thought you were alone."

Ava stared at Captain Headrick in horror. A large tear leaked from her eye and slowly slid down her cheek.

He leaned toward her. He took her hands and held them tightly. His voice was soft, but it was angry and the lines in his face were hard.

"Ava, the punishment for spying is death. I don't want to see you hung. They might go lighter on a woman, but this type of thing is punished harshly. Tell me what happened. If you aren't to blame, I will try to protect you.

"Did you meet with the enemy last night?"

Ava glared at him.

"He was your enemy, but he wasn't my enemy."

"You met your brother last night?"

"Yes."

"Did he come to you, or did you have an arranged time to meet?"

"Charlie came and scratched on my tent. I was going to shoot whoever was there, but he called me Sis. I knew then it was my brother. That was what Charlie called me when we were little."

"And he asked you to meet him in the trees?"

"Yes. And I did meet him. He is my brother and until last night, I hadn't seen him for over a year."

"You lied to the sentry."

Ava started crying. "I'm sorry. I—I wanted to see my brother so badly. He is the only family I have."

The captain stared at the small woman in front of him and cursed under his breath. So far, everything she said was true. Still, it didn't justify what she had done.

"And what did he tell you?"

"Charlie said our father had been killed by Bushwhackers, but I already knew that. Granny told me to run away before she died, and she wouldn't have said that if she thought Father was coming home."

"Did he give you anything?"

Ava's hands shook violently, and her breath came in gasps.

"He—he gave me a letter for his girl in St. Louis. He wanted me to post it for him. Charlie always liked girls, so I believed him. We didn't talk long after that. When he left, I hurried back to my tent."

"And did you post it?"

"No, I planned to post it this morning. Then I noticed the letter wasn't sealed completely. I knew I shouldn't open it, but I was curious about what kind of girl Charlie was able to meet during the war. I decided to read it." Ava avoided the captain's eyes, and another tear ran down her cheek as she struggled to continue.

Captain Headrick watched Ava closely as she spoke. He said nothing for a moment. When she didn't continue, he glared at her.

"And?"

"It wasn't a letter to his girl. It was a letter to someone giving information about this camp. It directed the receiver of who to shoot first. It also talked about your troop size and movements."

Ava's anguish was evident to Captain Headrick as he listened to her cry and talk at the same time. "That was when I studied the address. The name on the envelope was Charlotte Bowman, but we have no relative named Charlotte Bowman in St. Louis. I knew then it wasn't meant to be posted since it couldn't be delivered. That's when I knew there must be a spy right here in your camp.

"I—I didn't know what to do. There were orders at the bottom of who to kill first. I didn't want to be responsible for any of these men's deaths, but I didn't want to betray my brother either. I finally decided to burn the letter.

"I didn't think anyone saw me, but you were looking at me when I stirred the fire. I was hoping you wouldn't know what it was."

Silent tears ran from Ava's eyes.

"I'm so sorry. I love my brother, but I just couldn't bear the thought of being responsible for the deaths of more men."

Ava clenched her hands as she sobbed, "I want to save lives. I don't want to cause death, and I just don't know how to do both of those things in this war."

Captain Headrick could feel the relief rush through him. *This woman doesn't want to be a spy. She could have let my men die but she didn't.*

He asked softly, "How can I help you, Ava?" as he took her hands.

Ava jerked her hands away. She stood and sucked in a sob as she backed away. She stared at Captain Headrick a moment with wide eyes and then whispered, "I told you before—I don't want to like you. That hasn't changed. Please don't touch me."

Captain Headrick stood quietly and nodded. He looked back once as he walked toward the horses. His voice was soft when he spoke.

"I'm sorry you have to make decisions like this, Ava. If I could make it easier for you, I would. However, in the future, if anyone from the other side contacts you, you need to come to me. That is an order—even if it is your brother." He walked to his horse and waited for her as he held the reins to both horses.

Ava stared at him, but she didn't answer. *I pray my brother doesn't try to contact me again until this terrible war is over. Surely, since I failed, no one on his side will ask me to help them again.*

# Chapter 17

# DEUCE

**B**OTH AVA AND CAPTAIN HEADRICK TURNED TO LOOK when they heard a horse running towards them. The captain pulled his rifle from his saddle and dropped to one knee.

"Ava," he hissed, "get in the bushes."

Ava paid no attention to him. The horse was neighing, and she walked toward the sound with a smile on her face.

Captain Headrick cursed under his breath. He turned his horse loose and ran toward her just as a large sorrel crested the hill. The horse had a saddle and bridle, but no rider was in sight. It slid to a stop in front of the young woman, nickering softly.

"I knew you would come back, Deuce. Where have you been anyway? Just look at you. There are burrs in your mane and tail, and your legs are covered in scratches. Well, don't worry. I'll clean you up when we get to St. Louis." She hugged the big horse as she kissed his forehead. She turned toward Captain Headrick with a smile on her face.

"I raised Deuce from a colt, and we often played hide and seek. He finds me no matter where I am." Her face was glowing with happiness, and she wrapped one arm around the horse's neck.

The irritation in Captain Headrick showed in his voice when he spoke.

"You could have been killed you know. A Reb could have been riding that horse."

Ava's eyes sparkled and she laughed.

"No one can ride Deuce unless he wants them to. If he can't buck riders off, he rolls, and they come off that way." Her chin jutted out and she added, "Besides, I recognized his nicker." She laughed softly as she pointed at the horse. "Just look at that fine saddle. It would probably fit you, Captain Headrick. Most likely, some other snooty officer tried to ride him and lost it."

Captain Headrick stared at the small woman in front of him. He sputtered for a moment and before he responded.

"I think you just called me snooty!"

Ava's eyes sparkled and she finally laughed.

"You are always so stiff and proper. Yes, I think you probably are snooty. You never talk to me unless you are scolding me or angry with me for something I've done—something you don't approve of. And I don't think you approve of much that I do."

Captain Headrick frowned and then shook his head.

"I didn't think you wanted to be friends."

Ava glared at the man in front of her.

"I didn't say I wanted to be your friend. Perhaps we could just try to be civil to one another. It might make the rest of this journey more pleasant." When the captain continued to stare at her she added, "We don't have to like each other to be civil."

Captain Headrick pulled off his hat and ran his fingers through his hair. He was muttering as he turned around. He stopped just before he mounted and pointed at Deuce.

"Do you want me to switch saddles so you can ride Deuce? I think that saddle is too big for you."

Ava started to tell him no. She knew she could do it herself. However, she *was* the one who had suggested that they be civil.

"That would be nice. If you throw it up on his back, I can finish while you saddle the other horse. That way, we can catch your men sooner."

Captain Headrick said nothing as he switched the saddles. Ava was already mounted when he finished. He looked up at her and chuckled as he walked back toward his horse.

"Miss Bowman, I think I would have enjoyed your family. They must have been something to have raised such a stubborn, independent young woman."

Ava started to retort but instead she leaned toward Deuce's neck as she whispered, "I'm so happy you were able to escape and find me, Deuce. You and Charlie are the only ones I have left from all those I loved."

Her voice was soft, but Captain Headrick heard her. He didn't respond but his mouth became a little harder. *I had better not come across Sergeant Nielson or any of his Red Legs. I just might forget that I'm an officer.*

# Chapter 18

# "HER CAPTAIN"

AVA AND CAPTAIN HEADRICK RODE AT A LOPE UNTIL they reached the Union troops. As he turned his horse to ride around his men, he signaled for her to follow.

"I want you and Miss Moore to ride toward the front of the column for the rest of this journey. Lieutenant Lampkin or I will ride close to you.

"St. Louis is under Union control, but there is still unrest due to the Rebel loyalists scattered throughout the city. Since my job isn't completed until you are delivered to Benton Barracks Hospital, it is my duty to keep you safe."

When Ava looked at Captain Headrick in question, he added, "That is where you will receive your training before you are sent to your permanent posting.

"Miss Emily Parsons is in charge of the hospital there. It is the largest hospital west of the Mississippi River. The last I heard, there were over two thousand patients being treated there. Miss Parsons is a tough teacher but a great nurse. She will like your desire to heal so you should do well there."

Ava listened quietly and then asked, "How do you know her?"

"Some of my men were there for a time and I checked up on them. She is all about cleanliness and she treats all Union soldiers, both White and Colored. Some folks don't approve of that, but I believe that's how it should be. After all, they were wounded fighting for the Union cause."

"It is a training hospital?"

"Yes, but it didn't start that way. Nurse Parsons needs help so she will train anyone who wants to learn. There are quite a few volunteers working there every day."

His blue eyes drilled into her as he asked, "Do you have a problem working with Colored nurses?"

Ava glared at Captain Headrick.

"Not all Confederates approve of slavery, Captain. In fact, many of us have no slaves. And I have no problem working with Colored nurses. I don't care if they are green as long as they care for the patients.

"I am excited to learn more about nursing and treatment of war wounds. Most of the treatments I did at home were for ailments and infections along with a cut here and there. We rarely saw any gunshot wounds." Her frown became deeper as she added, "You certainly have many preconceived ideas about the South."

Captain Headrick stared at Ava for a moment. He finally answered quietly, "I am from the South, Miss Bowman. I grew up in southern Georgia. We were looked down on by many of our friends and neighbors when we freed our slaves. My father died when I was young, and my mother was sickly. She died when I was twelve.

"The Colored folks we freed stayed and worked for us until the war started. My brother and I were mostly raised by a Colored nanny whom we loved.

"Our plantation was one of the first to be destroyed when this war broke out because we were traitors to the Confederate cause. Besides, I was already a Union officer." Captain Headrick's voice was hard when he added, "I think I know a little more about the South and the people there than you credit me."

Ava stared at Captain Headrick in surprise and then she blushed.

"I—I'm sorry. I should not have assumed you were from the North." When the captain didn't answer, she added softly, "So much for that amicable relationship, I guess."

Captain Headrick looked over at Ava and nearly snorted.

"Miss Bowman, you are one of the most irritating, obstinate, opinionated women I have ever encountered. Maybe it would be best if we just didn't talk at all."

Ava was quiet for a moment. Her voice was soft but sarcastic when she replied.

"No, I imagine you prefer women who sit around and fan themselves because their corsets are too tight. I doubt you know many women who give you much sass."

When Captain Headrick glared at her, Ava spurred Deuce and fell in place beside Chloe. She gave her friend a bright smile.

"Look who found me! But then, Deuce always finds me."

Lieutenant Lampkin turned around to look for Captain Headrick. His eyes twinkled as the officer rode by. Captain Headrick's face was set in a frown and his back was stiff. Lampkin looked over at Ava and grinned.

"I see you an' Cap got ever'thing all worked out," he commented dryly.

Ava stared at the lieutenant in surprise. He had not spoken to her the entire trip, let alone joked about his captain. Then she frowned.

"Your captain is a difficult man. He calls me obstinate, but I believe he is used to having his own way."

Lieutenant Lampkin chuckled and nodded.

"That's true, but Cap, he's a good man. He cares 'bout the men in his command. He takes it personal when one of 'em gets hurt. We've only lost two men an' that's mighty low considerin' some of the missions we've been assigned.

"See, I've known Cap since we was tadpoles. My pa owned a place next to their plantation till we moved to Missouri. Cap was an ornery kid, but he had to grow up quick. His pa died when he was a youngster. His ma tried to run things, but she was sickly. I went down there for a spell ever' summer an' helped out." He flashed Ava a quick grin and added, "'Course, it was more of a vacation fer me. I don't mind workin' if I like the folks I'm helpin'.

"Cap stepped up after his pa died. They had 'em a foreman an' that ol' feller took Cap under his wing. 'Course we all called Cap by his given name of Noble back then.

"His ma, she wanted more fer Noble than bein' a farmer. She arranged fer 'im to attend West Point when he was seventeen. She died when he was twelve, but she made 'im promise.

"I reckon their pa's dyin' took some life outa her. Carolyn was her name. Pike was their pa's name, an' Carolyn counted on 'im fer 'most ever'thing.

"Noble didn't want to go to West Point. He thought he should stick 'round after their ma died an' help with Pete. A promise is a promise though." Lampkin pointed with his thumb toward the back of the column. "Pete there was jist a little tyke. He was born shortly 'fore their pa died.

"Cap graduated from West Point in '60. He was close to the top of his class. He pounded a cadet a year or so behind him shortly 'fore graduation. Almost got expelled. That feller's gal had some connections to some of the big dogs at West Point, an' her pa tried to run Noble out.

"Cap had the makings of a good officer though, an' several of his teachers went to bat fer 'im. He graduated with the rest of his class, but he was told he'd never be promoted higher than captain. That's a shame too 'cause he's a sight better officer than that arrogant little turd he pounded will ever be.

"Caster or somethin' like that was that cadet's name. I ferget. He's a big-dog officer now, an' he's jist as brash as he ever was." Lieutenant Lampkin shook his head and muttered something under his breath. He looked behind at the column of men but didn't speak anymore.

Ava listened quietly. When Lieutenant Lampkin stopped talking, she asked, "What was the fight about?"

The lieutenant shrugged his shoulders.

"Y'all cin ask 'im yore ownself. I reckon I talked too much the way it is." He pushed his horse to a gallop to ride beside Captain Headrick.

Chloe looked over at Ava and laughed softly.

"I think that is the most I have ever heard Lieutenant Lampkin talk. He has barely looked at me this entire trip, and he certainly won't carry on a conversation! I know because I have tried." She watched the two men visit as they rode and added, "I guess he must think a lot of your captain."

Ava glared at her. "He's not *my* captain. We can't even be civil to each other. He is the most irritating man I have ever encountered."

Chloe laughed but she said no more.

# Chapter 19

# BENTON BARRACKS HOSPITAL

BENTON BARRACKS HOSPITAL WAS A CONVERTED amphitheater. It was built on the outskirts of St. Louis on what used to be the fairgrounds.

Camp Benton, or Benton Barracks as it was called, was a training facility. It included over a mile of barracks built to accommodate up to thirty thousand soldiers. There were also warehouses, cavalry stables, and parade grounds.

Ava stared at the huge military encampment. Her eyes followed around the massive complex and finally settled on the hospital.

"My goodness. Look at the size of that hospital! How many wounded does it hold?"

"Three thousand when they are at capacity. I wonder how many doctors and nurses work here?" Chloe's eyes were as large as Ava's as they both looked in awe at the bustling facility.

Captain Headrick was all business.

"Ladies, I have orders to drop you at the front doors. Miss Bradley, I will put Deuce in the cavalry stable. You may keep him there as long as you are stationed here. I suggest you talk to the stablemaster about the fee. He might forgo it since you are a nurse.”

He helped the women down in front of the hospital. He smiled at both of them, but his eyes lingered the longest on Ava.

“Miss Bradley, I do hope our paths cross again. Hopefully not in a hospital though.” He bowed slightly and without waiting for Ava’s response, he mounted and rode toward the parade grounds.

Ava watched him a moment before she turned toward the hospital.

“Well, there is no point in waiting. We just as well get started.”

“You didn’t even say goodbye,” Chloe commented softly.

“He didn’t give me time to respond. Besides, he was glad to be rid of us—me for sure.”

Chloe pulled Ava around to face her.

“I don’t think so, Ava. I think he would have turned his horse around if you had answered. And I don’t understand why you are so abrupt with him. You are normally so friendly, but with Captain Headrick, you are almost rude.”

Ava stared at Chloe. She could feel the tears well up in her eyes. She swallowed hard and blinked to push them back.

“I don’t want to like him. He represents everything I hate.”

Chloe stared at her a moment and then asked softly, “And won’t the men inside this hospital represent the same thing? Captain Headrick is not your enemy, Ava. He wanted to be your friend, and you pushed him away. He was nothing but kind to us on this trip.

“How are you going to comfort the men in here who are dying if you can’t even treat them with kindness?”

“It will be different. They are injured. I have never had trouble treating anyone who was injured.”

Chloe studied Ava’s face. Her friend’s mouth was set in a firm line and her eyes blazed with defiance.

“Oh, Ava. I guess we will see. Now let’s go inside and see where we are needed.”

# Chapter 20

# SO MANY WOUNDED

THE NEXT WEEK WAS EXHAUSTING. NURSE PARSONS was in charge of the hospital, and she ran it with an iron fist. She was nearly forty and was a no-nonsense woman as well as an excellent nurse. Ava liked her, but Chloe was a little afraid of her gruffness. Nurse Parsons refused to flirt with the men and gave orders to the nurses in her charge to do the same. She focused on cleanliness and did her best to keep disease from spreading among her patients.

Also helping her was Belle Coddington. Nurse Coddington worked mostly with the quarantined patients. Many had measles which made them contagious. In addition, it was often a deadly disease, especially to compromised men.

Ava offered to help in the measles ward after Nurse Coddington contracted the disease herself, but Nurse Parsons refused.

"No, Nurse Bradley. I know you said you have already had measles, but you are going to be working with severely wounded men on the front lines of this war. I don't want you to carry any sickness with you that we can prevent.

"Besides, wound treatment and infection are what we are going to focus on first. We will train on other diseases next week." She frowned and shook her head as she looked around the large hospital. She added softly, "I am not sure how much more training I am going to be able to give you. You need much more than ten days, but I get wires everyday begging me for nurses."

A large number of the soldiers the nurses treated were missing limbs. They were there for treatment as well as rehabilitation. Some handled their missing limbs with a shrug of their shoulders. Others were convinced that their lives were over.

One young soldier whom Ava sat with was wasting away. He had no desire to become better. She had never seen anyone will themself to die, but that was exactly what this young man was doing.

"Will, you are only nineteen. You have your entire life in front of you."

The soldier looked at her with a numbness she had come to know. He lifted the stump of his leg and held up his bandaged arms.

"Doing what? I was a farmer. How am I going to work a plow or follow a horse with one leg and one hand? And the hand I have left barely works. Who will want to share a life with me now?

"I had a sweetheart at home, but she will want nothing to do with me when she finds out I am only part of the man she knew."

"Will, write her. I will even write her for you. Don't make that decision for your girl." She laughed down at him. "Besides, a banker only needs one hand and a quick mind. You have both of those. Change your profession but take your knowledge of farming with you. I believe you would be an asset to any bank who wants to work with farmers."

The young soldier stared at Ava a moment before he turned his head to face the wall. That night, Ava wrote to the address the young man had written on the picture of a pretty girl in his wallet. The girl's name was Evie.

*Miss Evie Smith*
*Columbus, Missouri*

*Dear Miss Smith,*

*You don't know me, but I am a nurse at Benton Barracks Hospital in Saint Louis, Missouri. Your friend, Will Tillman, is a patient here. Will has been injured and is very ill. He lost both a leg and a hand in this terrible war. If you can find it in your heart to still love him, please come and see him. I fear that he has lost his will to live.*

*I do ask that you please consider Will's wounds before you make this trip. If you don't believe you will be able to love him the way he is, I suggest you not come. Will needs someone to love him for the man he is, someone who will see him as complete and give him hope. I pray you will be that person and that your love is still true.*

*Should you decide to come, you could even train here to become a nurse. That would give you the ability to see Will often as well as support yourself too.*

*Sincerely,*

*Nurse Ella Bradley*

Ava sealed the letter that day and said a prayer before she handed it to the man who handled their mail. He sorted the envelopes as he turned around. He looked at the name on Ava's letter and smiled.

"Evie Smith is my niece, and she is planning to come to St. Louis for a visit this week. I will give her this letter myself." He pushed the envelope into his pocket and was whistling as he hurried to make the rest of his rounds.

# Chapter 21

# A SURPRISE VISITOR

**A**VA WAS HURRYING PAST THE FRONT OFFICE WHEN Nurse Parsons called her.

"Nurse Bradley, this is Miss Eva Smith. She would like to visit Private Will Tillman. Would you be so kind as to show her to his ward?"

Ava smiled brightly and nodded as she reached her hand out to Evie. She was just about to introduce herself when Nurse Parsons' voice reached her.

"And come back down here when you are done. I need to speak with you." Miss Parson's voice was firm, and Ava knew she was most likely going to be reprimanded for writing the letter to Evie.

Her face paled but she answered, "Yes, Nurse Parsons."

She turned back to the young woman and hurried her toward the stairs. She whispered, "You are Evie? I only posted a letter to you yesterday!"

"I am visiting my uncle here. He gave me your letter when I arrived this morning.

"Oh, please. May I see Will right away? I have been so worried about him. His last letter said that he might not write for a time, but he didn't say where he was. I was so afraid he was injured or even dead when I didn't hear any more."

Ava nodded and slowed her walk. She looked directly at the young woman.

"You do understand that Will has lost both a leg and a hand. He is not helpless, but it will be difficult for him to farm."

Tears filled Evie's eyes.

"I know. I talked to my uncle before I came today. Uncle Walt was injured when a tree fell on him, and he had to give up farming. He made some suggestions on job possibilities. He even offered to talk to some his friends who own businesses here in St. Louis. He said he was sure some of those friends would be willing to hire a wounded veteran.

"Father was planning to turn the farm over to Will when we married since I am the oldest girl. My younger sister is engaged now so I guess he can pass it on to her and her future husband.

"I don't care where I live or what we do for a living. I just want to be with Will."

"Well, I'm sure your visit will be a happy surprise for him." Ava looked sideways at Evie and asked, "Did you think at all about training to become a nurse?"

"Yes, I already told Nurse Parsons I would like to do that. She said I may start right away. She told me a number of her nurses are being sent to new posts this week, so she was pleased to have another trainee.

"This actually worked out perfectly. I came to St. Louis to look for a job. I was planning to stay with my uncle for just two weeks. If I didn't find anything during that time, my parents told me to return to Columbus.

"I certainly didn't know I would be able to find a job so easily."

Ava nodded as she stopped in front of an open door. The windows of the large room were open, and a light breeze was blowing through the room. It had rained the night before, so the morning was still a little cool even though it was nearly eleven.

"Just follow me. Our hospital holds nearly three thousand men, and we are almost at capacity."

Ava wove her way through the endless rows of beds. Some of the soldiers were laughing and talking while others just sat or laid in their beds and stared.

A tall soldier was standing by Will's bed. He had his back to the women, but Will was listening intently to what the man said. The soldier looked around when the two women approached, and a slow smile creased his face.

"Well, if it isn't my favorite nurse! How are you, Miss Bradley?"

Before Ava could answer, Will sat up in his bed. His face blanched white and he shoved his left arm under the sheet.

"Evie?"

"Will, oh, Will! I heard you had been wounded and I just had to come!" She dropped down on her knees by the bed and threw her arms around the young soldier's neck.

Ava slowly backed away and Captain Headrick followed her. He nodded over her head at the young couple.

"I asked Private Tillman if he was going to write to Evie and he said 'No.' I don't suppose you had anything to do with her coming here? Writing a family member or close friend like that would be against protocol…unless the patient gave you permission."

Captain Headrick's voice was quiet, and Ava frowned. She glared up at him, ready to retort when she saw him smile.

"Miss Bradley, I do believe there are no such things as rules with you."

"Oh, I believe in some rules, just not in *all* rules. In fact, I believe there are rules and there are guidelines. Rules you follow and guidelines are suggestions."

Captain Headrick stared at Ava a moment before he laughed. He nodded with his head toward the young couple talking excitedly behind them. Private Tillman was sitting up in bed, something he had refused to do since his leg had been removed.

"Well, it might have been just the right thing to do for the two of them. It doesn't always work that way though. Most stories don't have a fairytale ending." Captain Headrick's voice was a little sad and Ava stole a sideways glance at him. His hat had a second hole in the crown, and she could see where a bullet had cut through his pant leg.

"Has the last week been a difficult one?"

Captain Headrick nodded tiredly.

"It has. We lost two good men and three more were captured. We caught three Rebs though and we are hoping to trade." His voice was a little harder when he continued.

"One of the captured men was Lieutenant Lampkin. He can get out of just about anything he is tied with, but he won't escape unless he can take the other two men with him. I want to get them back before they are shipped off to some Reb prison camp."

# Chapter 22

# CIVIL CONVERSATION

CAPTAIN HEADRICK WAS QUIET FOR A MOMENT before he asked carefully, "Ava, would you like to have dinner with me today? I have a few hours before I have to head back out. Would you take the time to visit with a lonely soldier for a little while?"

When Ava looked up at him in surprise, he added with a grin, "Not as friends, of course. Just a little civil conversation."

Ava laughed in spite of herself. "I'll have to ask. Nurse Parsons is quite strict about us keeping our shifts. She does want to speak to me though.

"I need to give some medication and then I will ask her." She rushed away and Captain Headrick smiled as he watched her hurry up the stairs. He was still smiling when Nurse Parsons came out of her office.

Captain Noble Headrick was one of Nurse Parson's favorite officers. He always took the time to check on his men when he passed through St. Louis. The men appreciated it, and Nurse Parsons did too.

"Miss Emily, how about you let Nurse Bradley take dinner with me? I only have two hours and then we are headed out again. Ava is going to ask you, but I thought I might do it for her."

Emily Parsons cocked an eyebrow. "Ava? Ava who?"

Captain Headrick blushed. "I call her Ava, but she goes by Ella. Ella Bradley. She is one of the nurses we dropped off here last week."

Emily Parsons squinted her eyes as she looked hard at Captain Headrick's face. The man blushed and she laughed.

"Why, Noble Headrick, I believe you are sweet on one of my nurses. And the most headstrong one too. She is an excellent nurse, but she just doesn't think all of my rules need to be followed. Like writing to that young girl and asking her to come here. Those kinds of things don't always turn out well."

Noble nodded his head. His blue eyes were sincere when he looked at Nurse Parsons.

"I told her that, but you know, I think it might be all right this time. Will Tillman had no desire to get better, and now he is sitting up in bed. Maybe breaking a few rules here and there isn't such a bad thing."

Nurse Parsons stared at the man in front of her and laughed.

"Well, that is quite an admission, coming from Mr. Rules himself. I can't believe I just heard you say that."

Noble chuckled as he pulled a paper from his pocket.

"Here are those orders you have been expecting. Five of your nurses will be leaving tomorrow."

Nurse Parsons studied the list and shook her head.

"The brass seem to know how to skim the cream right off the top. Those are five of my best nurses, and now I am going to be short-staffed."

Noble grinned and leaned toward her as he whispered, "Then I guess it's a good thing Miss Bradley recruited a new volunteer for you, huh?" He turned around with a smile when he heard someone rushing down the stairs.

Ava faltered a bit as she looked from Nurse Parsons to Captain Headrick. She slowed her walking and brushed off her apron.

"You wanted to see me, Nurse Parsons?"

"Yes, but it can wait. Why don't you go eat with this handsome captain so he will get out of here and stop pestering my nurses. Be back in two hours." She started to turn away and then stopped.

"And, Nurse Bradley, please tell Nurse Moore that the two of you are leaving on the train tomorrow morning at seven o'clock sharp. Nurses Adams, Zahn, and Litchen are going with you as well. You may let them know when you return.

"You won't be assigned here again when you depart tomorrow so be sure to leave nothing behind." She smiled briefly at the startled young woman before she hurried down the hall to check on more of her patients.

# Chapter 23

# A FEISTY, STUBBORN WOMAN

CAPTAIN HEADRICK HELD OUT HIS ARM AND AVA slipped her arm behind his. He pulled her closer to his side and laughed down at her.

"I knew you would give in to my charm at some point in time." He faced forward and his smile became bigger when Ava didn't answer.

Finally, she glanced sideways at him and frowned.

"Your hat has another hole in the crown."

Captain Headrick nodded ruefully.

"Yes, but that one I didn't get trying to save a woman." He grinned down at her. "The first hole is the one that is most important to me."

Ava's eyes were wide when they met his.

"You have had several skirmishes since you left us here?"

"Yeah. It has been a little rough. We are one of the units called on to seek out Bushwhackers. Our battles are more guerrilla-style fighting."

"So you were ambushed?"

"You could say that. We came up on some Rebs we didn't know were in front of us. They know the area better than we do since this is where many of them grew up. A sniper just about got me. I had just pushed up my hat to wipe my forehead when he shot. If it had been down on my head, I wouldn't be here."

Ava was quiet as she listened. She felt her heart clutch at the thought of Noble being shot. She pushed away the feeling with irritation.

"Some of the men in the hospital talk about snipers. The South must have many of them."

"Both sides do but I think the Reb snipers were more effective early on. Our Union boys are catching up a little now.

"The Rebs have one sniper though that nobody has been able to catch. We call him One Shot because that's all he ever takes at a target. He rarely misses either.

"I don't think he's the one who shot at me. He wouldn't have missed a shot like that."

Ava's voice was tight when she spoke.

"Let's talk about something else. Like why you asked me to eat with you."

"Because you are the prettiest gal around mostly. I like sweet, submissive women, and I heard that is how most of you Reb gals are." He grinned down at Ava, and she laughed in spite of herself.

"Besides, I liked how you looked in your britches. None of the women I grew up with would have dared be so bold.

"You didn't wear them to be defiant though. You wore them because they were practical. You are a feisty, stubborn woman, but something about you makes me want to know you better."

Ava blushed slightly. She started to say something and then stopped.

"I don't even know how to respond to that. You are a bold man, Captain Headrick."

"Not bold but probably too blunt. I was hoping I would see you today when I stopped by the hospital to visit Will. He was injured in a skirmish before I met you, and I have been worried about him. I knew he was depressed so I made it a point to see him." His voice was a little softer when he added, "That was a fine thing you did to write his girl. I'm not saying you should break the rules all the time, but I believe you might have saved his life."

Ava was quiet a moment before she spoke.

"I thought Nurse Parsons was going to scold me. I knew she wouldn't approve when I did it. My reasoning was if he was going to let himself die, then what did we have to lose?" Her voice was soft when she continued.

"I try to write to the families of the injured soldiers but there are so many. We nurses have so many patients we are responsible for. Without the army of volunteers that Nurse Parsons has recruited, there is no way we would be able to handle it.

"I think she writes each family a personal letter when a man dies. I have seen stacks of envelopes on her desk. She works more hours than any of us. I don't know if she ever goes home.

"Nurse Parsons talks to us a lot about spreading disease too. She is particular when it comes to cleanliness, and I like that. She is stern and tough, but I believe she hides a tender heart."

"Like her best nurse?" Captain Headrick's face was friendly when he smiled at Ava, but his eyes were sincere.

"I don't think I am her best nurse. I just work fast, and she likes that."

They walked to a small eating house near the hospital. It was busy but the woman who ran it greeted them warmly.

"Right this way, Captain. I have a small table in the back. It is a little quieter back there. Hopefully, you will be able to hear each other." She gave Ava a friendly smile and hurried away.

The time passed quickly and all too soon, they were on their way back to the hospital. The captain stopped by one of the stables and led Ava inside. She heard Deuce's nicker when she entered the barn.

Ava rushed toward the horse. Deuce was pushing against the gate. Ava opened it and slipped inside.

"How did you know where he was? There are so many horses here!"

"I asked. I wanted to make sure he was being cared for properly. I really wanted to ask you to go for a ride, but I decided against it. Too little time. Besides, it's not so safe for you to be seen with me outside the city."

When Ava stepped out of the stall and closed the gate, Captain Headrick took her by the shoulders.

"Ava, would you let me kiss you?"

Ava's eyes were wide when she looked up at him.

"I—I don't think that is a good idea."

"I didn't ask you if it was a good idea. I asked if you would let me." He held her chin in his hand and when she didn't pull away, he kissed her lightly. Ava was trembling and he pulled her close.

"I am going to miss you. Will you let me write you?"

"How can you write me? I don't even know where I'm going, so you certainly don't."

Captain Headrick laughed down at her.

"You don't know where you're going but I know. I have connections, remember?" At Ava's look of surprise, he chuckled.

"I'll write you every chance I get. I may not mail all of them, but I will write you letters when I get lonesome. I'll pretend you are waiting for me." His voice was teasing but Ava knew he was serious.

"Don't say things like that. Someone might hear."

"If someone heard that, then they saw you come into this barn with me. I'd be more worried about that." He was laughing and Ava's eyes went wide.

"Good grief. I came in here to see my horse."

"How about another kiss before I take you back?"

Captain Headrick kissed her again and tears filled Ava's eyes.

"This is why I didn't want to be friends with you. I didn't want to like a Yankee, and I certainly didn't want to be waiting for one to come back to me."

Noble's eyes were intense as he looked down at Ava.

"So that means you want me to come back?"

"I want you to be safe, you and all your men, and Peter too." Her hands trembled as she clenched them together in front of her. "Yes. Yes, I do want you to come back."

When Noble tried to kiss her again, Ava backed away. She shook her head.

"No more kissing. You are too—too—I don't know what you are but no more kissing." She put out her hands.

"Stay away from me. I need to get back. It is almost one."

She rushed out of the stable followed by the laughing Noble. He caught up with her and took her hand.

"Ava, it is going to be fun writing to you. I'm so glad you want me to come back."

# Chapter 24

# THE FIRST POSTING

AVA AND CHLOE WERE ON THE EASTBOUND TRAIN BY six-thirty the next morning. The window they were seated beside opened to give them some fresh air. The two young women looked out the window as they talked excitedly.

A young soldier raced his horse toward the train. He waved his hand in the air as he hollered, "I have a letter here for Miss Ella Bradley. Miss Bradley!"

Ava stood as she caught her breath. "I'm Ella. I will meet you at the door."

She hurried to the door at the back of the train and rushed down the steps. The young man handed her the letter and grinned.

"Captain Headrick said to have safe travels." He grinned again and his whiskerless face turned pink.

Ava stared from the young soldier to the letter and her face turned a deep red.

"I—I—Please tell your captain I thank him for the letter."

The soldier doffed his hat and raced his horse away. Ava's hands shook as she stared at the letter. Then she cleared her throat, smoothed her dress, and walked calmly back to her seat.

Chloe jumped up when Ava reentered the car.

"Who is it from? Quick! Let's open it!"

Ava shook her head.

"Captain Headrick just wanted to wish us safe travels. I'll read it later. I'm sure it is nothing important."

Chloe looked at her friend closely and started to giggle.

"Nothing my eye! If it was nothing you wouldn't have to make yourself breathe slower or pretend you are calm.

"That's all right. You just keep telling yourself he's not 'your captain.' I'm pretty sure he thinks he is. Besides, I already know you had dinner with him yesterday. One of the new volunteers saw you and she told the rest of us.

"Nurse Parsons must think a lot of your captain to let you take off two hours to eat with him." Chloe squeezed Ava's arm and whispered, "I knew you would like him someday."

"Good grief, Chloe. It was just dinner. We talked some. That's all." Ava looked away but she could feel her neck sweating as she lied to her friend.

"You're a terrible liar, Ava, but I like you anyway. Now show me the surprise you have for me."

Ava lifted two aprons from her valise. They were made from the old pillowcase her grandmother had sent with her when she fled from her home. The apron strings were the stripes of cast-off cavalry britches. "Nurse Moore" was embroidered on the front of Chloe's apron, and two pockets cut from military britches were on either side. Ava handed it to Chloe and the young woman squealed in delight.

"It is beautiful, Ava! I knew you were working on something, but I had no idea you could embroider so beautifully. I thought you spent most of your time outside."

"I tried to spend *all* my time outside, but my mother insisted I learn to cook and sew. My granny is the one who taught me to be wild. She also taught me all I know about horses and healing. Mother tried to teach me to be a lady." Ava's eyes sparkled as she added, "I don't think that is as much fun though."

Ava touched one of the white aprons and added softly, "My granny sent a pillowcase with me when I hid from the Red Legs. It held the few things we had of value, and those few items are the only things left now that our home was burned." She smiled at Chloe and blinked back a tear. "There was enough cloth in that pillowcase to make two aprons, so I made one for each of us."

Chloe hugged Ava.

"I'm so glad we met and even happier we became friends."

Ava and Chloe were soon joined by the other three nurses who were traveling with them. Ava closed her eyes and listened with a smile until she fell asleep. The others carried on an animated conversation until they grew tired. All of them awoke when the train whistle blew.

The train was just coming into the station in Nashville, Tennessee, where they would have a half-hour stop. Chattanooga, Tennessee, was their final destination, and it was another four-and-one-half hours southeast.

# Chapter 25

# A FRIENDLY STRANGER

**I**T WAS NEARLY MIDNIGHT WHEN THE TRAIN ARRIVED in Chattanooga. Ava looked at the piece of paper Nurse Parsons had given her.

*Ella, look for a man waiting in a buggy. He will be wearing a red hat. Ask him to take you to the hospital. I included two bits for each of you for your fare. It may not be that much but certainly do not pay more. Someone at the hospital will show you to your quarters.*

*Please let me know that you made it safely when you get a chance, and remember, you may care about your patients but don't get emotionally involved. No courting while you are working.*

*Best wishes to all of you.*

*Nurse Parsons*

The five tired women stepped off the train and looked around. Ava pointed at a surrey parked on the side of the street with a lantern attached to each side. An old man in a red derby hat sat in the front seat.

"There. That is the man who is to take us to the hospital."

The old man looked up with a smile as the five young women approached him.

"Evenin', ladies. They call me Quick. Oscar Quick. I reckon y'all be the ones who need a ride to the hospital. Let me toss yore bags in the back an' I'll help ya up here. It were a long ol' ride, warn't it?"

Ava smiled and nodded.

"It was and we so appreciate you waiting for us. I know the train was a little late."

"Yeah, but she's always late. Trains in these parts don't run on much of a schedule any more. Too much cargo bein' packed around, an' too many troops bein' picked up an' left off.

"Now y'all jist relax a bit. It will take us nigh on twenty minutes to get y'all to the hospital."

Ava visited with the old man while the other women dozed.

"First time in these parts?"

"Yes, my home was on the border of Kansas and Missouri. It's gone now so I just go wherever I'm sent."

The old man commented quietly, "General Ewing's Order 11 warn't no good. The onliest ones what suffered was the old folks, women, an' little kids." He reached over and patted Ava's hand. He was silent a moment before he continued.

"I think y'all will like it here. Folks is friendly an' women is respected. Most of the time anyways. It ain't wise to ride out by your own self at no time anymore though. Not even the group of y'all together. Them durn guerrillas is jist unpredictable. Some of 'em be gentlemen an' others should jist be shot they own selves.

"Y'all didn't bring no hosses, did ya?"

"I did but a man on the train said he would take my horse to the closest livery. Once we get settled, I plan to check on him. I'd like him to be closer to the hospital if you know of another place I can keep him though."

"I tell ya what. Give me the paper what says all yore particulars, an' I'll take 'im out to my place. I jist live on the edge of town, an' that's less than a half mile from the hospital. Y'all kin walk out an' see 'im any time ya want."

Ava smiled at the old man.

"Thank you, Mr. Quick. I would appreciate that."

Oscar waved his hands around. "Chattanooga be a rail hub. We's located right along the banks of the Tennessee River, an' four major rail lines run through here. Both the Rebs and the Yankees want control of those lines. Right now, the Yanks hold this town. They captured it this summer, but the Rebs, they want it back. They lost it a couple of months ago with nary a fight, but they's a gonna be a big battle to get her back 'fore too long. In fact, she's already started.

"Rosencrans, he be the Yank general. He pushed Bragg back south of town. Now they's a gonna fight back an' forth to see who cin take the rail station. If the South don't take these lines back, they'll be in trouble. They need this rail hub to move men an' supplies south. 'Sides, if it stays like it is, Chattanooga'll open a door fer those Yanks to pour right down through Georgia.

"I know ya little gals was trained by the Yanks but in that there battle an' most of the others too, you'll treat Rebs right alongside the Yanks.

"I jist don't know who will win in this here fight. The Rebs be fightin' fer their homes an' the Yanks be fightin' fer a cause."

Once they reached the large hospital, the women were led toward the stairway. A young woman greeted them and pointed up the stairs.

"My name is Mavis. Please follow me. Your quarters are on the third floor."

A woman dressed in men's clothing came hurrying down the stairs. She nodded at the group of women and then stopped.

"I assume you are new nurses. Were any of you sent here as field nurses?"

When Ava and Chloe both nodded their heads, she replied brusquely, "Good. Be ready to leave at seven sharp tomorrow morning. We will be traveling south to set up a field hospital. I will expect one of you to drive a wagon or army ambulance. We will need all the supplies we can haul down there. And don't be late!"

Mavis watched the woman rush away and then looked back at the nurses with big eyes.

"That was Doctor Walker. She is a surgeon. She has been helping here for a time, but she was just assigned to the 52$^{nd}$ Ohio Infantry." Mavis leaned toward them and whispered, "She's an excellent surgeon but I'm kind of glad she's leaving. I think she's scary."

"I heard our men are skirmishing with the Rebs somewhere around Chickamauga in northwest Georgia. It is only fifteen miles from Chattanooga, but it is longer by wagon. I certainly hope the battle doesn't get this far north." Mavis paused and blushed slightly as she looked at Ava and Chloe.

"I'm sorry. Perhaps the battle will end quickly, and you will be able to return soon."

# GORDON HOUSE
## CRAWFISH SPRING FIELD HOSPITAL
### CHICKAMAUGA, GEORGIA
### FRIDAY, SEPTEMBER 18, 1863

# Chapter 26

# ORGANIZED CHAOS

AVA PULLED HER ARMY AMBULANCE TO A STOP. SHE and Chloe stared at the sprawling hospital complex. Crawfish Spring Hospital was set up along Lafayette Road. It was to the left and rear of the Union Army's initial position. Surgeons, stewards, and nurses were treating both Union and Confederate wounded.

A soldier grabbed the lines of Ava's ambulance and helped both women down.

"Report to that mansion over there. It's the Gordon House. We have ten division hospitals and seven are positioned near here because of the good water. The Gordon House is the main field hospital for one division. There are more tents down the hill near Crawfish Spring, and they hold the wounded too." He paused and added quietly, "I'm sorry you have to witness the carnage here, but we are pleased to have you. The wounded are pouring in."

Ava pointed to the supplies in the back of the ambulance.

"We brought supplies. Do you want me to deliver anything?"

"No, I know what is needed and where, so I'll take care of that." He smiled at Ava. "My name is Solon Hyde. I am part of the 17th Ohio Infantry and one of the hospital stewards here."

"Is there something we can carry to save you some time? Something they may be short on right now?" Ava could feel her heart beating quickly as she stared at the hospital complex. Hundreds of men were lying on the grass by the river and the spring that fed it. There were large shade trees everywhere, and she could see where numerous tents had been set up to make maximum use of the fresh water and shade.

Ava watched in horror as amputated arms, legs, feet, and hands were tossed from a window in the Gordon House into a wagon that was parked below. The pile of limbs grew quickly. When the wagon was full, it was driven away and emptied so it could be filled again.

Solon handed each woman a box.

"Take this with you and be careful. We are short on chloroform and the surgeons need it."

The two women held their boxes carefully as they hurried toward the large mansion. Doctor Walker joined them.

"The two sides have been fighting back and forth all around here, but the battle broke out in earnest today." Her voice was quiet when she added, "I think the casualties are going to be horrendous. Our ability to conduct war has outpaced our ability to treat the wounded."

Ava was quiet as she listened. She pointed an elbow at the mansion.

"Why are they performing so many amputations? Are we not able to save their limbs or is it because there are so many?"

Doctor Walker pointed toward a rifled musket laying on the ground.

"That is the problem. Those guns carry a conical ball. They weigh around an ounce and travel at high speed. The old round balls moved slower. They still caused fractures but not the amount of bone destruction. Not only are the new balls fast, but they spin. They shatter and splinter long bones when they hit. If the bullet hits close to a joint, we might be able to save the limb since the bone is softer there. If it shatters one of the long bones though, the limb has to come off and that amputation window is narrow. If the limb isn't taken off within the first twenty-four hours—and preferably less—infection will set in, and gangrene will follow.

"Abdomen wounds are nearly always fatal. Before, when the bullets moved slower, the intestines were sometimes pushed aside naturally allowing the bullet to go through without as much damage. Now…." Doctor Walker shook her head. "On the other hand, the round balls did more damage in the chest area. They often bruised and lacerated large areas of the lung while the faster conical ball leaves a clean-cut wound." She looked hard at Ava and Chloe.

"You nurses are going to have to evaluate the men as they come in. If this battle gets as bad as many think it will, you are going to have to make some hard choices on who gets treatment. And it will be the nurses making those decisions. Every doctor and surgeon will be needed to operate." She looked from one to the other.

"So…where do you want to be assigned? Who is willing to be out in front sorting the wounded, and who wants to help with surgery?"

Chloe looked over at Ava. Her eyes were wide.

"I—I'm not sure I can make those kinds of decisions."

Ava smiled at her friend.

"Chloe, you help with surgeries. I will help outside or wherever I am needed."

Doctor Walker nodded.

"Nurse Moore—you report to Doctor Thompson. I want to speak with Nurse Bradley before I come in." As Chloe hurried inside, Doctor Walker turned to Ava.

"Nurse Bradley, as I said, we are going to have high casualties with this battle. All the signs are here." She pointed over the sprawling hospital complex and the additional tents in the distance. "Seven field hospitals in less than a two-mile area. Since each general has his own field hospital, that tells me there are many men in the field." Her eyes were worried as she looked over the open field and then back at the hospital complex.

"You are going to have to maintain a calm manner. If you panic, the men in your care will be even more afraid. You reassure them and use every tool you have. The less seriously wounded should be treated in the tent hospitals down by Crawfish Spring. Initially, we will treat the most grievous wounds here in the Gordon House although that will likely change depending on the number of wounded.

"There should be chaplains around as well although many of them will remain on the field with the wounded. Use them if you see them. They all have the rank of captain so they can make decisions too.

"Most of all, I want you to make sure no unauthorized person enters that house. Cleanliness is one of my biggest concerns and I don't want a bunch of dirty men wandering around in there unless they are carrying patients. No curious onlookers.

"Wash your hands…and keep plenty of soap and water handy. You are going to need it."

# Chapter 27

# TOO MANY TO TREAT

DOCTOR WALKER WAS CORRECT. THE WOUNDED along with the dying and soon to be dead began pouring in the morning of September 19. At first, the dead were buried on the field where they fell, but soon, there were too many. The seriously wounded were often dead by the time they reached the hospital. The men were lined up in long rows. As hard as Ava tried to keep them separated, the wounded, dying, and dead were soon mixed together.

Ava sorted the wounded as efficiently and gently as she could. Those who could be treated without surgery were left outside. They would be taken to one of the tent hospitals to receive treatment. Those who could be saved were moved inside while the dying were offered comfort.

Time passed quickly. The rows of wounded were long. Some of the men moaned or cried out for help. Others stared vacantly and were silent as shock set in. It was nearly evening, and still the wounded kept coming. Ava took a ragged breath and rushed to meet the next wagonful of injured soldiers.

A young soldier touched her dress as she hurried by.

"Please, may I have a drink of water? I am so thirsty."

Ava stopped beside the young man and then looked again.

"Peter! I thought you were patrolling the Missouri River!"

Peter winced as he moved his leg and then tried to grin.

"We were but then this battle started churning up. We were sent to help here."

Ava lifted his pant leg carefully and let out a slow breath when she saw the wound. "Is this your only wound? You have not been shot in the stomach or chest?"

"Nope, that's it. I sure could use a drink though."

Ava pulled off his boot and handed it to him. "Hang onto this. If you lay it down, it will be lost." She handed him the canteen she carried at her waist.

"Let me wash my hands and I will treat your leg. Then I want you to go down to those tent hospitals by the river. Tell those men to stop relieving themselves so close to the water. We need that water clean."

Her hands shook a little as she cleaned and bound his leg. Peter was quiet as she worked on him. He finally commented softly, "Noble is healthy. He will be pleased to know you are here."

Ava looked up in surprise before she blushed.

"Your brother is a fine man, but I hope I don't see him here. Now take this crutch and go down by that spring. Wash your hands before you change that wrap and be sure to tell the soldiers by Crawfish Spring what I said." She kissed his cheek lightly.

"Be careful, Peter." She moved quickly as the wagon was unloaded and directed the men where to place the wounded. She stopped beside each man and talked to him before she moved on.

Peter watched her a moment before he hobbled away. He smiled to himself.

"Miss Ella is here. Well, Noble will be pleased to know that." He frowned before he muttered, "Then again, maybe he won't. He was hoping she would stay in Chattanooga.

"Our men are fighting with Wilder's Lightning Brigade. Noble keeps us on horseback, but Wilder's men like to dismount to fight.

"They have some darn nice guns too. Those Spencers can fire up to twenty rounds a minute. I know 'cause I counted some of them. Noble is going to see if we can get some of those." He turned around once to look at the chaos behind him. He stopped when he saw Sergeant Nielson and some of his Red Legs dismount in front of the mansion that Miss Ella said housed the main hospital.

"Now what is he doing here?" Peter turned around and began to hobble as quickly as he could toward the large house. He was nearly up the hill when he heard Nielsen laugh.

"Now, nursey, ya jist move outa the way. Major Burke here is a surgeon an' I am offerin' his help." The man Nielson pointed toward was a slovenly man with a tobacco stain on his chin. His hands and clothes were filthy. Long hair hung in greasy spikes from under his cavalry hat. The man spit in Ava's direction as he grinned.

"That's right. Stand aside, missy. I reckon there are some Rebs in there I cin cut on. What are we doin' a helpin' Rebs anyhow? They try to shoot us an' then when they's shot, we put 'em next to our boys? I'll jist help thin 'em down a bit."

# Chapter 28

# "DRAG THAT MAN OUTSIDE!"

**A**VA GRIPPED THE SIDES OF THE DOORJAMB. HER FACE was pale as she stared from one man to the other.

"I told you before. Only authorized personnel are allowed in here. Now you turn around and leave. Your kind of help is not needed or wanted."

Sergeant Nielson almost threw Ava aside. When she slipped and fell, he laughed at her.

"You're a pretty one but a mite too sassy. Mebbie I'll teach ya some manners 'fore I leave here."

Ava lunged to her feet and darted through the door to stand in front of the two men. Her voice was soft but steady when she spoke.

"I am asking you again to leave."

The patients who could move strained to sit up in their beds. As they watched the scene in front of them, some cocked revolvers hidden under their bed sheets. A murmur of angry voices began to fill the room.

Major Burke shoved Ava aside. He jerked the sheet off an unconscious man. The man's Confederate uniform was folded on the floor beside his bed. Burke laughed.

"Here's one of those lousy Rebs." He grabbed the man's limp arm and pulled a large knife out of his sheath.

"I cin hack this off now. Mebbie a leg too. That'll teach 'im fer messin' with us Northern boys."

A soldier in the bed next to the unconscious man struggled to sit up.

"That man saved my life on the battlefield. I was bleedin' to death an' he stopped it." He looked at Ava. "He said he was a surgeon. The feller who shot him thought he was tryin' to kill me but that ain't so. He was workin' to save me."

Ava jerked the revolver out of Burke's holster. She backed up beside the Confederate soldier and pointed it at the two men in front of her. Her voice was angry but steady when she spoke.

"You drop that man's arm now. I will shoot you if I must. And leave this hospital immediately."

Nielson stared at her in surprise and Burke laughed. He raised his knife and Ava shot into the floor in front of him. He dropped the man's arm as he jumped back and then charged Ava with his knife raised.

Ava shot him in the leg and quickly swung the pistol to cover Nielson. Her voice was hard and even when she spoke.

"Drag that man outside, and put him at the end of the last row. He will not be treated ahead of the men who were here before him."

Burke's screams were laced with curses as he shouted at Ava. He attempted to rise with the help of Nielson.

"I'll git you, you little—" His voice was cut off as Peter slammed him in the stomach with his crutch. Burke bent over and collapsed on the floor. As he gasped for air, he looked up to see Peter's pistol pointed at him.

"You finish what you were about to say, and you won't ever leave that floor." Peter looked behind the group of staff who had gathered and pointed his crutch at the startled steward.

"Find an officer and get him in here."

Just then, Captain Noble Headrick pushed through the crowded room. His eyes took in the wounded man on the floor and Ava's angry face. He shoved men aside stepping over Burke to stand in front of Nielson.

His face was angry as he stared at the sergeant. He pointed toward the floor.

"Get him out of here. And before you even think about speaking, this is a war situation. I can and will throw you in irons if you refuse an order."

Nielson's eyes narrowed down. He looked down at Burke who was writhing on the floor, still trying to catch his air. His mouth opened and then slowly closed. He grabbed Burke by one arm and a steward took the other.

"Come on, Burke. We'll get help somewhere else." As Nielson moved toward the door, he snarled at Captain Headrick, "This here deal ain't over. I'll report that nurse and have her thrown in the brig. Ain't no woman alive who has the right to shoot an officer in the Union army, especially one of General Ewing's Red Legs."

Captain Headrick continued to glare at him before he turned back to the scene in front of him.

"Nurse Bradley, please give me your weapon. And you need to come with me."

The noise in the room became louder as the men protested. Captain Headrick couldn't hear all they were saying but he did hear what they called Ava.

"Who in here saw what happened? Speak up now if you did."

The man who had spoken earlier pointed at the unconscious man in the bed beside him.

"I'm Sergeant Wilsey, sir, and it was a simple deal. Nurse Sweet was protectin' the life of her patient. That man is a Reb, but he saved my life. I told the sergeant that too but neither him nor the feller who said he was a surgeon cared. They just wanted to cause trouble." He looked over at Ava and added softly, "Nurse Sweet, ya shoulda killed 'im."

Ava patted the wounded soldier on his shoulder.

"Thank you, Sergeant. I probably should have. Now you lie back down. We don't want that leg wound to break open."

Captain Headrick looked around the hospital room at the angry men. He almost smiled. *It looks like my "Nurse Sweet" has won a place in the hearts of more men than me.*

"After you, Nurse Bradley." More of the men struggled to sit up in their beds, and angry murmurs in the room grew louder. Captain Headrick smiled as he looked around at the wounded men.

"At ease, gentlemen. I will have your nurse back shortly. I just have a few questions for her so I can fill out my paperwork.

"Private Headrick, you come with me too."

# Chapter 29

# NURSE SWEET

CAPTAIN HEADRICK FOLLOWED AVA OUTSIDE. WHEN they were a distance from the door, she stopped and glared at him.

"I don't have time for this. We have too many wounded men to worry about your paperwork. Besides, Peter was there. He can tell you what happened."

The captain looked down at the small, determined woman in front of him and chuckled.

"Nurse Sweet, huh?"

Ava blushed. "Only some of the men call me that. Not all of them do."

"Well, I'd say all the men in there agree with that title. I almost had an uprising when they thought I was going to arrest you." He looked over at Peter.

"Private Headrick, anything you want to add to what Sergeant Wilsey said?"

"No. I was headed down to the spring when I saw those Red Legs dismount. I hurried as fast as I could back up the hill. Miss Bradley had already bandaged my leg and found a crutch for me. She gave me her canteen too.

"I would have shot Burke if Miss Bradley hadn't beat me to it."

Captain Headrick studied his brother and then nodded slowly.

"You are dismissed, Private. Go to wherever Miss Bradley directed you before this incident."

Peter saluted his brother and then tipped his hat to Ava.

"That was a fine shot, Miss Bradley. You should have shot higher, but it was still a fine shot. I'd say you broke Burke's leg. Maybe he will lose it. That would be mighty just after what he tried to do to that wounded man." Peter smiled at Ava again before he hobbled down the hill.

Captain Headrick watched Peter for a moment before he turned to face Ava.

"Ava, what am I going to do with you? Everywhere you go, you get the men all stirred up." Noble's face was somber, but he was trying not to laugh.

Ava stared up at him briefly before she began to shake. She whispered, "I almost killed him. I *wanted* to kill him, and I almost did."

Noble pulled her close and kissed the top of her head. He hugged her tightly and murmured, "I saw him lunge at you but there were too many men between him and me to shoot. It was all I could do not to finish him off after you shot him." He slipped a small gun into her hand.

"Keep this in your pocket. It is only effective between three and four feet, but it will stop a man at that distance." He put his hands on her shoulders and smiled down at her.

"When did you read my letter?"

Ava blushed furiously.

"I am not going to discuss what you wrote in your letter."

Noble laughed and kissed her cheek.

"That you read it is enough for me. And as far as today, I wouldn't worry too much. I'll file a report when I get to it. It won't be for a time because I am regrouping my men and heading back out." He stared down at her and then pulled her close again as he smiled.

"Ah, Ava. I have so many things to say to you. I might not get to say them until this war is over though." He grinned at her as he backed away.

"Pretend I am hugging you when you read my letter again." He tipped his hat and strode toward his horse.

Ava watched him walk away and then rushed back to the hospital. Two more wagons of wounded men were being unloaded, and she began her dreaded job of sorting the men according to their wounds.

# Chapter 30

# ANOTHER BLOODY DAY

SUNDAY, SEPTEMBER 20, WAS ANOTHER BLOODY DAY. The wounded kept coming, wagon after wagon. By noon, Ava was almost staggering with exhaustion and Doctor Walker grabbed her.

"Nurse Bradley, I want you to lie down. You have been in this hospital since we arrived on Friday. If you don't get some rest, I will have another patient."

"But the men—there are more wounded and—"

Doctor Walker cut her off.

"Yes, there are many wounded, so we are going to have to do the best we can. Now you lie down for at least three hours. I put some blankets in a small room on the top floor. Go there and close the door. Come back when you have rested a bit." Her face softened just a moment before she added, "That's an order."

Ava climbed the stairs and shut the door to the small room. It was dark and hot inside. She wrapped her arms around her knees and buried her face. At first her sobs were slight, but soon her body was wracked with hard, silent crying. She could hear the cries and moans of the wounded even through the closed door.

"Lord, why is this happening?" she whispered. "The death and devastation of all these young men. Their blood has stained the floors of this house, and their dying words are carved into the walls. I just don't know if I can take it. Please give me the strength to continue and give our doctors the ability to save more lives."

Ava lay down on her side and fell asleep, her tears drying on her cheeks.

It seemed only minutes when she awoke to the sound of gunfire. She sat upright and listened before she rushed out of the small room. A bullet flew over her head, and she ducked instinctively as she ran for the stairs.

A steward grabbed her and pulled her down.

"Stay down! We are surrounded by Rebs. One of the surgeons is waving a bloody sheet to show them this is a hospital. We have to surrender because we have no way to defend ourselves. This house was used as Union headquarters for a time, so those soldiers probably don't realize it is a hospital."

Wild Rebel yells echoed through the valley and riders charged the hospital. Confederate soldiers shoved orderlies aside as they lunged through the door.

"This place is under our control now an' all ya Bluebellies are our prisoners.

"Stafford, start gatherin' blankets an' anything else we can use. Take 'em off those fellers in the beds. They likely ain't gonna make it anyhow."

Doctor Graham pushed through the loud soldiers.

"Who is in charge here?" His eyes moved around the soldiers until they rested on an officer who was just coming through the door.

"Sir, you have no business here. This is a field hospital, not headquarters for Union officers. We treat all the wounded here regardless of what color they wear. We have a great number of wounded we are trying to care for and not enough supplies to provide for them."

The man he addressed frowned and then waved an arm as he yelled, "I'm General Wheeler and I'm ordering you men out of here. You might be wounded bad enough someday to end up in one of these. Let's give these fellows the same treatment you'd like to receive."

One of the men cursed as he dropped the blanket he was holding.

"But, General, we got nothin'. Most of us don't even have shoes."

The officer pointed toward the rows of dead lined up outside the hospital.

"Take some of theirs but leave the wounded alone."

Just then, there was gunfire behind the Rebel troops. A man burst through the doors. He was shouting and pointing toward the forest behind him. Soon, the soldiers were charging away from the hospital, returning the fire of Union forces they could barely see through all the trees.

The fighting pushed away from the hospital and Ava ran toward the front of the mansion. The bullets had passed through the windows showering broken glass on some of the patients. However, the brick walls of the mansion were thick, and they stopped the bullets.

Ava and the rest of the hospital staff rushed to make sure their patients were safe. One of the soldiers pointed toward the open door.

"Rider comin' in fast. He's one of ours!"

The rider slid to a stop in front of the hospital and hollered through the door.

"You need to evacuate this hospital *now*!"

Ava's breath caught in her chest. She looked around at the rows of patients, many who couldn't walk. She ran to the door.

"We can't evacuate. There are too many wounded and most of them can't walk."

Lieutenant Noah Lampkin shook his head.

"Captain Headrick said everyone who can walk needs to leave now. The battlelines have been movin' all through this fight an' ya all are now behind enemy lines. It won't be long 'fore the Rebs take over this hospital." He looked hard at Ava and added quietly, "Everyone who is left will be a prisoner.

"Get ever'one who cin walk on their feet. Patients, doctors, nurses—ever'one needs to go an' go now!"

Lieutenant Lampkin held his horse as the animal danced impatiently.

"That means y'all too, Miss Bradley," he said. "Captain Headrick said to make sure ya leave." He seemed to want to add something. Instead of speaking again, he spurred his horse toward the heaviest gunfire.

Ava stared after the lieutenant briefly before she rushed to tell Doctor Walker. She grabbed a nurse who was assisting her and whispered, "We have been ordered to evacuate. Everyone is to leave. Any of the men who can walk must be moved now. We can fill the ambulances and wagons with the more seriously wounded. Please tell Doctor Walker now."

The nurse nodded. She hurried to Doctor Walker and spoke quickly.

The surgeon stared at the nurse. Her gaze caught Ava standing outside the door and she shook her head.

"Impossible. We have too many patients. Many are unable to travel. Absolutely not. It would take us at least a day to pack up this hospital and more time to move all of these men. I refuse to leave.

"Now pass me that scalpel."

Ava grabbed a steward.

"Please tell Doctor Graham. He is the chief physician. He must order an evacuation. We can at least start moving the men who can walk."

Stewards were soon passing the word between the cluster of tent hospitals. Doctor Graham found Ava and listened as she shared what she was told. He stared at the rows of men waiting to be operated on.

"If we leave now, even more will die. We must continue to operate until the last moment. You gather those who can walk. If they can carry a gun, try to find them one. Tell them to head north toward Chattanooga."

# Chapter 31

# A FRANTIC EVACUATION

**A**LL THE UNION SOLDIERS WHO COULD STAND WERE soon limping toward the door. Some of them supported a man between them who couldn't walk. Those who couldn't get out of bed cursed or stared silently. Some covered their faces so no one would see them cry while others watched stoically.

Ava ran outside.

"You men who can walk—hitch horses to these wagons and ambulances. This hospital is being evacuated. Please aid those who need help climbing in, and don't let any transport leave until it is completely full!"

She paused when she saw an orderly jump into an empty wagon. She ran toward him, but an injured soldier got there first. He jerked the orderly off the wagon and threw him on the ground.

"Where do you think you're goin'? If you can't do your job, then get on outa here. You'll go on foot though so get away from that wagon." When the orderly started to rise, the soldier moved closer and added quietly, "An' you had better make sure I never see you again or you just might be reported as missin' in action."

The orderly's eyes opened wide in fear. He climbed to his feet and began to run awkwardly toward the trees to the north of the hospital.

The soldier turned around and nodded toward the hospital.

"Nurse Sweet, I'm Private Gallagher. I'll help carry men out here if you can tell me which ones to grab." He pointed at two other soldiers who were hobbling toward him.

"Kirby and Callahan—get Feeney and grab two of those litters off the ground. Help me haul some of those men out here." He looked at the soldiers who were lying on the ground in front of the hospital.

"Any of you fellows who can move need to get to the wagons. The Rebs are taking this place over."

The Union soldiers stared at him in surprise. Some struggled to stand while there were ragged cheers from the Confederate soldiers. Still, a few Rebs helped wounded Union soldiers to the wagons.

The young Confederate doctor whom Ava had protected struggled to get out of bed.

"Let me take over the surgery. My head wound isn't serious, and I can work with a headache. Your army needs its doctors and nurses as much as we Rebs do."

Ava grabbed a pair of crutches and handed them to him.

"Surgery is to my right in the library. Doctor Walker might leave if you offer to take over for her. She has orders to evacuate." She stopped Chloe as the young nurse hurried by.

"You help those men outside to get in wagons, and you squeeze in one too."

Chloe grabbed Ava as she turned away.

"You have to come! Captain Headrick ordered you to leave!"

"I'm not going. There are too many men here who need help. I will just be a Confederate nurse now. Now go. Please let Nurse Parsons know I'm all right. I will write when I can."

Ava rushed up the porch steps and was soon outside with two more men leaning on her. She helped them to the last wagon.

"That's it, Nurse Sweet. We don't have any more room and we're out of wagons." Private Gallagher could barely put weight on his leg, but he helped squeeze a young man with a bloody stump onto the wagon seat.

"You drive, soldier, and I'll walk." Private Gallagher backed away from the wagon. The wound in his right leg from a musket ball was near the bone and was bleeding badly. Ava was convinced his leg was fractured or broken. However, the order for the hospital to be evacuated came before he could be thoroughly examined. Instead, the wounded soldier was handed a bandage and sent outside.

Private Gallagher was determined to follow the wagons on foot. *I might lose my leg if I have to walk all the way to Chattanooga, but that will still be better than losing it and my life in a Reb prison.*

Cavalry soldiers dismounted and placed wounded men on their horses. They wanted to evacuate as many of the remaining wounded as possible.

A smiling soldier offered to let Private Gallagher ride his horse. "I can walk, Private, but you aren't going to get far on that leg."

Private Gallagher shook his head. "Take this man. He's in worse shape than me." The man he helped on the horse had severe chest wound and was having difficulty breathing.

When the commanding officer saw this, he made all the walking soldiers return the injured men to the hospital.

Some of the wounded begged not to be left. "Please! Don't leave us here. Take us with you!"

Others cursed as they slid from the horses. "You have sentenced us to death. We'll never survive a trip to a Reb prison."

The man Private Gallagher helped, Private John Sweeny, just smiled. He shook the hand of the soldier who helped him to the ground and thanked him.

"It's all right. Maybe we'll be exchanged for wounded Reb prisoners. We'd only slow you down anyhow since most of us can barely sit on a horse."

As the last wagon drove away, Private Gallagher hobbled slowly behind. The soldiers in that wagon began to holler, "You can't leave Private Gallagher behind! He'll lose that leg if he walks on it much more. Besides, he's the one who made sure we all got a ride. Hold up now. We'll make a little room."

Ava smiled as she ran after the wagon. She thrust a roll of bandages and ointment into the young private's hands.

She whispered softly, "Wrap that leg wound, Private Gallagher. It could get infected if you don't take care of it. And have it examined as soon as you arrive in Chattanooga. We don't want you to lose your leg." She pointed at the driver and added, "Now move as quickly and as quietly as you can."

The soldiers in the wagon pulled Private Gallagher into the mass of bodies. Some of the wounded men groaned. Others tried not to cry out when their stumps were bumped.

The last wagon joined the caravan of wagons and ambulances on the road to Chattanooga. Most medical supplies and equipment had been abandoned to make room for the wounded. Ava had just turned back toward the hospital when a fast-moving wagon rattled by her. The wagon was piled high with musical instruments and each musician had a place to sit as well. No room was allowed for any wounded though. She tried to stop it, but the driver whipped his horses and the wagon rushed by. They were soon too far away for her to catch.

Ava muttered under her breath, "I guess their toys were more important than the men they could have saved." She glared again after the departing wagon before she hurried inside.

# Chapter 32

# BAD NEWS

**M**ORNING HAD BARELY BROKEN WHEN TWO MEN dressed in gray rode slowly up to the quiet hospital.

"Mornin'. We thought we might eat a bite with you folks. I'm General Forrest and this is General Cheatham." The two men proceeded to sit down. Food was quickly placed before them, and they enjoyed a quiet meal. They particularly appreciated the coffee.

"You all will be here for a time. We are trying to work out a prisoner exchange for the wounded men. We'll will allow your porters to continue to find and pick up any wounded who have not yet been retrieved." Cheatham frowned and his face became pale when he added, "Those fires from all the shelling cleared some big swaths of brush and grass. It burned some of the dead too." *Probably some wounded as well,* he thought, *but I won't say that out loud.*

The surgeon standing beside Ava rushed toward a wagon that was just arriving.

"Soldier, unload those men and get back out there as fast as you can." He looked at the billowing smoke. "Start with the ones closest to those fires." He pointed toward some of the wounded soldiers standing beside the hospital. "Two of you men who can walk and carry, go with them to help. We need to get those wounded away from that fire."

He turned his eyes toward the Confederate officers and added quietly, "We are short-handed. If some of your medical staff can help, we would appreciate it."

General Forrest shook his head. "We don't have any doctors to spare. In fact, y'all are Yankees, and as such, you are our prisoners."

Doctor Williams stepped forward.

"Sir, I am Lieutenant Reuben Williams with the Georgia Volunteers. I can tell you that men from both sides were treated equally in this hospital. I know this because I was wounded and was treated well here." He pointed at Ava. "In fact, that nurse protected me from a Red Leg who wanted to do me harm.

"I ask that you let us *all* do our work here and try to save as many of these soldiers as we can."

Two porters hurried toward the hospital carrying a litter.

"This man is a chaplain. He was ministering to the dying when he was hit."

Doc Williams backed out of the doorway and rushed toward the operating room in the library.

"Bring him in here. I'll work on him right away."

The chaplain pulled on Ava's dress as they carried him through the door. The porters stopped as they waited for the chaplain to speak.

"Are you Nurse Sweet? I have some letters for you." His eyes were sad as he added, "The top packet is from a captain who was shot near me. He was trying to pull one of his men to safety. He asked me to make sure you received this packet." The chaplain took a ragged breath and sagged back onto the stretcher.

"The rest are from—some—some of those poor boys I—I comforted as they were dying. They asked for someone to notify..." The chaplain sighed and his body went limp.

Another surgeon quickly checked him and shook his head.

"He is gone. Get those other wounded men in here now!"

Ava's eyes grew wide, and her breath caught as she recognized the leather packet the chaplain said he was to give her. Her hands shook as she tried to put the packet in her pocket.

A surgeon placed his hands on her shoulders and shook her.

"Nurse, there is no time for mourning. We have lives here to save. Now go down to the tent hospital and see if they have any laudanum. We are almost out, and we are going to need it for the amputations."

Ava nodded numbly and stumbled through the door. She tripped and a Confederate soldier caught her. He started to make a joke but stopped when he saw the tears she was fighting to hold back.

"Here, I'll walk with ya an' help ya carry whatever it is ya need. My name is Casten. Johnny Casten. I'm guessin' y'all are the Nurse Sweet I've heard some of the men talk about." Johnny gave Ava a quick smile and tucked her arm under his. His voice was quiet when he spoke.

"This here war has been hard on ever'body. I think it is harder on ya medical folks though. Us soldiers—we all know what we are goin' into. Y'all—the nurses an' doctors—have to pick up the pieces of the wounded an' dyin' an' try to put 'em back together."

When a sob slipped out of Ava's throat, Johnny put his arm around her shoulders. He steered her toward a clump of trees. His smile was kind as he held her arms.

"You go on behind there an' have yoreself a cry. I heard that doc say he needed laudanum. I know where to find some. I'll see what else I cin round up fer pain." He patted her arm and pointed behind the trees.

"Now go on. Ya ain't goin' to be good help till ya let yoreself cry a bit."

Ava nodded numbly. As Johnny disappeared, she sank to her knees behind the clump of trees and sobbed.

"Noble, why did you make me fall in love with you? Now you are gone and my heart is broken," she whispered brokenly. She pulled the leather packet from her pocket and opened it. When she felt the small ring inside one of the envelopes, she held it to her chest as she cried silently.

Ava leaned against a broken tree and stared at the fires in the distance. Tears ran down her cheeks as she whispered, "This land cries out as it is battered and broken while the rivers weep for the times when their waters did not run red with blood." She squeezed her eyes shut but the tears still came.

Finally, she dropped the packet into her apron pocket. She wiped her face on a corner of her apron and stood just as Johnny appeared. He had a satchel full of supplies and was holding something white. He was smiling when he approached her.

"I found a clean apron. Now let me untie the one y'all have on. A clean apron'll make the world seem jist a little more bearable."

Ava said nothing as Johnny untied her bloody apron. She pulled the clean one over her head. The apron was much larger than the one she had on. She wrapped the long strings around her waist and tied them in the front. She gave Johnny a brief smile.

"Thank you, Mr. Casten—for letting me cry and for the clean apron." She peered into the full satchel and looked up at Johnny in surprise.

"Where did you find all the laudanum? I thought we were almost out!"

Johnny grinned.

"I have my ways. My friends call me Johnny Luck 'cause I'm mighty good at findin' what we need…an' I ain't never been shot neither."

# Chapter 33

# HELPFUL SOLDIERS

JOHNNY INSISTED HE CARRY THE SATCHEL AS THEY hurried toward the hospital.

"It's mighty heavy an' we shore don't want to drop it.

"Why don't ya tell the porters where to put those wounded an' I'll take this inside to that surgeon."

Ava quicky diagnosed the wounded. Critical went inside while the rest of the wounded were placed on the ground outside. The dying were added to the rows under the trees. The dead were set in another row for identification before they were buried. Fires had been built between the rows the night before to keep the wounded warm, and it was a full-time job just to keep those fires burning

By noon, the rows were all blended together again. The smell of blood and the cries of the wounded were overwhelming.

A Confederate chaplain was ministering to the dying men. He looked around at Ava.

"Nurse, can you get me some fresh water. These men are all very thirsty."

Ava grabbed as many canteens as she could find and rushed toward Crawfish Spring. The water there was said to be the best around and she knew cool water would help soothe the wounded men.

As she hurried down the hill, another wagon stopped in front of the hospital. Two Confederate soldiers lifted a wounded man out of the back. The man was thrashing around on the litter and nearly fell off.

Ava stopped and almost turned back to help. She shook her head as she looked at the empty canteens and ran the rest of the way to the spring.

Another soldier offered to help her refill the canteens. When she told him where the water needed to go, he pointed to the hospital.

"Y'all go on back there an' take care of those fellers. I'll help the chaplain." He held up his hand as he winked at her.

"I only lost a finger. My buddies cauterized it 'fore I come up here an' it's barely bleedin'. A feller don't really have a need fer a durn little pinky finger nohow."

Ava gave him a quick smile. She grabbed two full canteens and hurried back to the hospital.

The two soldiers she had seen carrying the wounded man inside were standing inside the door. Both ducked their heads when Ava approached them.

"Gentlemen, no one is allowed in here unless he is carrying the wounded. Please step outside and make yourselves useful." She grabbed another armful of canteens and thrust them at the closest man.

"I would appreciate it if you could fill these and bring them back here. We are always short on water."

The soldiers turned around quickly. The taller one grunted a response, and they hurried toward down the hill.

Johnny Luck appeared. He looked at the empty wagon sitting in front of the hospital in surprise.

"Where are the men who was drivin' that wagon? They should be headed out fer more injured!"

Ava blushed slightly.

"I sent them for water. Here they come now."

Johnny grabbed the canteens and glared at the two soldiers.

"Get back out in the field! Porters don't stop their trips fer any reason."

Ava glanced at the two soldiers. Both had cavalry hats pulled down over their faces. The taller soldier ducked his head further before he turned and pointed toward a row of dead.

"Captain told us to take out a load of dead. He said y'all were goin' to be runnin' outa room."

Johnny slowly nodded. He bobbed his head to the side of the hospital.

"Those who are identified are all over there. Make sure ya don't take any wounded."

As Johnny turned away, the two soldiers hurried toward the dead soldiers. They began to carefully place them in the wagon. When they had fifteen bodies loaded, they rushed back inside the hospital. One soldier nodded at the nurse in front of him as they entered.

"We are goin' to git our friend. Doc didn't think he would make it, so I don't s'pose he did."

The two were back quickly with a stretcher. It held a still figure covered by a bloody sheet. The two porters lifted their friend carefully into the back of the wagon. His body was laid on top of the dead.

They drove the wagon toward the battlefield but swerved to the west once they reached the trees. They lifted their friend out of the wagon and quickly unloaded the bodies of the dead. Once the wagon was empty, they put their friend back in. They loaded the supplies they had stashed in the bushes and packed them around the wounded soldier, nearly covering him. They drove the wagon down a narrow path that curled through the trees. The taller soldier was whistling softly while the shorter man drove the team.

When they were about a mile away, the shorter soldier looked over at his friend with a grin.

"That was just a little too close for comfort. Now let's get Cap back behind our lines and in a hospital. And shuck off these Johnny Reb uniforms before we both get shot!"

Just then, the horse on the left shied violently. It reared as armed men pushed their horses out of the brush on both sides of the path.

"Where do you two think yore goin'? Our lines are to the south."

Corporal Blake hauled on the lines to get the horses under control. He hissed, "Answer like we talked earlier. I'll do as much of the talkin' as possible. Remember, Cap has on Yankee britches so we cain't claim he's a Reb."

# HER CAPTAIN'S LETTER

I**T WAS NEARLY MIDNIGHT ON SEPTEMBER 21 WHEN** the wounded stopped arriving at the Crawfish Spring field hospital. The porters couldn't see in the dark and had been picking up men in the fleeting moonlight when they heard them crying out. The night was dark and silent when they brought the last wagon in.

Ava was exhausted when she finally reached her quarters. She picked up a pitcher of water as she stared at her filthy hands. Blood was all over her arms and dried beneath her nails.

"I tried to wash them as often as possible today, but there was too much blood. Too many wounded and dying young men." She dropped her head down on the small wooden table and began to cry softly.

"Noble, I don't want to open your letter. I don't want you to tell me goodbye."

Slowly, she straightened her shoulders and stood. She turned her head in surprise when she heard a tap on her door. She wiped her face and opened the door a crack.

"Doc Williams said to bring some hot water over to ya. He said ya might want to take a bath. I have a tub here too."

Ava stared from the soldiers standing outside her door and the buckets they were carrying to the round tub one of them held.

Once again, tears welled up in her eyes. She forced herself to smile as she opened the door and stepped back.

"That was very considerate of Doctor Williams. A bath would be wonderful. Thank you all so much."

The soldiers soon had the tub filled. They left several buckets behind when they turned to leave.

The soldier who had spoken blushed slightly as he added, "There's more water there if y'all want to make it hotter." He twisted his hat and nodded at the smiling men behind him.

"We appreciate y'all stayin' to help out. Those Union boys told us they called ya Nurse Sweet, so we'll call ya that too.

"Ya jist let us know if there is anything else y'all need. An' don't try to carry that water out. We'll send a feller over in the mornin' to dump it." The soldier pulled his cap on. He tipped it to Ava and they all walked away smiling.

Tears slid from Ava's eyes as she closed the door. She dipped her hand in the water and added more hot water before she stripped down and climbed in. She could feel the dirt melt off.

Ava smelled the bar of soap Chloe had left and slowly scrubbed herself all over. When she finally stood, her skin was red, but she felt clean. She quickly washed and rinsed her hair before she threw her dirty aprons in the cool water. She scrubbed them and her dress with the strong lye soap the soldiers used. When she finished, she sat back on her heels and smiled.

She was still tired, but she was clean. The bath seemed to wash away some of her sadness too. She rinsed the clean clothes in the extra buckets of water and laid them out to dry.

"I'm exhausted but if I don't comb this curly hair out, it will be a mess in the morning." As she combed, her eyes went once again to Noble's leather packet. Her hand shook a little as she drew the comb through her hair for one last stroke. She opened the packet and climbed into bed.

She stared at the letter, "Noble, I hope upon hope that you survived today. I want you to be alive, but I am so afraid you are dead." She slowly opened the envelope and lifted the soiled letter out.

My Dearest Ava,

I am writing this as we prepare for battle. I can't give you a date or a location in the event this letter falls into enemy hands. However, it is a beautiful night. The sky is clear and bright—just full of stars. It is such a night as I would like to share with you someday.

It is my hope that this terrible war will end soon, and I will once again see you. I can almost hear your voice tonight. I see your eyes sparkle first with humor and then with anger. My, how you protect those soldiers in your care!

I encounter men everywhere who talk about their experiences of being wounded. There are so many miracles every day. Men who should have been killed or seriously wounded are still alive and doing well. I pray every night that the men in my command will be more of those miracles.

My men are a loyal bunch. Some of them told me that when I buy my ranch out West, they would like to work for me. I reckon that would be all right. A finer group of horsemen I have never seen.

Ava, I don't know where you are. I told you to leave when the hospital was evacuated but I'm guessing you didn't. I knew you wouldn't listen when I passed that message on, but I still had to say it. I fear for your safety on the front lines, but I know you don't want to be anywhere else.

I am going to ask you something tonight that I have been thinking on for some time. When this war is over and we are both free to go where we want, would you come West with me? Perhaps there will be a train that runs all the way to the Pacific Coast by then. I want to ride that train, and I want to ride it with you.

In fact, I think of you every time I ride a train. Never has a woman filled my head like you have. How lucky I was the day you were assigned to ride east with my detachment.

Rumors are going around that some of us will be sent West to protect settlements and those who are trying to carve out a life there. I'm sure it will require fighting with the Indians. I am so tired of killing. While I believe very much in ending slavery and holding the Union together, the fellows on the other side are fighting for their homes and their way of life. Some of them don't even believe in slavery. One prisoner told me that he was fighting for his state's right to stand up against a tyrannical central government. I didn't even know how to answer that. I kill men every day that I don't even know—men I would probably like if I knew them. We can't agree on much of anything, so we just keep killing each other—and nothing changes.

My commitment to the army ends in '66, and I won't be reenlisting. I am looking forward to standing in the door of my own house and looking at the sun setting over my ranch someday. Our ranch. You beside me and maybe a houseful of little ones. And Pete.

Ava turned to the third page. Noble's handwriting was darker and larger, so she assumed it had been written on a different day.

I only have a few minutes, but I wanted to finish this letter. We captured a couple of Rebs the other day. They were best friends. One was just a little younger than his buddy. They had grown up on the backs of horses and were the kind of men I'd enjoy talking to over a beer.

Those fellows didn't even believe in slavery. However, they loved their families and their home state of Kentucky. They said that was what they were fighting for.

They tried to escape last night. One was shot and died. It made me sad even though I was the one who killed him. The other one got away. I can't let my men see me cry but I sometimes cry inside.

We have lost so many men, and even more who are maimed for life. I always wonder if their wives and sweethearts will want them back if they aren't all in one piece. Enough of that though. If I keep this up, you will think I am a sad sack for sure.

Signing off for tonight. I'll write more tomorrow and will try to make it happier.          Noble

Ava put the letter back in the tattered envelope and opened the leather case again. She took out a second letter. This one was sealed. She could feel a small ring through the envelope and her hands shook as she opened it.

Ava, if you receive this leather packet, it means I am gone. This packet holds our family pictures and my mother's wedding ring. I would never part with any of this unless I believed I was dying.

Ava dropped the letter and began to sob. "No, Noble. I won't believe you are dead. I won't. I can't. You are my hope. You are who I look forward to seeing each passing day. I watch for you to ride up on your fine horse." She wiped her eyes and whispered, "And your smile. I want to see your smile again." She took a deep breath and picked the letter up again.

I'd like you to try to find Peter. I know this is an impossible request, but he should have Mother's ring and these pictures. They are all we have left of our life in Georgia.

Pete's not with me. I arranged for him to be sent back to St. Louis. He will be safer there. He wasn't happy with me though, and I am guessing about now, he is doing his best to be assigned to a unit headed back this way.

Do you remember the young soldier who helped you escape the day your family was killed? Well, Pete was that young man. I know it sounds impossible, but he took your quilt to keep it from being stolen. He told me he wants to give that quilt back someday. He keeps it wrapped as best he can so it stays clean. Somewhat clean anyway.

Pete doesn't know it was you. I figured that out. After you told me what had happened to your family, I did some checking. I wasn't too surprised when all the dates lined up with Pete's report. Then I unwrapped that quilt and looked it over. I found your grandmother's name, Libby Bowman, embroidered in one of the corners. Of course, Pete didn't recognize that name. You and me, our lives were intertwined even before we met.

Ava, I'm truly sorry I will never be able to ask you to marry, to be able to put this ring on your finger. That is my greatest disappointment. However, I cherish the time I had with you. I thank the Good Lord for bringing you into my life. You made it brighter and happier even though the time we spent together was brief.

Goodbye, Ava. I love you now and I always will. May you find love and happiness someday—and not with one of those stiff-necked fellows *who starch their longhandles! Smile for me now so I can keep your smile in my heart.*

*Yours forever,*
*Noble Headrick*

A single tear leaked from Ava's eye as she took the pictures out of the packet and laid them on the bed. She could see a little of Noble and Peter in both of their parents. Their mother's hair was brown like Peter's and their father's hair was black and curly like Noble's.

Ava put everything back in the leather packet but the ring. She slipped it on her middle finger, put the packet under her pillow, and cried herself to sleep.

# Chapter 35

# A SURPRISE VISIT

AVA CAME AWAKE WITH A START. THE SCRATCHING ON her door stopped and the doorknob began to slowly turn. She grabbed the gun off the box she used as a nightstand and spoke softly.

"You open that door and you'll have a hole in you so big you won't need a hospital."

The man outside laughed, and Ava cocked her gun.

"Sis, it's me—Charlie. Now move whatever ya have holdin' this here door so's I cin come in. If I git caught out here botherin' the hospital's favorite nurse, I could git shot by my own men!"

Ava gasped and rushed to the door. She pulled the heavy box of books away and jerked the door open. Charlie grinned at her as he stepped inside.

"Howdy, Sis. It's good to see ya."

Ava rushed into her brother's arms.

"Charlie! I can't believe it's you. When the Confederates took over this hospital and you never showed, I was afraid you were dead." She pulled back as she looked him over. He had a bandage around his arm but otherwise, he looked healthy.

"What unit are you with? Have you seen much fighting?"

"Why I've been busier than a one-legged man in an ass kickin' contest," Charlie declared as he gave Ava a big grin. "Yeah, crazy busy. My work is mostly done in secret though, so I can't talk about it." His fingers caught the ring Ava still had on her finger, and he raised his eyebrows.

"Looks like ya been a little busy yore own self."

Ava shook her head and tears tried to fill her eyes. She took off the ring and placed it in the leather pack.

"No, it belonged to someone I cared for. He asked that it be given to me when he was dying." A sob sipped out and Charlie hugged his sister as silent sobs shook her body.

"I'm ashamed of myself. Everyday, I have to decide what men take priority in this hospital. Families everywhere are crying for their loved ones who don't come home.

"I am no different than they are. Still…" Her voice trailed off. She straightened her shoulders and looked at her brother defiantly as she added, "His name was Noble Headrick. He was part of Merrill's Horse."

Charlie studied his sister closely. She met his eyes before she looked away.

"Yes, he was one of those Union soldiers I was with the last time I saw you." She glared at him and added, "And don't try to trick me into spying for you again. I am in this war to save lives, not to get more men killed."

"Was he a captain? Big feller with a loud voice? If so, I know who he is."

Ava gasped. "You know him?"

"Naw, but we was both in the last scrimmage I fought. I saw 'im go down. His men fought through gunfire to drag 'im off the field. That means he was liked. Some of those officers is self-centered chicken sh… they's not nice folks.

"He wasn't dead when I saw 'im last. 'Course, I only got close enough to their camp to count numbers. They was talkin' 'bout how to git that bullet outa him. They talked some of dressin' 'im in Reb clothes an' tryin' to sneak him into yore hospital. At least that's what I heard 'fore I slipped away."

When Ava stared at him, Charlie shrugged.

"If ya didn't see 'im, then I don't know. I don't know no more than what I just said. Sorry, Sis."

Ava turned away and Charlie could see her shoulders shake as she tried not to cry. He turned his sister around.

"I tell ya what. Let me do a little reconnaissance." He grinned at Ava and added, "I jist learned that there word, an' she's a big one. It means—"

"I know what it means. What are you going to do?"

"Well, ya see, I slip 'round undercover on both sides of this here war. If I play my cards right, I might be able to find out if yore captain is still alive an' where he is.

"'Course, I cain't talk to 'im. If I came right out an' told him who I was, he might have me arrested. Hung even. I hear he's a hard man." Charlie grinned at Ava.

"Don't know why ya couldn't fall fer a nice Southern feller. That would shore make my life easier."

"Your life?" Ava snorted. "You have barely thought of anyone but yourself since the day you were born." When Charlie grinned at her and winked, Ava laughed softly.

"And still, I love you.

"Now why did you sneak in here tonight? You could have come to the hospital tomorrow."

Charlie pulled a letter from his pocket.

"I have a letter here from yore friend, Chloe. She's a nurse up to Chattanooga." His grin became bigger when he added, "I was in there fer a time when the Union troop I was spyin' on got sacked by our boys. Since I had on a Union uniform, those Yanks all thought I was one of them.

"That Chloe is a right cute little gal. I'm thinkin' I might have to spark her some when this here war is over."

Ava reached for the letter eagerly.

"I'm so glad she is all right. The last I saw of her was when we evacuated the hospital before the Rebs took over." She looked from the letter to Charlie and frowned.

"She knows you are my brother? And a soldier in the Confederate Army too?"

"Now, Sis, I cain't answer all those questions. Jist know she's all right, an' she misses ya.

"I got to go now. I'll see what I can find out 'bout yore captain." He hugged Ava before he stepped back. He pointed at the letter.

"Don't talk 'bout that there letter. Chloe is a Union nurse so y'all are holdin' contraband. Might be a good idea to burn it once ya finish readin' it." He pointed at Noble's leather case. "The stuff inside there too." He kissed Ava quickly on the cheek and backed toward the door.

"See ya, Sis," and he was gone. Ava listened closely but she heard no footsteps. She couldn't read Chloe's letter without lighting a lamp, so she put it in Noble's case.

"I will read it in the morning and then I will burn it. I would have to say how I received it and that might get Charlie in trouble. I most certainly will not throw Noble's letters away though.

"I write letters to all the families of the fallen soldiers. That leather bag will be my case for keeping them." She looked at the finger where Noble's family ring had been and took a shaky breath. "Besides, he asked me to get his personal things to Peter and that is what I am going to do."

Ava lay down on her small bed, but sleep didn't come for a long time.

# Chapter 36

# ON ENEMY GROUND

PRIVATE HANSON GRABBED THE LINES ON THE HORSES so Blake could speak easier. The team was already spooked, and he knew if the horses bolted, both men would be shot.

"Howdy, fellers. Corporal Blake an' Private Hanson here. We done stole us a Yankee officer an' a buncha supplies. The captain was hopin' to take one of those Horse Soldiers prisoner, an' we got us one. They been wreakin' havoc on us boys an' he's a gettin' tired of it.

"We was headed back to turn him over to the captain. He wanted to see if he cin get some intel from 'im. Not sure what regiment this here feller's part of though. He was shot bad an' ain't come to yet."

The soldier in front kept his gun on them.

"I think yore lyin'."

Corporal Blake shrugged his shoulders.

"Look fer yore ownself. Don't mess with the wounded man though. The captain wanted 'im in one piece."

Several soldiers jumped up in the wagon. They dug through the supplies and pulled back the blanket that covered Captain Headrick.

"They have Yankee supplies all right. An' that wounded man looks like a Bluebelly to me. At least his britches says he is.

"I say we shoot 'im now. One less Yankee to worry about." He started to cock his gun but when he looked up, Corporal Blake's gun was pointed at him. Private Hanson's gun was pointed at the first man who had spoken.

Corporal Blake's voice was soft when he spoke.

"Ya fellers will likely kill us both, but we'll take some of ya with us. Now we cin go see yore captain or we cin shoot it out right here. An' that would be a durn shame since the South is short on fightin' men."

The soldier who had originally spoken slowly lowered his gun. He continued to stare at the two men and then shrugged.

"Captain Stegall took a bad one in the last scrimmage we had with Merrill's Cavalry outfit. He's back at that field hospital we took over several days ago.

"Turn that wagon around an' we'll see if he cin verify yore story. It sounds like hogwash to me." He stared from Hanson to Blake.

"I jist ain't shore. Y'all might be tryin' to desert. 'Course that ain't likely with a Yankee in the back. That leaves me to wonderin' if y'all are who ya say ya are.

"Mebbie yore a couple a Bluebellies yore own selves a tryin' to git away with a friend. We'll let the captain sort it out.

"Now wheel that wagon 'round an' head back to the hospital."

Private Hanson tried to hold his hands steady. He didn't look over at Corporal Blake, but he was scared. *Blake can talk his way outa 'most anything but this is goin' to be a tricky one. Shoot, Miss Bradley might recognize us an' then what? An' what if that Captain Stegall is still alive?*

Corporal Blake grinned at the men around him.

"So how did y'all happen to be out here? I mean if our boys moved, why didn't y'all?"

The man closest to him shrugged.

"Patrol. Word is we're a goin' to burn that hospital. We are short on men an' that hospital is right smack between us and the Yanks. When they figger out we ain't 'round, all our wounded will be in their prisons."

"What about the Bluebellies?"

The soldier grinned and shrugged.

"They ain't our problem. I reckon we'll leave 'em there. Ain't no way we cin haul all the men in that hospital now, an' we shore ain't a goin' to make no room fer a buncha Yanks."

Corporal Blake kept his face void of all expression, but he was concerned. *I hope Lampkin is around. We are going to need some help to get our men out of there.*

# Chapter 37

# BURN THIS HOSPITAL!

AVA AWOKE TO THE SOUND OF YELLING. SHE SAT upright in bed and listened.

A man shouted, "This hospital is being evacuated. Confederate troops will be transported south to our main hospital. The rest of you are prisoners and will be treated as such. We will load as many soldiers as will fit in the wagon. The rest will be on foot."

Ava pulled her dress quickly over her head and was buttoning her shoes when a knock sounded on her door.

"Nurse Sweet—come quick! Those Rebs are emptying our hospital! They are pulling the wounded from their beds!"

Ava grabbed her gun and rushed out the door behind the young orderly. She ran into the hospital and planted herself in front of the officer who was giving the order. Her voice was loud and angry when she spoke.

"You have no right to come in here like this. These men are seriously wounded. Many of them can't walk and some can't see. I demand that you remove your men at once."

The officer paused as he looked down at the angry woman.

Ava pointed her gun at one of the soldiers who was trying to drag a wounded man from his bed. Her voice was hard when she spoke.

"I will ask you nicely one time to remove your hands and then I am going to shoot. You have no authority in this hospital, and I want all of you out of here immediately." The man paused and Ava cocked her gun. "Now!"

All the soldiers except the officer backed up. He stared at Ava as he motioned his men back. She turned her gun toward him. The officer's face was tight, and he spoke softly.

"I can have you court-martialed for that."

"I'm not part of your army. I am a civilian working in a military hospital. The work I do is necessary, and medical personnel are in short supply. And I will not allow you to harm *any* man in my care." Ava spat out the words and her hand was steady as she pointed her gun at the officer.

The captain waved his hand toward the men behind him.

"You men go on outside while I get this straightened out." He turned toward Ava. "Ma'am—"

"It's Nurse Bradley. I am the head nurse of this hospital and have been since the Yankees abandoned it last week." She dropped her gun in her apron pocket and pointed at the wagons in front of the hospital.

"You don't have enough room to haul all these men and most of them cannot walk. All of our patients are seriously wounded.

"I suggest you take the soldiers who will survive your trip and leave the rest here."

The captain shook his head.

"I can't do that. I have orders to evacuate this hospital and burn it to the ground. All medical supplies that cannot be taken with us are to be destroyed. These men must leave."

Ava stared at him incredulously.

"The medical supplies were abandoned by the Yankees when your troops took over this hospital. And the Confederate officers I spoke to at that time were pleased with what was left behind. I was told the South was very short on medical supplies." Ava waved her hand behind her.

"I will send most of the medical supplies with you, but none will be destroyed. And you are going to leave the Union wounded here along with any Confederate soldiers who can't be moved. I will take the medical supplies I need to treat those left in my care but none of the seriously wounded are going with you."

"Lady—"

"Nurse Bradley."

"Nurse Bradley, I have my orders."

"And you have fulfilled your orders. The tent hospitals down the hill have been evacuated." Ava's eyes narrowed as she saw men trying to crawl away from the burning tents. She turned to the young orderly standing next to her.

"Ezra, get some stretchers. We are going to bring those men up here."

She wheeled around to the captain again.

"Surely you can spare a few men and a wagon to bring those men up here where they can be cared for. The blood smell brings in predators at night and those men will all be dead by morning with no protection—if your fires don't take them first. And if neither of those kill them, the cold will. This cold snap has taken a lot of our wounded already."

A young man stepped forward. "I can help, Captain. Wes and me will fetch them up here. That last wagon doesn't have anything in it."

The captain glared at Ava and cursed under his breath. He pointed toward a soldier standing close by.

"Private Andrews, take some men down there. Private Leiker can drive that wagon. Bring those wounded up here. And don't be too rough."

The private grinned and gave a rakish salute.

"Yes, *sir!*"

The captain started to respond but Andrews was gone.

"That man is completely undisciplined. I would have him court-martialed, but he is a good fighting man." He blushed slightly when he realized he had spoken out loud. He sighed deeply as he looked at Ava.

"So, Nurse Bradley, what do you suggest I do since you want me to defy orders."

"You aren't defying orders. You already burned all of the tents. However, if you find it necessary to try to burn this house, start your fire away from the walls so I will be able to put it out."

The captain laughed for the first time that morning. He put out his hand.

"Nurse Bradley, I am Captain Eberle. Now maybe you can point out the men who are fit to make this trip."

Ava shook his hand briefly, but she was all business.

"None of the men in this area. Follow me." She led Captain Eberle to a larger room. She smiled and spoke to each man as she walked by. She pointed to their beds as she spoke.

"Privates Watson, Michaels, Clewing, Jennings, and Downey could make the trip."

Captain Eberle commented softly, "And I suppose none of the men you pointed out are Yankees?"

Ava shook her head and answered firmly, "They are not but you said yourself you are short on space. Why leave one of your boys here when they could be taken with you today?

"Come, there are more men in another area."

By the time Ava was done, fifteen men were slated to be moved that day. None could walk so all would require transportation.

Captain Eberle frowned as he looked around at the remaining men.

"I can't fit any more in our wagons. I will have to send a detail back for the rest. I counted fifteen of our soldiers and over two hundred prisoners. It will take us about five days to get to Atlanta and another five to get back up here. I can leave a couple of men with you—"

"Leave me Privates Leiker and Andrews. They have both been wounded and that will give them a little time to heal. If you have a man who can cook, that would be helpful since I heard you say you are taking most of our hospital staff. I do ask that you leave my orderly, Mr. Diekman."

"I'll leave a soldier who lost an arm to help with the cooking. He can do more with one arm than most men with two." He turned and hollered, "Private Weatherby!" When the grizzled soldier appeared, Captain Eberle pointed at him.

"Private, you will stay here until we return. You are in charge so keep an eye on this nurse." Captain Eberle grinned at Ava.

"I don't trust you, Nurse Bradley, and that is a fact." His smile faded and he added, "And when I return, this hospital will be evacuated and burned."

Ava pointed toward the door.

"Please leave, Captain. I have work to do here. Mr. Diekman, you help Private Weatherby cook today. I have bandages to change."

Ava closed the door behind the captain. As soon as the wagons pulled away, she grabbed her orderly and whispered, "Ezra, tonight I am going to make some chicory coffee and put a little something in it to make those soldiers who were left here sleep. Then you and I will load as many men as we can. You will take them north to Chattanooga to the Union hospital.

"I don't think that captain will wait ten days to return. He will be back tomorrow or will send troops. Those Union wounded will never survive in a Confederate prison." She squared her shoulders and added softly, "They might not survive a trip to Chattanooga either, but they will at least have a chance. And one wagon will hold a mere pittance of those we need to send north." Her voice trembled and broke as she whispered, "War is so brutal. I am tired of deciding who will live and who will die."

Ezra smiled at Ava as he shook her shoulders gently.

"Nurse Sweet, you have saved many men on both sides of this war. You are a good nurse, and you are loved by the men you treat.

"Now if we are going to evacuate the Union soldiers first, how about we move them all to a room close to an exit door? Maybe that back door that faces the trees. That way we can move them out in the dark without disturbing anyone who might raise a concern.

"You come up with a reason and we will make an announcement."

"Simple. All the Confederate troops need to be at the front of the hospital so they can be moved out easily. We won't make an announcement. We can just explain quietly as we move them. Some won't ask so there is no need to upset anyone needlessly.

"Let's start now. We have a busy day."

Ava and Ezra began to move the patients. Privates Leiker and Andrews helped. Some of the healthier men quickly figured out that they were being segregated by army. One young soldier grabbed Ava's arm. He had lost a leg and had a severe chest wound as well.

"Are we being abandoned, Nurse Sweet? Is that why we are being moved?"

Ava smiled at the frightened young man.

"The Confederate Army is going to destroy this hospital so we must be prepared to evacuate. I want all of you as close to exit doors as possible." She smiled at him and patted his arm.

"I promise I won't leave this hospital until it is empty, and you will not be abandoned. I give you my word, soldier. Now, relax and lay back so we can carry you more easily."

# Chapter 38

# A FAMILIAR PATIENT

THE SOLDIERS ESCORTING CORPORAL BLAKE AND Private Hanson arrived at the hospital late afternoon on September 30. The one who appeared to be in charge rapped on the hospital door and called loudly, "I'm Sergeant Marley. I need to see Captain Stegall immediately."

Ava opened the door with a smile. She stood in the doorway as she spoke.

"Gentlemen, please don't shout. This is a hospital. Tell me quietly who it is that you need to see.

"Captain Stegall. I need him to verify what these two men told me." Sergeant Marley nodded behind him, and Ava noticed Corporal Blake and Private Hanson for the first time. She stared at them unsure of what to say.

Blake grinned at her.

"Nurse Sweet—this here feller don't believe that Hanson an' me are Rebs." Blake's eyes were piercing with intensity even as he smiled.

Ava walked toward the wagon and reached her hand up to him.

"Corporal Blake. Private Hanson. It's good to see both of you." She turned to Sergeant Marley.

"What is it you need to ask of me? Do I know these men? Yes, I do. Now, is that all?"

"How about that man in the back? He's the one I need to talk to Captain Stegall about."

Ava's face paled and she shook her head.

"Captain Stegall passed earlier this afternoon, so he won't be able to help you." Ava moved to the back of the wagon. She almost gasped when she saw Noble Headrick's pale face. She tried to hold her hand steady as she checked his pulse.

"Get this man inside immediately. He is bleeding."

"Was he treated at this hospital?" Marley's voice was sharp as he asked the question.

Ava stared at the wrapping around Noble's chest before she looked up at the sergeant.

"Possibly. That is a hospital dressing. I didn't treat him, but I rarely help with surgeries. Of course, since the Yankees abandoned this hospital, we don't do many surgeries here." She nodded down the hill.

"He could have been treated in one of the tent hospitals that was burned earlier today. I have no idea."

Ava peered into the wagon bed again. "Why is he in this wagon?" Her voice was almost angry when she said again, "Please bring him inside."

"We caught these two fellers west of here a piece. They claimed he was a Yankee officer an' that they had kidnapped him by orders of Captain Stegall. With Stegall dead, I cain't verify their story."

Ava helped Ezra move the unconscious man to a stretcher.

"We'll put him in that empty room toward the back. I need to clean him and change that bandage." She smiled at Blake and Hanson.

"Perhaps you two men would be so kind as to carry him in for me." As they jumped off the wagon and grabbed the stretcher, Ava smiled up at Sergeant Marley.

"Is there anything else I can help you with, Sergeant? If not, I have lots of work to do."

"No, I reckon not." He looked down the road and then asked, "How long ago did that detachment of wounded leave here, an' who was in charge? Mebbie I cin catch 'em."

"I'm sure you can catch them. They left this morning, but they were moving slowly. Captain Eberle was in charge. He said he would be back here in ten days to get the rest of the wounded."

Sergeant Marley hollered at Blake and Hanson.

"You two stay put an' don't ya try to sneak off. I'm goin' to find Eberle an' then I'll be back. An' I still say there is something off with yore story." Marley wheeled his horse around and his men followed as they all raced south.

Ava ran to open the hospital door. She led Blake and Hanson down the hallway and into a small room.

"Place him on that bed." She shut the door quickly. Her hands were shaking as she whispered, "You need to leave now. That man will be back, and someone will know you are not Confederates. And why did you have Captain Headrick in the back of your wagon?"

"We brought him in here yesterday because the Union hospital was too far away. Doc Williams took the bullet out of his chest. I'm guessing Doc knew he was a Yankee, but he didn't say anything. We cut his shirt off, but we couldn't get his britches off without hurting him worse. When Doc finished, we tried to sneak him back to our troops. We made it out of the hospital, but we got caught on the trail…and we won't leave him." Corporal Blake's face was determined as he spoke.

Ava stared from one man to the other.

"Can one of you ride to Chattanooga and get some ambulances down here tonight? These wounded Union soldiers must be removed immediately. I'm sure Captain Eberle will send troops and wagons back here tomorrow, and those men will never survive a Confederate prison."

Private Hanson nodded.

"I'll make that trip. I know this area, but I don't have a horse."

Ava grabbed his arm and led him out the back door. She pointed up the hill.

"Go straight up that hill. There is a cave that opens to a small corral in the back. It is almost completely hidden so try to make as few tracks as possible. Deuce is in the corral and his tack is in the cave. Whistle twice softly and he will come to you."

Ava pushed a hankie into Blakes hands. "Let him smell that before you try to saddle him." Tears filled her eyes, and she tried to keep from crying as she looked at Noble.

"Be quick. We need those wagons tonight and do ask them to come in as quietly as possible. I will give the two soldiers who were left here a little something in their chicory coffee to make them sleep heavily but let's be prudent.

"You've a fifteen-mile ride to Chattanooga. Once there, you need to convince the officer in charge there to help evacuate this hospital. You will need transportation for two hundred thirty severely wounded men. And we will run out of darkness if you run into any snags."

Both men stared at Ava when they heard the large number.

"Two hundred thirty! Why I doubt there are even that many ambulances in Chattanooga!" Private Hanson exclaimed.

Blake looked from Private Hanson to Ava.

"Let me make that trip, Hanson. You stay here with the captain. The brass up there might be more likely to see a corporal than a private." He grinned at both of them. "Besides, I can talk a cowboy outa his hat."

He shook Private Hanson's hand and touched Ava's shoulder.

"Don't worry, Nurse Sweet. I'll be back with the cavalry. The rest of Merrill's Horse was headed to Chattanooga after our fight down here. I know they'll come for Cap."

Ava nodded. Her hands shook as she touched Noble's face. She smiled at Private Hanson.

"I'm going to get some clean bandages. You stay here. I'd like to keep Captain Headrick as low profile as possible—and you too."

# Chapter 39

# A SASSY SWEETHEART

AVA WAS BACK QUICKLY WITH HOT WATER AND bandages. Ezra held Noble on his side while she cut off the dirty bandages. Her hands shook as she looked at the inflamed bullet hole. She motioned to Private Hanson.

"I need tree moss. There is a bucket by the back door. Fill that and return here as quickly as possible. And Ezra, get that tub of honey from the kitchen."

After the two men left, Ava kissed Noble's cheek.

"I thought you were dead! Please, Noble. Say something to me."

Noble stirred. He frowned and shook his head. Ava kissed him again.

"Don't you frown at me, Noble Headrick. I'm not going to let you die. You listen to me now. Your men have risked their lives to keep you alive. Even now, they are moving mountains. You owe them—and you owe me as well for making me think you had died."

Noble Headrick slowly opened his eyes. They were bloodshot and unfocused until they settled on Ava. He touched her face with a shaky hand and smiled.

"I thought I was having a dream. When you scolded me though, I knew my sassy sweetheart was real. Hello, Ava."

"I thought you died! The chaplain gave me your letter." Ava tried hard not to cry, and her chest shook as she sucked in the sobs.

"I just knew I was a goner, but my men drug me off the field after I went down. I don't remember much after that. I don't even know how I got here."

A tear fell from Ava's eye as she bathed him.

"Close your eyes, Noble. You need to rest, and I have to get you cleaned so I can dress your wound."

Noble's smile became wider.

"That's my Ava. First, she scolds me for not talking and then she tells me to be quiet."

The door opened quietly, and Ezra appeared.

"Here is the honey. I brought some of that dried root you had stashed there too. Echinacea, I think you call it. My pop always called it elk root. Out west where I was raised, the elk sought that root out. They loved it."

Ava looked at Ezra in surprise.

"I didn't know you were raised in the West. What area?"

"Dakota Territory. I joined the army out there after my pa was killed by Indians. I was shipped back here when this war broke out.

"I plan to head home when this war is done. Too much blood on this land for me to stay here." Ezra shook his head. "Folks say the Indians are brutal. Some of them are too, but I've seen more men killed here in just a few years than the Indians killed in my lifetime."

Ava leaned over Captain Headrick as she quickly applied the echinacea.

"Is your mother still alive?" she asked softly.

"As far as I know. She was when I left. I wanted her to move to town, but she wouldn't hear of it. She said her pop was moving in with her. With him and the few hired hands we had, she thought she'd have enough guns to hang onto the place until I made it home.

"We have a nice little ranch up there west of the Missouri River. The land on the east side of that river is more suitable for farming while most of the ranches are on the west side. We call our ranch West River Ranch.

"It's a mighty pretty place and I can't wait to go home. My military stint is up the end of this year. I haven't decided if I'll go home then or if I'll stick this war out until the end."

Private Hanson arrived with the moss and Ava began to pack the wound. After she applied the honey, she wrapped a clean bandage around Noble's chest. She pulled a blanket over him and set a canteen close to the bed.

"If you will sit with Captain Headrick today, Private Hanson, I will sit with him tonight." She touched Noble's face, but the man was asleep.

"Come, Ezra. We need to get a meal prepared. You find Private Weatherby, and I will show him what needs to be done."

# Chapter 40

# PRIVATE WEATHERBY

A WIZENED OLD MAN WITH ONE ARM WAS BANGING pots and cursing loudly in the kitchen. Ava's ears almost burned. The man had an excessive vocabulary of curse words and expletives.

"Private Weatherby, I am Nurse Bradley. If you can tell me what you need, I will be glad to show you where things are."

"I don't need no woman tellin' me how to cook. Jist 'cause you's a nurse don't mean ya know 'bout cookin'. I been cookin' in this here army long before this war broke out. I reckon I cin find what I need."

Ava stared at the old man a moment before she slowly nodded.

"Fine. We need food for two hundred thirty patients, four soldiers, and two medical personnel."

Weatherby glared at her.

"They all eat the same thing, don't they? Cain't ya jist say ya need food fer two hundred thirty-six?"

"See, that's the problem with women. They have to take a simple thing like cookin' a meal an' make it difficult. Now if ya want to make some helpful talk, tell me if any a those soldier boys don't eat much. Any of 'em 'bout ready to kick the bucket? An' are we feedin' those Yanks less food than our own boys? Now that there is useful information."

Ava glared at the old man.

"In this hospital, every man is treated equally. They all receive the same amount of food. If they choose to share it with a friend—and some do—that is their choice, but they will *all* be treated the same."

"Got any Colored boys? If'n ya do, ya ain't a goin' to give them the same amount, are ya?"

Ava clenched her fists and took a deep breath.

"I said *all* of them. And if this is too difficult a job for you, Private, we could use a new hole for the privy. Perhaps you would like to dig that instead."

Private Weatherby grinned at her.

"I knowed ya was tough an' I'll bet yore a Yankee. Yessir. Ya talk more like my ol' ma used to.

"Where ya from, gal? Illinois? Massachusetts? Lawrence mebbie, out Kansas way."

"Missouri. And just so you know, I am a Southerner. My brother is a soldier in the Confederate army and my mother was true southern belle."

"An' yore pa?"

Ava glared at him.

"We aren't talking about my family anymore. We both have work to do."

"I knowed your pa. An' I know yore name ain't Bradley. It's Bowman. I know that cause ya look jist like yore granny. She was my sweetheart, ya know, 'fore yore grandpappy swept 'er off 'er feet.

"She were a looker too, jist like you is. She were a sassy one—mighty sassy." His face became softer, and his eyes were sad when he added, "I heard she were killed by some Red Legs. I'm mighty sorry 'bout that."

Ava stared at the old man in surprise.

"You knew my granny and my father?"

"Shore did. My pappy's little farm butted up next to the Bradley place. Yore granny an' me—we growed up together. Yore grandpappy was my best friend. It were a hard day fer me when Libby told me she chose yore grandpappy over me.

"I jist couldn't be mad though. I liked both of 'em too much." Weatherby grinned at Ava and added, "'Sides, yore grandpappy was better lookin' than I was. He stood ramrod-straight an' he could cut a man in half with those gray eyes. Your granny said he was a 'fine figure of a man.' Now that didn't make no sense to me, but she believed it.

"Strong as a bull, he was, an' stubborn as a mule. They was quite the pair. An' they loved to dance." Private Weatherby's smile slowly faded and he shook his head.

"It were a sad day fer all of us when yore Grandpappy Alfred passed. Killed by an outlaw, he was. Shot down in the field while he plowed—shot fer the hoss he was usin'. Yore granny an' me, we set off after that feller. An' when we catched up to 'im, yore granny were the one who shot 'im.

"Oh, she give 'im a chance but he thought she were bluffin'. She weren't. We didn't bury 'im neither. Yore granny were tough.

"I wanted to marry up with 'er after yore grandpappy died but she wouldn't have it. She said she only ever loved one man, an' she wouldn't pretend to love another.

"Some years after that, she moved in with yore ma an' pa. 'Course, I was long gone by that time. Shoot, I been in this here army 'most as long as I am old. Made it all the way up to sergeant several times, but I always git busted back fer disrespectin' my betters." Weatherby grinned at Ava. "Don't much care though. I'm an ol' man now. Don't have no home 'cept the army. I don't kowtow to no one an' I don't care what the results is if'n the brass don't like it." His old eyes twinkled as he added, "And that right there is how I know yore last name ain't Bradley."

Ava walked slowly toward the old man. She pecked his cheek as she smiled at him.

"That was for loving my granny and for telling me about her. She never talked much about her early days and only a little about my grandpappy." Ava asked softly, "Did my father look like Grandpappy Alfred?"

"He shore did. He were quiet like yore grandpappy too." The old man's face broke into a scowl. "The word is he were killed by Bushwhackers. Don't ya believe it though.

"It were Red Legs. I even know the names of the men who done it." Weatherby's grizzled face broke into a brief grin. "'Course, they ain't 'round no more. They was a braggin' 'bout it one night an' I heard 'em a talkin'. I was a prisoner fer a time in a Bluebelly camp, ya see.

"Now, I didn't kill 'em outright. No siree. I jist made shore their saddle straps was cut through a little—an' I put a couple of cockleburs under their saddle blankets.

"I turned the hosses loose so there was nothin' else to ride but some mules, an' those mules they tried to ride was mean ones." Weatherby shrugged and winked at Ava.

"'Course, them there mules warn't broke to be rode. They was one bell mules, they was. They went to buckin' an' a kickin' an'…" The old man shrugged his shoulders again. "Those fellers was bucked off an' got plumb tangled up in their saddles.

"That there be the end of those durn Red Legs. 'Course, most of the Yanks in that camp felt the same way I did 'bout Red Legs. They jist didn't know how it all come to be." Weatherby frowned. "Durn Red Legs. They give real soldiers a bad name."

Ava stared at the old man in confusion.

"What is a one bell mule?"

"Wahl, mules' tails is cut accordin' to how they is broke. When they is broke to carry a pack, a notch is cut outa the tail. Folks call that a bell. When that same mule is broke to drive a wagon, a second bell is cut under the first one. When they works fer both of those jobs an' is good to ride too, a third bell is cut.

"Now, them there Red Legs didn't know nothin' 'bout mules—an' them mules only had one bell in their tails." The old man grinned at

Ava and winked. "I shore wouldn't want to git too close to a mule that ain't broke to ride so ya know I always look at their durn tails."

Ava finally laughed.

"Private Weatherby, I think I will keep an eye on you. I believe you are a dangerous man."

The old man chuckled and shook his head. "Naw. I'm an ol' feller an' I'm gittin' right peaceable.

"Now how 'bout ya tell me where things is so's I don't have to curse no more in the presence of a lady?

"An' if ya need help sneakin' those Bluebellies out the back, I cin cause a disturbance in the front." He winked at Ava's surprised face as he chuckled. "Don't ya worry none 'bout that big captain yore sweet on neither. He be a big dog in that horse unit, an' those Yank friends of his 'ill be hightailin' it down here tonight to snatch 'im.

"Ya picked ya a fine feller, girly. Yore granny would be proud."

# Chapter 41

# REMEMBERING

AVA BROUGHT NOBLE'S LEATHER PACKET TO HIS room that evening. She remembered what Charlie had told her about the contents being considered contraband. Besides, now that Noble was alive, his personal belongings needed to go back to him.

Her hands went still when she touched the letters Noble had written her. The sun was just going down and the room barely had enough light to read all of them. She stared at the letter she had written him that afternoon and a tear slid from her eye.

*Dearest Noble,*

*You have won my heart. I tried to despise you, but I wasn't able. I tried to ignore you and that didn't work either. When I thought you were dead, I tried to forget you, but my heart was broken.*

*Now you are wounded, and I must send you away. Please be careful. I don't think I can survive another letter like the last one you sent me when you thought you were going to die.*

I don't know how we will find each other when this war is over, but I pray we do. I am going to travel to the Dakota Territory. Ezra Diekman, my orderly, has a ranch there. He calls it the West River Ranch. He has invited me to go home with him and stay for a time until I can find a location where I want to settle.

I know I won't stay here. I have watched too many young men die, and their eyes haunt me. Some mornings I am just not sure I can face another day of death and dying. Sorting the wounded is the most difficult thing I have ever done in my life. Then, I look at all these young men we were able to save and my heart sings. I love nursing and helping people to heal. That is why I stay. I don't think I will ever get over the dying though.

Please take Deuce with you when you leave. I'm not sure when I will get back to Chattanooga. I am including one of my handkerchiefs. Let him smell it and he will go with you. Maybe he will even let you ride him one day!

I love you, Noble. Please remember that when you go into battle.

Yours always,

Ava

Ava slipped her letter between the letters Noble had written her and retied the ribbon that encircled them. She placed all of them inside his leather case.

"I'd like to keep your letters, but I can't. They could put both of us in danger if they were found by the wrong people," she whispered.

Noble's voice was soft when he spoke.

"What can't you keep? My ring? I'd like you to keep that—and when this war is over, I'd like to put it on your finger."

Ava jumped at the sound of his voice. She shook her head.

"No, I can't. I have no way to keep it safe."

She could hear the smile in Noble's voice before he chuckled.

"You could wear it. Then all my competition would think you were taken." His voice became more serious. "Please, Ava. Put it on a cord around your neck. It is certainly safer with you than with me." He struggled to open the pack, so Ava opened it and took out the ring.

Noble slid it on her finger as he smiled.

"There. I was able to put it on your finger. Now if I don't make it, I was the first."

Ava's breath caught in her throat.

"Don't talk like that, Noble. It almost killed me when I thought you were dead. I don't want to go through that again.

"I will wear it on my finger until I get a chain or a cord that is strong enough to wear it safely around my neck." She squeezed his hands and added, "Until I see you again."

Noble chuckled. "Ah, Ava. I certainly have missed you.

"Now tell me what the plan is tonight. Hanson had a few details, but he didn't know much. Old Weatherby knew more than he did." Noble's voice was sincere when he continued. "Weatherby is your friend. You keep that in mind if you ever get in trouble. He may not look like much but that that old man is a mover and a shaker. And he knows lots of important people."

# Chapter 42

# PLANNING A FORAY

AVA SMILED AT THE YOUNG SOLDIERS SEATED AT THE small table in the kitchen area.

"Where are the two of you from? And have you always been friends?" she asked as she poured each of them a cup of chicory coffee.

Private Andrews grinned at her.

"Not always. We were born a fair piece apart. Wes here was born in South Carolina an' I hail from Tennessee. After a few battles an' both of us gettin' lost, we ended up in the same unit." A shadow crossed his face as he added, "'Course, that wouldn't have happened if both our units hadn't lost so many men. Not even enough men left to fight a small scrap. They combined the men, gave our unit a new name, an' now we're pards."

Private Weatherby refilled their cups each time he walked by, and they each drank three cups of chicory coffee as they talked.

"And what will you do when this war is over?" Ava asked with another smile.

The two young men looked at each other and grinned.

"We've talked some on that. Don't neither of us have nothin' to go home to. Thought we might head west an' try cowboyin'. Wes ain't never been west of Georgia other than to fight, an' I was never outa my hometown 'fore this war.

"Shoot, we might take us a job with the railroad an' work our way west. We ain't neither afraid of hard work, so that won't bother us none." Private Andrews bumped Wes with his shoulder and grinned.

"We don't care much so long as we are together."

Private Leiker's head bobbed and almost hit the table. Private Andrews grabbed his shoulder and pulled him back.

"I think we'll call it a night, Nurse Sweet. Diggin' all those graves plumb wore us out. We'll see ya first thing in the mornin'." Private Andrews tipped his hat and led his tired companion away from the table.

Weatherby looked over at Ava and snorted.

"Ya know, yore a goin' to have to tap all three of us on the head. Probably should tie us up too. An' then, ya need to drink some a yore coffee. Otherwise, suspicion is a goin' to fall on ya fer this here deal."

Ava was horrified. "I could never hit such nice young men. Why I could damage their heads, maybe give them concussions."

"I'll do it then. An' have yore orderly whack me one. Shoot, we'll do it at the same time since there won't be no one else 'round to help.

"We'll keep ever'body's hats on 'em so's they don't get cut so bad. An' we'll wait till those wagons be gone an' those fellers is startin' to stir.

"Now mix up some more of that coffee mixture an' be ready to drink it down."

Ava's face was pale as she listened to Weatherby.

"I—I guess I didn't think about being a suspect."

"Durn right y'all will be. Has to be an inside job to git that many men outa here.

"Now ya start slippin' 'round an' tell the fellers who still be awake 'bout what's a goin' to happen this evenin'. Yore a goin' to have to move men out quick like, an' it needs to be quiet.

"Set the clothes and boots on top of them soldiers. When we start haulin' 'em out, we ain't a goin' to have time to stop an' fetch anythin'."

As Ava stood and began to rush around, she heard the sound of horses at the back door. Several of the wounded men tried to sit up. She patted their arms and shushed them as she hurried to unlock the door.

Lieutenant Lampkin grinned at her through the dark doorway. It was too dark to see his face, but she could see the shine of the moon on his teeth.

"We'll take Cap out first in the smoothest ambulance. Those things weren't made to carry many wounded so we're takin' our boys out lotsa different ways. We're a goin' to run a loop so's we don't drive down in front of the hospital.

"Now ya pick out the three most critical an' we'll put 'em in with Cap. The rest of the wagons 'ill be lots fuller.

"Light a couple of lamps an' let's go."

# Chapter 43

# "DON'T LEAVE ME BEHIND!"

AVA TAPPED THE SHOULDERS OF THE MEN SHE wanted to be in the first ambulance. As she tapped them, she pressed a colored scrap of rag into their hands. She turned to Lampkin.

"I will mark the ones to go first with a colored rag. Take them in any order but get those men out first." She turned to Ezra. "You take the rags as they are loaded and bring them back in here. If you can't keep up, don't worry about it. I think I have enough rags for the most seriously wounded."

"I'm hearin' a little stirrin' 'round from the men in front, so we need to be quick." Weatherby nodded toward the front of the hospital where the Confederate patients were sleeping.

"Nurse Sweet, ya go on out there an' calm anyone who might cause a stir. Tell em' there might be some raiders in the area what with all the hoss noise, an' they need to be quiet."

Ava hurried to comply.

Several of the Confederate soldiers were trying to sit up. One man had his gun out as he tried to peer out the window.

Ava hurried toward him. She spoke softly and touched each concerned patient as she passed.

"Be quiet now. Private Weatherby is checking things out. We heard the horses too but so far, there is nothing to be concerned about. Most likely, soldiers are just moving in the dark. It could be raiders though, and since this was a Union hospital, we need to stay as quiet as possible.

"Go to sleep now. I'm sure we'll be fine. This door is locked, and you men are all armed.

"How about Privates Leiker and Andrews? Where are they?"

"They dug graves all day and are asleep. I don't want to bother them.

"Now be quiet. Let's don't draw any more attention to ourselves than necessary." She patted a concerned young soldier and hurried from the room.

As she rushed to the next room that was being evacuated and hurriedly placed rags in the hands of various patients, one young Union soldier grabbed her hand.

"Nurse Sweet, ain't I goin' to git no rag? Don't leave me behind!"

"Don't worry," Ava whispered. "You are all going. I just have to prioritize the most seriously wounded first. Wound type determines the transportation method.

"Now hang onto your boots and britches. We have a short amount of time to get all of you out of here."

Soon ten ambulances were loaded and gone. A heavy wagon pulled up and ten more men were loaded in it. The loading of wagons of all sizes continued for nearly two hours. The last to arrive was a stagecoach.

Corporal Blake grinned at Ava as he pulled open the doors.

"The men who ride in this rig will have to sit up, but we'll move the fastest too. If we didn't count right, we can stick a couple more on top. Git 'em loaded."

Lieutenant Lampkin grabbed Ava's arm as she hurried by.

"Weatherby already whacked those two Bluebellies. Whoever comes to first cin untie the rest." He kissed Ava quickly on the cheek. When she stared at him in surprise, he grinned and shrugged.

"That was from Cap. I shore hope he heals quick. I don't want to be kissin' all his gals. Why, if I add them on top of mine, I might never get no fightin' done a'tall!" he drawled.

Ava could hear the humor in Lampkin's voice, and she was surprised. The quiet soldier rarely joked, and certainly not with her. She laughed quietly as he grinned.

As she hurried to cover the remaining soldiers with blankets, the rescue party loaded the last of the wounded. The quickly organized brigade of wagons, ambulances, and a stagecoach had removed two hundred thirty men in just over two hours.

# Chapter 44

# A SUCCESSFUL RAID

AVA TOOK A DEEP BREATH AS SHE LOOKED AROUND at the empty rooms. Her hands were beginning to shake as the realization of what they had just accomplished began to take effect.

Weatherby grinned as he poured a cup of chicory coffee. He thrust it toward Ava.

"Drink this down, gal. Then I'm a goin' to tie ya up. Be quick now. We's a runnin' outa time."

Ava lifted the cup but paused as she stared at Weatherby.

"Why, Mr. Weatherby—your head is bleeding!"

"I banged it on a durn tree whilst I was a runnin' 'round in the dark.

"Now drain that cup. These fellers need to go."

Ava drank the full cup quickly. Her legs almost immediately started to give way.

Lampkin caught her with a grin.

"Well, I reckon we know Nurse Sweet cain't handle chicory coffee when it's been doctored up some." He watched Weatherby tie her up and pulled on one of the ropes. "Now don't make them ropes painful tight. I have to give a full report to the captain when this here deal is done."

Ava was laid gently on the floor. Hanson took the key hanging on a cord around her neck and shoved it in his pocket while Blake positioned her just inside the door.

Weatherby tapped Ezra on the head from behind with his gun and the young orderly dropped heavily to the floor.

"Drag that feller outa here an' stick 'im on top a that stage. He's too good a medic to waste away in a Reb prison."

Weatherby's eyes shifted to Lieutenant Lampkin. "An' yore a goin' to shoot me. I want ya to jist graze my head. Make shore my gun's in my hand, an' drop me where those Reb boys cin see me go down. Give that Reb holler ya have after ya do it. That should confuse 'em some."

Hanson and Blake grabbed Diekman. When they had him on top, Blake climbed over the seat to take the lines and Lampkin jumped up beside him while Hanson stayed on top of the stage to support Diekman.

Weatherby pointed his finger at Lampkin.

"An' ya durn shore better not kill me. I know you's a good shot or I wouldn't trust ya with my sorry life."

Lampkin grinned and the stage wheeled around the back of the hospital.

Weatherby chased it as he hollered and cussed. He shot several times and then dropped down on one knee as he lifted his rifle. A shot sounded from the stage and the old man slowly fell over.

A rebel yell pierced the night and then all was quiet except for the sound of the departing stage.

The Confederate patients were soon all talking at once. Several of them called for Nurse Sweet.

"Do ya s'pose she's daid? Or mebbie they took 'er."

"Anybody in this room who cin walk?"

"I can hop if someone will pass me a crutch."

The men were quiet as a crutch was passed across the beds. Finally, one man stated, "That shore sounded like a Reb call. Ya s'pose our boys was out there tonight?"

"Musta been Yanks. They shot ol' Weatherby an' he's one of us."

The room became quiet again until a soldier stated softly, "Shore hope they didn't hurt Nurse Sweet."

Private Paneer finally had the crutch positioned to support him. The rest of the soldiers listened quietly as he hopped toward the back of the hospital. They could hear him talking to someone, but they didn't hear what he said. Soon two more voices joined his and feet were running.

"It's Nurse Sweet! Is she all right?"

"I don't know. She won't wake up."

"By all that holy! All those Yank prisoners are *gone*!"

# Chapter 45

# TAKING STOCK

I T TOOK SEVERAL HOURS FOR AVA TO COME TO. SHE stared at the men surrounding her in confusion.

She tried to stand but swayed and almost fell down.

"You all right, Nurse Sweet? Those Yanks hurt ya some?"

Ava shook her head.

"They didn't hurt me, but they did make me drink some kind of concoction. It must have made me pass out." She frowned as she looked around. "My mind is hazy. I don't remember anything after that.

"Are you men all right?" When they nodded, she looked around frantically.

"Where is Mr. Diekman? And Private Weatherby?"

"Diekman's gone an' they shot Weatherby. He's a layin' out front."

Ava's eyes were large as she listened.

"Private Leiker, will you and Private Andrews check on Mr. Weatherby? If he is alive, please bring him in here." She frowned as she looked at the number of men who were out of their beds.

"You men, get back in your beds. Whatever took place is over and done. There is nothing more we can do—and I do not intend to lose one of you because you broke open a wound."

The men grumbled but slowly returned to their beds.

Leiker and Andrews were back inside quickly, dragging Weatherby between them.

"He's alive! The bullet only grazed his head!" Private Leiker's voice was high with excitement.

Ava pushed herself up and held onto the table until she found her balance.

"Bring him back to the kitchen. I will treat him there." She gave the men a list of the things she needed. She frowned when she saw Private Paneer hopping after them.

"Private Paneer, you should not be up."

The young private grinned at her and shrugged.

"Nurse Sweet, I reckon I'll only have one leg for the rest of my life. I just as well get used to hoppin' around."

Private Leiker looked up with a smile.

"I'm handy with wood, Paneer. How about I fix you a wooden leg? That might be a little easier for you."

Paneer looked at Leiker in surprise.

"That would be just fine. And I might have all you fellers sign it. I'd wear it real proud if you'd all put yore names on it."

Ava touched Weatherby's head. When he stirred, she breathed a sigh of relief. Then her frown returned.

"Mr. Weatherby, you could be dead. If that bullet had been any closer—"

"It weren't though. Jist wrap it up. An' be careful of that cut on top of my head too.

"Now be quick. I have breakfast to cook." He glared at Leiker and Andrews. "An' ya two freeloaders cin help. No point in me doin' all the work 'round here." He winked at Ava and added, "'Course since all those Yanks got took, I ain't got to work so hard. Be better fer us too. We was runnin' outa food supplies."

# Chapter 46

# "THOSE YANKEE PRISONERS ARE GONE!"

SERGEANT MARLEY ARRIVED WITH TEN MEN AND three wagons shortly after breakfast that morning. He pushed his way into the hospital, shoving Ava aside.

"I have orders to burn this hospital. We'll only take the Yanks we have room for. The rest will be left here."

Ava glared at him.

"You have three wagons and fifteen of your own men who are wounded. You certainly have no room for any Yankee soldiers."

Marley grinned at her.

"Not my problem. As soon as we get our men out, I'm firin' everything. You best start now to get out as many of those Bluebellies as you can."

Ava didn't answer. She turned and pointed at the two young privates.

"Privates Leiker and Andrews. Please carry your friends to the wagons. Five per wagon and try not to crowd them any more than is necessary.

"Private Paneer, you may sit on the wagon seat but when your leg starts to hurt, I'd like you to lie down." She clapped her hands. "Quickly now. Sergeant Marley is anxious to destroy this hospital." She turned to Private Weatherby.

"Mr. Weatherby—"

"Yeah, yeah. Load the medicine an' medical supplies on one of those mules. Weatherby this, Weatherby that. Somebody's always a needin' somethin'."

Sergeant Marley finally noticed there were no Yankee soldiers being brought outside. He cursed as he ran into the hospital. His face was red, and he was cursing even louder when he returned.

"Where are those Yankee prisoners? Who turned 'em loose? I'll run 'em down if it's the last thing I do!" he shouted. He grabbed Ava's arm and jerked her around to face him.

Ava pulled back and glared at him without answering.

Weatherby stepped forward.

"I'm the one who was left in charge. Do yore hollerin' at me." He looked around and shrugged.

"Don't know exactly what happened. I heard some hoss movement last night in the trees. I made sure all our men was accounted fer includin' the fellers what brought in that last wagon. Then I slipped outside.

"What about Leiker and Andrews? Who was on watch?"

"I sent 'em to bed early. They'd been diggin' graves all day an' was plumb tuckered out. I took first watch. When I heard the noise, I went out in the trees and got whacked one.

"Next thing I knew, a durned stagecoach was a tearin' 'round the back of the hospital. A *stagecoach,* mind ya! I took a couple of wild shots, but when I went down on one knee to git a better aim, one of those fellers on top shot me. Liked to took my head plumb off.

"Lucky fer me he weren't no better shot than he were.

"Leiker an' Andrews was tied up an' missed the whole deal. When Paneer untied 'em, they said someone hit 'em over their heads too.

"They found Nurse Sweet by the back door. She was tied and unconscious. Said some soldiers made her drink somethin'. She was mighty confused when she finally woke up." He shrugged his shoulders and nodded toward the front of the hospital. "Nurse Sweet sent Leiker and Andrews outside to see if I was daid. They drug me in here.

"I guess those Yanks come an' got their boys. They ain't our problem now. Shoot, some of those fellers was in mighty bad shape. I doubt they'll all live through that trip to Chattanooga."

Marley glared at the three soldiers in front of him. He finally rested his eyes on Weatherby as he asked sarcastically, "And what makes you think they were headed to Chattanooga?"

"Ain't the Yanks in charge of that hospital now? 'Sides, that stage were headed north.

"No point in tryin' to catch 'em neither. They have a six-hour head start on ya an' should be reachin' Chattanooga jist 'bout now."

Marley mounted his horse. He leaned his hands on the saddlehorn as he stared at the small group in front of him.

"Somethin' stinks to high Heaven here. There ain't no way over two hundred men could be hauled outa here without no one knowin'. An' not in that short time neither. Somebody's lyin'.

"What about those two soldiers who claimed to be Rebs? An' that wounded man they said was a Union officer?"

Weatherby shrugged.

"They was around at supper.

"Those fellers fit right in with the rest of us. Knew all the same officers too, an' was in some of the same battles. They kept a close eye on that man they brought in though. One stayed with 'im all the time till Nurse Sweet took over last night. That feller was in bad shape.

"They mighta been Yanks. Ain't no way to know. 'Course, they is gone so either they is prisoners, daid, or part of that raid.

"Ever'thing was quiet from supper till 'round midnight. That's when I heard noises outside in the trees. Cain't say where ever'body was after that. Things was kinda fuzzy when I come to."

Private Paneer pointed with his crutch to the north.

"They coulda been Yanks, but one a those fellers sure gave a loud Rebel call when that stage was leavin'. Why he hollered one out better than me, an' I can give a good one."

Marley looked around.

"Where's that orderly? Did he go with them?"

Ava's jaw jutted out stubbornly.

"Private Diekman is gone but he would never have gone willingly. They must have forced him in some way. He had every opportunity to leave when we were ordered by the Union forces to evacuate this hospital—before the Southern army took it over. He chose to stay then to help care for the wounded. I know he never would have abandoned them now."

Marley smirked at Ava.

"This worked out just fine for y'all, didn't it? I knew ya was a Yankee nurse. I'm goin' to recommend ya be jailed when we get to Atlanta."

Weatherby grabbed Marley's horse. His voice was low and dangerous as he looked up at the angry sergeant.

"I don't reckon you'll do no such thing. I know this nurse an' I know her family. She's Southern through an' through.

"'Sides, ya try that an' I'll tell Eberle what ya did after that last battle. Shoot, I might tell 'im anyhow. Ya ain't much of a soldier, Marley, an' that's a fact."

Marley's face became pale as Weatherby spoke. His hand hovered close to his gun when he responded.

"Don't ya threaten me, Weatherby. I outrank ya. In fact, I think I'll recommend that y'all be court-martialed too. Ya shoulda stopped this deal."

"An' *y'all* shoulda left more men here but ya didn't. Ya didn't even leave any hosses so's we could chase them fellers. Naw, you'd better tread light, Marley. Yore already walkin' on top of a big pile a horse dung, an' ya jist might fall in if ya ain't careful." Weatherby's blue eyes were cold when he spoke. Marley's threats didn't scare him.

The two men glared at each other for a time before Marley turned away. He waved toward his men.

"Move those wagons out. We have a long haul in front of us."

Weatherby grabbed Ava's arm and hurried her toward the closest wagon.

"Ya fellers hold up there. Nurse Sweet needs a ride." He lifted Ava onto the seat and climbed up beside her. He hollered back at Leiker and Andrews, "Ya fellers better catch ya a ride or y'all be walkin' all the way to Atlanta."

# COLLEGE HILL HOSPITAL, UNION CONTROL

## CHATTANOOGA, TENNESSEE
## SATURDAY, OCTOBER 3, 1863

# Chapter 47

# A BITTER SOLDIER

CAPTAIN NOBLE HEADRICK GRIMACED AS HE SHIFTED his shoulders. "This laying around is overrated. I should be out with my men," he muttered as he stretched his legs. He had been in the hospital for almost four days and his irritation increased with each day.

The young soldier in the bed next to him looked over but he said nothing. He moved the stub of his arm to rest more easily on his chest. His face was bitter and angry. When the young nurse came in to change his bandages, he snapped at her.

Captain Headrick frowned as he looked over at the angry soldier. After the nurse left, he spoke softly to the man.

"Those nurses have a hard job trying to care for all of us. It would do you well to be a little more pleasant."

The young soldier snorted. "What do you know about nurses an' how hard they work? I lost an arm, an' I don't see nobody cryin' for me."

The captain's voice was soft, but it carried a hard undertone when he responded, "I watched a nurse as she sorted the wounded. She had to make fast decisions on who could be saved and who was going to die.

"I knew that nurse. She was a Reb, but she worked as hard to save us Yankees as she did her own countrymen. She did it without crying even though it broke her inside.

"You be nicer to these nurses. They are all here because they volunteered."

The young soldier was quiet for a time. He finally turned toward Captain Headrick and put out his hand.

"The name's Espy. Private John Espy."

"Captain Headrick. Pleased to make your acquaintance, Private."

The young man blushed slightly as he replied, "Sorry, Captain. I shouldn't have been so familiar. I didn't know you was an officer."

Captain Headrick nodded. "Things are a little mixed up in here." He glanced around the room at the other wounded men before he asked softly, "When did you lose your arm?"

"Couple of weeks ago. I had mustered out an' gone home. The wife an' me had a disagreement an' I reenlisted. Who knows where I'll go now." He raised the stump of his arm and cursed softly as he looked at it. "She didn't like me much before. I don't reckon she'll want me back now."

Espy was quiet for a time. He finally looked over at the officer beside him and asked, "You ever been married, Captain?"

"Nope. I've thought on it some though."

Noble looked over the young man's head as he thought to himself, *if this war goes on much longer, who knows what will happen? More will die on both sides. I'd sure like to marry Ava, but there's no guarantee I'll even live to see the end of this war. That last conflict just about got me.*

Private Espy nodded. His voice was soft when he spoke.

"I was married. I guess I still am, but I don't really know. We grew up together an' married young. Sal didn't want me to go off an' fight—an' fer sure not as a Yankee. She despised all Yanks. 'Course, her family did too.

"We had a little spread down in Texas. Our first baby was born just before this war broke out. That little girl is almost three now, an' I've only seen her once since I left.

"That was five weeks ago. I went home ready to pick up my life where I left off, but everything had changed. My wife had moved on without me. Our cattle were scattered all over an' nothin' was branded. Even if I gathered some of them, they weren't worth anything. Besides, I was a Yank in Reb country.

"Sal had a job in town at the mercantile store. A fancy feller ran it, an' the word was she'd taken up with him.

"Oh, she said we could start over, but she snarled an' bit at me all the time. Told me I'd changed.

"Our little Missy didn't even know me. She was scared of me an' wouldn't let me touch her—kinda like her ma.

"Sal wouldn't let me hug her neither. She hardly looked at me when I rode in. After barely talkin' for two weeks, I blew up. I told her I didn't want to be married to no woman who didn't like me. Sal, she just stared at me. Then she turned her back. As she walked away, she said, 'Things have changed, Johnny. Maybe it would be better if you did leave.'

"I stayed around another week, but things didn't get no better. I finally got to spendin' too much time in the town saloon. One of the gals there was mighty friendly. She tried to get me to go upstairs. I kissed her but that's as far as it went. She said I'd be sorry the next day.

"Shoot, I was sorry 'fore I took my lips off her." Private Espy's voice cracked, and he was silent for a time. His voice was soft when he continued.

"I love Sal. I've loved her since I was a kid. I carried a picture of her with me an' that picture kept me alive. I couldn't wait to get back home." Espy cursed softly and added, "Mebbie it was better I didn't know that fire done burned out whilst I was gone. I shore wouldn't have worked so hard to stay alive.

"I left an' headed east. I figured I'd just as well die in this war. Nobody cared about me nohow." He held up his stump. "Shortly after that, I got my arm shot off. My own durn fault too. I raised it up to wave at another feller an' one of those Rebs got me." Private Espy grinned for the first time since he arrived at the hospital.

"If yore goin' to lose an arm, ya should at least be a hero, don't ya think?"

Captain Headrick chuckled. "It sounds logical but that's not usually the way it works." He studied the young soldier before he asked, "So what now?"

Private Espy shrugged. "Don't know. The army don't think I can be of service with one arm." He lifted his stump and stared at it.

"I don't reckon it will slow me down much though. I broke my right arm when I was a kid an' it never did grow right. I learned to do everything with my left hand growin' up. I guess the Good Lord just let the right one get shot off so's it wouldn't be in my way all the time."

The young soldier looked out the window. His voice was soft when he spoke, "Mebbie I'll head west an' fight Injuns. I heard some fellers talkin' about how wild it is in some of those untamed territories. Nebraska, Utah, the Dakotas…any of 'em would be fine with me. I know I ain't goin' back to Texas." Private Espy didn't talk after that. He put his stump on his chest again and closed his eyes.

Captain Headrick heard the young soldier suck back a sob several times before he fell asleep. He shook his head. *This war has destroyed too many lives. And for what? Even if we beat the Rebs, will anything really change? I just don't know.* He frowned to himself and shook his head again. *That's a heck of a way for an officer to think. And after so many people sacrificed to save me.* Captain Headrick stared out the dirty window as he listened to the sounds of the wounded men around him.

*I wonder where you are, Ava? I left you tied on the floor to save myself. Not much of a hero—or husband material either for that matter. I should never have made those promises to you. I'm just not sure I can keep them.*

*And if we did marry, would we be like Private Espy and his wife? I don't think I could bear it if you didn't love me.*

# Chapter 48

# A NEW ASSIGNMENT

ON SUNDAY, OCTOBER 4, BREVET BRIGADIER GENERAL Lewis Merrill arrived at the College Hill Hospital in Chattanooga, Tennessee. He was led up several flights of stairs to a large room. It was full of patients from wall to wall. He frowned when he saw that enlisted men were bedded down beside officers.

He turned to the young nurse who had been his guide.

"Nurse, these men need to be separated. I can't have officers sharing the same quarters as enlisted men."

Nurse Chloe Moore barely held her temper as she glared at the officer.

"General Merrill, we are short on space. In fact, we are over capacity. We don't have the facilities to give your officers rooms of their own since more enlisted men are wounded than officers." Cloe's eyes sparked as she looked over at the general and added, "And I refuse to offer preferential treatment to any man, regardless of rank."

The general turned to look at the angry young woman next to him. He frowned and started to speak when Chloe interrupted him, "And please don't tell me it is my responsibility to follow your orders. I volunteered to serve as a nurse. I did not enlist in your army."

The cords in General Merrill's neck tightened as he stared at the young women. He slowly relaxed and smiled briefly before he nodded.

"That is a just explanation, Nurse Moore. Perhaps next time, you could explain it to our officers when they arrive so they aren't surprised."

Chloe blushed slightly and nodded her head.

"Captain Headrick is in the first row facing the window. He is the tenth bed from the wall. I have been asked not to enter this ward since I am working with soldiers with open wounds. I'm sure you will be able to find your way from here."

As Chole turned and hurried down the hall, she whispered to herself, "I can't believe I said that to General Merrill. Why, I almost sounded like Ava.

"I am so tired of losing these soldiers though. Too many of them die from infections as well as from their terrible wounds. I guess I am just getting more abrupt all the time." As she rushed down the stairs, her smile returned. "I do hope Ava is doing well," she whispered. "Perhaps that nice Lieutenant Charles will stop by again sometime with more news of her."

General Merrill walked briskly between the beds of injured soldiers. Those who were able tried to salute him. His walk slowed as he looked around. He stopped by the bed he was passing and shook a young soldier's hand.

"Hello, soldier. How is your treatment here?"

"Just fine, sir. The nurses are friendly and efficient even if they don't have time to talk. The food is mostly good, and they are saving a good number of us."

General Merrill slowly nodded. He moved from bed to bed visiting with each soldier who was able to speak before he came to Captain Headrick.

He saluted the injured officer, and Captain Headrick gave him a sharp salute in return even though it hurt his wound.

They visited briefly before General Merrill cleared his throat.

"Captain, as you may know, your company was organized to fight the Missouri State Guard. Your men have done a superb job in fighting those Rebs where they live, and your successes have been noticed.

"I have been asked to send some of my fighting men to the Western Frontier. Those savages are masters at attacking undercover, and they are killing too many of our soldiers. We need fighting officers out there who understand guerrilla warfare." He frowned as he studied the man in front of him.

"I chose you, Captain. I'd like to keep you here, but I was asked to send my best. When do you think you will be ready to ride?"

Captain Headrick pulled himself a little straighter and tried to cover his wince.

"Within two days, sir."

General Merrill chuckled as he looked down at the wounded man.

"I like your spirit, Captain Headrick. I will expect to see you at the Chattanooga train station on Friday, October 9. That is five days from now. Take two horses per man as well as extra guns and ammunition. I will have around seventy troopers waiting for you there."

General Merrill leaned closer and lowered his voice as he added, "You are going to be leading a group of Galvanized Yankees. Those are Reb prisoners who offered to fight in exchange for getting out of prison. When you reach Missouri, several Colored boys who saved an officer's life will join you. They are headed to Fort Leavenworth in Kansas to join a company there." Merrill stood upright and looked down at the man in front of him.

"I chose you not only because of your skill as a guerrilla leader, but also because you are from the South. I thought those fellows might be more likely to listen to another Southern boy.

"They are fighters too. I am giving you some of the toughest Rebs we captured. We don't want them fighting here because they would have to fight their own troops. Besides, we are not so sure of their loyalties or their willingness to abide by their oaths that we want to take that chance.

"And, Captain, regardless of what you hear, this is not a demotion. I specifically asked for you. I like your fighting style, and your men respect you. In fact, I am going to push for you to be promoted to major." General Merrill frowned and added, "I can't figure out why that hasn't happened already.

"You will receive your orders within the next few days. Any questions?"

Captain Headrick's jaw tightened as he looked at the general.

"Is there any way I can request some of the men from my current company? We are a fighting team, and I'd sure like to keep some of them around me."

The colonel frowned as he asked, "How many?"

"Five including my little brother. Peter is too young to be in this war, but he ran away after I left. I have been keeping an eye on him—well, I was until I was wounded."

General Merrill's face showed no emotion, nor did he indicate that he agreed.

"Who else?"

"Lieutenant Lampkin. He grew up in the hills of Missouri. He's a tracker and a dead shot.

"Corporal Blake. He's a fine soldier and true blue to the core. He's reasonable and will work with those Galvanized Rebs.

"Private Hanson. Both he and Corporal Blake would be assets to our unit. They are loyal to me—they put their lives in danger to get me away when I was wounded.

"The last one is Private Espy here." Noble pointed to the bed next to him. "Espy can do more with one hand than most men can do with two. I'd like him beside me."

Private Espy stared at Captain Headrick in surprise. When General Merrill drilled the young soldier with his hard eyes, Espy gave a left-handed salute.

"At yore service, sir."

"You'll be ready to ride by Friday?"

"I'm ready to go now, General. You just give the order. I'll have my horse saddled an' my guns loaded."

Merrill looked back at Captain Headrick and slowly nodded. "I'll approve those men, Captain.

"Lieutenant Lampkin just arrived from a scouting detail. I'll send him in. You can work out the details and locations of the other men with him." His eyes were hard and unyielding as he added, "But any man who isn't at the station when that train leaves on October 9 will not be joining you. I'm making an exception by allowing you to take some of your picks, but they won't hold up this mission if they are out in the field."

Captain Headrick saluted the general sharply.

"Yes, sir. I will make sure they are all ready to go."

# Chapter 49

# A HELPFUL LIEUTENANT

LIEUTENANT LAMPKIN SALUTED CAPTAIN HEADRICK when he stopped in front of the captain's bed.

"I have the list of men you asked for, Cap. Blake and Hanson were with me on patrol, so they are available. I don't know Private Espy though."

Captain Headrick grinned and pointed to the man in the bed next to him.

"Private Espy, meet Lieutenant Lampkin. He is my second in command."

Lieutenant Lampkin was quiet as he looked Private Espy over. He nodded slowly before he looked back at Captain Headrick. He cleared his throat and said quietly, "That just leaves Pete."

Captain Headrick looked hard at Lampkin.

"What about Peter?"

"He was with another unit. They was attacked an' lost some men. The rest was taken prisoner. They are all bein' held down to Atlanta in the old Fulton County Jail. Word is all the Yank prisoners 'ill be transferred to a Reb prison in the next few days."

Captain Headrick pulled himself up to sit on the side of the bed.

"Saddle my horse. We'll leave tonight."

Lieutenant Lampkin's neck turned red as he shook his head. "I cain't let ya do that, Cap. We need to make that trip in record time, an' ya shouldn't even be on a hoss. I thought I'd take Blake and Hanson.

"Private Feathers was in that outfit. Let us go down an' see what we cin come up with. I'll get Pete out, but I'd like to free all of 'em if I cin. Those Reb prisons is harsh. I don't want any of our fellers to spend the rest of this war in one if I cin help it."

Captain Headrick's face was set in hard lines, but his voice was soft when he spoke.

"Lieutenant, you have five days to get down there, find Peter, and get back. Each of you take three saddled horses. Trade off and make it a fast trip but be careful. You have nearly one hundred twenty miles to cover just to get there, and you'll be riding right into the heart of Reb territory." Captain Headrick's face settled into a scowl as he added, "And if you aren't back by Thursday afternoon, I'm headed south.

"Talk to Feathers before you finalize anything. Take him prisoner if you have to make it all work. I'd like to have him with me although he's mighty valuable where he is."

Lampkin grinned and saluted his captain smartly.

"Yes, *sir*." His grin became bigger, and he nodded over his shoulder. "Blake an' Hanson be right outside. Our hosses are saddled an' we're ready to go. All I needed was yore say so."

He backed away and was quickly gone. Captain Headrick eased back against the headboard and slowly lowered himself onto the bed.

Private Espy glanced over at him several times. He finally asked carefully, "How old is yore brother?"

"Peter just turned thirteen—way too young to be in this mess. I didn't want him to enlist but he ran away after I left." Noble cursed softly. "Darn kid. He lied about his age to be accepted. Now he's been captured, and I'm stuck in this bed."

Espy looked away before he spoke again.

"I don't mean to speak outa turn, Captain, but ain't three men a mighty small group to try to bust one man outa prison let alone a whole passel of 'em?"

Captain Headrick closed his eyes.

"Mighty few but those are three of the best soldiers I know. And Lampkin knows how to make things like this happen. He'll do it or die trying. I sure hope he gets it done.

"Now we won't speak of this again to anyone until they are all back. Good night, soldier."

# SOUTH TO ATLANTA
## THURSDAY, OCTOBER 1, 1863

# Chapter 50

# A HARD TRIP FOR THE WOUNDED

AVA WAS CONCERNED ABOUT THE LONG TRIP FROM Chickamauga to Atlanta. The wagons were heavy, and the road was rough making travel difficult for the wounded men. Marley didn't want to stop during the day, but Ava insisted.

"These men are wounded, Sergeant, and we have over one hundred miles to travel. I need to change their bandages and make sure they have water. I can't do that climbing around in the back of moving wagons."

Marley cursed but finally agreed to stop for dinner and camp early each night if they came across water. By that evening, several of the men were running fevers and Ava was concerned.

"Mr. Weatherby, I need some herbs that help reduce fever. Can you gather some for me?"

"Weatherby this, Weatherby that. Always somebody wantin' somethin'. I'll find yore plants, but one of those soldier boys who's been a ridin' all day cin do the cookin' tonight."

Marley pointed at Ava. "Yore Nurse Sweet can do the cookin'. She ain't been workin' all that hard."

Ava stood and placed her hands on her hips as she glared at Marley.

"I will be glad to cook, but the wounded come first. If your men want to wait until ten tonight to eat, then tell them to go ahead and make themselves comfortable. Otherwise, I suggest you figure something out." She dropped down to the ground and began to tend the man in front of her.

Marley grabbed Ava by the arm and jerked her up. Several of the soldiers began to protest and Weatherby cocked his gun. He planted himself between the men and Marley as he spoke softly, "Marley, I cin shoot ya here an' leave ya where ya drop. I know ya got this here job 'cause Captain Eberle couldn't spare no other officer. Now ya walk easy an' this here trip 'ill go smooth. Ya keep a buckin' an' a snortin' like ya are an' things is goin' to be difficult fer ya."

Weatherby pointed toward three privates who were lounging by the fire.

"Ya three—drag out those vittles an' git to cookin' supper. I know y'all was in charge of the cookin' on the way up here. Ya cin just be in charge on the way back too." He waved his hands at the rest of the men, "An y'all cin do the cleanin' so don't get too relaxed. Now drag some wood up here so's we cin all have us a nice fire tonight."

Weatherby was still muttering to himself as he tromped off into the trees.

"I declare. Nothin' would git done if Weatherby didn't do it. Weatherby this, Weatherby that."

Marley stormed off to yell at the soldiers setting up his tent.

Ava glared after him. She was still frowning as she gently removed the bandage from Private Paneer's stump.

"Mr. Paneer, you have been up too much today. Now I want you to lie down. Let's let your wound breathe a little before I bandage it again. And prop your leg up on this saddle. When Mr. Weatherby gets back with his herbs and hopefully some moss, I am going to treat your leg."

She looked around at the soldiers who were putting up tents.

"And you men—I want the wounded in those tents before anyone else is bedded down."

Just then, Weatherby appeared. He had a variety of plants and leaves. He dropped them on the ground by Ava.

"Leiker an' Andrews, y'all come with me. I found a pile of moss, an' I need some help carryin' it back. Too bad it ain't summer. We'd have us some honey too."

Ava looked up with a smile. "I have just a little left, Mr. Weatherby. I have been hiding it in case someone decided to eat it."

Weatherby grinned and nodded.

"Yore a right savvy little gal, Nurse Sweet. Right savvy."

# FULTON COUNTY PRISON
## ATLANTA, GEORGIA
### MONDAY, OCTOBER 5

# Chapter 51

# IN A REB PRISON

**P**ETER LOOKED AROUND THE CROWDED YARD AS HE was shoved through the large gate. Nearly fifty men filled the space no bigger than the small playground of the one-room school he had briefly attended. Most of them were young although several men with gray whiskers could be seen as well. He saw another young man about his age and wiggled through the crowd to stand next to him.

"Howdy. Been here long?"

"About three days. They are moving us out though. Word is we are being taken to a Reb prison. Shoot, we could be paraded all over this durn country just to get to one that ain't too full—not that those Rebs care much about too many prisoners." The young man was shivering. He wore no coat, just a thin shirt.

Peter put out his hand. "Private Peter Headrick. I was raised southeast of here a piece. I joined the Union army after my older brother enlisted."

"Jackson Lampkin. I'm from Missouri way. The folks was killed in all the border fightin' an' I heard the Union fed its soldiers better than the Rebs." He grinned at Peter as he added, "That was true too…till I was captured."

Peter studied his new friend for a moment. He finally commented softly, "I know a Lieutenant Lampkin. He hails from Missouri too. He any kin of yours?"

"Probably. There are a few of us around there. I had a cousin by the name of Noah who enlisted when this war started. We heard he was lost in action. Pop didn't believe it, but we never heard from him again so I ain't so sure."

Peter's eyes opened wide, and he nodded excitedly, "Your cousin is the lieutenant I know! He rides with my brother, Captain Noble Headrick."

One of the older soldiers bumped the two young men as he pushed between them.

"Keep yore voices down," he hissed. "There are spies in here an' if one of 'em hears that ya have kin who's an officer, he'll squeal an' you'll be shot right quick. These guards hate Yanks an' it don't matter how old ya are." He gestured slightly with his head.

"Meet me over against that far wall in a little bit. One of ya angle a different way an' don't foller at the same time." The old man limped across the least crowded part of the yard and pushed his way through the groups of men clustered together in the small space.

Peter watched the old man. It looked like he was talking to each group he passed. Peter turned to the left and eased his way across the yard until he came to the wall. He leaned against it with his knee bent and the heel of his boot resting easily. He saw Jackson from the corner of his eye. His new friend was squatting on the ground about thirty feet away, but Peter didn't look at him.

One of the men in a group Peter had walked through reached over and grabbed him.

"Ya little punk! Who do ya think ya are stealin' my tobacco?"

Peter's face lost its color, and he shook his head.

"I swear I didn't, mister. I don't even smoke."

The soldier slammed him down on the ground and straddled him. His voice was low, and he spoke quickly as he searched through Peter's clothing.

"We are gettin' outa here tonight. When ya see a wagonful of women come through that gate, you an' that other kid get as close to 'em as ya can. Act like ya ain't never seen a woman dressed like that before." He almost grinned as he added, "As young an' green as ya are, I doubt ya have." His face was serious when he added, "Some of us will gather 'round that wagon whilst one of our guys makes sure that gate ain't fully latched.

"Now I'm a goin' to punch ya jist to make this looks real. Act scared when ya get up an' stay away from everybody but the kid an' ol' man Feathers." He punched Peter once below one eye and slammed his fist into the boy's stomach before he stood. He held up a pouch of tobacco and hollered, "Got back my chew! Little thief. Ya try that again an' I'll pound ya good." He kicked Peter for good measure and was soon in a tight cluster of men.

Peter didn't have to fake pain when he climbed to his feet. Jackson grabbed his arm and helped him to the wall. Peter bent over holding his stomach. With the exception of the old man who had spoken to him earlier, the rest of the soldiers either glared at him or ignored him.

Feathers grabbed Peter's arm. "What did ya steal that feller's tobacco for? None of us have anything in here to trade with. Wouldn't do ya no good. An' I know ya don't chew 'cause I don't smell of it on ya." He pulled Peter upright and shoved him against the wall. He glared at the soldiers looking his way and they quickly turned around.

"This here deal has to happen tonight. Ol' Eberle left on the train an' took some of his officers with 'im. With him gone an' Marley pickin' up the wounded up to Chickamauga, there only be five guards left.

"Now Miss MaryAnn will bring a load of gals in tonight. Should be six of 'em. We want to get those guards distracted. 'Course, the two of ya don't need to worry none about them. Yore job is to ogle those gals when they get here. Get as close as ya can. Don't try to climb in that wagon though or one of the guards might try to shoot ya.

"Stare after the wagon as it passes but stay back close to that gate.

"Keep in mind that not ever'body in here knows what's goin' down. We ain't sure we cin trust all these fellers. Those Rebs like to plant spies.

"When that gate swings open, you fellers be among the first to run through. Head north an' run till ya cain't run no more. When ya come to a creek, turn left an' crawl under the riverbank. Hide out in the roots of a big oak tree a leanin' over the water there. I'll be along shortly an' we'll hightail it outa there.

"Now I'm a goin' to slap ya. An' don't neither of ya talk to me no more."

Feathers slapped Peter hard across the face.

"Ya stay over here by yore own selves. We don't tolerate no thieves." He pointed a big finger at Jackson and snarled loudly, "An' that goes for y'all too. Ya done picked yore company, an' ya picked the wrong friend."

Jackson's eyes were big as he watched the old man walk away.

"I ain't never talked to that old man before, an' I shore never saw him so mean as he is today. Shoot, he never talks to nobody, an' nobody talks to him."

Peter bent over and retched. He didn't have to pretend. His stomach hurt badly, and his pain was real. He slid down the wall to sit on the ground as he muttered softly to Jackson, "Just do what I do. We are getting out of here. Now, no more talking."

# Chapter 52

# PRISON BREAK!

ROUND SEVEN THAT EVENING, SOMEONE HALLOOED the gate from the outside. The soldier who was standing there peered through. He looked back toward the building and hollered, "It's women—a whole wagonful of 'em!"

The prisoners turned to look. They started to move as a body toward the gate. The guard who was in the yard snarled and fired his gun.

"They sure ain't here fer y'all. Now back up." He hollered to the man at the gate, "Let 'em in! There ain't no officers here so we'll have us a party!"

The gate swung wide, and the prisoners separated to allow the wagon to come in. Once it was in, the wagon was surrounded by men.

"Follow me," Peter hissed. He hurried across the yard and got as close as he could to the wagon. His eyes were wide as he stared.

"Lordy. I ain't never seen so many pretty gals at one time an' fer shore not wearin' so few clothes!" Jackson whispered as he crowded close to the wagon. Peter was beside him and he nodded.

The older soldiers pushed them back and the two young men were soon left behind as the wagon creeped slowly across the yard. Peter allowed himself to be pushed until his back was near the gate. He ignored the men behind him and continued to point at the women.

"Look at that little blonde, Jackson. Why she ain't much older than us. I'd say fifteen or sixteen tops. 'Course most of the gals I grew up with were married off by that age. She shore ain't though!"

The prisoners surged toward the wagon. Before long, it could no longer move. Soon, all five guards were in the yard. Peter watched in amazement as one by one, they disappeared in the sea of men. While some prisoners jumped on the wagon, others just stared. Suddenly, the gate flew open.

The sea of prisoners came to a halt as they stared from the women to the open gate. Most of the men ran toward the gate while two strolled up to the wagon.

"Well, lookie here, Balt. We have these gals all to ourselves," one prisoner commented. "How long cin y'all stay? I figger we have 'bout three hours 'fore Eberle gits back." He stared into the wagon and his eyes opened wide. "Ya brung whiskey? Why ya gals did come fer a party!"

The two prisoners climbed into the wagon and drove it up to the guardhouse. They helped the giggling women down and all of them went inside.

Soon, the yard was empty except for the five guards lying on the ground. Two were tied but the other three slowly sat up. One looked around and then staggered to his feet.

"The prisoners! They are gone and they have our guns!" Corporal Hemmer exclaimed. He grabbed the sitting men and jerked them to their feet.

"Height, untie those other two guards and meet us down at the horse corral. Double time!" As he raced out of the yard, he pressed his hands to his head.

"Eberle will shoot us for this. And if they took our horses, we'll die for sure."

The men skidded to a stop in front of the empty corral. All the horses were gone along with the saddles and bridles.

Hemmer threw his hat on the ground.

"This here deal was planned. There ain't no way those prisoners had time to steal all those hosses let alone our tack. An' look at us. On foot an' no weapons. They even took our sidearms.

"Let's get back to the jail. Just maybe a few of those Yanks were stupid enough to sneak back to those women. An' keep yore eyes open. There might be a few of 'em hidin' out 'round here.

"When we get back, we'll bust open that room where Eberle stores the extra weapons. We'll have to get us some horses from the livery, but four of us are goin' out tonight.

"We'll leave Height here to keep an eye on the place and guard any prisoners we find."

# FIFTEEN MILES NORTH
## OF ATLANTA
### MONDAY, OCTOBER 5, 1863

# Chapter 53

# NIGHT RAIDERS!

AVA SAT UPRIGHT AND STRAINED TO LISTEN. *I DID hear men running!* She slid off her bunk as quietly as she could and rolled to the other side of the tent. She grabbed the bag that held her meager medicine supply and crouched as low as she could get. She forced herself to breathe softly and slowly. Footsteps paused by her tent and the tip of a knife slid through the canvas. The footsteps retreated when a rebel cry sounded.

She rushed to the tent opening and peeked outside. She stared as the horses were stampeded through the camp. The campfire was trampled and some of the supplies that were stacked there were destroyed.

Ava recognized the rider. She almost laughed as she pulled her head back. She dressed quickly and stepped outside the tent. Marley was shouting orders, and his anger was obvious.

"Private Johns and Adams—put bridles on those mules and find those horses!"

"Sarge, those mules ain't broke to ride. Look at their tails. They only have two bells an' that means they ain't been rode.

"'Sides, there ain't no bridles, an' we cain't see in this dark."

Marley threw his saber on the ground as he glared at the men. His eyes finally reached Ava, and he stomped toward her. He grabbed her arm and jerked her around to face him.

"Look at ya, all dressed an' ready. Ya knew those Yanks was comin', didn't ya? I'll just bet y'all was part of this deal!"

Ava jerked her arm away and stepped back.

"Sergeant, I heard the horses running the same as you." Her voice was sarcastic when she added, "I see you are dressed as well.

"And while I knew nothing about this raid tonight, I am glad the mules were not taken."

Weatherby nodded toward the rope fence where the horses had been penned. "This here deal were all planned out. It took some mighty quiet fellers to pull off this heist an' they done it slick. Saddles, bridles, an' hosses all gone—an' us still fifteen miles from Atlanta.

"Anything besides the hosses an' tack taken? Nobody was hurt?"

As the men shook their heads, Weatherby frowned. He glanced toward Ava's tent and then walked around it to look a little closer. He poked his finger through the slit before he looked around at her.

"Those fellers cut yore tent?"

"I don't know who cut it. I heard someone outside my tent, and I rolled out of my bunk. I saw a blade start to cut through the canvas, but then it disappeared. Whoever it was ran away."

Weatherby's eyes were hard as he looked at Marley. The sergeant smirked as he looked from Ava to the old soldier. He raised his saber and waved it toward his men.

"Clean up this camp an' then get a little shut-eye. The sun will be up before long an' we have a long walk in front of us."

# Chapter 54

# FRIENDS AND ENEMIES

PETER AND JACKSON WERE WINDED WHEN THEY finally reached the river about a half mile north of the Fulton County Prison. They ran to the left and dove under the roots of a large tree that leaned over the water. They listened as other prisoners passed by, calling out to each other in the night.

Jackson started to answer but Peter clapped his hand over his friend's mouth.

"Feathers said not to talk to anyone. We are to wait for him," Peter whispered.

Jackson frowned and shook his head as he whispered back, "But we could be farther north if we keep goin'. It might be daylight before that old man gets here." He tried to stand but Peter jerked him down.

"Feathers said there were spies in that yard. Now I don't know who they were and neither do you. Let's just stay put until he gets here."

Jackson eased down beside his friend. His voice reflected his concern. "And what if old Feathers is a spy himself? Then what? I'll tell you what—then we'll both be sent north to Point Lookout, that's what."

Peter was quiet as he listened to his friend. He pulled his knees closer to his chest and replied softly, "Well, at least we will be together. I ain't had a friend my age since this war started, and I'm kind of liking it. If you'll agree to that, then hunker down here closer to me and be quiet."

Jackson gave his new friend a quick grin and nodded. "On the condition that we stay together when we leave here. Mebbie yore brother can use his influence an' take me with him too."

Peter smiled and the two young men listened silently to the movement of men all around them.

Before long, they heard someone panting as he ran along the creek.

Guns cocked and a voice rang out, "Who goes there?"

"It's Feathers, ya durn fool. Keep yore voice down." Private Feathers was so close that Peter and Jackon could hear him breathe.

"Private Feathers, I have orders to bring ya in an' I reckon this here deal will be enough to see ya hung. Eberle was convinced ya was an officer, an' after seein' how that breakout was organized, I reckon he was right."

"So ya was a spy, Bixby. Pretended to be a Yank, but ya was a Reb the whole time. An' what was goin' to happen to ya when we was all sent to Point Lookout? I doubt ya intended to let yore sorry hind end be stuck in that hellhole."

Bixby laughed sarcastically.

"Naw. After we git ya fellers back, I will mysteriously escape an' go on to my next assignment as a Yank. I'm not the only one neither. Shoot, there was four of us with y'all in the yard of that ol' jail." Bixby looked around and growled, "Where are those two youngsters? I know one is Captain Headrick's little brother. He's with Merrill's Horse, an' my sources just found out that the other kid is kin to a Yank lieutenant.

"Eberle 'ill want both of 'em for shore. We might be able to snag us some bigger fish if we dangle 'em out there fer a time."

Feathers was quiet. Both boys could hear him breathing heavily as he climbed up the bank to surrender.

"I reckon since I'm already dead, ya jist as well tell me who the rest a yore spies is. Ya say I'm an officer? If I am, I ain't much of one since I missed y'all."

"Balt, Sutter, an' Clement too," Bixby chortled. "An' ya thought Clement was loyal to ya. Well, he warn't. Balt an' Clement stayed with those women, but Sutter is out there now gatherin' up yore men. I reckon by tomorrow night, we'll have our hosses back an' most of those Yanks too.

"Now where are those boys?"

"Don't know. Didn't know 'em 'fore yesterday an' didn't trust nobody new, 'specially after one of 'em stole tobacco first thing. They was some of the first ones outa the gate though, so I reckon they be long gone. I would be was I them." His voice was soft when he added, "Did ya ever stop to think how all yore hosses come up missin'?

"I swung down by that corral to see if I could pilfer off a few an' they was already gone. Hosses, saddles, bridles—ever'thing.

"Now our boys didn't have time to do that, so I reckon y'all have other players wanderin' 'round out here in this brush. Was I y'all, I'd keep my voice down. As for me, I'm pleased to know there's other folks out here, 'cause I'm a guessin' they ain't Rebs."

Bixby cursed quietly. "Git in front of me. I ain't takin' no chances with ya.

"Now follow along this here path. It will lead us to a little cove, an' I reckon some more of yore men."

# Chapter 55

# RIDERS IN THE NIGHT

PETER AND JACKSON LISTENED TO THE SOUND OF Feathers' and Balt's fading footsteps.

Jackson looked at his friend. "Now what? This whole place is crawlin' with men, an' we don't know who's friendly an' who ain't."

"You know any of those names? Ya know what Sutter looks like?" Peter whispered.

Jackson shook his head. "Nobody talked to me an' I kept to myself." His breath was coming quickly when he spoke again. "How will we know who to follow?"

"Let's don't let on that Feathers told us where to go. I think he'll figure a way to identify any spies. That old man is a sly one." Peter frowned. "I sure wish I knew who had stolen those horses though. If we have friends out there, I'd like to know who they are."

The two boys crept up the path behind Feathers and Bixby. They went slowly and tried to stay quiet. When they reached a clearing, they stopped and hid behind some trees. The moon was full, and it was easy to see on the clear night. About twenty men could be seen scattered around like they were waiting.

One of the men lunged to his feet and hurried to meet Feathers.

"Sarge! We was hopin' ya would make it. Sutter here said you'd be along."

Feathers looked around the clearing. "Anybody else make it this far?"

The man who had spoken shrugged his shoulders. "Not that we know of. Balt an' Clement chose to stay with the women." He snorted. "Durn fools. Ain't no roll in the hay worth stayin' in prison."

Feathers looked around the group of men. His eyes studied each face before they moved on to the next man. "That's 'cause they's spies!" He folded over with a grunt as Bixby slammed him in the stomach with his gun.

"This man is the spy. Y'all held him up as a big man, but he ain't no feller to be proud of. He went an' got the rest of the fellers caught. That's why they ain't here. Now if they show up, be quiet. There're more spies out there."

Just then, ten more men came rushing into the clearing. The last one spoke excitedly, "We need to get movin'! There are a bunch of horses movin' out there in the dark an' horses mean riders."

When the men saw Bixby with his gun on Feathers, they slid to a stop.

"Why ya pointin' yore carbine at the sarge, Bixby? He's the one who got us all out." The man who spoke moved slightly to the side as his friends spread out around the clearing.

"'Cause he's a durn spy, that's why. Ya seen any of the other fellers? An' what horses are ya talkin' 'bout?"

The two men who had spoken didn't answer but another man across the clearing spoke up quietly.

"I saw those horses. There were only two fellers drivin' 'em. Has to be more men than that out here though. No way two fellers coulda slipped in an' stole 'em on their own."

Bixby nodded. "We need to keep movin'. Let's try to move quiet. Mebbie we'll come up on the rest of our men."

Feathers glared at him, and Bixby hit him again in the stomach. He tied his neckerchief around Feathers' mouth and threw the rope he had tied to his belt toward a couple of soldiers.

"Two of ya—grab 'im an' tie 'im up. We don't need 'im makin' no noise when we find the rest of the fellers. I want 'im with us though so's he cin hang when we git to Chattanooga." The men were quiet. Some frowned as they followed Bixby while others glared at Feathers.

The last group of men to arrive were at the end of the little column. As the last prisoner passed by, Peter tripped him with a stick. The man cursed as he fell. When he saw Peter and Jackson waving at him from the bushes, he called to the men in front of him.

"Karl, I tripped and twisted my durn ankle. You and Mert help me up. I ain't sure I can walk without help." The two men stopped to help, and the rest of the column kept moving.

The man who had fallen pulled his friends into the bushes. He grabbed Jackson as he looked the two boys over and asked carefully, "What are you fellers doing out here? Why didn't you come in with the rest of us?"

Jackson's eyes were wide. When he started to respond, Peter bumped him. "Keep your voice down," he hissed.

"Bixby is a spy," Jackson blurted out in a harsh whisper. "He caught Feathers down by the water when we was hidin' there. He said Balt, Sutter, an' Clement are all spies too. Balt an' Clement didn't leave the yard so they're out of it. Sutter ain't though. He's is tryin' to catch all us escaped Yanks. That's why Bixby hit ol' Feathers, an' we don't know who Sutter is."

The three men listened carefully, and the first one slowly nodded.

"How about we find those horses? Let's see who the rest of the folks are roaming around out here tonight."

# Chapter 56

# "THEY MIGHT NOT BE FRIENDLY!"

**THE SOLDIER NAMED KARL STEPPED FORWARD. "THIS** way," he whispered.

"I heard them over by that little spring when we were running. We'd better go in quiet though. They might not be friendly."

"Yore right," a quiet voice replied. "I might not be friendly. Now who are ya an' what are ya doin' out here?"

Peter started to turn around and the man who had spoken jabbed him with his rifle.

"Stand still. I don't want to fire this weapon, but there be other ways to die."

"Private Hanson, it's Pete, Peter Headrick! What are *you* doing out here?"

Hanson let out a low chuckle and lowered his rifle.

"Pete, we come down here lookin' fer you. Cap is fit to be tied. He woulda come his own self but he went an' got himself shot. He's doin' fine now but it were a little touchy fer a time there.

"Who are these fellers ya have with ya?"

"Private Jackson Lampkin…but I don't know who these other men are. We were all prisoners together down in the Fulton County Jail."

The tallest of the two soldiers put out his hand. "Lieutenant John Hermann and my brother, Karl. Karl here is in the cavalry, but he was caught with us." He grinned at Hanson and added, "Karl is a scout. He knows this country like the back of his hand. Private Mert Dixon is the short one over there."

Hanson shook hands. He looked hard at Jackson.

"You say yore name is Lampkin? Any relation to Lieutenant Noah Lampkin? He's wanderin' 'round out there somewhere."

A soft voice sounded behind them, and all six men jumped.

"I shore 'nough am, fellers. Pete, I'm glad ya made it out. I didn't have ever'thing all planned out yet when ya boys come pourin' outa that gate. Blake an' Hanson were to steal the hosses an' I was to break into prison." His teeth showed white in the moonlight when he grinned. "I thought 'bout ridin' in with those gals, but I heard 'em talkin' an' figgered there was somethin' in the works. I decided to wait it out, an' I'm shore glad I did." He shook Peter's hand before he squinted at Jackson.

"Well, I'll be durned. I shore never thought I'd see any of my own kin in this here scrap. Good to see ya, Jackson. How're yore folks?"

When Jackson looked down at the ground and didn't answer, Lieutenant Lampkin squeezed his shoulder. "I'm sorry to hear that, Jackson." His eyes moved to Peter.

"Cap 'ill be plumb tickled to see ya, Pete. I am too 'cause ol' Cap woulda skinned me if I was to come back without ya." He looked around at the rest of the men and grinned. "Let's go get the rest of our boys."

Peter hesitated before he said quietly, "They might not all be Yanks. I know two for sure are Rebs, and I don't know about the rest."

Lieutenant Lampkin's eyes glinted in the moonlight.

"Ya leave that up to me. We'll find 'em first an' then we'll sort 'em out."

# Chapter 57

# SPIES AND SUCH

LIEUTENANT LAMPKIN LED THE WAY THROUGH THE trees and brush following the sound of the men in front of him. When they caught up with the group, Peter, Lieutenant Lampkin, and Jackson stayed in the brush while the other three soldiers led Private Hanson into the clearing.

"I found one of the fellers who's been roamin' around out here." Sergeant Herman pointed to Private Hanson. "That feller right there—he's your horse thief."

Bixby looked up quickly. He was maneuvering to place Hanson in front of him when Lieutenant Lampkin spoke softly from the brush.

"Drop yore weapon, Bixby. An' unloose that man in front of ya." When Bixby hesitated, Feathers slammed his elbow into the man's stomach and dropped to the ground. Bixby whirled around to fire into the brush, but a knife slammed into his side. He dropped to the ground, moaning softly.

Feathers jerked the bandana off his mouth. Peter stepped up beside him and cut the ropes that bound his hands. The old man pointed toward another soldier.

"Sutter, ya dirty traitor. This here's the last time ya betray yore own men."

Sutter looked around quickly and then made a dash for the bushes. Some of the prisoners stared in surprise but the closest man tackled him. When Sutter started to yell, another man slammed him in the side. Once he was lifted off the ground, a rag was stuffed in his mouth. While the two men held Sutter's arms, another soldier tied his hands behind his back with his bandana.

Lieutenant Lampkin stepped out of the brush and nodded at Hanson.

"Get that rope off my hoss. We're goin' to string that feller up right here. Let Eberle find 'im whilst he's a chasin' us."

When some of the prisoners started to mutter, Feathers glared at them as he pointed at Sutter.

"That man is a spy. He intended to turn all of ya over to Eberle. Ya think yore trekkin' north? Well, ya ain't. Yore headed east an' 'fore long, you'd be headed back south.

"Now any man who thinks I'm wrong, well ya just keep on a keepin' on. The rest of us is goin' to find those nags we been hearin' out there in the brush. Once we do, we'll hightail it fer Chattanooga."

Hanson quietly handed his rope to Lampkin who tied one end around Sutter's neck. Sutter struggled to speak but with the rag in his mouth, only muffled screaming could be heard. Feathers tossed the other end of the rope over a tree branch. Lampkin and two other soldiers lifted the struggling man while Feathers pulled up the slack on the rope and snugged it tightly to the tree. The three men who were holding Sutter dropped their prisoner. His body twitched and kicked as it swung below the thick branch.

Lieutenant Lampkin looked around at the quiet men. His voice was soft when he spoke.

"We have forty-two hosses an' forty-three of us Yanks. Pete an' Jackson be the smallest, so they'll ride double. We'll probably have to trade off some unless one of those hosses is a big one." He glared at the rest of the men. "Now if there's any one of ya who don't want to make this hard trip, jist speak up an' we'll leave ya right here. Extry horses would be welcome." He grinned and added, "'Course, I'll report ya fer desertin,' but yore free to make that choice."

"You have that many horses?" Lieutenant Hermann asked Lampkin incredulously.

Lampkin grinned at him and slapped Private Hanson on the back.

"Shore now, while Corporal Blake an' me was gatherin' the Reb's remuda in Atlanta, Hanson here paid a visit to Sergeant Marley. Marley's 'bout five miles from here with a few soldiers and several wagons of wounded Rebs. Marley was right generous too—he offered to give us seven hosses plus his own. That was right neighborly of 'im, don't ya think?" When the soldiers began to grin, Lampkin added, "An' we need to move out now to take advantage of the night.

"Hanson here likes to play 'round in the dark, an' Karl over there knows these woods. They cin guide us. Those soldiers behind us 'ill be gittin' hosses from the livery as soon as they cin, an' come first light, they'll be on our tail. That means we need to move out fast, an' stay as quiet as we cin. We have over a hundred miles to cover, an' we need to do it quick. We be in Reb country, so ever' man we meet is likely an enemy.

"Private Hanson, show us where those hosses be stashed."

# CHATTANOOGA, TENNESSEE
## THURSDAY, OCTOBER 8

# Chapter 58

# SOME HAPPY PRISONERS

LIEUTENANT LAMPKIN PULLED HIS TIRED HORSE TO a halt in front of the livery. The sun was almost down, and the last slivers of light showed between the buildings. He grinned when Captain Headrick appeared in the doorway. Even though exhaustion showed all over him, he gave a sharp salute before he spoke.

"Evenin', Cap. These here are those Yankee prisoners ya asked me to collect. Forty men—thirty-six privates, three sergeants, an' one lieutenant." He waved behind him as Peter pushed his way to the front. "An' that includes one brother," he added as his grin became bigger.

Captain Headrick nodded at the soldiers beside Lampkin. He squeezed Peter's shoulder before he addressed the other men.

"Corporal Blake and Private Hanson—I need to see you in my quarters in fifteen minutes. Lieutenant Lampkin, you come with me now.

"The rest of you men take care of your horses and then get some vittles. I told the cook to make extra this evening." He waved toward the barracks. "And I want those horses rubbed down as well as fed and watered before you eat.

"When you finish, find some empty bunks and get some rest. You will report for duty at reveille, and that is about nine hours from now.

Lieutenant Lampkin will get you lined out after chow." Captain Headrick paused as he studied the horses, and a slow grin filled his face.

"It looks like you acquired some fine horseflesh. Make sure you care for them well. They might be your mounts going forward." He saluted them and said, "Dismissed," before he turned stiffly. He started to lead his saddled horse into the livery.

Peter slid off his horse and took the reins from his brother.

"I'll take care of your horse, Nob—I mean, Captain. It won't take me long."

Captain Headrick smiled at Peter and nodded. He looked back at the tired soldiers one more time.

"Welcome to Chattanooga, men."

Lieutenant Lampkin fell into step beside his captain as they walked toward the officers' quarters.

"Did you have some trouble? I thought you might be back this afternoon."

Lampkin shrugged. "A little. Some Reb spies was mixed in with the prisoners, an' we had to sort 'em out. Good thing we got there when we did too.

"Captain Eberle had taken some of his men south fer a meetin' with some bigwig officers. He sent Sergeant Marley an' ten men up to Chickamauga to burn the hospitals.

"We almost run into Marley when he was headed north. I think ya know 'im—arrogant, loud-mouthed skunk.

"Once Marley burned everythin', he was to haul the Reb wounded down to Atlanta. I think he planned to leave our boys in there when he set the place afire—that or shoot ever'body 'cause he didn't allow no room fer 'em." Lampkin's face was hard as he spoke, but he broke into a grin when he added, "He was a mite disappointed there warn't no Yanks there.

"That big house didn't burn neither. The grass was too wet an' the walls was brick. Marley was madder than a hornet. He couldn't even git no torches to light.

"Any fighting on your way down?"

"Naw. We went 'round 'em. That Hanson cin see in the dark, an' he figgered about where they'd be when we headed back north.

"Didn't have no trouble stealing those Reb mounts in Atlanta neither. Those Reb soldiers was so shorthanded they didn't even have a man guardin' their hosses. It took us longer to saddle all of 'em than anything else."

When Captain Headrick looked up in surprise, Lampkin added, "We had jist planned to take 'em bareback to save time, but some of those local folks offered to help us saddle those hosses when I told 'em we was in a hurry to catch some Bluebellies. 'Course, we had on borrowed Reb uniforms." Lampkin gave Captain Headrick a grin and a wink.

"Once Hanson and Blake got those hosses headed north, Hanson cut out. He sneaked up on Marley an' stole their mounts. Tack too. He didn't try fer their guns though. He figgered he'd better leave with what he had." Lampkin gave Captain Headrick another quick grin as he added, "We was only short one hoss by the time Hanson got back.

"Ol' Weatherby heard Hanson come in. He kept an eye on those Rebs but they was all in their tents. Weren't nobody 'round the fire. Hanson whacked the sentry watchin' the hosses an' those Rebs didn't know what hit 'em till Hanson gave his own Reb yell.

"We didn't take their wagon mules though. We figgered those wounded Rebs probably needed to ride an' they warn't no threat to us."

"You didn't have any problem getting the men out of the prison?"

"Nope. By the time Eberle an' Marley left, there was only five men guardin' that prison in Atlanta. Well, five plus the spies mixed in with the prisoners.

"Those prisoners had already planned to break out 'fore we got there. The word is old Feathers planned it.

"I didn't know how I was goin' to get that gate open till a wagonful of women showed up. I finally figgered out they was part of a plan. It were a good one too. After those women was let in, things happened mighty fast. The prisoners rushed the gate an' all but two men got out. I found out later the two prisoners who stayed was Reb spies.

"It took us some time fishin' all our boys outa that brush though. Once we had ever'body gathered up, we found out there was two spies in the group. I knifed one when he tried to shoot me, an' we hung the other.

"Speakin' of spies, that Feathers feller wants to speak with ya. He said he has some information the brass should have."

Captain Headrick nodded. His voice was quiet when he asked, "Was Ava with Marley's men?"

"She was. Hanson watched the camp fer a time 'fore he went in. He said that gal was as cool as a cucumber. She didn't back down to Marley neither." He frowned and shook his head. "That Marley is a mean man. He didn't care much more about those wounded Rebs than he did our men.

"Nurse Sweet did though. She made him stop regular-like so's she could change those wounded fellers' bandages."

Captain Headrick's eyes were hard as he listened.

"Hanson said when he rode through that camp, Marley was cussin' a blue streak. Nurse Sweet poked her head outa her tent. When she saw the wagon mules was still there, she never said a word.

"I told Hanson it was a good thing he left those mules. Nurse Sweet loves all her wounded soldiers, an' she mighta shot 'im her own self if he'd tried to strand those wounded men out in the middle of nowhere by takin' the mules." Lampkin chuckled and added, "That Hanson could sneak up on an Injun. 'Course, that fool Marley had his soldiers stack all their guns, an' Hanson ran those hosses right over top of 'em. Those Rebs didn't even have time to get their sidearms out 'fore he stampeded those hosses through their camp. They was some confused too when he give his Reb yell.

"Nurse Sweet warn't confused though. She recognized 'im. Hanson said he saw her smile as he ran those hosses past 'er. Said it was all he could do to keep from wavin'."

"Did you take her horse?"

"Nope. He's stabled outside town. Blake rode 'im up here to find help the night we spirited all of ya outa that hospital. Yore Nurse Sweet give 'im a hankie with 'er smell so's he could catch 'er hoss. Blake said Deuce was a smooth ridin' hoss an' they made good time. He still don't trust 'im much though. He said that hoss don't appear to like men. Blake left Deuce here after he told us where y'all was."

"Nurse Sweet met Oscar Quick whilst she was here, an' ol' Oscar took a likin' to her." He grinned at the captain and added, "An' if ya ain't dug through yore letter packet, ya might want to do that. There be a new letter in it to ya. I read it since ya couldn't. Y'all are to take her hoss with ya when we leave here." When Captain Headrick looked surprised, Lampkin grinned.

"I saw 'er stuff a hankie an' that letter in yore packet 'fore we whisked ya outa there." Lampkin's grin became wider when Captain Headrick blushed. "Not sure if that was fer her hoss to smell or fer y'all to sniff now an' again." Lampkin winked before he added, "I ain't so dumb as I look, Cap. I see things—especially things folks do quiet-like."

Lampkin waited but Captain Headrick didn't ask him any more questions. The lieutenant finally nodded over his shoulder. "Nurse Moore works in this here hospital if you'd like to git a message to Nurse Sweet 'fore ya leave," he added softly.

Captain Headrick frowned as he looked across the grounds.

"I don't know what I'd say. She's already risked her life to save me. I don't want her taking any more unnecessary risks or waiting on me either."

Lampkin stopped suddenly and Captain Headrick looked at him in surprise.

"She loves ya, Cap, an' that ain't goin' to change jist 'cause ya ain't around. You write that note an' I'll see it gits delivered." He blushed slightly as he added, "Besides, that Nurse Moore is a right cute little gal. I wouldn't mind tellin' 'er goodbye."

Captain Headrick's eyebrows lifted in surprise, and he finally chuckled. His smile slowly disappeared, and he shook his head.

"I can't ask anyone to do that. Miss Bradley is miles away, smack in the middle of Reb territory. Whoever might try to deliver that message would be in danger. Besides, I can't say where I'm going, and I sure don't know how long I'll be there.

"If she did by chance get a letter, it wouldn't be until she was sent back up here…and that's not likely since she is with the Rebs now." Captain Headrick shook his head. "No, a letter is pointless."

"Ya write that letter, Cap, an' let the Good Lord figger out the rest. This here war won't last forever, an' Nurse Sweet'll be ready to leave. She's got no home, an' I don't think she'll want to stay 'round here. Ya done already invited her to head west an' find ya while y'all was outa yore head. I reckon she'd appreciate a letter from her feller when he's a talkin' sense.

"The West ain't all that big. I figger if she smiled sweet at jist 'bout any officer, he would point her in the right direction."

Captain Headrick blushed slightly and grinned.

"I reckon so. You clean up and eat something. I'll have that letter ready for you tonight. And be sure to let me know when those Galvanized Yankees arrive." Captain Headrick frowned and paused.

"On second thought, never mind my letter. You make your visit and get back here. I'll have one of those new recruits drop it off tonight or first thing tomorrow. You don't need to play messenger for me."

Lieutenant Lampkin grinned and saluted. "I reckon I'll make that visit right now so's I can be back here to line out yore Reb detachment when they come in on the train."

Lampkin grabbed a young private and pointed him toward Captain Headrick's departing back.

"Follow that officer, Private. He has a letter that needs to be delivered, an' it needs to go out today."

Private Pack O'Neill nodded and grinned. He saluted and hurried after Captain Headrick.

# ATLANTA, GEORGIA
## TUESDAY, OCTOBER 6

# Chapter 59

# RED LEGS ON MY POST!

EVERYONE WAS TIRED WHEN AVA AND THE THREE wagons of Rebel wounded arrived in Atlanta the afternoon of October 6. Captain Eberle was shouting at the soldiers in the prison yard.

"What do you mean those Yankee prisoners all escaped? How could they escape? Who opened the gate?" He whirled around when he saw Marley limping toward him.

"And you, Sergeant Marley—why did you take so many men with you? All you had to do was pick up the wounded, and it didn't take ten men to help you do that." He stared at the wagons and his eyes narrowed.

"Where are those wounded Bluebellies?" he ground out as Marley hobbled forward and stood stiffly in front of him.

"They was gone—all of 'em—by the time we arrived." Marley pointed at Ava. "An' I think that nurse was part of it. We should lock her up for the rest of this war an' see how sassy she is then."

A slow murmur began to build, and Private Paneer pulled himself to his feet.

"I don't reckon that's so, Captain. Nurse Sweet was unconscious, an' it took her some time to come to. She—"

Captain Eberle cut him off.

"Marley, you and Private Weatherby meet me in my quarters *now*." He spun around and began to stomp away.

Ava stood. She spoke quietly but firmly.

"Captain, the wounded men have been in these wagons far too long. Where would you like us to house them?"

Before Eberle could answer, the sentry called from his lookout point, "Soldiers comin'. They look like ours."

Weatherby turned to look. He leaned forward and cursed. His voice was soft when he spoke to Eberle.

"Captain, I recognize that first feller. He's a Red Leg an' I don't reckon he's here to do no good. I don't know the rest of 'em, but that feller is fer shore a Bluebelly."

Captain Eberle only paused a moment before he began to bark orders.

"You soldiers who drove those wagons in—get them down to the train station and get the wounded loaded. That train leaves for Columbus in five minutes and I want all of them on it. You too, Nurse Bradley.

"Weatherby, you go with them. If you know that Red Leg, he probably knows you. Now move! If there's gunfire, I don't want those wagons in the middle of a fight.

"Once the wounded are loaded, all you men but Weatherby get back up here. Come in behind the jail. Get a weapon if you need one from that gun rack by the door. Spread out around those windows. The rest of you, take your positions and cover me. If I say anything about rabbits, that is your cue to disarm those soldiers. Wait until I separate them from their officer though. Now *move!*"

There was a scurry of activity as the men jumped to the captain's bidding. Weatherby tossed Ava into the wagon. He climbed up beside the driver and they raced toward the train station.

Captain Eberle watched the soldiers slowly riding toward him.

The soldier in front pulled his horse to a stop and grinned down at the lone captain.

"Kinda quiet 'round here, ain't it?"

"I like it quiet. What unit are you men part of and what brings you here? I didn't receive any wire announcing you."

The soldier who had spoken peered around the small jail. He appeared relaxed but his eyes missed nothing.

"We are lookin' fer a spy. She claims to be a nurse but she's workin' fer the Yanks. Perty gal. Small but mighty sassy."

Marley gave low curse and started to move forward, but the man beside him shoved him back. His voice was barely a whisper as he hissed at the sergeant.

"Weatherby whispered somethin' 'fore he took off. I didn't hear it all, but I think he mentioned Red Legs. Those fellers might not even be Rebs. We have our orders. Now keep yore gun on that feller talkin' to the captain."

Eberle was quiet as he watched the soldiers in front of him.

"We don't have any women on this post. In fact, there are darn few in this town. Those who are around are old gals who have been married longer than both of our ages added together. I'm quite sure I'd remember someone who fits your description."

The soldier stared long at the captain. His voice was hard when he spoke.

"We followed a gal's tracks right up here. She was travelin' with three wagons likely filled with wounded an' eleven more men walkin' and ridin'. Their tracks said they was soldiers."

Eberle's voice was soft but equally hard when he replied, "Could have been wagons. The lousy Red Legs burn out everything in their path so lots of folks are on the move.

"What's your name, soldier?"

The train whistle blew, and the train began to creep slowly down the tracks.

The insolent soldier grinned.

"Sergeant Mosby. We are on our way to meet up with our outfit down south a piece." His eyes narrowed and he added, "In fact, we jist might catch that train now."

"Not until you verify who you are. Now show me your papers."

Mosby cursed under his breath as he pulled a packet of papers from inside his shirt.

"It's all right there. I got my orders three days ago. We met some of our boys south of Nashville an' they said Reb soldiers burned the field hospitals at Crawfish Spring. Now I'm a bettin' that nurse was with the wounded when they left."

Captain Eberle frowned as he studied the orders. He turned the page over and read everything slowly before he reread the entire paper.

"According to your orders, you are to rejoin your unit in Coumbus, Georgia, if you don't find that nurse as you pass through here. These papers don't give you permission to deviate from your route nor to make her your mission.

"I will keep an eye out for her. If she shows up, I'll notify your captain." Eberle looked behind him toward the train in the distance.

"Looks like you'll have to catch the train at the next station. Why don't you have chow with us and then you can be on your way." Eberle didn't wait for an answer. He turned and called behind him, "Privates Andrews and Nichols—you are in charge of mess tonight. Skin those rabbits you shot and get them in a pot." The smile on his face didn't reach his eyes when he added, "Go ahead and dismiss your men, Sergeant. Have them care for their horses and you come with me. I'd like to hear some news from up north."

Mosby tried to keep the anger off his face. He cursed softly and backed away, but Eberle was ready.

"Drop your weapons, Sergeant Mosby. You and I are going to have a talk." The rest of Mosby's men looked up in surprise. While they stared from their sergeant to Captain Eberle, they were quickly surrounded and disarmed.

Mosby slowly began to unbuckle his revolver. As it began to drop, he grabbed the gun and jumped on his horse. He charged it through the surprised soldiers and into the cluster of horses, slipping to the side to keep from being a target. As he raced his horse around the jail, the other horses spooked and ran with him.

Eberle dropped to one knee as he tried to aim. However, the running herd gave him no target. He spun around and pointed at Marley.

"Send out a wire. Tell headquarters a spy is going to be arriving in Columbus. He will be riding a worn-down sorrel and will be alone. Arrest him and notify me."

As Marley raced toward the small building where the telegraph was located, Eberle wheeled to face the new soldiers.

"You men are under arrest. Your sergeant is a spy and I'm going to assume the rest of you are as well until I can sort this mess out. Now file into the jail. Andrews, you and Nichols get them in irons." Captain Eberle jerked off his hat and shoved his hand through his hair.

"What an unholy mess I have here. Two major prisoner escapes and now I lost a Red Leg on my own post!"

# Chapter 60

# A CHANGE IN PLANS

AVA WAS TREMBLING WHEN WEATHERBY HELPED HER from the wagon. She had recognized the voice of the soldier who had spoken to Captain Eberle. She clenched her hands to keep them from shaking and took deep breaths as Weatherby hurried her toward the train depot.

Private Weatherby bought Ava's ticket and rushed her back to the train. He looked down at her and frowned as he asked, "Ya recognize those fellers?"

"I recognized the voice of the one who was speaking. He was one of the Red Legs who terrorized my mother and grandmother. He came back later with his men and killed them. He tried to find me, but I was hidden in one of the caves that bordered our home. I never saw their faces though." Ava took a shaky breath. There were tears in her eyes when she spoke.

"Mr. Weatherby, I am afraid. I'm afraid for myself as well as for the soldiers in my care. What if that man follows us? Those soldiers will try to protect me. That means I am putting them in danger."

"I been thinkin' on that too. I think we need to send ya away, an' I don't rightly know which direction. If we ship ya east, you'll likely be in a field hospital. That means it could change hands like the one at Chickamauga did." He studied her face and added softly, "Maybe ya should head west. Ya could care fer those Union boys tryin' to whip the Injuns out there.

"'Course, I don't know where you'll end up. I ain't even sure how far west the trains run." The train whistle blew and Weatherby grabbed Ava's arm.

"I know one thing fer shore. We cain't put ya on this here train."

"If we cin find some folks headed back north, we might send ya with 'em." Weatherby rubbed his chin and nodded. "Yes sir, Chattanooga might be the safest place fer ya, fer a time anyway."

Just then, an older woman with an extravagant hat and colorful cloak hurried toward the train. The man following her was carrying several crates of food. She smiled at Private Weatherby as she passed.

"Mr. Weatherby, I didn't know there would be so many soldiers on this train. If I had known, I would have organized meals for all of them."

Weatherby stood and bowed before he winked at the woman. He took her arm and led both her and Ava away from the train. The woman looked at the old man in surprise. Her eyes were watchful, but she continued to smile.

"An' if I had known Mary Fowler was goin' to be at this here station, I'd a taken a bath first!" Weatherby's smile was wide as he pulled Ava around to face the older woman.

"Mary, this here young lady is one of the best nurses 'round, an' I reckon those soldiers back there would agree with me.

"Nurse Sweet, this lovely lady is the wife to one of my oldest friends. Mary Fowler, Ella Bradley." Ava stretched her hand toward Mary Fowler and forced a smile.

"It is wonderful to meet you, Mrs. Fowler. Mr. Weatherby has been a wonderful friend to me as well."

Mary smiled as she took Ava's hand, but she frowned slightly when she glanced at Weatherby.

"Take a quick walk with me, Mary. I have a problem I'm a hopin' ya cin help me with." He pointed toward a small bench behind the train depot and guided Ava toward it as he spoke, "Ya take a seat here an' have ya a little rest, Nurse Sweet. I'm a goin' to talk to Mary a bit. I'll be back in a shake."

When Ava started to protest, Weatherby gently pushed her onto the bench. It was in a clump of trees and was hidden from the front of the station.

"We's all plumb tuckered out, Nurse Sweet. Now ya relax fer a time an' let me get this here deal all worked out."

Weatherby took Mary's arm as he pointed toward a group of nuns who had just stepped off the train. They were gathered around a wagon and were obviously leaving soon.

"How well do ya know those good sisters, Mary? I'd like to know where they's a goin'."

Mary looked at Weatherby in surprise as she laughed.

"Why, Mr. Weatherby, I didn't think you even noticed women, and especially not nuns!"

"It's Nurse Sweet. There're some durn Red Legs after 'er. They showed up jist as we was planning to catch the train.

"Now I know Captain Eberle will try to arrest 'em, but where there's one Red Leg, a passel more be lurkin' 'round somewhere.

"They killed Nurse Sweet's family an' now one a those fellers showed up here lookin' fer her. I'm a guessin' he musta gotten wind that she survived. I'm thinkin' I need a decoy an' that group of nuns might be jist her ticket.

"Nurse Sweet ain't no nun so they won't pay those sisters no mind. Maybe they cin huddle 'round 'er an' keep 'er hid. If she leaves with 'em, we cin spirit her outa here right under those Red Legs' noses. What do ya think?"

"Mr. Weatherby, I think you are just as devious now as you were forty years ago when you tried to trick me into marrying you!" Mary Fowler's smile was big as she looked at Weatherby.

"Let me see what I can arrange."

"She needs to go now. Sergeant Nielson was a leadin' that pack back there, an' he's one mean son of a gun. Those fellers with him didn't act like no Red Legs though. I reckon he managed to get assigned to 'em to make hisself look like a Reb."

"I'll give her a little travelin' money. She has pay comin' but it might not ever git here as mixed up as the Union is on funds."

Mary Fowler turned quickly and called as she hurried toward the nuns, "Sister Marie Christi, may I talk to you?" She whispered to the tall nun who seemed to be in charge. The nun looked confused but when Mary spoke again more urgently, the nun nodded. She whispered to the cluster of sisters around her. The shortest one smiled and quickly grabbed a bag from the wagon.

Six sisters hurried toward Ava. They lifted her up and surrounded her as they hurried toward the privy. They were all smiling as they pulled Ava into their cluster. One pushed Ava into the privy and the rest of the sisters gathered in front of the door.

Weatherby grinned at Mary and kissed her cheek.

"Ya remind Red what a lucky feller he is. An' when this durn war is over, you tell 'im we need to kick back an' drink a little of that hooch he makes."

Mary laughed and hurried into the train car, smiling and talking to those she passed. She passed out her food to the wounded soldiers as well as to anyone who looked hungry.

Ava was soon out of the privy and dressed like the nuns surrounding her. They all climbed into the waiting wagon, and Sister Marie Christi turned the team north. Some of the soldiers had been watching out the train windows. They were staring in confusion when Weatherby entered the car alone. He stopped and poked the man in front of him as he whispered, "Rouse the men an' do it quiet-like."

Word passed quickly and the soldiers were soon alert. Weatherby spoke softly.

"Men, the feller leadin' that pack of soldiers back there were a Red Leg." Some of the men sat up straighter and all of them looked grim as they listened closely.

"Now he be lookin' to find Nurse Sweet. They burned 'er out an' killed 'er family. We're a gittin' 'er outa here, but I want ya fellers to all have the same story should ya be questioned.

"Nurse Sweet helped git us on the train here in Atlanta, but she was busy an' didn't sit down. Ya didn't see 'er once we all reached Columbus. Ya jist assumed you'd see 'er at the hospital. When ya arrived, things was busy an' ya don't know if she ever made it there or not. Several of ya thought ya saw her but didn't none of ya talk to 'er.

"If they ask what she was wearin', look confused. Say ya never noticed nothin' but that bandana she wore over 'er hair an' 'er white apron.

"Now y'all got that? It's important all yore stories be the same."

Private Paneer struggled to his feet.

"There ain't a man on this train who wouldn't give his life to save Nurse Sweet. Want us to create a ruckus to keep folks watchin' us when we get off?"

Weatherby grinned and nodded.

"I reckon that would be all right. A couple of ya fall down the steps when we stop. Make a big scene. The rest of ya push through the door all at once." He looked at Timpkins, one of the men who had a bad chest wound.

"Not y'all, Timpkins. If Nurse Sweet hears one of ya busted open yore stitches, she'll be back to tan my hide.

"Now don't none of ya be a lookin' out the windows. An' when we git there, don't nobody pay attention to nothin' but the ruckus in front of ya.

"I'll be behind ya hollerin' like I'm yore captain or somethin'." Weatherby grinned at the men and added, "I feel like I'm a durn sergeant even if I keep gittin' busted back to private.

"Ever'body clear?" Weatherby waited until the men nodded and then he grinned.

"Ya jist as well git some sleep. This here ride should take us nigh on six hours, so we'll likely be on here a fair piece longer. Now eat that food Mrs. Fowler give ya. I'll fill yore canteens at the next fuel stop." He saluted the men and winked as the train chugged out of the station.

"Git some rest so's y'all be ready to carry out yore parts."

# Chapter 61

# FRIENDLY DECOYS

AVA TRIED TO SEE MR. WEATHERBY THROUGH THE cluster of nuns but he was nowhere to be seen.

"Where—where are we going? Are you sure I am to go with you?"

The young nun beside her smiled and pulled Ava's veil higher on her head.

"You will be safe with us. We travel back and forth through both lines of this terrible war. The hospital in Chattanooga is short-staffed so some of us will help there for a time. The rest are being sent to a small mission in the Dakota Territory.

"Our mother superior is Sister Marie Christi. She never tells us specifics until it is closer to the time." The small nun smiled and put out her hand.

"My name is Sister Felix. What would you like us to call you?"

Sister Marie Christi spoke without turning around. "Her name is Sister Augustina. We will make an exception of what she is called on this trip only. When we arrive in Chattanooga, Sister Augustina will just disappear. Now no more talking. Let us begin the rosary."

Sister Felix smiled at Ava and squeezed her hand. The sisters soon had rosary beads in their hands and began to pray. Their voices were soft and lilting. Even though Ava had never heard most of the prayers, she found herself relaxing. She could feel the peace around her, and it had been a long time since she'd had that sense of calm.

The sisters prayed for nearly an hour and then all was quiet in the wagon. Benches had been placed against the sides and nine nuns, along with Ava, were seated there. Sister Marie Christi was driving, and another older nun was on the seat beside her.

Ava leaned forward and spoke softly to address Sister Marie Christi.

"Sister, I know several good campsites with water if you are not familiar with this route. I came this way just a few days ago."

Sister Marie Christi nodded without looking around.

"I would like to make twenty miles today, so we won't camp until this evening. If you know a place we can fill our canteens though, that would be helpful. I would like to take a break around eleven."

"There is a little spring with clean water about an hour from here. I stopped there with the wounded soldiers I was caring for. We also camped beside a river about fifteen miles from here so that might work for tonight."

Sister Marie Christi nodded again, and Ava slid back on the bench. None of the sisters were talking and her head soon began to bob. Before long, she was asleep with her head resting on Sister Felix's shoulder.

# Chapter 62

# RED LEGS PAY A VISIT

EVERYONE WAS TIRED WHEN THEY ARRIVED THE FIRST evening at the campsite Ava had spoken of. She grabbed the stack of canteens and hurried toward the river. She had just finished filling them when she heard horses and a man's loud voice.

"Where are ya nuns headed? Yore a mighty long way from anywhere."

Sister Marie Christi's voice was quiet but firm when she answered.

"We are headed to Chattanooga to help in the hospital there."

"How many of ya are there?" He watched the nuns as they hurried back and forth, taking items from the wagon and preparing the evening meal. Sister Felix appeared carrying an armful of wood and another nun followed her.

"Sir, if you can't count then our number is irrelevant. Now please, step aside so we may complete our evening duties."

Sergeant Nielson tried to grab one of the younger nun's arms, but Sister Marie Christi stepped between them.

"My novices are not allowed to speak to men. I will kindly ask you to direct your questions to me."

"My name is Sergeant Nielson, an' I'm lookin' fer a gal who poses as a nurse. She's a spy an' I have orders to take 'er in. Ya seen anybody on this here trail? I know she was in Atlanta an' she bought a ticket to Columbus. I went all through that train though, an' I didn't see 'er."

"I saw no riders today, nor did we meet any horse-drawn carriages of any kind. Now please, take yourself on down the road. I can give you no more information."

Sergeant Nielson's eyes narrowed, and he glared at the quiet nun in front of him.

"I'll go but I think yore lyin'. I'm headed north, but if I don't find 'er, I'm comin' back. We'll continue this talk then."

Sister Marie Christi didn't respond until Sergeant Nielson pulled his horse around.

"May God ride with you, Sergeant, and may he guide your hands as well as your heart."

Nielson snorted and several of the men with him laughed.

"I don't need God to do my job, Sister."

"We all need God. You may not *want* Him around, but we *all* need Him…and He rides with you even if you don't ask Him to." She smiled and added, "Good day to all of you."

Sister Marie Christi turned quickly to face the silent nuns. She clapped her hands and smiled at them.

"Quickly now. Seat yourselves and let us pray."

She took out her rosary and held it up. The nuns quickly followed her lead. Nielson snorted again at the praying nuns.

"Come on, boys. We have more ridin' to do before dark." He led his men out of the little cove on the run.

Ava appeared with the canteens, and Sister Marie Christi handed her a rosary without missing a word. When they finished, she smiled again at her nuns.

"Quickly, Sisters, get in line. Sister Felix, fill your plate and hand it to the sister behind you. Sister Augustina, please follow me." Sister Marie Christi led the way through a line of trees. She smiled at Ava and pointed to a rock in front of her. "Please sit down.

"Miss Bradley, I would like you to help with chores outside camp on our trip north. I fully expect that sergeant to return, and I would like to keep you away from his prying eyes as much as possible."

"Maybe I should travel alone. I'm afraid I am putting you in danger." Ava's face was tight when she spoke.

"Nonsense. You will travel with us, but I think it would be prudent to keep our eyes open." Her face softened and she asked quietly, "Do you have any family still living?"

Ava took a deep breath and nodded. "My brother. Charlie is in the Southern Army." Her voice was angry when she added, "That man who was here killed my mother and my grandmother. He would have killed me too, but I was hiding.

"Red legs are killers, and I hate them all," she added bitterly.

Sister Marie Christi was quiet when Ava finished. When she spoke, her voice was soft.

"They are all children of God, Miss Bradley. Some of them have lost their way and we must pray for them. However, to hate is not God's way. Even though it is difficult, we must forgive.

"I know that is hard, especially after what you have been through, but you must pray for God's help." She pointed at the rosary Ava was holding. "Put that in your pocket so you have it when we begin to pray. You will stand out as different should a stranger notice you are not using it." Her eyes twinkled as she added, "After five days, you may even know how to say the rosary yourself.

"And please, do not talk to my sisters about your family or your loss. You may speak to them about nursing though. In fact, if you know where to collect moss and dandelions, I would like to teach the novices about the different plants here we can use to aid healing."

Ava nodded. "I do know where to find some moss, and we will pass many patches of dandelions. I have echinacea root and honey in my bag if you would like me to share about that as well."

Sister Marie Christi nodded. She put her hand out to Ava and pulled her up.

"Come. Let us go eat." She smiled and added, "I can tell you have a passion for the sick and wounded, Miss Bradley. No wonder your soldiers call you Nurse Sweet."

Ava looked at the tall nun in surprise, and Sister Marie Christi laughed before she led the way back to the fire.

# Chapter 63

# A FEARLESS NUN

ON THE EVENING OF THE FOURTH DAY, THE SISTERS had just made camp when Sergeant Nielson raced his horse into camp. The man he was dragging behind him was bloodied and bruised. The sergeant dismounted and pulled the man until he was lying in front of Sister Marie Christi.

"Take a good look at those penguins, boy. Tell me which one you were to deliver that letter to."

The young soldier on the ground could barely speak. Both eyes were swollen nearly shut. He tried to shake his head, and his voice was barely audible when he spoke.

"I told you I don't know her. I was asked to take that letter to the hospital in Chattanooga, but I was sent out on patrol before I could deliver it."

Sister Marie Christi's eyes were angry.

"Sister Augustina, help me take the rope off this man." Ava stepped forward and deftly loosened the rope while Sister Marie Chrisi slipped it over the wounded man's head. She clapped her hands and pointed at a young nun.

"Quickly—bring me my medicine kit from the wagon."

Nielson's face turned dark with rage. He pulled his gun, but Sister Marie Christi stepped between him and the man on the ground. Ava quickly pulled the soldier back and the small group of nuns encircled him.

"Sergeant Nielson, you brought this man here. He is now in our care. I will deliver him to the hospital in Chattanooga tomorrow.

"If you wish to file some kind of charge or complaint, feel free to use my name. I am Sister Marie Christi. However, you will not take this man when you leave here."

Nielson began to yell as he waved his gun around. "I could shoot all of ya an' no one would know who done it!"

Several of the soldiers with Nielson shifted uncomfortably in their saddles. One finally spoke.

"Sarge, let's go. That feller didn't tell us nothin'. All he had was a letter. He don't know who the nurse is or what she looks like.

"I think our best bet is that train. I think she was on that train headed south an' we jist didn't find her. I'm guessin' those wounded soldiers was hidin' her. We should ride on down to Columbus an' be waitin' when that slow train arrives. I'm thinkin' we can catch her when she tries to sneak off—we know she bought a ticket."

Sergeant Nielson stared at the nuns while the soldier spoke. He cursed and threw the letter he was holding in the fire. The wind caught it and dropped it on a rock. It was burning when Nielson turned away. Sister Felix stomped on it to put out the fire, and the Red Legs rode out of camp slowly.

Nielson pulled his horse around to stare at the group of nuns. He studied each of their faces and his voice was dangerously soft when he spoke.

"I know ya, each one of ya. I'll get even with ya fer takin' my prisoner. I'll make ya pay, ever' single one of ya." His eyes rested on Sister Marie Christi last. "An' *y'all* most of all. I'll kill ya fer what ya done here today."

The tall nun said nothing, and her facial expression didn't change.

Nielson wheeled his horse around and raced it after his men. They argued loudly for a time and finally turned their horses south.

Ava watched the riders race toward the south before she spoke softly to Sister Marie Christi. Concern showed on her face and her voice was anxious.

"Sister, I think we should break camp and move. We should try to go at least five more miles or possibly more if the horses aren't too tired. Maybe even push on to Chattanooga tonight.

"I don't trust that man. He's a killer and he could try to sneak back here tonight. He could even send some of his men."

Sister Marie Christi studied Ava and slowly nodded.

"I believe you are right, Miss Bradley. We will wash this man's wounds and then prepare to leave. He will come with us, of course." She looked hard at Ava. "I will leave his care up to you. Can you treat him while we travel?" When Ava nodded, Sister Marie Christi turned to her waiting nuns.

"Come, Sisters. Help me reload this wagon. Leave room for the wounded soldier between the benches. You may have to hold some of the supplies if they won't fit around your feet.

"Sister Felix, fill those canteens. Sister Martin, fill that pan with water from the creek and help Sister Augustina clean this man's wounds.

"Quickly now. I want to leave here in ten minutes."

Sister Felix grabbed the partially burned letter from beside the fire. She frowned. Most of the letter was burned. The name on the envelope was not even visible. She stuffed it in her pocket and poured water from one of the canteens she held over the fire before she rushed to the creek.

The moon was bright, and the sisters drove through the night. They reached Chattanooga at six the next morning. The horses were tripping with exhaustion, and the nuns were tired. Most of them had walked the last five miles to spare the horses.

They pulled the wagon up to the hospital and several orderlies appeared to carry the wounded soldier inside. Once he was out of the wagon, Ava took the lines.

"Sister, you get your nuns settled in. I will take care of the horses." She smiled at the tired group of nuns who had become her friends. "Thank you for letting me travel with you. I will wash this habit and leave it with Mother Bickerdyke." As she started to turn away, Sister Felix thrust the letter into her hand.

"I think this was likely meant for you," she whispered. "I hope you find whomever it's from." She hugged Ava quickly and hurried to join the rest of the sisters.

Ava opened the letter. Most of it was burned and the writing that was still there was blurred from moisture. None of it was legible and the signature was gone. Her hands shook as she studied it.

"Noble, if this is from you, I can't read it—and for the sake of the sisters and myself, I can't keep it."

She petted the horses and whispered, "Come now. I'll get you some feed and water if Oscar isn't around. I'll rub you down too. I think you earned that." Ava tripped as she led the team toward the large livery stable. She shoved the letter into a manure pile as she walked by.

════════  *Chapter 64*  ════════

# AN OLD FRIEND

**O**SCAR POKED HIS HEAD OUT OF THE SMALL ROOM HE called his office. His face broke into a grin when he recognized Ava.

"Howdy, gal! Did ya give up on that uppity captain an' become a nun?"

Ava laughed and shook her head.

"Some kind nuns spirited me out of Atlanta. We just arrived and I told them I would take care of their horses. They all have army brands so I was hoping you would be around this morning to tell me where to put them."

Oscar nodded and took the lines to the team.

"Ya go on in my office an' change. I reckon it would be best if no one saw ya in that git up. Then they cain't bother those good sisters with questions." He looked sideways at Ava and asked, "Hard ol' trip, were it?"

Ava nodded and the smile left her face.

"Sergeant Nielson showed up with some of his Red Legs. He was hunting me in Atlanta and the kind sisters took me with them. Nielson visited us twice on the trip up here. The second time, he threatened all of us and promised to kill Sister Marie Christi.

"He dragged a wounded man into our camp. Sister Marie Christi took charge and protected the wounded man. He wanted that young soldier to identify me, but the soldier didn't know who I was. I didn't know him either. In fact, I had never seen the man before.

"When the soldier couldn't do it, Nielson attempted to shoot him. That's when Sister Marie Christi stood between them."

Oscar slowly nodded. His old eyes glinted, and he asked softly, "That Sister Marie Christi—she jist a little older than you? Mebbie thirty or so? Tall gal with piercing, gray eyes? Looks mighty severe until she smiles?"

Ava's eyes were wide as she nodded.

"Yes! I don't know her last name, but she looks just as you described. Do you know her?"

Oscar chuckled and nodded.

"I knowed her when she was knee-high to a grasshopper. Tough, plucky little gal. Got in a lot of trouble in school fer bein' sassy.

"Her folks shipped her off to a convent when she was sixteen. They was afraid she'd end up killin' someone. She caught the feller she was sweet on with one of those saloon gals in a compromisin' situation, an' she warn't happy.

"Had her a terrible temper. Carried a pistol an' warn't afraid to use it neither. She was to stay in that convent till she was eighteen and finish high school.

"She surprised ever'body when she took to that life an' decided to stay. Her folks told me her religious name, but I lost track of 'er.

"Who'd a knew little Sassy Ann would become a nun. The Good Lord goes after mighty unlikely folks sometimes." He grinned at Ava and bumped her. "Better look out. He might have His eye on you. They say when the 'Hound of Heaven' is after ya, there ain't no point in runnin'!"

Ava laughed and shook her head. "I don't think so although I do have my own set of rosary beads now—and I know how to use them too." She was smiling when she turned toward Oscar's little office.

"Give me a little bit to change and I will be out to help you rub the horses down."

# Chapter 65

# A BRIEF STAY

AVA HURRIED TO THE HOSPITAL. SHE CAUGHT Mother Bickerdyke as she was coming down the stairs. The older woman frowned, and her steps slowed as she looked at Ava.

"I didn't expect to see you so soon, Nurse Bradley. Where are you being moved?"

Ava blushed as she spoke.

"Mother Bickerdyke, may I speak to you in private?"

The head nurse nodded. She opened the door to her office and stepped aside for Ava to enter.

Ava shared the events of the last few weeks with Mother Bickerdyke including the threats from the Red Legs. When she finished, there were tears in her eyes.

"I didn't want to leave the men but an old soldier, Private Weatherby, sent me up here. We were both concerned that my presence might bring danger to the wounded soldiers I was traveling with." Ava looked down and twisted her hands. She was trying not to cry when she looked up again.

"I love being a nurse, but I don't know where to go. Private Weatherby planned to send me south. He changed his mind though when those Red Legs arrived.

"I am a danger to anyone I am around, especially the wounded men who might try to defend me."

Mother Bickerdyke drummed her fingers on her desk as she stared at Ava. Her finger movements slowed, and a brief smile crossed her face.

"Nurse Bradley, I am going to send you west. I am going to put you on a train to St. Louis. Of course, there are large numbers of soldiers moving around because of this war. If one of those westbound divisions needs a field nurse, you go with them. Otherwise, when you get to St. Louis, you report to Nurse Parsons at Benton Barracks Hospital.

"Colonel Bonneville is the commander of that post, and he can direct you as well. I will send a letter for you to present to him in case you need it. I am guessing either of them will be delighted to have an experienced field nurse at their disposal." She glanced down at Ava's apron with "Nurse Bradley" embroidered on it.

"And take off that apron. We are going to keep your presence here as quiet as possible. There are stacks of clean aprons outside my office door. Take one of those.

"Now go to the nurse's quarters and get cleaned up. You can help in our intensive care unit this afternoon but be ready to leave on the westbound train tomorrow morning at seven. And be sure to wash and press Sister Marie Christi's habit before you bring it down here.

"You are dismissed, Nurse Bradley."

Ava hurried upstairs. A soaking bath sounded wonderful, but she didn't have time. She washed the habit and hung it up to dry. "I'll press it tonight," she whispered to herself as she sponged herself off. She was tired and hungry, but she rushed down one floor to the intensive care unit. She took a deep breath and smoothed her apron before she opened the door.

She stopped in front of a group of nurses. "Mother Bickerdyke sent me to work in this unit today. I am a field nurse and would be glad to help wherever you need me."

The charge nurse studied Ava and finally nodded. "Come with me. We are shorthanded today as always. What should we call you?"

Ava paused and then smiled. "Nurse Weatherby or Nurse W. is fine too."

"Very well, Nurse Weatherby. You may help in here." The charge nurse paused before she opened the door. Her voice was soft when she spoke.

"Most of these men are terminal. However, some could be saved with proper treatment—or even a will to live. See how many you can save today. I am sure you have experience in both of those areas or Mother Bickerdyke would not have sent you." The nurse's smile was tired when she opened the door. She whispered, "Offer encouragement, Nurse Weatherby. Often, hope is what will bring them around. That and faith."

# Chapter 66

# "WOULD YOU EVER LOVE A MAN WITH ONE LEG?"

AVA FORCED HERSELF TO SMILE AS SHE ENTERED THE room. She could smell decaying flesh and the telltale signs of gangrene. She stopped at each bed and visited with the man there briefly as she followed the smell she feared the most.

A young soldier was in the back corner of the room. His arm was gone, and his leg wound was the cause of the smell. Ava smiled at him.

"Good morning. I am a new nurse and I have been asked to check your wound." She reached for the bandage around his leg, but the soldier grabbed her hand.

"Leave it. I know I'm going to die."

Ava gently loosened his hand. "But *I* don't know you are going to die. Please—let me look at your wound. I have had much experience with wounds such as yours."

"Are you a Reb nurse?"

"I am both a Yankee and a Reb nurse. We treated both sides at Chickamauga." She smiled at him again as she began to unwrap the discolored bandage.

"When were you wounded?"

"Three days ago on patrol. Some Red Legs shot me and left me to die. They took my horse, and I drug myself as far as I could."

"Those Red Legs are worse than the Bushwhackers an' all that freedom to terrorize makes 'em downright mean. They're supposed to be Yankees but if they're on our side, I might join the Rebs." The soldier's voice was bitter when he spoke. He added, "My folks are Southern Sympathizers, so I reckon that would make 'em right happy."

Ava's mouth tightened but she didn't respond. She smelled his leg and then leaned back on her knees as she looked at him.

"Your leg needs to be treated immediately. You appear to have the beginning of gangrene, and it is spreading. If we take your leg off today, you will still have your knee. If you wait another day, you may lose the entire leg."

The young soldier lifted his stump of an arm.

"I'm already missin' an arm. What can a man do with one arm and one leg? No point in livin'."

Ava smiled at him. "I'm sure your mother would disagree. Besides, lots of men are surviving this war with missing limbs. You will have most of your leg. You can still ride a horse and rope with your left hand."

The soldier stared at her.

"Would you ever love a man with one leg?"

Ava's eyes sparkled and she laughed softly. "I guess that depends on how fast he would hobble if I chased him. If he just sat there and did nothing, I'm not sure. But if he tried to chase me back, I think I would let him catch me."

The young soldier grinned for the first time in three days.

"How bad will it hurt?"

"It will hurt when you awake, but we can give you something to make you sleep during the surgery." She squeezed his hand and stood.

"If you'll agree, I'll find a doctor and schedule you immediately."

The young soldier slowly nodded. "I reckon I'll agree. My name is Reid. Private James Reid." He tried to sit up and winced as he lay back down. "Say, you didn't see a Private Pack O'Neill in here did you? He was took by those same Red Legs. They found a letter he was carryin' for a nurse in this hospital. He didn't know who she was, so he couldn't tell 'em anything. That's when they started on me. I didn't even know he had a letter so I couldn't tell 'em nothin' neither.

"Lucky for me I was found by some of our boys."

Ava was quiet as she listened. She patted Private Reid's shoulder.

"I only arrived this morning, but I will ask Mother Bickerdyke to speak to you. She is in charge here, and she might be able to give you some information." Ava lifted the rosary from her pocket and smiled again at the young private.

"Are you Catholic, Private Reid?"

He shook his head and Ava laughed. "I'm not either but this rosary gives me comfort. You hold onto it while you are in surgery."

Ava rushed toward the front of the room. Several doctors were talking quietly, and she tapped the arm of one. He turned and looked at her in surprise.

"Doctor, I am Nurse Weatherby. Private Reid in the back corner has agreed to have surgery on his leg. I believe it has gangrene and so his surgery must be done immediately."

The doctor glanced from Ava to the direction she pointed and shrugged his shoulders.

"Doubt it will make a difference. Besides, we can't get to it today."

Ava glared at him.

"If that leg is not taken off today, he will lose his knee as well. Now if you don't want to do it, point me to someone who will!"

The surgeon's face turned red but before he could respond, another doctor took her arm and led her to the side. Ava recognized Doctor Williams, the young Confederate doctor she had saved at Chickamauga.

Her eyes opened wide, but Doctor Willams shook his head slightly as he led her away.

"I was captured and escaped in a Yankee uniform. They don't know I'm a Reb," he whispered. He grinned at her and added, "I'm helping in this department because they give poor care to the Reb soldiers. In fact, the doctor you talked to does little for anyone.

"Now show me your patient, Nurse Bradley—and my name is Doctor Jones." Doctor Williams kept his face still, but his eyes smiled.

Ava laughed as she shook his hand. "Nurse Weatherby, Doctor Jones. I guess we both have new names today."

# Chapter 67

# NEW NAMES

AVA LED DOCTOR JONES QUICKLY TO THE CORNER OF the room. Private Reid once again struggled to sit up. Ava smiled at him before she pointed toward the surgeon standing beside her.

"Private Reid, this is Doctor Jones. I have known him for some time, and he is one of the best surgeons I have ever worked with. He will be doing your surgery today." She squeezed the soldier's hand and smiled again at him.

"I will see you when your surgery is completed, Private. I will pray for a quick and successful procedure." Ava turned to the surgeon beside her.

"Doctor Jones, it is wonderful to see you here. I hope to have the pleasure of working with you again sometime."

Doctor Jones nodded as Ava hurried away. He smiled at his patient. "I just want to check you over before I schedule your surgery." He quickly checked the young private, pushing gently on the skin around his wound.

"Yes, we need to do surgery today. I will get it scheduled." Doctor Jones paused briefly. "Do you have any questions? I know you refused to do this yesterday, so I want to make sure you understand that your leg may possibly need to come off."

"Below the knee Nurse Weatherby said. Don't take any more than you have to." The young soldier gritted his teeth and muttered, "Let's get it done. I just as well get used to being a cripple."

Doctor Jones shook his head. "Just because you are missing part of your leg doesn't make you a cripple. I have fashioned six wooden legs for men since I have been here and most of them walk with just a slight limp. I would be glad to do the same for you…if your leg must come off.

"Let's don't get ahead of ourselves though. I will take your leg only if absolutely necessary." Doctor Jones patted the young man's shoulder.

"I will be back for you in fifteen minutes."

Doctor Jones hurried away, barking orders to nurses and orderlies. The doctor who had refused to do the surgery glared after him.

"That young whippersnapper thinks he can waltz in here and take over. I've a notion to schedule a surgery just to spite him."

The other doctor shook his head. "I don't think he's arrogant. He's an exceptional surgeon, and he's willing to try or do whatever is necessary.

"I've watched him, and he studies all the time. He constantly has books open on his desk long after we all leave. He told me that some of the surgeries we do take too long. He wants to figure out ways to make them shorter and less traumatic for the patients.

"He's good, McCay. I know he's better than me, and he might be as good as you. You and I don't like to take risks for fear they will fail. Doctor Jones will try anything to save a man's life or limb. He is who I would want operating on me."

"Yeah, well I think he's a Reb. I'm going to report him when I finish today. We don't need any more Rebs in this hospital than we have now. I only like *dead* Reb soldiers, so we sure don't need a Reb doctor in here trying to keep them alive."

Doctor Watt looked at his colleague and shook his head. "Then let me do it. I worked all night so I can report to Mother Bickerdyke when I leave here today."

As he walked away, Doctor Watt muttered under his breath, "I'll file a report all right. I'll suggest that Mother Bickerdyke pay this ward a surprise visit.

"McCay is a fine surgeon but he's not an asset here. He only wants to operate on officers, and flesh wounds at that. Maybe she can get him reassigned to some fancy officer who never sees any combat. I doubt we'd miss him."

Chloe was asleep when Ava finally made it to the nurses' quarters. She shook her friend awake and then signaled for her to come out on the balcony.

"Ava!" Chloe whispered excitedly. "When did you get here! I have been so worried about you."

"Just this morning and I am leaving at seven to catch a train headed west. Mother Bickerdyke is sending me to St. Louis and likely beyond." She hugged her friend.

"It is so good to see you. I do have a favor to ask though. A young soldier in the Tenth Ward had surgery today. Private Reid. Doctor Jones didn't take off his leg, but he said the wound will need lots of special treatment if it is going to be saved. He removed quite a bit of tissue.

"Would you check on him? I'm not sure how good the care is in that ward."

Chloe nodded. "Mother Bickerdyke is going to inspect that ward first thing tomorrow, and I am to go with her. I think she is moving me there.

"She didn't tell me there was a problem, but while I was waiting outside her office to give my daily report, I heard a man talking to her. When he left, I saw it was Doctor Watt. He is a surgeon in that ward. Mother Bickerdyke was angry when she followed him out the door.

"She had her 'Somebody is in trouble!' look on her face. I've heard rumors about a doctor up there, and I'm guessing Mother Bickerdyke has too.

"Now enough talk about the hospital—tell me what you have been doing. Oh, Ava. I have missed you so much!"

# LOUISVILLE, KENTUCKY
## SUNDAY, OCTOBER 11, 1863

# Chapter 68

# "I'LL SHARE MY NAME!"

AVA HURRIED TOWARD THE PONTOON BRIDGE THAT spanned the Ohio River between Louisville, Kentucky, and New Albany, Indiana. The trip north and west from Chattanooga to Nashville, Tennessee, had been long with all the stops they made, but the leg up to Louisville at nine hours had been even longer. October weather was often chilly at night, and the hard seats made it difficult to stay warm.

They arrived just before midnight. Even though it was dark, the train station was well lit. It was busy too. Rails stretched in all directions, covered by a variety of trains. Nearly all held passengers and cargo. Several were boarding soldiers as well. Often, there was no room for them inside, so they rode on top of the cars.

The last leg of Ava's trip had been particularly cold. She shivered. However, she stopped complaining to herself as she watched a group of Yankee soldiers climb stiffly down from the top of the train, rubbing their hands against their legs to warm them.

Kentucky was considered a border state and was still part of the Union. However, the citizens of the state were divided. Some of the towns they passed through on their way north were definitely more inclined toward the South. Louisville, on the border of Indiana, was a Union stronghold.

Ava slowed her rush when a large group of children pushed in front of her. Several women were with them. One was young and smiled a lot. The other was older and looked severe. Her dress was black, and her lips barely moved when she spoke.

"You children line up here so I can count you. And don't take those tags off. They tell us who will be taking you. Eight children will remain here, and the rest of you will find homes farther west."

The younger woman smiled as she placed the children in line.

"Your tags tell us who your new mommies and daddies will be! Isn't it exciting that you will soon have a home?"

One little boy glared at her.

"I reckon that ain't quite true. I been on this here train three times now."

The older woman jerked him around and shook him until his teeth nearly rattled.

"If you would behave, Owen, someone would want you. Bad as you are, we'll be lucky to ever find you a home." She shoved him toward a wagon that was waiting to take passengers across the pontoon bridge. The tag on his jacket showed his passage was already paid.

"Go find a seat in that wagon. And make sure you sit on the floor. Maybe you will behave better if you miss breakfast *and* dinner."

Ava stared at the woman in surprise. She guessed the boy was around five or six. She didn't have children of her own and hadn't spent much time around them. Still, she was sure he was younger than seven. As the little boy shuffled toward the wagon, Ava followed him. Gas lights from the train station shined across the water and covered the waiting wagons with a faint glow.

The little boy climbed into the back of a wagon. Benches were positioned along the side, and he climbed onto one of them. Ava pointed at the spot next to the angry boy. "May I sit with you? I am traveling alone, and I know I will be lonesome. Maybe we can keep each other company on this trip."

The little boy looked up at Ava in surprise before he hooded his eyes and shrugged.

"Sit where ya want. Folks say this here is a free country." His voice was barely audible when he added, "I sure ain't seen it though."

Ava smiled and sat down. She opened her bag and removed a large sandwich. Slabs of meat and cheese were stacked between two large slices of thick bread.

"Goodness, this is a huge sandwich. I don't believe I can eat all this myself, and if I don't, it will be wasted." She sighed and broke the sandwich in half. "Well, perhaps someone on this ride will be hungry." The young boy licked his lips but said nothing.

Ava pointed to herself. "I'm sorry. I didn't even introduce myself. My name is Agnes Weatherby. And what is your name?"

"Owen. Just Owen. Don't know my last name."

Ava leaned toward him and whispered, "Agnes Weatherby isn't really my name either, but I'll share my last name with you. The old man to whom it belongs wouldn't mind at all."

Owen stared at Ava. A glimmer of hope passed over his face and Ava put out her hand. "Owen Weatherby, it's nice to meet you." She winked at him. "Shall we be cousins? I don't think I'm old enough to be your mother."

"How about my big sis? I ain't never had a sister."

"Big sister it is. Now, how about half of my sandwich. Family should share, you know."

As Owen reached for the thick sandwich, he glanced up at Ava in amazement.

"I ain't never had this big of a sandwich to myself before. Back in New York, we all ate outa the trash piles—till those folks at the Aid Association took us in.

"Then we ate regular, but we shared everything. I never did get full."

Ava took a bite. She frowned slightly. After a moment, she asked, "So why were you on that train?"

"Some folks call it a Baby Train, but those old gals call their trains of kids Orphan Trains." He frowned at his sandwich and talked around a large bite. "I call it the Lost Kid Train. Kids that get on one of 'em just disappear. They never come back, an' no one knows what happens to 'em.

"That's why I act bad. Then no one wants me, an' they take me back to New York. I don't like it in that Aid House but it's better than just disappearin'. This time when I go back, I'm goin' to run away. I had friends on the street. I was always hungry, but at least I had pals to play with."

Ava stared at Owen. "Surely you didn't sleep outside! How did you stay warm in the winter? I've heard New York gets lots of snow."

"We piled up like dogs. If we slept in piles, it were't so bad—unless you was on the outside. I remember one time. It started to snow. Snowed all night. We was all mighty cold, an' come mornin', Billy was froze stiff. We tried to wake him up, but we couldn't even bend his legs. We took off outa there an' stayed under a bridge the next night with the bums. They always had a big fire.

"Most of 'em left us alone. Some of 'em was mighty scary though."

Ava's eyes opened wide. "And no one took you in?"

Owen looked at Ava sideways. When he saw she was sincere, he shook his head.

"Too many of us. Those old gals at the Aid House said there was thousands of us kids livin' on the streets. That's why they started the Aid Association. 'Course, not all the kids they took in was orphans. Sometimes they took kids whose folks was at work.

"That's what happened to my friend, Paul. Him an' his little sis was on this train. They left Paul in Nashville." A big tear rolled from Owen's eye before he looked away. "See, this train stops in different towns an' they leave kids along the way.

"Paul was the best pal I ever had. His little sis was barely older than a baby. He took care of her while their folks worked. Those ladies over there give his little sis to one family an' Paul to another. They was both a cryin' when little Millie was took away." He looked back at Ava and whispered, "I hate those women. I hate 'em for takin' Paul an' Millie from their folks. An' I hate 'em more for splittin' 'em up. An' that's why I'm runnin' away when I get back to New York."

Ava felt the lump in her chest growing. She cleared her throat.

"But surely part of it is good. You said you get to eat regularly. Besides, you have a bed."

"Naw, we mostly sleep on the floor. There's too many of us an' there ain't enough beds. After they put us down at night, all of us on the floor pile together.

"It ain't too bad though. Those wood floors warm up after a time."

"If it's so crowded, where do you play?"

"Back at the Aid House, we don't play much. They are always tryin' to teach us somethin' that will make us more—more—I don't know what that big word is."

"Adoptable?"

"Yeah, that's it. But I don't want to disappear, so I won't learn. I'm in trouble all the time, so those old gals won't let nobody play with me. They say I'm a bad seed. I don't even know what that means, 'cause I sure ain't no seed."

Ava's heart broke for the little boy. She could feel anger welling up inside her, and she worked to push it down.

"Do you have folks back in New York, Owen?"

"Ma died some time back. She kept company with lotsa men, but none of 'em stayed around. She always sent me outside when her manfriends come to visit, so I never talked to any of 'em.

"She didn't tell me their names either. Ma said she didn't even know their names. I thought that was kinda funny 'cause they was always pleased to see her. I always hoped one of 'em would be my pa, but I guess none was. Ma wouldn't never talk about him.

"I think she knowed some of those fellers though. When she was dyin', she called out men's names. Mostly, she cried out for Macon. I think maybe that was my pa's name. Ma didn't say his name though unless she was feverin'. She never told anybody her last name neither." He looked over at Ava.

"You have folks?"

"No, they are gone too. Now it's just me." She bumped Owen and laughed as she added "And my little brother!"

# Chapter 69

# A BIG SIS

THE TWO AID SOCIETY WOMEN HURRIED SOME OF the children into Ava's wagon. The rest were placed in the wagon behind them. The seats filled quickly, and the younger of the two women climbed onto the wagon seat with the driver. She turned around and smiled at Ava.

"Now if Owen bothers you, just let me know. We can trade places."

"Oh no—we are fine. In fact, we just found out that we have the same last name."

The young woman stared from Ava to Owen. She frowned but before she could speak, Ava added, "I always wanted a little brother or sister. You let him sit right here. We are having a great conversation."

Owen glared at the young woman and refused to talk after that. He finished his sandwich and soon his head began to bob. Ava put her arm around him after he dozed off, and he nestled his head beneath her arm.

The wagon began to slowly roll. As it moved onto the pontoon bridge, the boards beneath them shifted and moved with the water. Ava gripped the bench and tried not to show her fear. She looked down at the water and shivered. The waves were black in the shadows, but the light of the moon covered them with silver shimmers.

"I wonder if these things ever collapse or break," Ava whispered to herself. Then she looked across at the terrified children on the other bench. Some of them had their eyes squeezed tightly shut while others were crying. She leaned toward them and smiled.

"Isn't the water beautiful? Look how it shimmers and shines." She pointed up at the moon and forced herself to laugh. "See, the moon is God's eye. He is watching over us to make sure we arrive safely.

"Hang onto the bench but don't be afraid. Lots of soldiers cross this bridge every day. They check it to make sure it is safe for us all to cross."

A little girl sobbed. Her eyes were terrified. Ava held out her arms and the child stumbled across the rocking wagon floor toward her. Ava pulled her onto her lap and hugged her tightly.

"Shush, sweetheart. Don't be afraid. Close your eyes and pretend you are in a rocking chair. Lean your head back now. I won't let you fall."

Even though she gripped Ava tightly, the little girl slowly began to relax. She looked up with big eyes and whispered, "I don't have a momma or daddy. Do you think I will get one who will hug me like you?"

Ava pushed back the sob in her throat. She kissed the child's grimy cheek and smiled.

"I'm sure you will, but let's say a quiet little prayer right now. We will ask Jesus for a nice mommy and daddy for you."

The little girl squeezed her eyes shut. Ava could only hear parts of the prayer the little girl whispered. She did hear the ending though.

"And please let my new mommy hug and kiss me, and let my new daddy bounce me on his knee. Amen."

The wagon pulled to a stop in front of the New Albany rail station and was quickly surrounded by couples with papers in their hands. A young woman rushed toward them. She gripped her paper tightly. When she saw a number and a name on the little girl sitting on Ava's lap, she scooped her up.

"Annie, oh Annie!" She kissed her as she cried. "I am your new mommy, and this man is your new daddy." The man put his arms around both of them and hugged them tightly as he tried not to cry.

Annie smiled. She waved at Ava as she was whisked away. The young woman with the Aid Society jumped down from her seat and tried to catch the couple, but they were quickly lost in the crowd. One by one, the rest of the children were given to their new parents. Papers were quickly handed out and the new families clustered around the Aid Society women to finish their paperwork.

Finally, only one angry woman was left. She was thin and her dress hung in rags. The shoes she wore were tied to her feet. A whiskey bottle protruded from one pocket. She looked in the wagon and shook her paper as she hollered, "Where is my kid? I ordered a girl to help me with my work. Annie is her name. Where is she? I want that girl I was told I could have free to work for me!" She dropped the paper she was holding and Ava picked it up.

The Aid Society women were confused. The older one whispered something to one of the soldiers and the drunken woman was dragged away.

Ava looked at the paper she held. She shivered when she saw that the woman's number was the same as the one Annie had worn. Then she smiled. "Thank you, Lord," she whispered. "Thank you for putting little Annie with people who will love her and not with that woman."

The pier was busy. All around them, people were arguing and voices were shouting. Just then, a group of soldiers appeared. The wagon drivers were told to step down and the passengers were to line up in front of their wagons.

Ava shook Owen awake and grabbed his hand. She lifted her small bag as she stood and whispered, "Now don't talk." They quickly climbed over the side and were pushed up against the wagon.

"They are probably going to board some soldiers here and want to make sure they can do it safely. Or maybe they are looking for someone," Ava told Owen softly. "I don't know what's going on so be still."

A soldier held a lit lamp in front of each woman. When he reached Ava, he grabbed her arm. He held his lamp closer as he peered from the paper he held in his hand to her face. He wheeled around and hollered, "Is this her? Is this the gal we were told to find?"

People turned to stare, but Ava looked at the soldier calmly. Owen jerked his head up. He glared at the swarming soldiers and pointed his thumb toward Ava.

"This here is my big sis, Agnes Weatherby. I'm Owen an' we're from New York. An' my sis sure ain't never been in trouble with no coppers!"

The soldiers looked confused. There was some discussion, but Ava and Owen were eventually allowed to walk to the train station. They were followed by the Aid Society women. Both women were busy with children, and neither heard the soldier question Ava. They didn't seem to miss Owen either. Ava hurried him to the opposite side of the platform.

Owen whispered, "Are they Johnny Rebs?"

"No, they are Union soldiers. Now hush."

One of the soldiers cursed and slapped his whip against his leg.

"I knew this was a wild goose chase. We have more important things to do than flag down trains lookin' for a gal who is supposed to be a spy. Shoot, we don't even have a picture, just an approximate age." He scribbled on a piece of paper and growled again as he shoved the paper toward the soldier next to him.

"Private Leiker, give this to the conductor. Ask him to send a wire at the next town to Sergeant Nielson in Chattanooga. We didn't find his spy, and I'm not wasting any more time.

"Mount up, men. We have a war to fight."

As the disgruntled passengers hurried to board, Ava and Owen were pushed farther from the train. The conductor paused beside them.

"Be careful climbing up those steps because it's dark in there. Go toward the back and take the first seat you find. Sit down quickly because we will be leaving soon." He frowned and shook his head.

"We are picking up soldiers here in New Albany, so things will be crowded tonight." He paused as he looked at Owen and then added, "There are a couple of privies just south of the tracks and off to the east if you need to make use of them. Be quick though or you won't have a seat."

Ava grabbed Owen's hand.

"Come, Owen. Let's find those privies. Hurry now so we can find a seat on that train."

# Chapter 70

# A CROWDED TRAIN

**S**OLDIERS WERE CROWDING AROUND THE TRAIN CARS when they returned. They parted to allow Ava and Owen to pass through. One offered Ava his hand to help her up the steps. She smiled and thanked him as she hurried Owen into the car. Lamps were lit outside, but inside the railcar, it was extremely dark.

Ava felt her way to some open seats. She sat down and pulled Owen down beside her. Before long, the car was completely full, and some passengers were without seats.

Owen leaned over and whispered, "Was those soldiers lookin' for you? Did you do somethin' bad?"

Ava kissed his cheek as she smiled. "I didn't do anything wrong. I think they were just confused." She added softly, "You are a quick-thinking young man, Owen. I'm glad you are my little brother."

Owen stared up at Ava and slowly grinned. "I reckon all those times I had to run from the coppers paid off. I got mighty good at lyin'."

Ava paused and her face paled slightly as she hugged the little boy.

"Owen, lying is something we really shouldn't do. We'll talk more about that later."

Owen wiggled in his seat. He finally quit fidgeting and asked, "Where are we headed next?" He wiggled again as he complained, "This here seat is hard."

"I'm not sure how many towns we'll go through, but St. Louis is our last stop. It is nearly three hundred miles from here though, and that is a lot of hours.

"Now go to sleep and we will eat when you wake." Ava covered both of them with her light blanket.

Owen was quickly asleep. His little face was innocent and relaxed. Ava pulled him closer.

"I wish I had a warm quilt to cover us. Of course, that would be too heavy to carry." She looked down at the small boy beside her and whispered softly, "I don't know how I am going to take care of you as a single woman, Owen, but you are getting off this train with me."

An angry man stopped beside Ava. He grabbed her arm and tried to pull her up.

"You are in my seat. Get up or I'll throw you out."

A derringer appeared in Ava's hand, and she pressed it against the man's chest.

"You are mistaken, sir. This is my seat. Now unloose my arm or I *will* pull this trigger."

"You wouldn't dare shoot me! I am an important man in these parts," the man stated loudly. "Up with you now!"

"Sir, I don't know who you are, but in three seconds I am going to scream and then shoot. No one will fault me for protecting my honor."

"You wouldn't dare!"

"One—"

"I say, move that gun or I'll—"

"Two."

The man backed away and Ava faced forward in her seat. Owen's voice was quiet when he asked, "Did ya ever shoot anybody, Agnes? You shore backed that feller down an' you wasn't even scared!"

"Shush, Owen. It is late and folks want to sleep. I know you have already had a long ride, but we are on the last leg now. Take a little nap and we will have an apple when you awake."

Someone bumped Ava's arm, and she peered up through the dark.

"Begging your pardon, ma'am, but would that seat next to your son be taken?"

Ava felt through the dark and found an empty seat. She stood and slipped past Owen to sit down.

"Take that outside seat. I'm sure you will be less crowded."

The soldier sat down with a sigh and laid his head back. Owen was already sleeping, and Ava put her arm around him. She was tired but her mind was racing in many different directions.

"Lord," she whispered into the night, "please guide me. You put Owen in my care, and I am afraid. He is a wonderful little boy, but I don't know how to care for a child and be a nurse too." She shifted in her seat and finally fell asleep.

The soldier opened his eyes when he heard the woman near him whispering. He listened and shook his head. *This war has displaced so many folks. I wonder what her story is.*

# Chapter 71

# A FRIENDLY MAJOR

AVA OPENED HER EYES WHEN SHE HEARD THE SOLDIER ask, "So where are you and your ma from, Owen?"

She sat up and smoothed her hair as she listened to the soldier.

Owen shook his head. "She ain't my ma. She's my big sis. We're from New York."

Ava blushed and patted Owen's leg as she smiled at him.

"Don't bother the nice soldier, Owen. He probably wants to get some sleep since he has a seat."

The soldier laughed and nodded.

"I should but there is too much noise on these trains. I'm used to sleeping lightly and that isn't paying off for me now." He pointed toward himself and added, "I'm Major John Reynolds, lately from St. Louis."

Ava smiled and put out her hand. "Agnes Weatherby. I see you have met Owen."

The major laughed again and nodded. "I sure have. Why, I reckon we've been talking for the better part of an hour. Your little brother wants to be a soldier.

"Where are you and Owen headed, Miss Weatherby? He said you'd been on this train a long time and he didn't know when you were getting off."

"To St. Louis. I'm a nurse and I will likely be posted at the hospital there unless some military unit needs a field nurse." Ava smiled and ruffled Owen's hair as she added, "And will allow a little brother to tag along."

Major Reynolds winked at Owen. His eyes were twinkling when he said, "Owen, I am guessing just about any officer would make room for you and your pretty sister—even if she wasn't a nurse."

Ava blushed and Owen frowned.

"I would need a job though," Owen commented. "I can't just be sittin' around all day." His eyes lit up and he added, "Say, maybe I can learn to play one of those drums some of the fellers carry. I've seen boys beat on 'em, so I reckon I could learn."

Major Reynolds nodded somberly. "Why I think that would be just fine. Of course, I could use a fellow to deliver messages for me too. Important messages that I can't trust just anyone with. And fill canteens too. We never have enough canteens filled."

Owen's eyes shone with excitement. His smile slowly faded as he looked up at Ava.

"I don't have a uniform though. A feller should have a uniform if he is goin' to be a soldier."

Major Reynolds laughed and Ava smiled.

"We'll see, Owen. Let's don't get too far ahead of ourselves." She glanced toward Major Reynolds.

"Do you have family close, Major?"

"Not too far away. My family is from around Hardscrabble, Illinois, but folks are calling that town Unionville now. It is north of Peoria. We have a farm there." He grinned as he added, "A hardscrabble one.

"I always wanted to be a cowboy, so I left home when I was fifteen and headed west. I was riding for a ranch down in Texas when this war broke out.

"Most of the fellows I was riding with enlisted with the South, but I headed back home and enlisted as a Yankee." His brow furrowed and he added softly, "I hope I never have to fight any of those cowboys. I made some good friends down there, and they were mighty handy with their pistols. Rifles too." Major Reynolds shook his head slightly and added, "I don't know what those ranchers will do with all their young men gone. I don't think there are enough riders left in that country to handle all the cattle down there.

"Texas provided beef for the Southern Army but that ended when us Yanks put up blockades." Major Reynolds frowned again. "Don't know what will happen to all those cattle either with no market. I reckon there is a glut of beef on the hoof in that country by now."

"So is your family still in Illinois, Major?"

"My ma and pop are. My little sis signed on to be a nurse when the war started, and she is hoping to get transferred to St. Louis.

"I tried to tell her that I wouldn't be there much, but Jessie doesn't listen to me." He frowned and muttered, "Jessie doesn't listen to anyone unless they condone what she wants to do."

"Ah, the blessings and difficulties of being an older brother!" Ava laughed and her eyes sparkled.

Major Reynolds grinned and nodded. "How about you and Owen? Are your folks in New York?"

"Our folks are gone. Now it is just the two of us." Ava smiled at Owen. "We were separated for a time, but from now on, he is going to be stuck to me like glue."

"Where all have you shared your nursing skills, Agnes? Owen told me you were the best nurse around." Major Reynolds' face was somber, but his eyes were laughing as he spoke.

"Not the best but I have traveled some. I started out in St. Louis and then was sent to Chattanooga for a time. From there, I was a field nurse at Chickamauga during that battle. Now, I am being sent west again."

Major Reynolds' face showed his confusion. "You never did any nursing in New York? Most nurses are put to work where they volunteer."

Ava's face paled slightly, and she looked away before she answered.

"I was staying with my granny in Missouri when this war broke out. It changed everything for me." She patted Owen's head and smiled. "For both of us. I'm glad we were able to find each other in all the chaos this war has caused."

Major Reynolds nodded.

"That border between Kansas and Missouri is a mess. I was posted in Lawrence when it was sacked. It seemed to me that was the beginning of all the conflict out there."

Ava frowned. "No, the border conflict started long before then. And the destruction of Lawrence was payback for the ongoing brutality of the Unionist raiders, especially the Red Legs."

Major Reynolds cocked an eyebrow as he looked at Ava.

"That almost sounded like a Reb talking."

Ava looked at the major cooly and shrugged her shoulders.

"In the beginning, I did lean more one direction because of what happened to my family. However, after working with both sides, I have seen good and bad soldiers in both colors of uniforms. In the end though, most soldiers are just men fighting for their homes or what they believe in."

"You worked in a Reb hospital?"

"In a field hospital in Chickamauga, Georgia. When the Rebs took over the Union field hospital at Crawfish Spring, I stayed. Medical personnel were all told to evacuate, and most did. However, there were severely wounded men there from both sides. I stayed to do what I could.

"A wounded Reb surgeon who had been a prisoner stepped up and finished surgeries that had been started but not completed.

"We treated both sides there. Of course, that is common in battle situations." Tears tried to fill Ava's eyes, and she looked away. "So many young men killed and maimed," she whispered. "It was terrible."

"Is that why you left?"

Ava frowned and shook her head. "No, I take my orders the same as you.

"After that hospital was burned by the Rebs, I attended the wounded soldiers who were left. Then I was sent back north to Chattanooga… and I left because Mother Bickerdyke ordered me to go west." She faced forward in her seat and didn't talk any more.

Owen had listened to all that was said. His eyes moved from one adult to the other and he frowned. *Since Agnes won't talk to this here soldier, I reckon I won't either.* He folded his little arms across his chest, glared at the major, and refused to talk any more.

Major Reynolds leaned back in his seat. *I think this gal would be the perfect spy. A little truth and some lies all tangled up together. Or maybe it's all the truth, just not the complete truth.* He stole a glance at the young woman from the side of his eye. Her eyes were closed but he could see the dampness of a tear on her cheek.

*She is passionate about treating the wounded though. Gutsy too. I think I will see if Colonel Bonneville will allow her to be our regimental nurse. We could use a nurse with field hospital training. Besides, I could keep an eye on her just in case she is working with the enemy.*

# Chapter 72

# A HAPPY LITTLE BOY

OWEN JUMPED FROM HIS SEAT AND PRESSED HIS FACE against the window.

"Holy smokes—look at all that water!" He looked back at Ava and asked hopefully, "Think we can go swimmin' in that water sometime?"

Ava laughed and shook her head. "I don't think so. That river is much too dangerous." She was quiet as she looked out the window. She smiled at Owen and asked, "Do you like to swim, Owen?"

"Ain't never been but I heard tell of it. I'd sure like to learn sometime. Didn't have much water back at the Aid House, an' sure not enough to swim in." Owen watched intensely as the train approached the river. He was quiet when he sat down.

"Agnes? Are you goin' to keep me or are you sendin' me on with those other kids?"

Ava put her arms around the little boy and tears filled her eyes as she kissed his cheek.

"I am going to keep you forever, Owen. Just know I don't make much money so we will likely be poor. My hours will be long too so I might not see much of you during the day."

Owen's smile was so big it almost broke his face. He jumped at Ava and hugged her tightly.

"I sure am glad you found me on this here train, Sis. I reckon I won't run away no more now."

Major Reynolds stirred in his seat and sat up. Owen bounced from leg to leg in front of him. His eyes were shining, and his smile was huge.

"Did you hear that, Major Johnny? Sis is goin' to keep me forever! I don't have to live in that ol' Aid House no more!"

Major Reynolds glanced at Ava before he replied. Her face paled but she met his eyes.

He leaned forward and shook Owen's hand.

"Owen Weatherby, I reckon you'll make a fine soldier, and I'm mighty pleased that you and your sister came west on this train."

The train jerked to a stop and both Ava and Owen nearly tumbled out of their seats. Major Reynolds caught Owen and gave Ava his hand to help her up.

He stood and smiled down at the two of them.

"Miss Weatherby—Owen. It was nice to meet both of you. I hope to see more of you during your stay in St. Louis." He turned abruptly and loped down the steps as soon as the door opened. He was talking to several men when Ava and Owen finally made it to the platform.

Ava gripped Owen's hand and followed the soldiers to the dock. Her ticket showed passage across the river, but she had no ticket for Owen. "Maybe he'll be able to slip aboard," she whispered as she straightened her shoulders.

Major Reynolds appeared beside them. He lifted Owen easily and offered Ava his arm. He took the ticket from her hand and guided her toward the ferry. She murmured a thank you before she stepped quickly onto the ferry. Major Reynolds nodded at the man who was in charge.

"Ferris, these folks are traveling with me. Miss Weatherby is a new nurse at Benton Barracks and Owen here is her little brother." He handed the old man Ava's ticket and his pass.

The old man looked from Ava to the major and snorted. He muttered something about officers expecting privileges but finally stepped aside.

"You hang on, lady, and keep that kid away from the edge. We don't stop to fish no one out of the water. And, Major, you'd better be carryin' that boy when you get off or I'll tell my boss you sneaked him on."

Major Reynolds put Owen on his shoulders and walked around with the little boy until the ferry docked. He helped Ava ashore before he set Owen down carefully. He grinned and winked at her before he spoke.

"Miss Weatherby, I hope to see you soon." He bowed and was quickly gone.

"Think we'll ever see Major Johnny again, Sis?"

"I don't think so, Owen. Benton Barracks Hospital is huge and so is St. Louis. Now take hold of my hand. If I lose you here, I may never see you again either."

Ava hurried Owen toward a waiting buggy. When she saw who was driving, she smiled.

"Good afternoon, Uncle Huck! Would you be so kind as to give us a ride to the hospital?"

Huck Layton grinned and nodded. He jumped down to lift Ava and Owen into his buggy.

"An' who is this fine-lookin' feller ya have with ya?" He cocked his head as he studied Owen. "I reckon ya be 'bout fifteen or so, ain't ya?"

Owen snorted and shook his head.

"I'm six an' this here is my sister. We be Agnes an' Owen Weatherby."

Oscar nodded solemnly. "Weatherby, huh. I know a feller with that last name. Stump we called 'im 'cause he only has one arm."

Owen looked up at Ava.

"It that the feller whose name we took?"

Ava blushed when Huck grinned at her, but she nodded her head.

"Yes, that's the one." She turned to Huck. "I need to check in at the hospital, but I'd like to feed Owen first. He has barely eaten since

Louisville, Kentucky. Do you have any suggestions of something quick and not too pricey?"

Huck nodded and wheeled the wagon around.

"I know jist the place. I have a little time, so I'll take ya myself." Huck turned off the crowded, main throughfare and wound through a series of crooked streets lined with houses of all sizes. He stopped in front of a neat little cottage with a picket fence and flowers in the yard. A dog barked as it ran out to greet them. Owen started to jump down but Ava grabbed his arm.

"No, Owen—we don't know if that dog—"

Huck chuckled. "That there dog be as harmless as me.

"Git on down, Boy, an' I'll help yore sis. Ya play out here fer a time an' ya come on in when yore ready to eat." Huck waved toward a creek in the back of the house.

"Ya might want to stay outa that there creek though. She's a little muddy an' I doubt yore sis wants ya to git yore shoes all dirty."

Ava frowned and started to speak but Huck squeezed her hand as Own rushed off. He whispered, "Let the boy play. 'Sides, ya need to tell me why ya are usin' a different name. And where'd that little feller come from?"

Huck led Ava up the sidewalk and knocked on the door. A pretty older woman with lots of white hair in a bun pulled it open quickly with a smile on her face. Her smile remained but her face showed surprise as she looked from Ava to Huck.

"Lucy, this here is Ella Bradley, but Agnes Weatherby be the name she is usin' now. She brought a young feller with her on the train from Louisville over in Kentucky, an' they both be mighty hungry. Agnes, this is Mrs. Lucy Sneed." He winked at Lucy and added, "I was hopin' ya might have some extra vittles, Lucy."

Lucy pulled the door open.

"Of course! Friends of Huck's are friends of mine. Now you wash up over there and then sit down in this chair. I was expecting Huck for supper, and I always make extra for him to take home." She smiled at Huck and blushed prettily.

Lucy soon had food on the table. Ava looked nervously toward the door and started to get up, but Huck pushed her down.

"Ya go ahead an' eat. I'll git that boy."

Lucy filled Ava's plate. She chattered about the weather and the town as Ava ate. She finally sat down across from her and asked quietly, "Who are you hiding from, Ella?"

Ava's breath caught in her throat. She slowly let it out and began to talk. She told Lucy about the Red Legs who had burned her home and killed her family as well as meeting Private Weatherby. She even told Lucy her real name.

"I met Owen in Louisville. He was on an Orphan Train. The older woman who was with him made it clear she didn't see him as adoptable. I did so I took him." Ava's voice was soft when she added, "Those two women never looked for him the entire trip. I don't know if they were just busy with all the other children or if they assumed I would bring him back. Regardless, I never spoke to them again. Now here we are, and we are both Weatherbys." Ava laughed and added, "I am sure Mr. Weatherby won't mind me using his name though."

Lucy laughed and nodded.

"Did Huck tell you that I too grew up in Missouri?"

Ava's eyes were wide, and she shook her head. "No, he didn't, but I didn't tell Huck much either, not since I arrived this time anyway. I didn't want to talk about those things in front of Owen.

"I was sent out here because of Sergeant Nielson's attempts on my life. Mother Bickerdyke and Mr. Weatherby were both concerned my presence would put the soldiers I'm to care for in jeopardy."

Lucy studied Ava's face and then laughed.

"You must have been a favorite nurse if those soldiers were willing to give their lives for you."

Ava blushed but didn't respond. Just then, Huck appeared with a very dirty Owen in tow.

"Found 'im down in the creek, knee-deep in the mud."

Ava rose and grabbed Owen's hand. She led him outside.

"Take off your clothes, Owen. I want to bathe you before you eat." She whispered, "We don't want to get mud all over Lucy's floor. We are guests in her house."

Owen slowly took off his clothes. He held up his clean shoes.

"These ain't muddy. I took 'em off 'fore I went in." His looked up at Ava and stated softly, "That there was the first time I ever played in clean mud."

Ava almost cried. She hugged the nearly naked little boy and then wiped the tears and mud off her face.

"Owen," she whispered, "I'm so glad you are my little brother. Now let's give you a quick bath so you can eat."

# Chapter 73

# A NEW ROUTINE

**H**UCK OFFERED TO TAKE AVA'S LETTER FROM MOTHER Bickerdyke to Nurse Parsons. "I'll tell her y'all is plumb worn out an' I bedded ya down at a friend's house. I'll have ya at the hospital bright an early tomorrow.

"Now no arguin' with me, gal. Ya ain't much good when ya cain't think." He nodded to where Owen was digging in a corner of the yard. "Besides, that there feller needs some 'man time' an' ya need to be thinkin' on that. In fact, I jist might take 'im fishin'. I been meanin' to go an' jist ain't took the time. Won't be many nice days left 'fore winter sets in." He grinned at her and asked casually, "How's that captain you was sweet on—the big, grumpy one?"

Ava's face blushed a deep red and she unconsciously touched Noble's ring that hung from a cord inside her dress.

"I don't really know. I haven't seen much of him since I left Chattanooga the first time. I don't know where he is posted, and he doesn't know where I am either."

Huck nodded and rubbed his chin. "This here war ain't made courtin' easy, has it? Ya worry cause you's afeared fer his life an' ya don't know where he is to boot.

"Let me do some lookin' into that. He mighta left word at the Barracks in case ya showed up. I'll see if Nurse Parson's knows anything when I speak to 'er.

"Now ya let Lucy show ya to a nice, clean bed. Things'll fer shore look better after a good sleep."

"You will keep an eye on Owen?"

"Yep. I'll take 'im fishin' soon as I get back from the hospital. Now ya go on to bed. Let Lucy an' me take over fer a time."

Huck waited until Lucy came outside. He pecked her cheek and winked at her. Lucy laughed and turned pink.

"You are a scallywag, Huck Layton, but I sure like it when you come around."

"I'm headed up to the hospital. I'll be back shortly to take that feller what's diggin' fer worms out to scout some fishin' holes. Then you an' me cin have us a talk 'bout what to do with these two kids."

Lucy nodded. "Did you tell Ava that her Mr. Weatherby is my brother?"

"Nope. I figgered you could be the one to tell that—when it's time."

Huck strolled outside.

"Hey, kid. I'm a headed down to the Barracks to talk to yore sis' boss. Now ya make sure ya dig where Lucy tells ya.

"I'll be back in a shake an' we'll go check out some water holes."

Owen stood and watched Huck closely.

"Like fishin' water holes?"

"Yessir, that is exactly what I mean. Now be good fer Lucy an' I'll be back. Be quiet though. Yore big sis is takin' herself a nap."

Owen walked all around the yard. He checked every inch of the fence for holes before he opened the gate. He and the dog began to run circles around the fenced yard. Their circles were bigger and bigger until they were once again by the creek. He sat down and stared at the wonderful mud with his arm looped over the dog's neck.

"I think I'm a goin' to like bein' Sis' kid brother. An' I'll just make like Huck an' Lucy are my grandfolks."

# A TERRIBLE ACCUSATION

AVA SMILED. OWEN NEEDED A SECOND BATH BEFORE he went to bed. He wouldn't stop talking about the fishing holes Grampy Huck had shown him. His blue eyes were shining, and he talked all through supper. When Ava finally calmed him enough to go to bed, he was tired but still smiling.

"Sis, I had the best time. I'm mighty glad you found me. Grampy Huck—he told me I could call him that—why we talked pertineer all afternoon. He knows *everything*. An' he answered all my questions without yellin' at me."

Ava laughed softly. She had been able to take a bath while Huck and Owen were gone. She felt refreshed and relaxed, especially since Lucy offered to watch Owen during the day while she worked.

Owen was delighted. He was convinced that Grampy Huck and he would go fishing every day.

Ava had just finished washing the supper dishes and was wiping off the table when someone pounded on the door. Lucy jumped and Ava gripped the towel she was holding as she turned to face the door.

Huck jerked the door open. Before he could speak, four soldiers pushed their way in. Three kept their guns aimed at Huck and Lucy while the fourth approached Ava. He unrolled a piece of paper and read the words printed there.

"Aveline Olivia Bowman—you are under arrest for treason, collaborating with the enemy, and the attempted murder of an officer in the Army of the United States of America."

As the three civilians stared at him, he added in a loud, monotone voice, "There will be a hearing tomorrow, October 13 at one o'clock. If a trial is deemed necessary, your trial will be Wednesday morning, October 14. Sentencing will be announced at that time.

"You will be incarcerated in the Benton Barracks Prison until you are sentenced or released." He handed his paper to one of the other soldiers and pulled out a pair of handcuffs.

"You will come with us now." He jerked Ava around and snapped on the cuffs. When Huck tried to speak, one of the soldiers smashed him over the head with a gun. The old man staggered and almost fell down. He pulled himself to his feet and gripped the back of a chair to keep himself upright.

The first soldier paused and growled, "We have permission to shoot anyone who tries to stop us." He almost threw Ava out the door when he shoved her.

"Take care of Owen!" Ava screamed as they dragged her to the wagon.

Lucy rushed to Huck.

"You are bleeding!" She grabbed a clean rag from a cupboard and washed his head before she bound it.

Huck looked at her with bleak eyes.

"I need to get hold of Captain Headrick. I am goin' to hitch a horse to yore buggy an' send a wire. The express office is closed but Dixon will open fer me." He tried to walk and almost fell down. Lucy guided him back to a chair.

"Let me put a little whiskey in your coffee. That might help clear your head. Now sit in that chair until you get your senses." She paused and added softly, "I will write up a message for you to wire to Stump and another for Mother Bickerdyke in Chattanooga. And you send Stump's message exactly as I write it—don't let Dixon change any of the words."

Evie Smith Tillman paused in front of her door and stared at the noise coming from Lucy Sneed's house. She recognized the woman who was being dragged by the soldiers as Ella Bradley, the nurse who had written her the letter about Will. She rushed into the house where her husband was already asleep.

"Will! Will! Wake up! I went outside to use the privy and that nurse who wrote to me about you—Miss Bradley. She was being dragged from Lucy Sneed's house by soldiers. I think they arrested her!"

Will Tillman sat up and swung his good leg to the floor. He rubbed his eyes and ran a hand through his wild hair as he frowned.

"Hand me my wooden leg. I'll saddle Nel and ride down to the Barracks. We'd better find out what's going on." His frown grew deeper and he added, "Maybe you should ride with me. You can talk to Nurse Parsons. If Nurse Bradley is here, it is probably to work at the hospital." Five minutes later, they were riding south toward the Barracks.

# Chapter 75

# GETTING THE WORD OUT

**H**UCK SHOVED A PIECE OF PAPER TOWARD THE telegraph operator. Dixon glared at him as he rubbed his eyes.

"This had better be dang important, Huck. You know I don't like being dragged out of bed for just any reason."

"These here messages be important, an' I want 'em sent pronto. The first two go to the College Hill Hospital in Chattanooga, an' the third one goes to Captain Headrick at Columbia, Missouri."

Dixon peered at the messages. He cocked an eyebrow as he read the one for Pat Malarky. His face showed his irritation.

"I'll send them, but the only reason I'm sending this one to Malarky is because I'm already up." He was mumbling under his breath as he tapped out the first message. He studied Lucy's message again and looked up at Huck with irritation.

"Huck, what in Sam Hill is this? Can't Lucy ask someone here how to treat that horse?"

"You know Lucy, Dix. When she sets her mind to somethin', there ain't no changin' it. Now she thinks Malarky is the onliest feller what cin treat her horses so who am I to git in the middle? Jist send the message like she wrote it."

Dixon tapped out the message and shook his head as he handed the piece of paper back to Huck. "You ever going to marry that widow? You're over there just about every evening. It would save you both time and money if you'd just get hitched."

Huck grinned and shoved the messages into his pocket. "I'm workin' on it but Lucy's a thinkin' woman. There ain't no rushin' 'er."

Dixon snorted. He looked closer at his friend as he frowned.

"Say, what happened to your head? Lucy whack you with a frying pan for trying to get too friendly?"

Huck touched the bandage on his head and shrugged.

"You'll know by mornin', but ya ain't gonna hear it from me." He put out his hand. "Thanks, Dix. I appreciate ya gittin' these off so fast."

The old man put his hand to his head and was muttering as he hobbled out the door. "That durn soldier. I'd like to whack him one like he did me. Mebbie I'll git the chance someday. Ya jist never know." As he climbed into his buggy, a horse raced by him up the dark street. Huck followed it slowly.

"That looked like Evie and Will. I wonder what they be doin' out so late."

He chuckled as he thought about the message Lucy had written her brother.


**Mr. Pat Malarky—that filly you sent me has weak back quarters. I am keeping her in a small stall but she's not doing well and is going down. What can I do to help her recover? I fear my only other option is to shoot her. Please respond quickly. Lucy Sneed**

# Chapter 76

# AN URGENT WIRE FOR CAPTAIN HEADRICK

**C**APTAIN NOBLE HEADRICK STARED AT THE WIRE Lieutenant Lampkin handed him. He frowned and read it again.

"This is all you received?"

"Yep. Come in last night. You want I should go to St. Louis? I cin take that report ya filed in Chattanooga 'fore ya left. Ya said ya made several copies. That might clear up some of this. I'm a guessin' it has to do with Nurse Sweet shootin' that Red Leg down to Chickamauga."

Captain Headrick cursed and paced the floor.

"They should have had my first report weeks ago and the addendum to it last week. But then, who knows if either was filed or if any of the information in them was sent on.

"Yes, you get ready to leave now. I'm going to send two copies with you. Give one to Nurse Parsons to hold for you and give the other to Colonel Bonneville." He scribbled a note and signed it. "Present this note when you arrive. It should help to arrange a meeting with the colonel." He handed Lampkin a leather package.

"Both copies are in there. Make sure you give Nurse Parson's her copy *before* you meet with the general. Ask her to hang onto it and not to give it up for any reason. I want her to have that copy in case this goes even further but pick it up before you return." He gripped Lampkin's hand and finally smiled.

"I am going to send Corporal Blake with you. He was with Nielson when they stopped at the Bowman place. He can testify that three of Nielson's men camp left camp the night her family was killed.

"Take six horses for the two of you and trade off about every ten miles. This needs to be a fast trip so you can't afford to wear out your horses before you get there.

"And ride carefully. We are around a hundred miles from St. Louis and there are Rebs everywhere—and some of them will be in our uniforms." Captain Headrick called to a young private standing guard outside his tent.

"Private Handley! Find Corporal Blake. Tell him I want to see him immediately. Then, get down to where the horses are picketed and saddle three mounts for Blake. You know which ones he likes to ride."

He turned back to Lampkin and gave him a quick salute.

"You are dismissed, Lieutenant."

Lampkin saluted. He was running as he shoved the leather packet inside his shirt. When he reached the area where the horses were picketed, he grabbed a private and pointed at two long-legged bays.

"Wrangle those two an' give me Deuce as well. I jist might leave 'im in St. Louis since Nurse Sweet is there. An' make it quick."

Private Handley arrived as Lampkin was saddling his horse and selected the three mounts he wanted for Corporal Blake. The two soldiers led the horses up the hill to Captain Headrick's tent.

Blake met them there. He shoved a packet of food in his saddlebag and handed a second to Lampkin. He grinned at the Lieutenant.

"I ain't as good as you in the brush so lead off. And don't get us lost!"

Lampkin flashed a grin, and the two men raced out of camp.

# Chapter 77

# A FAST TRIP

LIEUTENANT LAMPKIN AND CORPORAL BLAKE RODE into Benton Barracks at eleven in the morning on October 13. Both men were worn down and their horses were tired as well. They stopped at the livery and handed them over to the soldier in charge. Lieutenant Lampkin returned the salute the young soldier gave him.

"We rode all night so make sure ya rub 'em down an' give 'em some good feed. Grain too—not jist hay. Water 'em first." He started to turn away but stopped and looked back.

"Can ya tell me where to find Colonel Bonneville?"

"He is in his quarters, sir, but he doesn't like to be bothered before he has chow."

Lampkin nodded before he turned away. He led the way quickly to the hospital and knocked on Nurse Parson's door.

A woman's loud voice growled, "I'm busy. You will need to come back later."

"Nurse Parsons, I have a report fer ya from Captain Headrick."

Emily Parsons jerked the door open and glared at the two men in front of her. Corporal Blake almost stepped back, but Lampkin grinned.

"How do, Emmy. Yore shore lookin' fine this mornin'!"

Nurse Parsons was a no-nonsense woman. She had never married and was old enough to be legitimately considered an old maid. She was all business both in and out of the hospital, and none of the soldiers teased her—except Lieutenant Lampkin.

Nurse Parsons' serious face cracked into a grin, and she hugged Lampkin.

"Come in, Noah. If you had introduced yourself, I wouldn't have been so abrupt." She led the way through her crowded office to a small desk. She pointed at two chairs as she sat down.

"I hope this visit has to do with Nurse Bradley's hearing today. I am very concerned about the direction it seems to be going."

Lampkin nodded and presented Nurse Parsons with Captain Headrick's report.

"Cap wanted ya to have this copy of his report. He said fer me to bring it back when this deal is all over." Lieutenant Lampkin's smile was more of a grimace when he added, "I think the captain believes this here trumped-up deal is a gonna blow up. Maybe ya cin help straighten things out if ya know all the facts."

Nurse Parsons' eyes narrowed as she unfolded the papers. She quickly glanced through Captain Headrick's neat and precise account of past events that could be used against Nurse Bradley.

"Bowman? Her name is Bowman?"

"Before 'er granny died, she told Nurse Sweet to use 'er family name which was Bradley. She was afraid the Red Legs who attacked 'em would try to get 'er granddaughter. The old gal was right too."

Nurse Parsons cocked an eyebrow. She stared at Lampkin in surprise as she pointed toward the paper she was reading.

"Nurse Sweet?"

Lampkin grinned and shrugged.

"The soldiers she treated all loved 'er. Not sure if the Yankees or the Reb soldiers started callin' 'er that, but it stuck. There was quite a few of our boys there when Nurse Sweet shot that Red Leg. I wish some of those fellers was here now. She could use their help."

Emily Parsons' eyebrows raised again but her eyes twinkled.

"I think the brass may have dabbled a little too deeply in this matter. Nurse Bowman has some unlikely friends, and they aren't shy about helping her." She stood and put out her hand to Lieutenant Lampkin.

"Thank you for bringing this by. I will read as much as I can. If you'll give me a minute, I'll send a message with you that I want wired to General Merrill in Chattanooga."

She hugged Lampkin and added, "Come again when you have time to drink a little coffee with me." She pushed him toward the door. Blake was following quietly, and Nurse Parsons glared at him.

"And you, whoever you are—leave this hospital. Don't come back unless you have something to contribute."

# Chapter 78

# A MEETING WITH THE COLONEL

LAMPKIN AND BLAKE HURRIED TO THE EXPRESS office. They waited until Nurse Parsons' wire was sent before they turned toward Colonel Bonneville's private quarters. Lampkin knocked loudly until an aid answered.

"Lieutenant Lampkin with a message for Colonel Bonneville from Captain Headrick, 2nd Missouri Volunteer Cavalry."

The aid put out his hand. "Give it to me and I will make sure Colonel Bonneville receives it."

Lieutenant Lampkin shoved the note in his pocket and gave the soldier a hard look.

"I reckon not. I rode all night to deliver this here message. I was told to give it to Colonel Bonneville directly an' that's what I intend to do."

The soldier glared at Lampkin. His frown became bigger when Lampkin grinned. He finally disappeared but was back quickly.

"Colonel Bonneville said he is not familiar with Captain Headrick, and the 2nd Missouri Volunteer Cavalry is not posted here." He tried to close the door, but Lampkin put his boot inside the doorjamb.

"Mebbie he's familiar with General Merrill. Now, this here message is urgent so…" Lieutenant Lampkin's voice trailed off when Colonel Bonneville appeared in the doorway. He withdrew his boot quietly and both men saluted the colonel smartly.

Colonel Bonneville saluted back and nodded at his assistant.

"I'll take it from here, Corporal." His eyes moved to the soldiers in front of him. "State your business, gentlemen."

Lieutenant Lampkin handed Colonel Bonneville the note from Captain Headrick. Both men were quiet as they waited for the colonel to read the message.

Colonel Bonneville looked up after reading Captain Headrick's letter. "You have some reports for me?"

"Yes, sir. Captain Headrick already filed 'em, but since that was in Chattanooga, he sent copies of ever'thing in case ya ain't seen 'em yet."

Colonel Bonneville flipped through the reports. He stopped several times and reread passages. His eyes were hard when he looked up.

"There are some serious breaches of conduct in here. I hope you have witnesses who can back up this nurse's innocence."

"We have some an' are workin' on more."

Bonneville studied the faces of both men. His years of military service had taken him all over the American West, from mapping travel routes to fighting Indians. In addition, he had led men in both the Mexican American War and now the Civil War. He was known for his low tolerance for slackers, and he judged men quickly. Colonel Bonneville liked the looks of the men in front of him.

"I would like to study these reports more thoroughly before the hearing. You will be staying?"

"Yes, sir. An' fer the trial as well if the charges ain't dismissed."

The colonel nodded and saluted the men before he turned away.

"I'll see you this afternoon then."

As they turned away, Corporal Blake asked, "Now where?"

"Let's go see Nurse Sweet. We'll make shore she's bein' treated right."

# Chapter 79

# SO MANY NUNS!

WHEN LAMPKIN AND BLAKE OPENED THE DOOR TO the jail, they looked around in surprise. The waiting area was full of nuns, and they could hear a woman's voice in the cell area.

"And I am telling you, sir, that cell is filthy. No one should be expected to spend time in there let alone a woman. And how is she supposed to relieve herself?

"I demand that you open these doors immediately. I will escort her to the privy and help her to tidy herself. My sisters will clean this cell while we are gone."

A man started to speak, and the woman interrupted him.

"Open this cell now, soldier. This woman is innocent until proven guilty. Now open it or give me your keys."

"Sister, I cain't. I have my orders."

"Then give me your keys. I only take orders from the Lord." A jangling of keys was followed by the creaking of the cell door.

Lampkin and Blake were grinning when a tall nun appeared with Ava in tow.

Ava looked at the two soldiers in surprise and their smiles became bigger.

"Cap sent us. We already met with the colonel an' Nurse Parsons. Cap told us to stay till this here deal is settled, an' Blake is ready to testify." The two men backed up and took off their hats. They both nodded at the nun as she hurried Ava by.

The noise in the cell became louder as the swarm of nuns moved in with buckets, brooms, and scrub brushes. Some were quickly out again with a filthy mattress that they threw on a burn pile. One nun set it on fire while the rest hurried back inside.

The soldier who was in charge of the jail fled as he shouted, "I'll have y'all arrested! Ya cain't come in an' take over. I'm in charge here an' I ain't give ya permission!"

One of the nuns stopped in front of Lampkin and Blake. She smiled as she looked from one to the other and asked, "Would you gentlemen be so kind as to find some food for Miss Bowman? She has had nothing to eat today. And some cold water as well." She smiled again and darted away, assuming her request would be fulfilled.

The men stepped outside. Lampkin stopped by the nun who was burning trash.

"Thank you, Sister. We are Miss Ava's friends, an' we shore appreciate ya takin' over."

"Oh, this was all Sister Marie Christi. She is fearless. We just follow her orders." The nun smiled at them and quickly turned away to push some loose straw into the fire.

The men sauntered down to the mess hall. They grabbed three plates and waited for them to be filled. They ate quickly and carried the third plate back to the jail.

The jailor was back but the nuns had locked him out of the cell area. They set the plate down along with milk and water. "That there food be fer yore prisoner, an' she durn shore better git it," Lampkin growled before the two soldiers strolled away.

# Chapter 80

# AN ABRUPT HEARING

COLONEL BONNEVILLE BEGAN THE HEARING AT thirteen hundred hours sharp. His gavel banged on his desk. The courtroom grew quiet—not so much a result of the colonel's gavel but because of the cluster of nuns who hurried into the room. Everyone stood and men moved to give them seats. The six sisters in their long white habits nearly filled the entire second row.

Ava's hands were in cuffs when she was brought in, and the spectators' voices showed their disapproval.

Colonel Bonneville frowned.

"Remove those cuffs. They are not necessary for this hearing." He looked at the judge advocate general who was presenting the case against Ava.

"Major Minsky, present your charges."

"Sir, we are here today to show that this woman collaborated with the enemy and attempted to kill an officer while stationed at a field hospital in Chickamauga, Georgia. Because of her traitorous behavior, we plan to charge her with treason."

"And who is defending her?"

Major Reynolds stood.

"I am, sir, but I am still receiving information that I believe will prove her innocence. I would like to see this hearing postponed until next week so I can fully prepare."

"Do you have witnesses and exculpatory evidence in front of you which can exonerate the accused?"

"Sir, I just received this case this morning and am trying to track people down. However, the witnesses are scattered all over."

"So, you do not have anything that will prove her innocence today?"

"I—I—no, sir, I do not."

"Then this case will go to trial tomorrow. We will begin at nine hundred hours. Until that time, the prisoner is released in the care of Sister Marie Christi. She and her nuns will be held responsible, and they *will* be arrested should the prisoner not appear by eight hundred hours on Wednesday."

He banged his gavel and stated, "This hearing is adjourned."

Lampkin and Blake sat in shock. They thought surely some evidence to show Ava's innocence would be presented. They, along with the spectators in the packed courtroom, began to murmur. That noise grew to a loud crescendo.

Colonel Bonneville banged his gavel. He stood and shouted, "I want everyone to sit." He slammed the gavel on his desk again and shouted, "Be seated or I will have you thrown in the brig!"

Once he had the courtroom under control, Colonel Bonneville stated, "If you believe you have information or testimony that will help prove Miss Bowman's innocence, please stand. Major Reynolds will take your names."

Nearly half of the room stood, and Major Reynolds began to smile. He quickly sent aids to collect names and addresses. Both Blake and Lampkin stood as well as all of the nuns.

The judge advocate shouted, "This isn't right! There can't be that many witnesses. These people are just making a scene to slow this process!"

Colonel Bonneville leaned forward and pounded on the desk with one fist. His voice was so loud that the windows rattled.

"Major Minsky, you were excited to take this case last night. In fact, you had this woman arrested and drug out of her home in the dark of night.

"You have until tomorrow morning to prepare your case."

Major Minsky's face was red, and he was almost twitching in anger.

"There is also the matter of those nuns forcing their way into the jail and taking the prisoner from her cell. I want to file charges against them—"

Colonel Bonneville's voice became even louder as he pointed his finger at Major Minsky.

"You and your jailors are responsible for cleaning the filth out of the rest of that jail. In addition, I am fining each of you $10 to be paid to Sister Marie Christi and her order." He paused and held up his hand when Sister Marie Christi tried to speak, "For reimbursement for the labor they provided to do your work. That money is to be used as needed for the orphanage they are building." He glared at Sergeant Nielson.

"And if I find these are bogus charges or that they have been exaggerated in any way, the parties who began this prosecution will be charged themselves.

"Now clear this courtroom unless you want to testify and have not yet spoken to either Major Reynolds or Major Minsky."

Lampkin and Blake were laughing. When they turned to leave, a long line of wounded soldiers was waiting to talk to Major Reynolds.

Lampkin chuckled and poked Blake.

"Yes sir, this is goin' to be a humdinger of a trial. Too bad Cap cain't be here to see it."

# Chapter 81

# A LIVELY TRIAL

ON WEDNESDAY MORNING, OCTOBER 14, THE GROUP of nuns once again entered the courtroom silently. Most of the people were quiet and respectful. Men removed their hats and folks made room for them to pass. Someone had even posted a sign on the second row of seats that said, "Reserved for the Good Sisters."

However, one man leered at them. "Sure didn't know Catholics had white penguins too!"

Corporal Blake slammed his elbow into the man's stomach and another soldier followed up with a punch to the chin. As the man slid soundlessly to the floor, Blake and the other man removed their hats and nodded at the nuns as they filed quietly by. The rest of the onlookers stepped aside to allow the unconscious man to be dragged outside. Several men chuckled but most said nothing as he was tossed down the steps. However, if anyone had been watching Sister Marie Christi closely, they would have seen just a dash of humor pass through her eyes.

Every seat in the courtroom was full with additional men standing. The witnesses for the defense were all seated on the left side, and they nearly filled that section. The room was quiet as they waited for Colonel

Bonneville to start. Since trials were always a form of entertainment, no one wanted to be ejected, and this one looked to be particularly lively.

When Ava entered the room, most of the men stood again and removed their hats. Colonel Bonneville was torn between smiling and glaring. *If this woman is found guilty, we could have a riot in here.*

The colonel slammed his gavel down and said loudly, "This military court is now in session." He looked around the room at all the people and added, "There will be no talking during these proceedings. Anyone who cannot follow that order will be ejected.

"Let's begin. Major Minsky, state your charges."

"The Army of the United States of America charges Aveline Olivia Bowman with treasonous behavior. She fraternized with the enemy on numerous occasions, aided Confederate soldiers, and attempted to murder an officer in the Union Army."

Colonel Bonneville looked toward Major Reynolds.

"And how does your client plead, Major?"

"Not guilty, sir."

Ava listened quietly. *Actually, I am guilty of all of those charges—and I would do it again. They had better not ask me about remorse.*

Major Minsky called his first witness, Sergeant Nielson. Once the man was sworn in, the questioning began.

"Sergeant Nielson, can you explain what happened on September 19, when Major Burke was shot."

Nielson pointed at Ava. "That woman who claims to be a nurse tried to kill Major Burke. He was a surgeon an' only wanted to offer his services in a field hospital near Crawfish Spring during the Battle of Chickamauga."

"And where is Major Burke today?"

"When that nurse shot 'im in the leg, her bullet shattered some bones. The major had to have his leg took off. When word come that the Rebs was goin' to take over that field hospital, the patients was put in wagons an' hauled north. Major Burke died on the trip to Chattanooga."

Surprise showed briefly on Ava's face, but she masked it quickly. *I didn't know Burke died. I guess he did get his just deserts.*

Major Minsky asked several more leading questions before Major Reynolds questioned Nielson.

"Do you know why Nurse Bowman wanted to shoot Major Burke?"

Nielson's face turned red, and he shouted, "'Cause she's a bloody Reb, that's why!"

The soldiers who were in attendance lunged to their feet and chaos erupted.

Colonel Bonneville quieted everyone and threatened to eject the soldiers if there was another outburst. Major Reynolds paused near Nielson and asked loudly, "It wasn't because Major Burke tried to cut the arm off an unconscious man?"

Nielson lunged to his feet and began to yell. Major Minsky grabbed him and shoved him back into the chair while Colonel Bonneville pounded on his desk and roared at everyone.

When things quieted again, the colonel pointed at Major Minsky.

"Major, you keep your witness under control, or I will have him thrown in the brig." He looked over at Major Reynolds. "Do you have any more questions for this witness, Major?"

"No more, sir. I would like to call Sergeant Wilsey."

Once Wilsey was seated, Major Reynolds asked, "Sergeant Wilsey, were you present when Nurse Bowman shot Major Burke?"

"Yes, sir. It was in the Gordon House at Crawfish Spring. I was in the bed next to the feller Major Burke tried to cut on."

Major Minsky lurched to his feet in protest. "I demand that accusatory testimony be struck!"

Bonneville slammed the gavel down and shouted, "Denied! And you will conduct yourself as an officer and a gentleman in this court or I will break you back to sergeant!"

Minsky was trembling with rage as he slowly sat down. He began to scribble furiously.

"Can you tell me a little more about the patient Nurse Bowman was defending?" Major Reynolds asked.

Sergeant Wilsey looked from Major Reynolds to the angry colonel and hesitated.

The colonel's face was still red, but he nodded abruptly and said, "Continue, Sergeant Wilsey. And try to keep your description a little less colorful."

"The feller in the bed next to me was a Reb doctor. He told me he was a surgeon when he treated me on the battlefield. I had been shot in the leg an' was bleedin' out. He stopped the bleedin'. Our boys saw he was a Reb an' thought he was tryin' to kill me. They shot him but he saved my life." Sergeant Wilsey looked at the colonel and added, "Nurse Sweet was kind to all us wounded men, Yanks an' Rebs alike. She didn't protect that feller 'cause he was a Reb. She stood between Nielson an' that wounded man 'cause he was her patient."

"Nurse Sweet?"

Wilsey blushed slightly and grinned. "That's what all us wounded soldiers called Nurse Bradley or Miss Bowman as you say her name is. Rebs and Yankees—she treated everybody the same regardless of their uniform, an' she had gentle hands.

"She kept a tight hand on that field hospital too. She wouldn't let anyone in unless they were carryin' a wounded man. She wanted things clean. She worried about infections, an' she was always checkin' our wounds."

"Was the Confederate doctor conscious during this time?"

"No. He come to sometime later. I thought mebbie he would die, but he said he just had a concussion."

"So why did Nurse Sweet—"

Bonneville interrupted Major Reynolds.

"You will call the defendant Nurse Bowman or Miss Bowman."

"Why did Nurse Bowman shoot Major Burke?"

"He come in with Sergeant Nielson over there. 'Course none of us knew their names. Major Burke claimed to be a surgeon, but I don't think he was. He was mighty dirty—slovenly is what my old ma would have said.

"Burke, he offered his services but Nurse—uh—uh—Nurse Bowman wouldn't have nothin' to do with him."

"When he found out the man beside me was a Reb surgeon, he pulled a knife. He grabbed that Reb doctor's arm an' was goin' to cut it off. Said he might take his leg too.

"That's when Nurse Sweet—I mean, Nurse Bowman grabbed Burke's gun. She threatened to shoot him if he didn't back off."

"And did she?"

"She fired in the floor once. When he lunged at her with his knife and yelled, she shot him."

Major Reynolds nodded.

"Thank you, Sergeant. No more questions."

Major Minsky almost ran to the witness stand.

"Sergeant, how do we even know you were there? That battle was just a few weeks ago and you are posted here. You could be fabricating this entire story just to protect a nurse you are obviously in love with," Minsky stated sarcastically.

Sergeant Wilsey leaned forward in his chair. His eyes were angry, but he kept his voice even.

"You can check my records, Major. They will show I was wounded, what day, an' where I was treated. An' I don't appreciate bein' called a liar by a—"

"That is enough, Sergeant Wilsey. Respect for superior officers is still required, even on the witness stand." Colonel Bonneville glared at Minsky.

"Any more questions, Major Minsky?"

Minsky shook his head and almost stumbled as he walked back to his seat. He turned to Sergeant Nielson. His face was red with anger as he whispered, "You didn't tell me he tried to kill her! We just lost this trial."

Sergeant Nielson glared at him. "Don't make no never mind. She is a traitor through an' through."

# Chapter 82

# MORE DAMNING EVIDENCE

COLONEL BONNEVILLE'S VOICE WAS ABRUPT AS HE addressed the two lawyers.

"Next witness."

Major Minsky was studying the paper in front of him, but Major Reynolds arose.

"I would like to call Corporal Boston Blake."

Major Minsky looked at Sergeant Nielson in surprise. He hissed, "Why would he call that soldier? Do you know him?"

"We rode with 'im briefly, me an' some of my men. He didn't like me none so he's likely to make somethin' up."

After Corporal Blake was sworn in, Major Reynolds asked, "Is there any reason Sergeant Nielson would want Nurse Bowman to be charged with treason?"

Major Minsky surged to his feet.

"Sergeant Nielson is not on trial here! Leading question. I demand it be struck!"

Colonel Bonneville glared from one lawyer to the other.

"Major Reynolds, you had better have good reason for asking this question or I will have all of Corporal Blake's testimony struck from the record."

"Sir, it is necessary to show why Sergeant Nielson has been pursuing Nurse Bowman from the border of Kansas and Missouri to Georgia and now here."

"May I remind you that Sergeant Nielson is not on trial."

"No, but he is the reason Nurse Bowman changed her name to Bradley." Major Reynolds asked carefully, "May I continue?"

"Unless Corporal Blake can show that Sergeant Nielson threatened Miss Bowman, I will have his testimony struck."

Major Reynolds nodded.

"Corporal Blake, were you there the day Miss Bowman's family was killed and their farm burned?"

"I was there the morning before their farm was burned. They were killed that night."

"But you think you know who did it?"

"I don't think—I know."

"Please explain."

"Miss Bowman was not around when we stopped, but her grandmother and mother were. The Red Legs I was with gave them fifteen days to get out. Sergeant Nielson gave the order to steal all their horses as we were leaving. He wanted their chickens too.

"I was mad and told him that wasn't right. Nielson said he had permission from General Ewing to handle things as he chose. A little while later, he pulled Private Mitchell and a soldier he called Slug aside and whispered to them.

"I didn't trust any of them so when I saw Slug and Mitchell sneak back into camp before sunrise, I checked their horses over. One had a loose shoe, so its tracks were easy to follow. The other horse had small feet. I didn't see Sergeant Nielson come in, but his horse was ridden after they were bedded down for the night. I know that because I rubbed it down earlier.

"I studied those men's tracks too. Mitchell walked off the side of his boot and I found his tracks around the horse he rode. I couldn't sort Slug's footprints from the rest of the boot tracks there. Sergeant Nielson wears a boot with a higher heel, so his tracks were easy to pick out too.

"I tracked three horses early the next morning. They led toward the Bowman farm. I didn't go any farther than the edge of camp though.

"The next morning when our company went out to the Bowman place, I found some of those same tracks around those dead women's bodies."

He looked over at Nielson and added bitterly, "I wish I had heard them leave. Maybe I could have stopped that killing."

Major Reynolds nodded. "No more questions."

Major Minsky strolled up to Sergeant Blake.

"So, you *assume* Sergeant Nielson, Private Mitchell, and this man called Slug were going to the Bowman farm, but you don't know. In fact, you don't even know what Slug's real name is or you would have used it just now. You also don't know if those men were riding the horses you claim are theirs.

"Your testimony is all supposition, Corporal. I'm betting you didn't tell your captain either since you likely were farther than the *edge* of camp."

"I reported what I had seen to Captain Headrick the first thing the next morning. He said we couldn't prove anything, but he was worried.

"Then, I found those same boot tracks with the broken-down heel all around those women's bodies.

"Captain Headrick was furious. He told Nielson an' his men to dig three graves. When Nielson refused to take orders, the captain ran them off."

Minsky snorted. "You still have no proof that those men killed anyone. For all we know, you killed those women yourself.

"And what does that have to do with Miss Bowman? She was not attacked."

"No, but Nielson thought she knew who did the killing an' he has been after her ever since…an' that is why she changed her name."

"All projection. I demand that Corporal Blake's testimony be stricken."

Colonel Bonneville drummed his fingers on his desk. He frowned and turned his eyes toward Nielson. The man grinned at him and shrugged.

The colonel's face turned a mottled red and he hit the desk with his gavel.

"The testimony stands. Next witness."

# Chapter 83

# A NUN ON THE WITNESS STAND

MAJOR REYNOLDS STOOD. "I WOULD LIKE TO CALL Sister Marie Christi."

Major Minsky jumped to his feet.

"I protest!" he shouted.

"On what grounds?"

"I—I—she doesn't have any reason to testify. We are not looking for character witnesses."

Colonel Bonneville looked from the tall nun to Major Reynolds. "Well?"

"Sister Marie Christi has testimony I believe is necessary to show the bias of this charge against Nurse Bowman."

"Accepted."

The soldier who was to swear in the witnesses, looked from the nun to Colonel Bonneville.

"Do I still swear her in? She's a woman of the cloth!"

Sister Marie Christi smiled at him. "Proceed as you should, soldier. Being a nun doesn't make me a saint." Her eyes were twinkling, and the soldier responded uncomfortably with, "Yes, ma'am—I—I mean, Sister." The tall nun placed her hand on the Bible, and the soldier swore her in.

"Sister Marie Christi, can you tell me how you came to know Nurse Bowman?" Major Reynold's voice was soft but clear.

"She was in Atlanta when we sisters arrived by train. We had arranged for a wagon to travel north, and a mutual friend asked that we take Miss Bowman with us."

"Were you aware of who she was?"

"I was the only one who knew her name or knew why she needed to leave Atlanta quickly."

"And why was that?"

"I was told that a man was pursuing her with intentions of killing her."

"And you knew that to be true?"

"As I said, I did not know her, but I did know the person who requested my help."

"And who was that person?"

"Mary Fowler. She lives in Atlanta and often helps us when we need to arrange transportation."

"Is she a Southern Sympathizer?"

Sister Marie Christi's eyes drilled into Major Reynolds, but she faced the people in the gallery and answered quietly, "We sisters travel back and forth between both lines. Our service is to the Lord. The fighting that is taking place causes many casualties. The people we meet, civilians and soldiers, are our concern—not which side of this terrible war they are on."

"And did you take her with you?"

"Yes. We gave her a novice habit and left town immediately."

"But the other sisters didn't know anything about her?"

"No, just that she needed help."

"Did she share anything about her past on that trip?"

"When I asked, Miss Bowman told me she heard the men talking after they killed her family. She didn't know who they were and didn't see them. However, she could identify their voices if she heard them again. She believed they had found out she was still alive and wanted to kill her.

"I told my sisters nothing about her, not even her name. I said on our journey that she would be called Sister Augustina. I asked Miss Bowman, or Miss Bradley as she called herself, not to share anything about her personal life with my sisters. She did as I asked."

"Did you have any trouble on your trip north?"

Sister Marie Christi pointed toward Sergeant Nielson.

"Only from that man. He visited us twice. The first time was to threaten us. He was sure we were hiding Miss Bowman. The second time, he dragged a soldier into our camp who was tied behind a horse. Sergeant Nielson had a letter that he said was to the woman he was looking for.

"The Union soldier he was dragging was wounded and bloody. He had been severely abused. He said he knew nothing of the letter's contents, only that it was to go to a Nurse Sweet. He didn't even know what the woman looked like or her real name. He said he was to leave it at the hospital in Chattanooga but was called out on patrol before it could be delivered."

The courtroom was still when Major Reynolds asked quietly, "And what happened to that soldier?"

"The man identified today as Sergeant Nielson tried to shoot him."

"But he was stopped?"

"I stood between him and the injured man. Then my sisters surrounded the wounded soldier."

A slow murmur began and the noise in the gallery continued to increase.

Major Reynolds looked from Sergeant Nielson to the nun. "And did his men do anything to stop him?"

"Several of them spoke up in protest. I don't think they were comfortable with the situation." Sister Marie Christi's eyes made contact with each man in the courtroom who had been there that day, and she added, "Perhaps they will learn from this and make things right with their Lord."

The three men in the audience she had directed her comments to turned red and looked at the floor. However, no one noticed. All eyes were on Sergeant Nielson. He jumped to his feet and began to shout.

"I knew you was hidin' her! Yore nothin' but a—" He stopped when a man behind him shoved a gun in his back.

"Ya want I should shoot him now, Colonel? It would save us all lotsa grief."

Colonel Bonneville snorted and beat on his desk with his gavel. He finally climbed on top and roared, "Clear this courtroom! Put those guns away and get out—every last one of you who is not involved in this trial."

His finger shook as he pointed it at Nielson.

"Sergeant Nielson, you are on the edge of being court-martialed yourself. Now you leave this room quietly."

He moved his finger to point at Lampkin and Blake as he shouted, "You two soldiers help clear this courtroom. I don't want anyone in here but Miss Bowman and both lawyers.

"Now everyone *out!*"

Lampkin and Blake began to push the spectators toward the door. The sound of a gunshot behind them was muffled, and as they turned, a man near Nielson dropped to the floor.

Nielson pushed his way into the aisle and rushed toward Sister Marie Christi shouting, "I shoulda shot the lot of ya!" He hollered at his men in the crowd behind him.

"Y'all are nothin' but cowards! Shoot that nun—she's why that nurse ain't daid already!" He lunged as he pointed his gun.

Ava was already running. Nielson's first shot barely missed Sister Marie Christi. It clipped the edge of her veil and caught Ava's shoulder as she ran between the nun and Nielson.

"No!" Ava screamed as she threw herself over Sister Marie Christi. Nielson's second shot hit Ava in the back and the shocked nun caught her as she collapsed.

As Sister Marie Christi turned her over, Ava whispered, "I'm—I'm sorry. I didn't mean to put you in—"

Her body went limp, and the rest of the nuns rushed to surround both women.

Lampkin whirled around. He shoved his way to the front of the courtroom just as Nielson ran through a side door, firing a wild shot as he ran.

The bullet grazed Lampkin's arm, but he kept running as he yelled, "Stop that man! He shot Nurse Sweet!"

# Chapter 84

# KILLERS AND THIEVES

SERGEANT NIELSON HIT THE OUTSIDE DOOR WITH his shoulder and almost fell through the opening. He jumped on the first horse he saw and spurred it toward a side street.

The three men who had been with him allowed themselves to be pushed out of the courtroom. Slug and Mitchell watched Nielson race away and then strolled slowly toward the livery.

Slug turned around and asked, "You comin', Goat? Ain't nobody after us. Those nuns are the onliest ones who knowed we was with the sarge, an' they're busy now." He grinned and added, "Them an' that nurse. I reckon she's a goner though. Looked to me like that bullet hit a lung."

"Naw, I'll take my chances. I only rode with you boys fer the fun of raidin'. It's a little too hot 'round here now. I saw a couple of fellers I knew in that courtroom. I'll mebbie join up with them an' head west. We can hit some of those wagon trains out in the middle of nowhere. There won't be so many soldiers around out there. Too much law here fer me."

Goat lifted his hand as he turned away muttering, "If I stick with those fellers, I'm a goin' to die way too early. I don't mind robbin' folks or even a little shootin' now an' then, but I don't believe in shootin' men in the back. Those fellers are killers." He frowned and added, "'Sides, I didn't like the way that nun looked at me. Made me feel all dirty inside. Why, it was like she looked down in my soul an' saw ever' bad deed I ever done…an' I've done a sight of wrong."

Slug glanced at Mitchell as they watched Goat walk away.

"We cain't take a chance on him a talkin'," he commented quietly.

Mitchell frowned. He turned to look for Goat, but the man had already disappeared in the crowd.

"I think we'd better git outa town. We need to meet Sarge at that ol' shack we agreed on. If he ain't there, we'll head west too. Less law an' lotsa loot on both sides of the Missouri border." He grinned and bumped Slug's shoulder.

"Mebbie we should take a few extry horses with us in case Sarge is chased." He frowned and added, "It worries me some to be ridin' with him though. He's a marked man now."

Slug looked in the direction they needed to ride to meet Nielson and then behind them at the angry crowd. He slowly nodded.

"Let's head fer that border now. If Nielson gits strung up, I don't want to be nowhere around."

"That's what we'll do. Now make sure the extra hoss ya take don't have a military brand. No need to make any soldier boys suspicious."

As the two men entered the livery, they looked around. Mitchell pointed toward a horse in the first stall.

"Say, look at that long-legged sorrel. Now that's the one I'm a takin'."

Slug stared at the horse.

"I think that's the one that nurse rode, ain't it?" He looked closer and the horse pulled back, throwing its head in the air as it reared. "Yeah, it is. It's a fine hoss but too spooky 'round men fer me. I don't want a hoss I know will throw me first chance it gits."

"I'll break it from that. Mebbie I'll work it over some with a whip. 'Sides, it's a good one to take since that nurse is dead." Mitchell grinned at Slug as he hooked a rope to Deuce's halter. "Now grab ya some fast ones an' let's go."

# Chapter 85

# UNCLE HENRY

HENRY MCCUNE JUMPED OFF THE TRAIN IN ST. LOUIS. He unloaded his big mule and led it to a water tank. He stared up the street at the angry crowd in front of one of the military buildings.

"Musta had a lively trial today. Too bad that eastbound train didn't git here no earlier. I always enjoy me a good argument." The old man shifted the large buffalo gun he carried to lay more easily across his arm, mounted his mule, and rode slowly up the street. He listened as he rode through the crowd. He soon learned that a nurse had been shot, and the would-be killer had gotten away. He stopped when he spotted a man he recognized and rode toward him with a grin.

"Well, if it ain't little Noah Lampkin. Whatcha doin' here, Boy? I thought you'ins was headed west—least that's what yur cranky captain said when he tried to steal my durn mules.

"Squeaky cheapskate. I never seen the like. He knowed I have the best mules in the country an' he still tried ta dicker me down ta where I pertineered give 'em away."

Lieutenant Lampkin grinned as he reached up to shake the old man's hand.

"Badger McCune! What are ya doin' in St. Louis?"

"Come to talk to yore brass 'bout buyin' some a my mules. I told Colonel Bonneville that I'd make one trip. I'd be ridin' the type a mule I have fer sale so he cin take my mules fer the price I want, or I'll sell 'em ta other folks." Badger grinned at the younger man and added, "They's 'nough wagon trains headed west that I cin purty much set my price an' not have ta dicker with a bunch a stuffy army officers what has their britches cinched up so tight they squawk when they walk.

"Wouldn't a sold 'em cheap ta yore captain but I knowed his pa. Liked 'im too. That boy reminds me of his ol' man—fer shore when it comes ta partin' with his money."

Badger nodded toward the crowd in front of a sign that said, "Trial Today!"

"See ya had a big trial today. Musta been a lively one seein' as how the crowd is still all riled up."

Lampkin's smile left his face, and he swore softly.

"Dad-blamed Red Legs. They was after a nurse we know. Real nice little gal. Accused 'er of spyin' an' all sorts of stuff. Things was lookin' good fer our side when a Red Leg by the name a Nielson tried to shoot a nun who was testifyin'. That little nurse jumped in front of the good sister an' that feller shot her instead.

"Looked mighty bad when they carried 'er out. We tried to git in to see 'er, but the hospital won't let no one in but family.

"Shoot, that little gal don't have no family but a Reb brother. Red Legs killed all of 'em." Lampkin's face was angry when he added, "Cap sent us up here to keep an eye on things. I think he knowed this here trial would be stacked against 'er." His face softened and Lampkin added quietly, "Cap is sweet on 'er."

Badger's blue eyes became hard, and he looked toward the hospital.

"Nurse Parsons still in charge over there?"

Lampkin nodded and Badger winked at him as he laughed evilly.

"Let's go see 'er. I got me a way with the ladies." He pointed toward Blake as he nodded behind him.

"There's a bottle in my saddlebag. Grab it but be mighty careful. Stick it inside yore coat an' act all innocent-like when we go in there. Nurse Parson's 'ill shore 'nough frisk me some but she might not you'ins."

When Blake returned, Lampkin grinned and took the bottle.

"I'll take it. Nurse Parsons don't like Blake here much, but she won't worry 'bout me." He looked at Badger curiously, "Her name is Ava Bowman. You goin' to claim to be family?"

"Don't have ta claim. That little gal used ta spend pertineer ever' summer over ta my house. Her granny an' me growed up together. 'Course I moved to Kansas City 'fore she married, but we was always friends.

"I bought all their breedin' hosses fer 'em. Granny knowed her blood lines so she told me what ta buy. I even sold Granny that big mule she used ta ride. 'Course, that was 'fore her accident." Badger's eyes became hard again.

"I heard they was burned out. Nobody seemed ta know if little Ava was alive. I knew she was though. Granny woulda sent 'er to the caves first chance a trouble.

"I mentioned that little gal to yore captain an' he turned red as a ripe tomater." Badger grinned at Lampkin and added, "So you'ins didn't have ta tell me he was sweet on my little Ava. I already knowed."

"Now let's git over to that hospital an' check on my niece."

# Chapter 86

# "YOU ARE NOT COMING IN HERE!"

**B**ADGER PULLED OPEN THE DOOR TO THE HOSPITAL and pushed through. Lampkin and Blake followed. Several orderlies tried to stop them, but Badger was shouting, "Emmie, ya come on out here! This here's Henry McCune an' I come to see my niece."

Nurse Parsons was coming down the stairs. Her steps slowed and she glared at Badger as she walked toward him.

"Henry McCune, you are *not* coming in here. I know you don't have a niece because you only have one brother and neither of you married."

"Now, Emmie, are we a goin' ta stand out here an' jaw or do I have ta give you'ins my durn life story?" When Nurse Parsons continued to glare at him, Badger added, "Ava Bowman's granny be Libby Bradley, an' Libby's ma be my ma's sis. I reckon that makes little Ava my niece. Why, that little gal spent 'most as much time with me as she did her own folks, 'fore her granny come to live with 'em that is.

"Now tell me where she is. I come a long piece ta see 'er."

Nurse Parsons glared at Badger and spoke sarcastically, "Henry, that makes you cousins and distant ones at that. Besides, I know you didn't come all this way to see Miss Bowman. That trial was only this morning."

Badger grinned and shrugged. "I reckon I be too old ta be a cousin ta that little gal so that makes me 'er uncle…an' since I'm here, I want ta see 'er." His face became somber as he added, "I heard she be in a bad way."

Nurse Parsons continued to frown but she finally nodded. She pointed toward Badger and Lampkin.

"Follow me." When Blake took a tentative step to follow, she pointed at him and barked, "Not you. I know you are not family, and you have no business here." She turned to the orderlies.

"Throw him out if he won't leave."

Blake's face paled and he backed toward the door. He shook off the two orderlies.

"I'll leave an' I don't need yore help." He muttered under his breath as the orderlies opened the door, "I shore don't understand why that woman despises me so."

One of the orderlies chuckled. "Nurse Parsons doesn't like most men. She doesn't think we are useful. For some reason though, she took a liking to Lieutenant Lampkin. Him and his captain. I think they are the only two men I have ever seen her smile at…and that includes us."

Corporal Blake was still growling as he walked away. He turned around once and glared at the closed door. Then his face cleared. He strolled over to a bench where he had a clear view of the hospital and the front of the livery.

"I'll just keep an eye out. You never know what I might see or hear whilst I sit here."

# Chapter 87

# A MIGHTY SICK NIECE

AS BADGER AND LAMPKIN FOLLOWED NURSE PARSONS up the stairs, the old man asked softly, "So how is my little Ava? I heard she took a slug."

Nurse Parsons paused and looked back at the two men. Her face softened.

"Miss Bowman was hit by two bullets. One grazed her shoulder, but the second one came extremely close to one lung. Doctor Whitman removed it. The surgery was a long one, and now she is fighting infection.

"Our patients are too close in here, and I fear a bug of some kind was carried from one of the sick men to her." Nurse Parsons shook her head.

"I emphasize cleanliness and hand washing, but sometimes that just isn't enough."

Nurse Parsons stopped in front of what looked like a closet and spoke softly as she looked up at the two men.

"I put her in this small room. It was used as a closet at one time.

"Miss Bowman is very ill. If we can't stop that infection and break her fever, I'm not sure she will live."

Badger and Lampkin said nothing. Nurse Parsons pointed toward a basin. There was also a pitcher of water and soap.

"Wash your hands before you go in. Don't stay too long and let her rest if she doesn't wake. She hasn't responded to anyone since she was shot."

Major Reynolds looked up in surprise when the two men entered. Badger introduced himself and the major nodded at Lampkin. He looked over at Ava and his voice cracked.

"This is my fault. I should have known how Sergeant Nielson would react. This could have been prevented if I had been thinking."

Badger looked from the major to Ava's pale face.

"That don't make no never mind now. You'ins go on out. I'd like a little time here with my niece."

Major Reynolds nodded and walked slowly toward the door. He looked back at the two men as he left.

"I'll stop in tonight. She hasn't spoken since she collapsed. I'm not sure if she is sleeping or unconscious."

Badger didn't answer. He was leaning over Ava as he felt her head. He spoke to Lampkin without turning around.

"You'ins stand in front a that there door. I'm a goin' to treat this little gal, an' I don't want no nurse ta come a bustin' in here.

"Now hand me that bottle you'ins has in yur boot."

Badger pulled a chair close to Ava's bed. He leaned over and kissed her cheek.

"Hello there, gal. How's my favorite niece a doin'?"

Ava stirred and slowly opened her eyes. They opened wider when she saw Badger. She tried to smile when he took her hand.

"Uncle Henry! I was just thinking about you and our rides together on your mules. What are you doing here?"

"Wahl, I come to dicker with the colonel on some mules fer his cavalry. When I heared ya was shot, I come right over." He pulled a can from his pocket and took off the lid.

"I brung some medicine with me. We's a goin' ta treat ya so's you'ins cin git outa this here bed. Ya done enough layin' 'round ta last a fair piece."

Ava's face was flushed with fever. She shook her head and squeezed her mouth shut. She finally opened her eyes and whispered, "I don't want any of your smelly medicine, Uncle Henry. I know how bad it tastes."

"Shore now, she be nasty tastin', but she heals feverin', an' you'ins has ya a bad one.

"Now Lampkin here'll help ya sit up an' I'll git ya a cupful. 'Fore ya drink it though, I'm a goin' to put this here salve on those bullet holes. An' I know you'ins like the salve. Ya used to help me treat my hosses an' mules with it."

Ava smiled again and closed her eyes. She inhaled deeply.

"I remember that smell. It makes me think of home." Ava opened her eyes. Her smile disappeared and a single tear slid down her cheek.

"Those Red Legs killed my family, Uncle Henry. Charlie and I are the only ones left."

"Don't write me off, gal. I figger I have me a few good years left. Shoot, I ain't even found me a wife yet so I cain't be a kickin' the bucket jist yet." He grinned and winked at Ava.

"Noah, shove that here chair against that door. Brace the back under the knob. Then you'ins hold little Ava up whilst I untie this rag and put on my salve." He shoved a can into Lampkin's hand. "Now hold that there salve up close to Ava's nose. She cin smell that whilst she's a drinkin' my tonic. I reckon that libation will do 'er more good than anything Nurse Emmie tries ta give 'er."

Ava tried to hold her nose, but Badger pulled her fingers away.

"Now don't be a doin' that. Too much chance ya might choke. Jist drink it down." As Ava took a big swallow, he nodded. "Keep a goin'. Ya know you'ins don't want ta take a breath in the middle there."

After Ava swallowed the last of Badger's tonic, she shuddered violently. He smiled and patted her back.

"I'll jist sit here with ya fer a time, Ava." He looked over at Lieutenant Lampkin and winked. "'Course, Noah here could share what you'ins says in the next few hours. That cranky captain a his might like ta hear it."

Ava grinned loosely. "If you're talking about Captain Headrick, he's *my* captain. That's what Chloe calls him. I told her he wasn't, but I lied." She pulled a ring from the top of her gown that hung on a heavy cord.

"He gave me this to keep for him until I see him again." Her eyes became wide as she looked from one man to the other.

"He almost died! I just don't know what I'd do if he died."

Lieutenant Lampkin leaned over and kissed Ava's cheek as he smiled.

"That there is from yore captain. I reckon I'd better git back to our camp so's I cin give Captain Headrick a full report. I've seen how yore uncle's tonic works on folks. I'll tell Cap yore a goin' to be fine."

Lampkin tipped his hat to Badger.

"Good to see ya, Badger. I'll tell Cap ya still ain't happy with the deal he got." He grinned and walked out quietly. His smile slowly disappeared, and he muttered, "I didn't need to hear all the things Miss Ava was a sayin'. Weren't none of my business an' it shore looked like she was a goin' to spill her guts all over the place.

"I'll put Badger's mule up too. No sense in that big feller standin' out there all night. I'm a guessin' Badger will stay till Miss Ava is outa the woods.

"Wonder if Mule be as testy as he was in the past." He reached for the reins and the mule tried to take a bite out of his arm.

Lampkin jumped back and grinned.

"Yep, yore as nasty as ya always was. Now ya come along with me gentle-like an' I'll get ya a feed bag." He dropped the reins and turned away without looking back. The mule snorted once and then slowly followed Lampkin.

Blake stood when he saw Lampkin, and the two men strolled toward the livery.

"Miss Ava goin' to be all right?"

"Shore is. Badger give 'er some of his elixir. I call it his potion. He's been makin' that stuff fer lotsa years. Cures ever'thing from hosses an' mules to people.

"An don't ask me what's in it 'cause I don't know. I jist know the seeds floatin' on top come from the tail end of a buffalo or mebbie a deer. I jist hope I don't never get sick 'nough to ever need it."

Blake nodded silently.

"How long have you known this Badger feller? An' where'd he come up with a name like that?"

Lampkin grinned at his friend.

"He earned it, that's how.

"Jist open the door to that first stall an' stand back so's Badger's mule cin git in there. I'll hook this here feed bag on a board an' then let's git a move on. A special passenger train be headin' west tonight with some big dog railroad fellers on it. We cin offer to provide security an' they jist might let us ride inside as far as Centralia. That 'ill put us close to where Cap planned to camp tonight."

# CAPTAIN HEADRICK'S ENCAMPMENT

## TWENTY MILES WEST OF CENTRALIA, MISSOURI

### THURSDAY, OCTOBER 15, 1863

# Chapter 88

# GOAT

**I**T WAS NEARLY DARK WHEN LAMPKIN AND BLAKE rode into the Union camp. They dismounted and looked around. Most of the soldiers were gathered at one end.

Lampkin glanced around. He walked to the edge of camp and asked the sentry, "What's goin' on? Cap catch 'im a spy?"

"That's what he's tryin' to figger. The feller was ridin' alone, no uniform or nothin', but we found a red sash in his saddle bag.

"Cap don't like Red Legs an' he figgers this feller is one of 'em."

Lampkin pushed his shoulders back and flexed his arms.

"Well, Blake, it's been a long day an' it jist got longer. Let's go see who Cap has cornered."

The two men strolled into the clearing. Several soldiers held their rifles on a man in front of Captain Headrick. Just as they arrived, Captain Headrick whacked the man across the shins with his rifle barrel.

"Let's try that again. Goat is not a name. Tell me your name."

"Dad-blame it, Captain!" the man exclaimed as he rubbed his shins. "That there is called torture."

"Torture!" Lampkin snorted. "Let me use my knife an' I'll show 'im torture," he growled as he lifted a large knife from inside his shirt.

Captain Headrick's face was hard as he glanced back at Lampkin and Blake.

"Good to have you men back." He nodded at the man who called himself Goat. "You recognize him from anywhere? He says he's a civilian on his way home. Said he grew up by the Washita River close to No Man's Land down in Indian Territory."

Lampkin lit a match and held it closer to the man's face. He looked over at Blake.

"He look familiar to ya?"

"Yeah, he was sittin' by Slug an' Mitchell at Nurse Sweet's trial. He didn't leave with 'em though, an' none of 'em rode out with Nielson. 'Course, Nielson left on the run so they mightn't had time."

Captain Headrick stared at the man a moment longer. He finally growled something before he spoke loudly.

"Private Hanson! Pick a couple of men and tie that prisoner up. Put him over there by those mules McCune sold me. Several of them like to kick if they're bothered. Maybe they will keep him quiet tonight. We'll deal with him in the morning.

"Lieutenant Lampkin and Corporal Blake—you come with me. I need a full report."

As the three walked toward Captain Headrick's tent, he asked softly, "Miss Bradley?"

Blake didn't answer but Lampkin said, "Well, first of all, her name ain't Bradley or Ella neither. It's Ava Bowman an' I think it was good ya sent both of us down there. Blake here testified. I jist listened and watched.

"Things wasn't lookin' good in the beginnin', but they started to look up when folks began testifyin'. A nun she traveled north from Atlanta with was last, an' that's when things got squally. Sergeant Nielson tried to shoot the nun an' Miss Ava jumped in front of 'er. She caught a couple of slugs. One grazed her shoulder an' the second hit 'er in the back.

"A buncha soldiers she treated was there, an' they carried 'er to the hospital. Nurse Parsons wouldn't let nobody in to check on 'er till 'er Uncle Henry showed up." Lampkin grinned at Captain Headrick.

"I shore didn't know Badger was related to 'er but he was. Nurse Parsons didn't want to let 'im in neither but she finally did. He give me his elixir to carry. I stuffed it in my boot an' Emmie didn't even check me.

"Badger dosed Miss Ava with it. He was with 'er when we left. He's cured lotsa folks with that potion he makes. Horses an' mules too. It smells like the Devil 'imself but it works.

"I knowed she'd get better after that, so we come on back." He frowned and added, "As far as that Goat feller goes, I think he was with Nielson when they busted in on those nuns whilst Miss Ava was travelin' with 'em. I watched that head nun's eyes when she was testifyin'. She landed 'em on Slug, Mitchell, an' the feller ya called Goat.

"I'd never seen 'im before the trial, but I'd lay a wager he was with Nielson—fer a time anyway."

Captain Headrick cursed softly. "You have anything to add, Corporal Blake?"

Blake shook his head. "I didn't see nothin' suspicious. That Goat feller musta left right after the trial 'cause I shore didn't see him around."

Captain Headrick nodded. "That will be all, Corporal Blake." He started to turn but added, "Why don't you and Private Hanson pitch a tent close to the mules. If that feller wants to talk in the middle of the night, I'd like to have some men close to hear him." He grinned and added, "And I think he will. There is a jenny in that group that has a nasty temperament. She's fine as long as you don't get too close to her, but she is particularly testy at night.

"Badger called her Minot. He said she "might not" be friendly, but she could go for hours—if she liked the feller riding her. Hanson took a liking to her, and I think she likes him too."

He saluted the corporal and then shook his hand. "Good to have you back, Blake."

After Blake walked away, Captain Headrick cursed long and low.

"I knew Ava was in danger. I should have kept her safe. I should have—"

"Cap, there weren't nothin' ya coulda done. Nielson follered her all the way from Georgia an' brought up those charges. Mosta what that lawyer said was true—he jist didn't give *all* the facts. That's why it went to trial. As folks testified at the trial though, the truth come out. An' believe me, there was lotsa fellers who wanted to testify.

"That head nun was the one what surprised me. She's who Miss Ava was tryin' to protect when she jumped in front of Nielson's bullet. 'Course, if he coulda shot Miss Ava, he would have.

"An' as far as that Goat feller goes, ya could always make 'im be a soldier." He grinned at Captain Headrick as he nodded back toward the men. "Mosta the men in yore command are Galvanized Yanks anyhow. What difference will one more discontented soldier make? We might need his gun when we reach Injun country.

"Speakin' of that, how come we're still in Missouri? I didn't think ol' Grant wanted these Reb soldiers 'round other Rebs."

"He doesn't but with all the fighting east of us as well as on the border, the North is short on men.

"New orders did come through while you were gone though. We leave tomorrow. We are to meet the train in Centralia and ride it west to Kansas City. That's just a little less than one hundred-fifty miles. Our orders are to guard some railroad tycoons as well as the wives of some top Union brass. We'll leave the railroad bigwigs in Kansas City and escort the officers' wives on to Leavenworth.

"Some of Colonel Bonneville's troopers will ride the train from St. Louis to Centralia. We will meet them there and take over. It looks like a lot of security to me, so whoever they are, the brass wants them protected well."

# Chapter 89

# GALVANIZED YANKEES

CAPTAIN HEADRICK GATHERED HIS MEN TOGETHER the next morning.

"We will be riding the train west tomorrow morning from Centralia. Most of you will be on top since the cars will likely be full of passengers. I expect you to conduct yourselves in the courteous manner expected of all servicemen. You especially will not talk to the women.

"You will be there as security—to provide protection and to escort that train through hostile territory." The captain looked from man to man and added, "I know you are part of this army not because you are loyal to the United State Government but because you didn't want to serve out the rest of this war in a Yankee prison. However, you are all fighting men, and we are one unit now."

One soldier called from the back, "I heard you have orders to shoot all deserters. Is that true, Captain?"

Captain Headrick eyed the man coldly and nodded. "That is correct. However, I would much prefer to have you fighting with us than to use our guns against you.

"It is the hope of all of us that this war will be over soon. You will all muster out in 1866 like the rest of this unit. You may return to your homes or make new homes in the West. I know for many of us here, there is nothing to go home to.

"Now mount up and stay in formation."

Captain Headrick put Private Hanson at the head of the column. He was to range back and forth, looking for Bushwhackers or tracks. Lieutenant Lampkin brought up the rear, and soldiers who were specifically chosen by the captain rode on either side of the column. Captain Headrick sent his brother to the back while he rode at the front of the column behind Private Hanson.

"Private Headrick, I want you to report to Lampkin. You be an extra set of eyes. If you see any shenanigans taking place, let him know since he will be watching our back trail."

Peter nodded and pulled his horse around to ride at the back of the column.

Two men watched him from the sides of their eyes as he rode by.

"That kid is the captain's little brother. If we break loose, we should take him with us," said a surly soldier with a big mustache. The men called him Fuzz. The man to whom he spoke shook his head.

"I don't think so. He's a favorite of the officers an' has made friends with half the fellers in this command too. They might turn on us.

"Nope, when we make a break, we do it on our own. An' don't try to git a buncha men to foller us neither. We'll keep this here deal quiet."

Fuzz looked over at his companion and snorted.

"Ya shore are cautious since we was hauled outa that there jail. What's come over ya?"

The other soldier didn't answer for a time. He finally hissed, "Jist be ready. I won't give ya no warnin'. I'll jist jab my hoss with my spurs.

"An' ya better be right behind me 'cause I ain't a waitin'."

Fuzz glared at the man riding beside him. He muttered under his breath but didn't speak out loud anymore.

Blake watched the two men talking furtively. He frowned. He knew the one they called Fuzz had been talking. Whatever he said, the man beside him heard and replied.

"I think those two bear watchin'. In fact, I'll suggest Cap change fellers up to ride different positions. That way, they'll be ridin' by somebody new each time we head out."

When they broke formation at noon, Blake reported to Captain Headrick what he'd seen.

"Think we ought to split those fellers up each time we stop? That might keep 'em from gettin' too chummy on this ride."

Captain Headrick slowly nodded his head. "We'll have them line up and then move the right line up eight positions." He grinned at Blake and slapped his shoulder.

"Good thinking, Blake. You keep an eye on them. My guess is they are making plans to make a run for it. Especially watch the smaller one. He's got the brains and the boldness."

Later that afternoon, they rode down a small hill. There were trees on both sides of the trail. Blake pulled out his rifle and stopped his horse beside the column. The smaller soldier whom he had pointed out to Captain Headrick suddenly spurred his horse and made a break for the trees. Soldiers pulled their uneasy mounts around to keep them from charging after him.

Fuzz saw a break in the line of soldiers and spurred his horse through the hole just as Blake shot the first rider. He tried to pull his horse up, but all the confusion excited it. It raced after the first horse. Blake calmly shot Fuzz as well.

He carefully shoved his rifle back in its boot and hollered, "Keep movin'!"

Some of the men murmured angrily but most rode on with no emotion. All were seething inside though. Lieutenant Charlie Bowman, Missouri State Guard, watched from the trees.

"Sis' captain ain't no sugar cake an' his men ain't neither. I'd better keep my head down an' stay quiet. I hope ever'thing works when we bust those officers out. I wasn't countin' on Headrick bein' the officer in charge."

# Chapter 90

# NEW ORDERS

CAPTAIN HEADRICK GLARED AT THE OFFICER WHO gave him new orders.

"I was told we were escorting railroad executives and officers' wives. I have mostly Galvanized Yankees in my command, and they shouldn't be anywhere near high-level Reb officers. Besides, this is an unvetted passenger train. Prisoners shouldn't be on here at all."

Major Johnson shrugged his shoulders.

"It wasn't my call so don't bark at me. These orders came straight from General Merrill." He squinted his eyes at the men behind Captain Headrick.

"I didn't even know we had Rebs wearing blue uniforms." He snorted. "What kind of deal is that? I doubt you have a man among you who is loyal." When Captain Headrick didn't respond, the major asked, "How about I send some of my men with you? I have two who are mustering out in two days. I can send them as well as Sergeant English and Corporal Barnes.

"I planned to send them to Fort Leavenworth with a message for Colonel Ault. He is the temporary commanding officer there. I don't want to send that message by wire so this will help me too."

Captain Headrick slowly nodded. "Send them down to our camp this evening. I want to talk to them."

Lampkin listened as the two officers talked. When Major Johnson left, he spoke softly to his captain.

"Mebbie I should mosey up here 'fore daylight. Once we git those prisoners loaded, we'll pull the shades in their car. We'll load those bigwigs once we're done. You bring the men up 'bout six. I'll make shore the prisoners are on by then.

"I reckon they'll be housed in the jail overnight, so ya might want to look that over." Lampkin nodded toward the soldiers.

"Keep Espy an' Blake up here to oversee their unloadin'. They cin sleep in the jail tonight an' make shore those Rebs are up an' movin' first thing tomorrow."

Captain Headrick glanced at the men and frowned. "That will work. You take the men down to the camping area. I'll be there as soon as I escort these prisoners to the jailhouse." He wheeled around and began to bark orders.

"Privates Hanson and Headrick, go with Lieutenant Lampkin—you spread out and keep your eyes open. We don't know which of these men we can trust.

"Corporal Blake and Private Espy—you are with me.

"Fall out and make camp."

Captain Headrick waited until the rest of the passengers were unloaded before he opened the prisoners' car. He recognized some of the Confederate prisoners as friends from West Point. However, his face showed no recognition.

"You men will be taken to the privies one by one. One arm will be handcuffed to your britches when you enter, and it had better still be there when you come out.

"We'll stop at the water tank so you can wash off some. Your handcuffs will be affixed, and you will be taken to the town jail where you'll spend the night.

"I don't want any talking and I want this done quickly so move along."

Some of the officers purposely wasted time. Captain Headrick spoke softly so only they could hear.

"You men get your job done or you will be wearing what you are trying to hold. Now move."

One man looked at him in surprise.

"Come on, Noble. We've been friends for lots of years."

"Maybe, but right at this moment, we are not friends. You are enemy prisoners. Now move."

The prisoners were taken to the privies and then quickly herded to the jail. Several complained about their treatment but most of the twenty men were quiet.

When the cell door closed, the prisoners could hear the thudding of Captain Headrick's boots as he stomped away. They didn't see him jerk his hat off though or quietly curse before he pulled it on again.

"Neighbor against neighbor, friend against friend. I despise this war."

# Chapter 91

# TRAINER FREEMAN

CAPTAIN HEADRICK STRODE DOWN TO THE encampment. He slowed and the frown left his face when he saw several Colored soldiers working with the horses. He stopped beside them. One was checking the horses' shoes while the other two were grooming them.

Captain Headrick watched them for a time before he spoke.

"Did you men just arrive? I'm Captain Headrick and I don't have you on my roster."

"Yes, suh. We come in on the train from St. Louis. We's to go with ya as far as Fort Leavenworth an' then we'll be assigned to a Colored unit. Buffalo Soldiers we is told, but I ain't real shore why they's called that."

Captain Headrick chuckled. "Me either." He waved for the other two men to join them.

The two soldiers stood. They joined the first man and stood at attention.

"Did an officer assign you men to the horses?"

"No, suh. We jist know hosses."

"What is your name, soldier?"

"Trainer, suh."

"Trainer? Is Trainer your last name?"

"Jist Trainer. Never had me no other name. I only was ever called Trainer."

"You worked with horses before this war, Trainer?"

"Yes, suh. I was a hoss trainer on a plantation. The massuh had racin' hosses. I rode 'em an' broke 'em. Took care of 'em when they was sick too. My pappy was Trainer 'fore me an' his pappy 'fore that.

"When this war broke out, the three of us runned away. We signed on to fight fer the North with the first fellers in blue we come across. We figgered this army would be a safe place fer runaway slaves."

Captain Headrick grinned at the soldier and nodded.

"I reckon that was partly right. Since you are part of this company though, you need a last name so I can add you to my roster. I need the papers you were given in St. Louis too so I can make everything match.

"Now what would you like to be called?"

"I never wanted nothin' but to be a free man, suh."

Captain Headrick chuckled.

"Well then, I guess your name chose you. I'll call you Private Trainer Freeman."

The soldier's face broke into a huge smile.

"I like that jist fine, suh. An' how 'bout my friends? They is Walker an' Tinker. What do ya think their names should be?"

"I reckon you should ask them. Talk it over and I will update your records tonight.

"And Private Freeman, from now on, you, Private Walker, and Private Tinker are in charge of the horses. I want you to make sure they are fit to travel, from brushing them to checking their shoes. Make sure they are hobbled every night and have them saddled and ready to ride every morning." Captain Headrick smiled and put out his hand to Trainer.

"It's a pleasure to have you as part of this company, Private Trainer Freeman. I appreciate a soldier who takes care of his horses."

Captain Headrick saluted the three soldiers, and they quickly returned the salute. The other two men stared after Captain Headrick as he walked away.

"Ya think that captain means what he says?"

Trainer watched Captain Headrick walk toward a small creek and nodded.

"I reckon he does. His pappy owned the plantation next to Massuh Preston. The captain's pa bought the massuh's hosses. The captain knows his hoss flesh an' he treated his Colored folks right nice.

"'Course, they was all free folks. I ain't real sure when they was set free, but they was free by the time I knowed of him. They stayed on an' worked there some long time after they was all given their freedom. They was even paid.

"When this war broked out, the captain, he joined up with the North. He told his Colored folks he didn't think there'd be nothin' left of his land when he come home. He told 'em it was all right if they all left. He give 'em each a paper sayin' they was free.

"I seen one a those papers. The feller what showed it to me, he said he was a goin' to put it in a frame someday. He said it be the most prized thing he ever did own.

"The captain was right 'bout his plantation too. It be the fust to burn. Some a those Colored folks died tryin' to save the house an' barn—an' the captain's little brother. Those Colored folks hid that little feller. They managed to save a few hosses too. They sent that kid away on one. He said he was goin' to find his brother, an' I reckon that's what he did 'cause there's a young feller here now by the name a Pete Headrick.

"Yes suh, I reckon we have us a mighty fine captain. Now let's git these hosses fed an' watered so's we cin pick some names."

Trainer grinned at his friends.

"I think Fastly Walker an' Goodly Tinker be fine names. 'Course, ya cin always take my last name if ya want. I like Trainer Free Man."

# BENTON BARRACKS
## ST. LOUIS, MISSOURI

# Chapter 92

# OLD FRIENDS AND GOOD MEMORIES

**H**ENRY MCCUNE PRESENTED HIMSELF TO THE soldier in front of Colonel Benjamen Bonneville's door. He poked the young man with the end of his buffalo gun and pointed it toward the colonel's quarters.

"Tell the colonel that Badger McCune is here to dicker with 'im on them there mules the army needs fer its fightin'."

The young soldier shook his head.

"Colonel Bonneville said he was not to be disturbed. You will need to come back tomorrow."

"You tell the colonel that *I'm* already disturbed an' if'n he don't see me, I'm a gonna turn my mule loost in his livery stable."

Colonel Bonneville jerked open the door. He was trying to contain the grin on his face, but he failed.

"Badger McCune. You old sidewinder. Get on in here." He pointed at the surprised soldier and waved his hand.

"Bring me some of my best whiskey and a couple of pieces of that apple pie Mrs. Sneed brought by. And I'll be busy for several hours so see to it that I'm not bothered."

The young soldier rushed off to fulfill the colonel's wishes and was back quickly. He handed the bottle and the pie to Colonel Bonneville and backed away as the colonel shut the door.

"Colonel Bonneville don't receive anyone unless they're big wigs." He thought about the wizened old man visiting the colonel and shook his head in surprise. "This Badger McCune don't look like much, but he must be some important to get this kind of a reception." Sergeant Wilsey moved to the side of the door and stood rigidly trying not to favor his bad leg.

Colonel Bonneville opened the bottle and handed Badger a glass.

"So…you are willing to sell the army some of your best mules."

"My mules is all best an' you'ins knows it or I wouldn't be drinkin' yur oldest whiskey an' eatin' yur favorite pie."

Colonel Bonneville chuckled. He pulled out a chair and pointed at it.

"Badger, it's good to see you." He dropped into a chair beside his friend as he grinned.

"Every time I hear your name, I think about the time that big badger got in your chicken coop. How old were we? Eight or nine?"

Badger grinned but didn't answer.

"I don't think either of us knew how mean badgers could be, but we found out! Why that old devil chased us clean out of that chicken coop. I ran up a tree, but you stopped and grabbed a wagon hammer. You said that badger had chased you one too many times.

"I was hollering at the top of my voice—I just knew you were going to die.

"That badger came at you, and I was terrified. Its claws were nearly two inches long. It hissed once to show its teeth and then charged. You were small and you dodged around until you were where you wanted to be. You held that hammer with both hands and slammed it down on top of that badger's head. Your old pa always said you'd only have one chance to kill a badger, so you'd better make the first hit count. You stunned that badger and it dropped. Once it was down, your pa tossed you his big knife. Why, I bet you stabbed that badger fifteen times or more. Your pa told us, 'Never assume a badger is dead—make sure he is,' and you did.

"Your pa just spit his chaw on the ground and said, 'Ya didn't hit quite square on top a his head, Boy. Ya got to hit 'em right smack in the middle to kill 'em. That durn badger jist 'bout had ya.' He never blinked an eye or made a move to help. He just assumed you'd get the job done. You did too.

"We cut off his feet. We strung those claws on a cord and were going to wear them like the Injuns did. Those claws were so sharp though that they cut our shirts and us too. We decided we'd just hang them on our walls.

"You made a scruffy-looking top hat out of that pelt and wore it for the next six or seven years. It was full of holes from all the knife cuts, but you didn't care. And that right there is how you got the name Badger. The hat finally wore out, but the name Badger stuck." Colonel Bonneville chuckled and lifted his glass.

"To old friends and good memories."

Badger grinned and did the same. The smile slowly left his face, and he leaned forward to speak.

"I come ta talk ta you'ins 'bout my niece. Ava Bowman or Nurse Sweet as some a yur soldiers call 'er."

Colonel Bonneville's eyebrows lifted.

"Your niece? I thought we were going to dicker on mules."

Badger chuckled and shook his head.

"I done told ya my price. Take it or leave it—it's all the same ta me. Now my niece is another matter.

"I want ta take her home with me, but I want the word out that she's daid. That durn Nielson put on lotsa miles ta run 'er down, an' yur soldier boys let 'im git away.

"Now that hole in 'er be a bad one an' I want the word leaked out that she died." Badger paused and added, "An' while yur thinkin', why is that salty Captain Headrick still a captain? Why he's one a the toughest officers I ever did run into—an' you'ins know I don't like many officers."

Colonel Bonneville's face turned a mottled red and he started to bluster.

Badger snorted. "An' don't tell me it's military business. I know the whole durn story 'bout how he pounded that feller at West Point." He snorted again. "A fight with a cocky little nincompoop an' that ruined his career? What kinda outfit you'ins runnin' back East? Ain't ya s'posed to be teachin' them thar young fellers ta fight? Ya want ta lose this here durn war?" When Colonel Bonneville didn't answer, Badger grinned and added, "I done said my piece.

"Now back ta my niece. Can ya help me spirit her outa that hospital? I know that cranky ol' Nurse Parsons what runs that place won't work with me none, but she'll take orders from you'ins."

The color in Colonel Bonneville's face slowly returned to normal. He pondered for a moment and finally nodded.

"I'll give my permission but how do you propose to get her out?"

"They put dead folks in coffins, don't they? I reckon we cin take her out that way." He grinned. "I'll give 'er a dose a my elixir an' she'll sleep like a baby. Won't even know we'uns moved 'er.

"I'll ask that head nun ta help me. We'll take little Ava over ta where those nuns be a stayin' an' fill that coffin with rocks. Then we'll have us a fine funeral." Badger chuckled and added, "Shoot, if'n there's a lost soul that needs a buryin', we cin put their body in that box. I'll even pay fer the durn funeral.

"Ava cin stay in that nun house till she's fit enough ta travel. I figger that'll be four or five days at least.

"We'll do the buryin' right away an' then I'll leave ta git yore mules. When I come back, we'll spirit Ava outa that nun house.

"This all has ta be done quiet though or else we'll have half the soldiers in yur durn army at that fake funeral."

Colonel Bonneville grinned at Badger and shook his head.

"Badger, when I listen to you right now, it makes me think of all the shenanigans you planned when we were growing up. Why if half the stuff we did was known, I doubt I'd even be an officer in this army let alone a colonel."

The two men visited a while longer before Colonel Bonneville stood.

"You talk to Sister Marie Christi, and I will talk to Nurse Parsons. We'll plan on a funeral first thing tomorrow morning. In fact, why don't you spend the night at the hospital? Have the nuns arrive at the hospital right after reveille, and I'll meet you at their residence with the chaplain."

Colonel Bonneville chuckled and added, "And I'm just guessing you're right. Sister Marie Christi will have some lost soul in that coffin once she hears about this. She's never been one to miss an opportunity."

# Chapter 93

# A DEVIOUS PLAN

SISTER MARIE CHRISTI AGREED TO HELP BUT ONLY IF the casket held a person in need of burying.

"I certainly won't pray for rocks or waste a new coffin. We have many poor souls who pass through here with no one to bury them properly.

"When you arrive tomorrow, I will have a body ready for burial. And of course Miss Bowman may stay here until she is fit to travel." Sister Marie Christi stood. "If you leave money with me, I will make sure she is properly outfitted to travel by train.

"Good day, Mr. McCune. I have a full evening of work and no more time to chat."

Badger almost did a little jig as he went down the steps, but he stopped himself. *This here is a serious deal an' I need ta look sad. I best git on back to the hospital an' git that room locked down. I'll tell Nurse Parsons I be sleepin' there tonight. Maybe one a those little nurses cin send me up some food.*

Nurse Parsons wasn't in her office, but there was a plate of warm food on her desk. Badger grabbed the plate and rushed up the stairs.

The sisters arrived quietly the next morning. Ava agreed to take another dose of Badger's elixir only after he explained what was going on. He didn't tell her that she would be leaving in a coffin though. He knew she'd never agree to that.

It was a somber group of nuns who helped Badger carry the coffin down the stairs and to his wagon. Several of the nurses stopped to stare, and the rumor mill was soon ripe with new information.

Huck Layton and Lucy Sneed arrived at the cemetery with Owen. The little boy did a fine job of pretending to cry. Badger could barely contain his laughter while Huck forced himself to frown.

*We need to git this kid outa town an' put 'im to work. With all his early trainin' an' natural talent, he could become a criminal with jist a little push.*

Lucy was quiet. She was concerned news of the funeral would leak and soldiers would arrive. She needn't have worried though. Colonel Bonneville sent lots of patrols out early that morning…and all of them contained soldiers who knew Nurse Sweet.

The good sisters didn't tell anyone, but the body they carried to the cemetery was that of a young prostitute. They had taken her in when she became ill. She had died in childbirth, and her baby was buried with her.

Badger knew who was in the casket, but he said nothing. He had a wreath of flowers made and even hired a woman to sing. He carried out the funeral just as he would have for his own kin.

The sisters smiled. The young mother was given a sendoff that she could never have hoped for. *And one she deserved*, thought Sister Marie Christi. *That little mother tried hard to change her life. She wanted to raise her baby differently than the way she was forced to live.*

The chaplain wasn't told the entire story. However, he knew a young prostitute had been taken in by the nuns, and he correctly assumed it was she in the coffin. He was told not to use any names for security's sake. That was surprising, but as an army chaplain, he was used to following orders without questioning them. His sermon was about love and his eulogy was simple.

When the service was over, Badger gave the man who had dug the hole some money and a marker. It said, "Child of God. May She Rest in the Lord's Loving Arms."

The gravedigger frowned and asked, "Don't ya want no name on there?"

Badger glared at him. "The Good Lord knows 'er name. That be enough. Now put up that marker."

As the quiet group left the cemetery, Lucy took Huck's arm. When they arrived at her house, she sent Owen down to the creek to play.

Owen's eyes lit up. "Can I get muddy?"

"You may get as muddy as you like. Now go and play but know you are going to take a bath when you return to the house." Lucy kissed his cheek and smiled as she watched him run. She turned to Huck and her eyes were soft.

"Huck, you have been pestering me for two years to marry you. I will say yes on one condition."

The old man grinned at Lucy and nodded. "I agree. Now tell me the deal."

"I want to go with Ava and Owen. We are Owen's grandparents, and we should be around to watch him grow—to play with him. I'm just not sure I could bear it if Ava left and took him with her."

Huck pulled Lucy close.

"I was jist thinkin' the same thing. Ya write yore brother. He cain't come, but he's yore onliest kin an' he should know. I don't have nobody to tell, but I reckon Stump 'ill be right happy when he hears the news. We'll plan to tie the knot in four days.

"We'll have to put yore place up fer sale, but houses is in short supply here. I doubt you'll have trouble sellin'. I rent my place so all I have to do is saddle my hoss an' ride away.

"I'll come over this afternoon an' help ya pack. We cain't take much though. We might be travelin' fer a time what with Miss Ava bein' a nurse."

Huck kissed Lucy gently and smiled at her. "I reckon this here is the happiest I've ever been. Now let's go tell our grandson that we're gettin' hitched…an' that we be goin' with him an' his sis when they leave."

# CITY RAIL STATION
## CENTRALIA, MISSOURI

# Chapter 94

# KANSAS BOUND

**C**APTAIN HEADRICK'S ORDERS WERE SPECIFIC. "IT will be nearly a nine-hour ride from here to Fort Leavenworth. If the prisoners need to relieve themselves while we are traveling, there are chamber pots under the front seats. You can dump those when we stop for fuel."

The three soldiers stared at Cap. They frowned but before they could respond, Major Johnson appeared and thrust a paper into Captain Headrick's hand.

He leaned forward and whispered, "You've been promoted. Congratulations, Major Headrick."

Noble stared at Major Johnson in surprise and the man grinned.

"General Merrill. He can make things happen. He pushed until this came through."

Captain Headrick glanced at the paper and then thrust it in his pocket. He was already yelling as he moved on to give the next round of orders.

A young officer was the last prisoner to board. He commented quietly, "Howdy, Blake. I didn't expect to see you on this train."

Corporal Blake looked at the bearded man in surprise. Recognition showed on his face briefly before he guarded his expression. His voice was gruff when he ordered the man to sit. He cursed softly as he slammed the door.

Espy caught the brief exchange. He asked softly, "Friend of yours?"

"Cousin," was Blake's answer. He cursed once under his breath but didn't look at his cousin again.

Private Espy and Corporal Blake had the prisoners loaded and the shades to the railcar pulled before the rest of the soldiers arrived at the station. Sergeant English had checked each man as he was loaded to ensure all handcuffs and chains were secured.

Espy and Blake were to stay in the front of the railcar with the prisoners and two of Major Johnson's men climbed on top of the livestock cars with their shotguns. Sergeant English was to stay at the back of the prison car while Corporal Barnes rode between the prison car and the first livestock car.

Espy ran his eyes over the prisoners as he worked his way to the front of the railcar. He muttered, "I ain't cleanin' out no chamber pot. Those fellers cin take a leak out the door as we're movin'. We cin hang onto their chains. If they try to jump, they'll end up under the railcar."

Blake stared at the younger man a moment and then shook his head.

"Nope, Cap said to use thunder buckets so that's what we'll do. It ain't like we have to do this more than one day." Still, he knew the smell would be terrible and the thought made him sick. *Maybe these officers took advantage of the privy before we left, and it won't be so bad as we think.*

*Humiliating for these soldiers too.* Blake shook his head. *I'll be glad when this war is over. I'm tired of seein' men I don't know as enemies. An' some I love like brothers too.*

The officers were angry when they were told the rules. Still, they knew they were prisoners and most understood even though they didn't like it. Several complained but Corporal Blake refused to budge.

"Take it up with the brass in Leavenworth. I don't make the orders—I just follow 'em."

Blake was quiet as he took his seat, but his thoughts were angry and bitter. *I would ask to be removed from this detail but there ain't anyone Cap trusts enough to take my place.*

He leaned against the side of the railcar with his rifle in his hands. *This is going to be a long old trip an' one I certainly won't enjoy.*

The prison car was near the middle of the train while the private car carrying the railroad executives was the last in line. Captain Headrick had been ordered to ride with the rail executives. He was irritated and pointed out that was not the way to protect them. However, those were his orders.

The horses were in three railcars behind the prisoners, and the soldiers rode on top of the livestock cars. A passenger car separated the livestock cars from the executive car.

Peter and Jackson were on top of the first and second livestock cars. One of Major Johnson's men was with each of them, and Goat climbed up to join Peter. Lieutenant Lampkin rode on the third livestock car. Hanson stayed on the ground until everyone was loaded. He checked the men's positions and signaled to Captain Headrick before he climbed aboard.

Espy took a seat across from Blake and muttered softly to himself, "She's a mean ol' war. I'm jist not sure we will all come back together when this here deal is over."

He glanced at Blake again, but the soldier's face showed no expression. *This is one of the times I'm glad I don't have much kin. Was I Blake, I'd be tempted to help my cousin escape.*

Espy settled back against his side of the railcar. He put one leg up on the seat beside him and frowned. He watched as Sergeant English took a seat at the back of the car. English cocked his shotgun when several of the officers started to talk. After that, the inside of the train was quiet.

# Chapter 95

# A REB FIRST AND ALWAYS

THE RAIL EXECUTIVES PEERED THROUGH THE windows of their car when the train made its first fuel stop, but they did not disembark. There was nothing at the stop but the water tank.

The fireman climbed down from the tender car that carried the wood. His job was to keep the firebox full, and it was hard, dirty work. He stretched and slowly walked toward the water tank. He swung the long waterspout over the boiler and pulled the rope that opened the spicket. The engineer watched the water level and signaled to the fireman when it was full.

The wood was burned to heat the water, and the steam that was produced powered the train. The locomotives required not only lots of wood but ample water as well.

Lampkin climbed down the side of the train and crawled inside the last livestock car. He wanted to check a horse that had spooked during loading and cut its leg. He lifted up the trembling animal's leg and then cursed. "That cut is mighty deep. I should treat it 'fore I climb back on top." He looked between the slats of the livestock car, but all was quiet. He lifted some salve out of his pocket and pulled off his bandana. "I'd better do this fast. I don't want to be caught down here if there's trouble."

The train slowly pulled away from the water tank. It reached full speed going down an incline and pulled steadily into the hills. While the two new soldiers on top distracted the men, Corporal Barnes climbed around the livestock cars until he was in front of the passenger car. The coupling wasn't locked down, and he quickly unhooked it, dropping the last two cars. The rest of the train moved away from the slowing cars. Trees were close to the tracks and the long branches shielded the last cars from those in front. He quickly moved around the railcars once again until he was behind the tender car.

All was quiet inside the prison car. Corporal Barnes waited until the train went down another incline. He unhooked the coupling between the prison car and the tender car just as the train was ready to start up the next hill.

Men stood as the prison and livestock cars slowed. Private Espy pulled up his shade to look out. Reb soldiers charged from the trees.

Corporal Blake yelled, "Bushwhackers! Get ready to hold this car!"

Both men were quickly subdued by freed prisoners. Blake cursed when he realized that Sergeant English, instead of checking their cuffs, had actually handed the prisoners keys. The sergeant pushed his shotgun against Blake's chest and started to pull back on the triggers. Blake's cousin knocked the gun barrel away.

"No unnecessary killing. Now get those horses unloaded."

The doors to the first two livestock cars were pulled open and Reb soldiers began to quickly unload the horses. Guns were pointed at Hanson, Pete, and Jackson. Most of the Galvanized Yankees stayed on top of the cars and watched while a few jumped off to join the freed Confederate officers.

One of the officers pointed at the soldiers still on top.

"You men get down here! You are still part of the Southern Resistance!"

The Galvanized soldiers climbed to their feet. Some stood uncertainly while others jumped to the ground.

When the doors to the last livestock car were pulled open, Lieutenant Lampkin began to shoot.

Several officers went down as well as some of the clustered soldiers. He continued to fire steadily. Those officers who were mounted spread out and raced away. They rode low over their horses to make as small of targets as possible. The rest of the prisoners were scrambling for horses. Several of the Galvanized Yankees escaped too even though Lampkin made each shot count.

Lampkin held his gun on the soldiers clustered around the horses.

"Ya men drop to the ground. Put yore faces in the dirt. I still have bullets an' I ain't afraid to use 'em." He swung his gun toward the soldiers holding Peter and Jackson.

"Ya fellers better unloose 'em or I'll blow ya apart. "Besides, yore already in enough trouble." When the men stepped back, Lampkin nodded at Peter.

"Pete, ya take a hoss back fer Cap an' ya stay with that last railcar. Now git!" His eyes moved toward the prison car.

"Hanson an' Goat, keep yore guns on those fellers on the ground an' ever'body else sit down!" Lampkin swung his eyes toward the prison car.

"Blake an' Espy! If ya ain't dead, git out here."

The two men staggered from the railcar supporting each other.

"Either of ya shot?"

"Naw, just pounded good," Blake growled.

"Any weapons in there?"

Blake held up the shotgun. "Just this an' both barrels are empty."

Lieutenant Lampkin pointed toward the last of the fleeing prisoners.

"Get mounted an' see if ya can catch some of those prisoners. Loose hosses too. Be careful though. More Rebs might be waitin' out there."

Goat was still on top of the railcar and Lampkin waved him down.

"Put yore gun on these fellers. We are goin' to lock them in the same car their officers was in." He added quietly as the man passed him, "An' be ready. At this point, they ain't got much to lose."

Lampkin looked around and finally asked, "Where's Hanson?"

Goat pointed toward the trees. "He took off by himself after a couple of those officers. Never said nothin'—jist took off."

Lampkin looked toward the trees. He started to say something but shook his head. Instead, he addressed the cluster of Reb soldiers on the ground.

"Ya fellers broke yore word. Ya promised to remain loyal to the United States Government. Now, y'all be sent to Fort Leavenworth an' be tried as traitors." He glared at them. "All ya had to do was sit back an' do nothin'."

One man stood and spat on the ground. "That what you'd a done? I doubt it. We's Rebs first an' always. I only signed up fer this deal to get outa that prison. We'll take our punishment. I jist hope the rest of those officers git away." He added bitterly, "'Sides, y'all are the ones who lied. We wasn't s'posed to fight our boys an' that's what we'd a done if we hadn't helped. What was those Reb officers doin' on this here train anyway?"

Gunfire sounded from the trees, and all heads turned to look that way. Lampkin's gun was steady when the men on the ground looked back at him.

"Git in that car. Cap cin sort this out when he gits here."

# Chapter 96

# DECEIT AND TRICKERY

IT TOOK THE ENGINEER NEARLY AN HOUR TO BACK UP and reconnect all the cars. The railroad executives were furious and planned to talk to General Ewing as soon as they arrived in Kansas City. They wanted Captain Headrick to be disciplined for endangering their lives. While they were shouting at him and making all kinds of threats, he snorted and walked away.

"I have more important things to tend to than a bunch of railroad bigwigs whose schedules were interrupted," he muttered. He cursed and shoved his fingers through his hair.

Of the twenty Confederate officers on the train, two were dead, three had life-threatening wounds, and six had escaped. Only nine would be delivered uninjured to Fort Leavenworth. In addition, four of the Galvanized Yankees in his command were dead, three had escaped, and six more had likely taken part in the prison break. Hanson did capture one of the Bushwhackers who had assisted in the heist though.

What made the captain the angriest was that men had died through trickery he had missed. "This deal required a lot of planning. Major Johnson was obviously working undercover to rescue the Confederate officers. In addition, the soldiers he sent to help were plants to make sure the prisoner heist took place."

Lampkin saw a Reb soldier with blond hair ride out of the trees to assist the escaping officers. He swore he saw the same man in a Union uniform at the Yankee hospital in Chattanooga. *And I'm guessing that fellow is Ava's brother. It sounds like the soldier she saw attacking our transport train when I first met her.* Captain Headrick's scowl became deeper, and he cursed again.

Captain Headrick ordered Lieutenant Lampkin on top of the last livestock car again. The Reb infiltrator was forced to climb up after him. All the other prisoners were in the prison car. Privates Hanson, Goat, and Espy were inside as well. Hanson had the shotgun and was sitting in front of the large hole in the side of the car. Corporal Blake was with the executives and the rest of the soldiers were on the first two livestock cars along with Privates Headrick and Lampkin. Captain Headrick waited until everyone was in position. Then he climbed on top of the prison car.

When the train arrived in Kansas City, Missouri, all passengers were ordered off and no new passengers were allowed to board.

The engineer demanded that ticketed passengers board, but Captain Headrick abruptly refused.

"Absolutely not. None of these people have been vetted. We are delivering these prisoners to Fort Leavenworth. Once they are unloaded, you can resume your normal schedule.

"Now arrange passage across the Missouri River so I can continue on my way. Make it quick because this train isn't coming back until my prisoners disembark. Also, the train we take from the river to Fort Leavenworth will only carry military personnel—no passengers will be allowed on nor will any civilians cross the river with us."

Once the train was on the Kansas side of the Missouri, Captain Headrick climbed onto the car beside Lieutenant Lampkin. He glared at the prisoner in front of him. "You have five minutes to tell me what I want to know. If you don't talk, I am turning you over to the authorities in Fort Leavenworth and recommending that you hang."

The soldier stared from one man to the other and slowly shook his head.

"I reckon not. I'll take my chances in your courts." He smirked at Captain Headrick and added sarcastically, "Besides, y'all plumb missed all the plannin' an' figurin' that took place. The officers we wanted got away an' I shot the ones who we was told might spill the beans."

He laughed at the surprise on Captain Headrick's face.

"Shore 'nuf. Whilst y'all was restin' easy down there with all the railroad bigwigs, we was pickin' an' choosin' who should git away.

"Our mission was accomplished an' y'all helped us. But don't expect me to tell nothin' like that to yore uppers. No siree. Somebody on yore side wants y'all to roast, an' I reckon this here deal will do ya in."

Lampkin looked over at Captain Headrick.

"I say we throw 'im off this here train when we reach the next canyon. We cin always say he tried to escape."

Captain Headrick didn't answer, and the prisoner began to protest.

"Y'all cain't do that! It's murder!"

"No reason to keep ya alive if ya ain't a goin' to talk, an' these here train tops cin be right slippery." Lampkin pointed toward the edge of the roof. "Now move over there."

One of the men in front shouted, "Bridge comin' up! Ever'body hang on!"

The train slowed but it still wobbled as it crossed the wooden bridge.

The soldiers grabbed for the rails that ran along the tops of the livestock cars and the prisoner saw his opportunity. He lunged to his feet. He tried to drop over the edge as they approached the bridge. Whether to swing himself off the train or to commit suicide, no one knew. He hit a support beam on the bridge, and the speed of the train flung him back to bounce off the rocks below.

Once the train was on solid ground, Lampkin sat up and grinned. "I reckon that saved me throwin' 'im off."

"Yes, but we have no proof of what he told us either," Captain Headrick replied quietly.

"Wouldn't have nohow. He was ordered to put ya away, Cap. Somebody with connections wants ya outa command an' in jail. Don't guess we'll see no friendly faces when we reach Fort Leavenworth."

# FORT LEAVENWORTH, KANSAS
## SATURDAY, OCTOBER 17, 1863

# Chapter 97

# NO WARM RECEPTION

CAPTAIN HEADRICK JUMPED OFF THE TRAIN. HE grabbed the first soldier he saw.

"I need to speak to your superior officer. I have some high-ranking Reb officers in my care who are slated for your prison."

The soldier stared at him. He stuttered several times and finally said, "We don't have a prison here, sir. All we have is a small jail and it's full."

When Captain Headrick glared at him, the soldier saluted quickly.

"I will find an officer. He will tell you where to put them." The soldier raced away. He was soon back with a confused major.

"Captain, we have no orders for Confederate prisoners to be incarcerated here. We don't have the facilities. I can show you where to put them overnight. I will ask Colonel Ault about incarceration here, but I am guessing they will need to be sent on to Fort Scott. We don't have the capabilities to separate high-ranking Confederate prisoners from the general population—and we certainly don't want to combine them."

Captain Headrick was seething. He tried to contain his anger as he and Lieutenant Lampkin followed the major to an empty storage shed. The Reb officers were locked inside, and the enlisted men were confined in another small building. Once they were jailed, Captain Headrick asked to see the fort commander, Colonel Ault.

"Captain Headrick reporting, sir. I have placed fifteen men in two of your storage sheds. Nine Confederate officers and six Galvanized Yankees who may have taken part in the attempted escape. My men are guarding them."

Colonel Ault pulled his pipe from his mouth and frowned as he stared at Captain Headrick.

"I received no information about any prisoners to be housed here. We don't have room. I must refuse them." He glared at the officer in front of him and growled, "Who gave you your orders, Captain?"

Captain Headrick placed his orders on the general's desk.

"These are the orders I received. I was told they were from General Merrill, sir. However, I now believe the soldier who gave them to me was a Confederate posing as a Union officer."

Colonel Ault lurched to his feet. His face turned pale and then a deep red.

"How is it that you know he was an enemy soldier?"

"I was not told about the order change until I reached Centralia, Missouri. Before then, all I knew was that I was to escort some railroad executives and officers' wives through Rebel territory to Kansas City, Missouri. Major Johnson, whom I now believe to be a Confederate, presented me with new orders in Centralia. I told him that my company was composed primarily of Galvanized Yankees." Captain Headrick paused and added, "Those are…"

"I know what Galvanized Yankees are, Captain."

"The new orders stated that I was to escort twenty high-ranking Confederate officers to Fort Leavenworth. I tried to tell Major Johnson that we should not be escorting Confederate prisoners with unvetted civilians and certainly not with my Galvanized Yankees. I also told him I did not have the manpower or enough cars to do it correctly. However,

Major Johnson insisted. I conceded when he showed me General Merrill's signature." Captain Headrick pointed at the signature on the paper."

"But you questioned the orders?"

"The orders were not written as I would have expected them. However, I have seen General Merrill's signature many times and it looked legitimate."

Colonel Ault's face was turning red again. His voice was hard when he grated, "Continue."

"Major Johnson offered to send four of his men with me to help guard the prisoners. Two were mustering out in two days. Sergeant English and Corporal Barnes were to deliver a message to you. Since they were all on their way to Fort Leavenworth, he ordered them to help transport the prisoners."

"And where are those soldiers now?"

"One died and the other three led the escape of the Confederate officers."

"So out of twenty high-ranking Reb officers, how many escaped?" Colonel Ault's breath was coming quickly, but Captain Headrick remained calm.

"Six escaped. Two were killed during the escape. Three were seriously wounded, and one of them died on the way here. The two wounded officers are with my men outside and will require hospitalization. The other nine officers are jailed in one of your empty storage sheds."

"Where were you when all this was taking place?"

"I was ordered to stay in the private car at the end of the train with the railroad executives." Captain Headrick's face was red as he added, "I knew that was not where I should be to give protection, but the orders were specific."

"And your Galvanized Yankees helped in the escape?"

"Some of them, sir. The railcar I was in was released from the rest of the train, so I did not see the escape. However, my men gave me detailed reports."

"And how do you know not all of your Galvanized Yankees were involved since you were not even present during this escape?"

"My men, sir. Lieutenant Lampkin, Corporal Blake, and four privates were all present. Lieutenant Lampkin is the one who shot some of those who were killed. We also captured one of the enemy soldiers whom Major Johnson sent with us. He said they were given orders of which officers to shoot in the event that not all could escape. He said he shot two himself."

"Where is this man? Can he corroborate your report?"

"No, sir. He died between Kansas City and Fort Leavenworth. He tried to escape when we crossed a bridge."

Colonel Ault slowly sank down in his chair. He glared at the man in front of him and finally shook his head.

"You do realize how preposterous this all sounds—especially when I have orders here for your arrest for aiding the enemy in a prison break of Confederate officers." Colonel Ault lifted a paper off his desk and shook it at Captain Headrick. "And the only reason I am not arresting you now is because no officer who planned such an escape would be *stupid* enough to show up here with those who did not get away." His face changed and he added softly, "Or it would be a very smart way to cover his tracks." He glared at Captain Headrick for a time, but the officer said nothing.

"Is there anything else you need to tell me?"

Captain Headrick pulled the promotion papers from his pocket and laid them on the desk.

"I now assume these papers are not legitimate either so I will leave them with you."

Colonel Ault grabbed the promotion order, scanned it, and threw it on his desk with a curse.

"You are dismissed, Captain. I expect to see you tomorrow morning at ten-hundred hours." He stared hard at Captain Headrick. His voice was brittle when he added, "And I am going to recommend that you be court-martialed."

"And the wounded officers, sir?"

"Take them to the hospital. I will put one of my men with them so don't leave until he arrives."

Lampkin met Captain Headrick as he left Colonel Ault's office. The lieutenant had a letter in his hand and held it out to Captain Headrick.

"A company of soldiers arrived this morning from St. Louis. A sergeant by the name of Wilsey asked them to deliver this to you. He told them it was private and important." Lampkin fell in step with his friend and asked softly, "Was it bad?"

Captain Headrick pushed his hat back and wiped his face with his bandana. "Yeah, but it will be worse. Colonel Ault wants me court-martialed."

Lampkin stopped so suddenly that he almost tripped.

"But ya was jist followin' orders!"

"Orders I should have questioned.

"I need to get those wounded Rebs over to the hospital. Hanson, Goat, Pete, and Blake can help carry them. You and Espy get the mounts to the livery. Make sure the men get their horses rubbed down and fed after they are watered.

"I want to see all the men before they are shown to their barracks, so keep them close until I'm done here." Captain Headrick squared his shoulders and led the way to the hospital.

It was dark when the captain was finally shown to his quarters. There were no lamps lit, so he laid the letter on the stand beside the bed and pulled his boots off. He shook his head as he thought about what was to come. *Who orchestrated this deal? It was planned down to the last detail. If Lampkin hadn't gone inside that livestock car to treat a horse, more men would likely have been shot, and those officers would have all gotten away… along with more of my Galvanized soldiers.*

A deep frown creased his face. *I sure hope Ava's brother wasn't part of this. If he was and they can connect him to me through her, I will go to prison for sure.*

Captain Headrick stripped down and laid back on the bunk. He was exhausted but sleep didn't come for a long time.

# Chapter 98

# MORE BAD NEWS

CAPTAIN HEADRICK WAS UP BEFORE REVEILLE. HE grabbed the letter and headed for the privy. His hands shook as he read the short note.

*October 16, 1863*

*Captain Headrick*
*Fort Leavenworth, Kansas*

*Captain Headrick, my name is Sergeant John Wilsey. You probably don't remember me, but I was in the bed next to the Reb surgeon when Nurse Sweet shot that Red Leg doctor at Chickamauga last month.*

*There was a trial here in St. Louis and Nurse Sweet was shot. That was several days ago. We all thought she was getting better, but she must have taken a turn for the worse. She passed sometime* during the night of October 15. Her uncle was there. Him and those nuns buried her this morning.

I'm real sorry to send you this sad letter, Captain, but I thought you should be told. I know you thought a lot of Nurse Sweet. Shoot, most of us soldiers loved her.

I heard someone call her uncle by the name of Badger, but I didn't catch a last name. I don't even know where he was from. Word is he left town right after the funeral.

My chest and leg wounds are healing just fine. The Reb surgeon that Nurse Sweet saved is the doc who worked on me. He took over surgeries after the Yankee doctors were ordered to leave. We were all mighty lucky to make it out of there before the Rebs tried to burn down that hospital.

The doctor here in St. Louis said I will be back with my regiment in Kansas soon. That's all I have to say. I'm sorry I couldn't give you good news.

Sergeant John Wilsey
11th Kansas Cavalry
Benton Barracks
St. Louis, Missouri

Captain Headrick bent over. He sucked so hard to keep from crying that he almost threw up. He slowly stood, straightened his uniform, and strode down to the livery. Lampkin told him that Deuce had been stolen in St. Louis around the time of Ava's trial. The chances of getting him back were slim and Captain Headrick had little hope of seeing him again. Still, as he walked, he listened for the horse's distinctive nicker.

"Maybe you are with Ava, Deuce. You probably wouldn't let anyone ride you, so I'm guessing you have been abused. Or maybe they sold you before you were ruined. I just don't know."

Captain Headrick walked through the barn until he found his company's horses. They looked well rested.

"That's good because we have some long miles in front of us." He stopped and added quietly, "Well, you do. I'm not sure what is going to happen to me."

Goat appeared in the barn. He saluted the captain and commented softly, "I recognized one of those Rebs that come outa the trees to help those officers escape."

When Captain Headrick looked up sharply, Goat added quickly, "Not at first. I thought he looked familiar, but I couldn't place 'im.

"That soldier's name was Lieutenant Charlie Bowman. Nielson called him Bachman so he must not have knowed his real name. That Reb used several other names, but Bowman is his actual moniker.

"I think he might be related to that nurse who was on trial. They have the same last name anyway.

"Bowman is a spy. He works both sides, but his loyalty is with the South. He met us a couple of times when I was with Nielson. I don't think he approved of Neilson's ways, but they knew each other.

"The next time I saw him, he was in the hospital in Chattanooga. He was pretendin' to be a Yankee. He was with some Yanks and was wounded. I think he was shot in the arm."

Goat's face colored slightly, and he added, "I made a couple of runs with some of those Red Legs. I was with Nielson when he threatened those nuns too." He added hurriedly, "But I didn't take part in abusin' or shootin' those two young soldiers. I tried to talk Nielson outa botherin' those nuns too." He cleared his throat before he continued.

"I was in the courtroom the day Nurse Sweet was shot. That head nun recognized me. That's when I decided to leave town.

"Nielson is the one who told me that feller was a spy. He laughed and said he sold Bachman information on troop movement. That Nielson is a snake. If I ever get a chance to shoot him, I'm goin' to do it." Goat's voice trailed off and he added softly, "I just wish I had seen Bowman sooner. We could mebbie have stopped that prisoner heist."

Captain Headrick listened quietly. Bile came up in his throat and he turned away. *Ava's brother was involved, and I have the letters she returned to me showing that I care for her. I can feel those prison bars around me now.* He let out a deep breath and shook his head. *Somehow though, I just don't care. I've lost Ava.* He turned to face Goat.

"Private, if you are asked to testify, don't you try to cover for me. I don't want to be responsible for any man taking an oath who is later court-martialed for lying."

Goat grinned at him.

"Don't you worry none, Cap. I won't lie—not much anyway. I sure won't tell all I just told you though. In fact, the brass will have to ask me some mighty specific questions to get any information outa me at all. I got my own skin to worry about, an' I like *me* a lot!"

# Chapter 99

# THE DECK IS STACKED

COLONEL AULT'S HEARING WAS BRIEF AND TO THE point. He wanted Captain Headrick to face a court-martial, and he wanted it to happen immediately.

"This hearing is dismissed until thirteen hundred hours today." He slammed his gavel on the desk and walked out without saying another word.

Major John Reynolds was representing Captain Headrick, while Major Lew Minsky represented the United States Government. Major Reynolds was worried.

"Captain, is there anything else you can tell me? Something that will throw some doubt on your guilt? Right now, all the evidence indicates you were either careless or complicit…and Major Minsky is going to try to prove you planned the entire thing."

Captain Headrick slowly shook his head.

"I received the new orders when we arrived in Centralia. General Merrill's signature was on them. I know him well and have seen his signature many times. I questioned the orders, but the signature looked legitimate. Still, he's a thorough planner and this deal did not sound like something he would order." Captain Headrick cursed under his breath and shook his head.

"I didn't agree with the orders or the proximity of the two groups. In both cases, I was told that I had no say. The railroad refused to put empty cars between the prisoners and my soldiers. If I had received extra cars, I could maybe have controlled the situation better.

"I didn't want the livestock cars at the back of the train, but I had to separate the two groups somehow. I put my Galvanized Yanks on top of the livestock cars. I put a couple of men I could trust on the top of each car as well. Still, my new troops were too close to the Reb officers."

Major Reynolds drummed his fingers on the table as he watched Captain Headrick.

"Were you aware that one of the escaped Confederate officers was related to Corporal Blake?"

Captain Headrick stared at his lawyer in shock. His face was pale when he shook his head.

"No. I had a list of prisoner names and didn't see any Blake on there. If I had known, I would have reassigned him. I oversaw the loading and made assignments, but then I left for the executive car.

"Of course, names are sometimes inaccurate. Some soldiers, and especially officers, don't use their given names when they are captured."

"Did you know any of the prisoners?"

"Yes, three of them. Two were friends from West Point and a third I knew growing up." Captain Headrick's face was hard when he added, "But that fact didn't matter to me. In fact, I told one of them that very thing."

Major Reynold's frowned as he made notes. He looked up and stated softly, "Those three officers were among those who escaped.

"Have you been told that one of the soldiers you said Major Johnson sent with you is said to be a spy?"

"No, but I am not surprised. The Reb's wouldn't use ordinary fighting men to try to pull off a deal like that. Of course, at the time they joined us, I thought they were legitimate Yankee soldiers."

Major Reynolds stood and waved at the guard.

"You may take Captain Headrick now. Lock him in the supply room to keep him away from those Reb prisoners. And get him some food." He looked back at the captain.

"I am going to try to reach General Merrill. The last I knew he was in Chattanooga. If we can find him—and that is a long shot—maybe he can verify some of this in a wire. If not..." Major Reynolds shrugged and shook his head. "Things are not looking favorable, Captain. I will do my best, but Major Minsky has already said he is calling some of the Reb prisoners to testify. I'm guessing some of them will lie if they think it will hang a Union officer. Some of your Galvanized Yankees are going to be called as well...and I don't have one unbiased witness to verify your story."

# Chapter 100

# A TALKATIVE WITNESS

**THE MILITARY COURT CONVENED THAT AFTERNOON.** The first witness called was Goat.

"Private Goat—what is your first name?"

"Billy."

When some men in the room snickered, Goat added with a grin, "My folks had a sense of humor. 'Course my Pa's name was Harry, so I guess his folks did too." The chuckles became louder, and Colonel Ault slammed his gavel on his desk.

"Order…Order!"

"Private Goat, where were you when the prisoners escaped?"

"On top of the first livestock car."

"Did you try to stop the escape or shoot at anyone?"

"Nope. I was mostly confused. We was told our company would not have any contact with Rebs, so I was mighty surprised Rebs was on that train. Most of our soldiers are Galvanized Yanks. Not me but most of the other fellers are.

"When the ruckus broke out, I couldn't tell who from who an' which from what. The rest of the fellers mostly knew each other. They all come outa Yankee prisons, and most of them was tight with each other. I signed up when I met Captain Headrick and his men on the trail, so I don't know ever'body yet."

"Did Captain Headrick coerce you into enlisting?"

"Naw. I wanted to travel west an' I figgered it would be safest to do that with the army. When Cap come along with his cavalry, I figgered that was my lucky day. My hoss was worn down an' I was outa food. Lonesome too so I joined up." He grinned at the room of officers and added, "I like good conversation, ya see."

"Why didn't you try to shoot those prisoners when they escaped?"

"Well, first of all, they was Reb officers. They was brung west 'cause the brass didn't want 'em with the enlisted prisoners. I figgered that meant they was some important an' they should be caught, not shot. I wasn't sure what to do so I just sat there on top of that train car. Besides, like I said before, I couldn't tell who ever'body was."

"You didn't take part in the breakout?"

"Nope."

"Look at that group of men over there. Did all of them take part in breaking those Rebs out?"

"Not all of 'em."

Major Minsky's voice went up in pitch. "Which ones didn't take part?"

"The two fellers on the right and the short man on the left. Those three in the middle was the ones who took up their guns against Captain Headrick's company."

"You're sure?"

"As sure as Harry Goat was my pa." He frowned and scratched his head before he added, "Although there is some question with that." When the entire courtroom stared at Goat in shock, he grinned.

"See, my brothers didn't like me so much. They said I was spoilt. I wasn't spoilt but Ma did treat me special. She said it was 'cause I was the littlest. Those five big brothers of mine said it was 'cause I was adopted." He grinned around the courtroom and added, "Ma said I weren't though.

"Most folks said I looked just like my pappy, an' he was a handsome devil—least that's what Ma always said. 'Course, I never thought Pappy was good-lookin', so I always figgered there was a *chance* I wasn't his."

"Now, my cousin Ferd—we all know he ain't—"

"That's enough, Private Goat. You are only to answer the questions I ask you.

"Did you know Corporal Blake had a cousin amongst the prisoners?"

"Who's Corporal Blake?"

"He's that man over there." Major Minsky pointed toward Blake.

Goat squinted his eyes. "Did he have a beard before? A big, bushy one? He musta shaved it off 'cause that feller don't look familiar at all."

"Private Goat, how is it that you could ride with these men for *five days* and not know one of the officers?"

"Well, first of all, I lost my spectacles out there on the prairie. In fact, that's how Captain Headrick come up on me. I was a crawlin' 'round on the ground lookin' for 'em. Without those durn glasses, I cain't hardly see my hand in front of my face."

Major Minsky's voice was sarcastic when he suggested, "So, you couldn't help stop the escape because you couldn't see who was who."

Goat grinned widely.

"Shore 'nuf. When I shoot at animals or Injuns, I just shoot at their hazy shadows, but when good folks an' bad folks is all mixed together, I just cain't tell no one apart without my spectacles."

"So how is it that you know the three men you pointed out earlier were not involved?" Minsky's voice dripped with sarcasm and disbelief.

"'Cause of how they's shaped. See, the feller on the left is a short feller. He's so short that his hands pertineer reach his kneecaps. Now the feller to the right—he's mighty tall an' humps his back. When he walks, he drags his left foot. Musta gotten runned over by a wagon or mebbie a hoss rolled on 'im when he was a kid. The other feller is shaped like a durn ball. He can barely hook his britches. When he mounts his hoss, he gives three heaves. If he don't make it up on the third try, that tall galoot puts a boot in his—I mean, he helps him up." He grinned at the courtroom and again received quiet chuckles.

Minsky snorted.

"Private Goat, you are dismissed."

"I just have one more story I'd like to tell. Y'all didn't let me finish tellin' how we all know that Ferd ain't really my cousin. See, he—"

Colonel Ault slammed his gavel down and Major Minsky grabbed Goat. He jerked him from the witness chair and shoved the grinning man toward the door.

Goat stopped in the doorway and hollered, "Any of ya fellers who want to hear the rest of that there story, I'll be—"

Colonel Ault began to bellow, and the guard pointed his gun at Goat. The ornery soldier darted out the door singing "Peas, peas, peas, peas—eatin' goober peas," as he ran down the hallway. Most of the officers didn't recognize the Confederate song about peanuts but Captain Headrick did. He ducked his head to hide his grin.

# Chapter 101

# A SKEWED TRIAL

MORE WITNESSES WERE CALLED ON THE SECOND AND third days of the court-martial trial. By day three, Captain Headrick knew he was not going to get off. He watched as the parade of men moved in and out of the witness chair. Some of the witnesses talked about details that never happened while others said the captain was drunk when he boarded the train. Major Reynolds tried to have their testimony thrown out, but Colonel Ault overruled him.

On the afternoon of the third day, the courtroom door suddenly burst open. Brevet Brigadier General Lewis Merrill strode into the room. Captain Headrick stiffened. He leaned forward in his chair as he frowned.

General Merrill waved his arm around the room.

"I want this room cleared of everyone except the officers presiding over this trial. Witnesses, lawyers, defendant—I want them all out."

When the room was cleared and the door closed, General Merrill glared at Colonel Ault.

"I want to see those orders that supposedly came from me."

Colonel Ault was silent as he handed Merrill the orders.

General Merrill studied the orders briefly. He quickly wrote his signature under the forged one on the paper in front of him. The two signatures were nearly identical. He threw the papers toward Colonel Ault before he leaned across the desk to address him.

"You were told there was a Confederate spy ring operating out of this area. You were also told that Confederate officers would be arriving in Centralia and that their presence was top secret.

"Where were the men I ordered to escort those officers to Fort Scott? They certainly were not in Centralia nor were they on that train with the prisoners."

Colonel Ault's body was stiff, and his face was a mottled red when he answered.

"I am short-staffed. With all the Indian depredations and so many settlers being attacked, I didn't have ten men available to escort twenty prisoners. Major Lewis—" He pointed to the back of the room and then looked around in surprise.

"Where did Major Lewis go? He is the one who offered to arrange the escort for me. He said he had some soldiers being moved through this fort and he could spare a few to help me out."

General Merrill almost snorted.

"Who is Major Lewis?"

"He just arrived at the fort a week ago. He said he was joining Major General John Fremont with the 2nd Missouri Volunteer Cavalry."

"Did you verify that information?"

Colonel Ault sat back in his chair. Fury leaked from him as he spoke.

"I didn't think it necessary. His papers were in order.

"And who are you to question me? *I am in charge here.* You are a general and you answer to *me!* How dare you threaten me!" Colonel Ault was almost shouting as he lunged out of his chair.

General Merrill slammed a paper down on the desk. It gave General Merrill permission to take command of Fort Leavenworth and was signed by President Lincoln. Merrill pointed at it.

"That paper gives me permission to question you and to throw you in the brig if I deem it necessary.

"You turned this mission over to a major you barely knew. And in doing so, you did not verify the authenticity of his papers. You failed your office, Colonel Ault, and now you want to court-martial my best officer because your sloppy oversight and lack of judgment caused this mess." General Merrill looked at the court-martial panel.

"I am ordering this court-martial be dismissed." Brigadier General Merrill's voice was soft when he added, "And I want a new one opened to investigate the actions of Colonel Ault."

Colonel Ault lurched to his feet.

"You can't do that! I only have two months before retirement. You will destroy my career!"

"I didn't ruin your career—you did when you tried to blame your ineptitude on a junior officer." General Merrill's eyes narrowed when he saw Captain Headrick's promotion order on Colonel Ault's desk.

"And why wasn't Captain Headrick promoted like I ordered?"

Colonel Ault sank down in his chair. His voice was barely above a whisper when he replied, "I—I thought that signature was forged as well."

General Merrill glared at the officers in front of him. His eyes finally settled on Colonel Ault.

"Colonel Ault, out of courtesy, I will not remove you from this courtroom in irons. However, your court-martial will begin tomorrow morning at nine hundred hours." He pointed at one of the officers in front of him.

"General Dickson will be the presiding officer per President Lincoln's orders.

"I suggest you pack your belongings, Colonel Ault. Regardless of how your court-martial turns out, you will be removed from this post." General Merrill picked up Captain Headrick's promotion papers and saluted the silent officers.

"Gentlemen." He strode out the door, his back stiff and his boots stomping loudly.

"I will never understand how incompetent men like Ault make it to the top," General Merrill muttered. "That man should have been thrown out of the service years ago for some of the things he pulled. Now fifteen years later, here he is a colonel." He snorted and added, "But I doubt he will be when this is over. I have a trove of information on his actions over the years, and I will pass that along to General Dickson.

"We'll shake this post up a little, and when it's over, they will have a commanding officer here who can handle the job.

"Now to find Captain Headrick and give him this promotion."

# CITY OF KANSAS
## MOUTH OF THE MISSOURI RIVER, KANSAS SIDE
## WEDNESDAY, OCTOBER 28, 1863

# Chapter 102

# "THOSE FELLERS IS LIKE RATS"

**B**ADGER RODE ONE OF HIS MULES SLOWLY DOWN THE main street of the City of Kansas although many were beginning to call the town Kansas City. He was going to the livery to collect a horse that had arrived there yesterday. The owners had tried to rob a bank in town and were in jail. The new sheriff was going to shoot the horse because it was dangerous. However, the man who ran the livery convinced him to contact Badger.

"There's a feller outside town who takes in sick hosses an' mules. Let him look that hoss over an' see if it can be calmed down. He was a fine hoss in his day. He's jist been abused an' neglected to the point that he is mean.

"Give Badger the durn hoss an' you'll save yore own self the cost of disposin' of 'im."

Badger stopped first at the jail to get the needed papers from the sheriff. As he signed for the horse, he asked, "So who be these here fellers what tried to rob the durn bank? You'ins need any help ta hang 'em?"

"Strangers and they won't tell me their names. I'm guessing they are deserters based on their army pants. 'Course that isn't for sure. If I knew they were, I'd turn them over to the officers at Fort Leavenworth. They won't take anybody though that ain't for certain a deserter though. They said they have their hands full the way it is." The sheriff cursed.

"This damn war. We have riffraff from both sides terrorizing folks around here." He studied Badger and added, "I'm surprised you haven't had any trouble."

Badger grinned at him. "Naw, I be prepared. I have my road paced off so's I know how far Ol' Betsy here kin shoot. An' I shoot anybody what don't answer when I call out.

"'Sides, I turn Mule loost at night. When I'm gone too. He be kinda like a watchdog. He patrols the place an' takes care a the bad element if'n they try ta sneak in." Badger chuckled and added, "Got me my own little fort an' I like it out there." He nodded toward the cells.

"Mind if'n I take a look at them there fellers. Could be I might recognize 'em."

"Go ahead. I doubt they'll talk but feel free to try."

Badger strolled back to the cells and stared at the surly men incarcerated there. He caught a glimpse of red before one of the men shoved the red strip in his hand into his pocket.

Badger almost cursed. *Likely friends a that scallywag Nielson, the dirty bugger who tried to kill my little Ava. I know two or three more was with 'im at that trial. Sergeant Wilsey said that head nun's eyes pointed 'em all out.*

"So why ya fellers in this here jail? Be ya Rebs?"

"Rebs! We ain't bloody Rebs. We's part of General Ewings special fightin' forces, an' when he finds out we's in here, he'll send someone to git us out."

"That General Ewing, he tells ya ta rob Union banks too, does he?"

The man stopped talking and turned to face the wall.

Badger chuckled.

"Don't make me no never mind. I don't keep my money in banks. Don't trust no banker enough to hand my hard work over to 'im.

"Well, ya fellers enjoy yur last day on this here earth. Word is you'ins be hangin' tomorrow mornin'. I ain't seen me a good hangin' in some time. Might stick around or I might head home. Ain't rightly decided." Badger turned and stalked toward the door.

One of the prisoners called after him softly, "Mister, if ya cin whisk us outa this here jail, we'll make it worth yur while."

"Not unless you'ins cin tell me where ta find Sergeant Nielson. Nielson an' me go way back, an' I been tryin' ta catch up with 'im." Badger turned toward the two men briefly but neither answered. One frowned and the other looked down.

"I reckon I'll see you'ins at yur hangin' then," he stated and strolled toward the front of the jail. He stopped by the jailer and commented softly, "They's Red Legs, an' those fellers is like rats. When one shows up, a passel more of 'em be close by.

"Keep yur eyes open."

# Chapter 103

# A HAPPY REUNION

**B**ADGER STOPPED BY THE LIVERY AND PICKED UP THE horse he had been asked to take. The young stud showed good breeding, but he was in poor condition. He had been abused and fought when Badger tried to hook a rope around his neck. Suddenly, the horse stopped fighting the rope. He sniffed Badger's shirt and nickered softly.

"Whatcha smell, feller? Ya think I have some food fer you'ins? I don't have none here, but I do back home. So yur a goin' ta foller me? I reckon we don't need no rope then. Let's go see yur new home."

The farther they rode from town, the more excited the horse became. When they were about a half mile from Badger's ranch, the stud threw up his head and neighed. He raced down the narrow lane and charged into the yard. Ava stepped out of the barn and the horse nearly ran over her in its excitement. Ava threw her arms around the horse's neck and cried as the horse nickered softly and nuzzled her.

"How in the world did you find Deuce, Uncle Henry? I thought he was gone forever!" Ava was laughing and crying at the same time as she hugged her horse.

"I reckon that there hoss smelled somethin' of you'ins on me. Once he sniffed me, he calmed right down an' follered me out here." Badger looked closer at the horse and nodded.

"Shore now. He be a son of ol' Jewel. Well, I'll be. Guess ya cin start that hoss farm you'ins always wanted if'n that cranky Captain ever slows down long 'nough fer ya to catch 'im."

Badger smiled as he watched Ava. She had been recuperating on his ranch for nearly two weeks and the bloom was back on her cheeks. Her back and chest were still stiff, but the wounds had healed well.

"Guess it's time ya decided what you'ins is a goin' ta do, gal. Go to Fort Leavenworth an' work in that hospital or go back ta St. Louis an' work there."

"I think I'll go west. Noble told me that the army camps are short on medical staff so I can help in one of those."

"Jist any ol' camp or does ya have a certain one in mind?" Badger's blue eyes were sparkling. When Ava looked up quickly, he chuckled.

"I reckon it's time ya moved on, but you'ins come back ta visit any time now. This ol' house'll be plumb quiet when you's gone."

Ava ran to Badger and hugged him.

"Uncle Henry, thank you for letting me stay here. I have so enjoyed myself, and Owen has too. Huck and Lucy are such wonderful grandparents. They just spoil him rotten." She kissed the old man and whispered, "And you are a wonderful grandfather too. Owen calls you Grampy Badger. You will have to come and visit once we are settled."

Badger didn't answer. He was looking down the long lane that led to his house. He pointed at Ava.

"You'ins git that hoss in the barn. Put 'im in a stall an' keep 'im quiet. We's about to have company an' I ain't so sure they's friendly."

Ava rushed toward the barn with Deuce right behind her. She could see some small figures on the lane, but the cluster wasn't much bigger than a bug.

"Uncle Badger has eyes like an eagle. You be quiet now."

# Chapter 104

# "I'VE BEEN INTRODUCED TO THAT MULE"

**B**ADGER STEPPED TOWARD THE SMALL BUILDING HE used for his blacksmith shop. He lifted his big gun and whistled.

A large mule charged toward him and slid to a stop.

"Mule, we's about ta have some folks show up an' they ain't here fer a social visit. I'm a goin' ta need yur help so you'ins be ready."

The mule snorted and swung around to look in the direction Badger pointed. It edged closer to him and snorted again. It wasn't long before three men rode into the yard.

The first one looked around carefully. When he was satisfied that Badger was alone, he pulled off his hat and ran his fingers through greasy hair.

"Howdy. My partners an' me are in need of some pack mules. The feller at the livery said ya might have some fer sale."

"Mebbie I do 'an mebbie I don't. Depends on how you'ins treat yur livestock."

The stranger's face became hard, and he waved his hand at the group of mules in the corral.

"Look, mister. We need some mules. How they'll be used don't matter—they're jist mules."

"It matters ta me. These here mules is like my kids, an' I take family serious." He studied each of their faces. His eyes lingered on the third one the longest before his gaze returned to the first man. He asked, "Where ya fellers from? Ain't never seen ya 'round before."

The second man laughed. "We hail from down in Georgia. We were out here on business an' lost our pack hosses to some renegades. We need some mules to haul our personal effects." He pointed at the large quilt tied behind his saddle.

"Ma sent this quilt with me when I left home an' I intend to keep it safe. It's so durn thick that I can barely get my leg over this hoss with it on the back of my saddle. I need a mule to haul it an' some other goods I left back to the livery.

"Two mules for the three of us would be plenty. We have money an' we'll be glad to pay."

Badger's bright blue eyes studied the three men again. The more he looked them over, the more irritated the one in front became.

"Look, old man. We don't have time to wait around while ya think. Do ya want to sell us some mules or not?"

Badger spat the tobacco in his mouth toward the fence behind him.

"Git on down an' look 'em over. Ya tell me which ones you'ins be likin' an' I'll tell ya the price."

The man in front pointed at the mule beside Badger.

"I like that jack. He looks like a good one."

"He be my best mule. He don't take to jist anyone though so walk easy when ya come up on 'im."

The third man in the group had been quiet the entire time. He kept his hands on the saddle horn and spoke carefully.

"I reckon I'll come back another time. I just remembered something I need to take care of back in town."

"Go on an' git outa here. An' don't ya bother ta come back again neither." Badger's eyes were cold as he stared at the quiet man.

The first man swung his horse around with a curse.

"Mort, ya leave now an' there ain't no need fer us to ever meet up again."

The man called Mort nodded and slowly turned his horse around. He looked back as he spoke quietly, "I reckon that will be fine with me." As he rode his horse slowly down the lane, the first man jerked his pistol out of his holster. Before he could cock it, Badger's voice sounded behind him.

"I don't know what kinda argument you'ins be havin', but there won't be no backshootin' today." His buffalo gun was ready, and both men knew he would shoot.

The second man held up his hands and shook his head.

"My partner was only funnin'. Now let's talk mules. We'll take that big jack and the black one on the east side of the corral—the one that's off by itself." He pulled some money out of his vest.

"$200 be enough?"

When Badger turned his eyes toward the second man, the first one whirled his horse around and fired at Badger. The old man was ready though.

He whistled, and Mule charged with an open mouth. The horse screamed and reared as it tried to get away. Mule whirled and kicked. His back feet hit the horse in the shoulder and knocked it over backwards.

The second man dropped the money. When he made a grab for his gun, Mule lunged. He grabbed the man by his leg and drug him off his horse. He tossed him in the air and came down on the screaming man with both front feet. Then he wheeled around and charged the first horse that had just struggled to its feet. When the horse shied, its rider fell off. His boot stuck in the stirrup, and he screamed as the horse's movements pulled his leg. His boot slid off and he grabbed his leg as he fell back on the ground.

Badger whistled and Mule stopped.

The man on the ground held his leg as he cursed.

"That mule broke my leg! Give me my gun an' I'll show 'im a thing or two!"

Mule grabbed the downed man by the leg and began to drag him toward the corral. Just then, Ava stepped out of the barn. She held a rifle, and it was pointed at the screaming man.

Her voice was shaking and could barely be heard above the man's cursing.

"That's him. That's Sergeant Nielson. He's the one who ordered the killing of Mother and Granny—and he's the one who shot me."

Badger took the rifle from Ava's hands. His voice was soft when he spoke.

"No need fer you'ins ta use that. Mule cin finish things up here." He pointed at Mule and ordered softly, "To the crick, Mule. Take 'im to the crick."

The big Jack released his hold and grabbed the cursing man by a knee. He trotted toward a grove of trees with Nielson bouncing over the rough ground beside him. They disappeared in the trees. The screaming briefly increased in intensity and then all was quiet.

Mort could hear the noise behind him, but he didn't look back.

"I think it's time for me to leave Kansas, and California might not even be far enough. I've been introduced to McCune's big jack before, and that one meeting was enough for me.

"Yessir. I think I'll head west. Nielson said we were going to get some pack horses. He never said anything about mules or Badger McCune. If he'd mentioned either, I wouldn't have ridden out here today." Mort spurred his horse and disappeared over a hill.

Ava sank to the ground and began to sob. Badger lifted her up and tried to guide her toward the house. She stopped when she saw the quilt lying on the ground. She gasped and ran toward it. She cried and hugged it to her.

"My quilt! It was taken by a young man the day the Red Legs came. He was going to try to keep it safe for me. He must have lost it."

Ava untied her quilt and shook it out. It was dirty and had a few holes but was in decent shape for the miles it had traveled. Her breath caught as she touched her grandmother's name.

Badger lifted the quilt and took Ava's arm again. He hugged his niece.

"It's all over now, gal. Mule done took care a ever'thing. Now you'ins go on in the house an' pack yur things. It's time fer ya ta make a new start. All of you'ins."

Once Ava was in the house, Badger walked slowly toward the frightened horses. They shied away and rolled their eyes as he approached them.

"Easy now, fellers. Let's git these saddle off an' look you'ins over." He dropped the saddles to the ground and led the horses into the barn. He fed them and rubbed them down as he talked quietly.

"We'll find you'ins a new home." He grinned and added, "An' one that don't have no mules 'round neither. Nope, I reckon from now on, ya both be mighty concerned 'bout gittin' too close ta mules.

"Owen'll be needin' 'im a hoss. Mebbie I'll jist send ya on with my little Ava. That gal loves hosses an' she'll baby ya back ta not bein' so afeared." He applied some of his ointment to the injured horse's shoulder and left the barn quietly.

# Chapter 105

# TIME TO FIND A HOME

OWEN BOUNCED IN HIS TRAIN SEAT EXCITEDLY AS HE asked, "Where we goin, Sis? Will we live on a ranch? Is one of those horses Grampy Badger showed me really mine? When can I ride it?"

Ava laughed and hugged him.

"I'm not sure where we are going but wherever we go, you will have your grandparents with you. And Grampy Badger promised to visit us when we get settled.

"As far as the horses go, they are on this train too. We need to stay for a time in Fort Leavenworth to let that injured horse heal so I will try to get a job in the hospital there. And yes, one of those horses will be yours." She smiled at the excited little boy.

"Which one do you think you will choose?"

"I like the one with the hurt shoulder. He has friendly eyes. I think I'll call him Gimpy 'cause he limps when he walks.

"I don't mind that though. He's a nice horse."

Ava nodded her head.

"He is a nice horse. We want to make sure he heals correctly because a lame horse shouldn't be ridden." She hugged the excited little boy and whispered, "You have a tender heart, Owen, and I think your heart will help Gimpy heal."

"Now try to get some sleep. Fort Leavenworth is a busy military post so it could be loud tonight." She put her arm around Owen. It took him some time to stop fidgeting, but he finally went to sleep. Ava smiled as she looked toward Huck.

"How will we travel when we leave Fort Leavenworth? I know the train tracks don't reach all the way to Lawrence yet let alone farther west."

"We'll probably hook up with some soldier boys." He grinned at Ava and added, "If ya hadn't already packed yore heart away fer that durn captain, we could let ya flirt a little. Then we'd have an invitation to travel in no time."

Ava blushed furiously and whispered, "Good grief, Huck. Don't talk so loudly. You make it sound like I am chasing him."

Huck grinned and winked at her.

"Well, ain't ya? We shore didn't travel this way 'cause we had a new home. Yep, you's a hopin' to catch that captain an' we all know it. Nothin' wrong with that neither." He pointed at the quilt Ava had draped across their laps.

"Kinda surprisin' thing to find that quilt after all this time. Wonder what all places it traveled 'fore it come back? An' yore hoss too." Huck frowned and shook his head.

"Not sure Deuce woulda lasted much longer bein' treated like he was. An keep in mind that's a goin' to affect how he acts 'round folks. We'll need to pen 'im alone from now on. In fact, mebbie ya should castrate 'im. Might make 'im a little easier to handle."

Ava glared at the old man.

"Deuce is fine around me and he will calm down. He was as gentle as a kitten when he was taken. He's just nervous, that's all.

"Besides, he is the only horse remaining from the bloodline my granny created. With him and that filly Badger gave us, I have the start of my horse ranch."

Lucy laughed. "Now Huck, you leave that girl alone. I know you said that just to rile her." She shook Huck's arm when he grinned. "Let's all relax and get some rest."

The train wheels suddenly locked and metal screamed. Ava grabbed the back of the seat in front of her with one hand and pushed Owen back with the other. Men's voices could be heard and soldiers in blue uniforms swarmed around the train.

A man shouted loudly, "I want every car searched. That killer was said to be traveling on this train, and we need to find him.

"And if anyone has a quilt or blanket of any kind draped over their seat, make them stand while you search. A man could crawl under those seats and hide."

Ava grabbed the quilt and stood as she tried to fold it. It was large and fell over the seats as she struggled with it.

A man's voice behind her ordered softly, "Ma'am, I'm asking you to step away from your seat. The rest of you folks too."

Ava froze and then slowly turned around.

"Noble? Oh, Noble!" She threw her arms around the surprised soldier as she tried not to cry.

The officer's face was pale as he took Ava's arms. He held her away from him and his breath came quickly.

"Ava? But you died! I was sent a letter. There was a funeral! I—I—is it really you?"

Ava touched his face and pulled a sturdy chain out of her bodice. The small gold ring that hung on the end glistened in the sunlight.

Noble pulled Ava close to him. He hugged her so tightly she could barely breathe. Owen stood and jerked on his uniform.

"Mister, you are a squeezin' my sis so hard that yur knockin' the air clean outa her. Now step back an' let 'er breathe." He glared as he spoke and jerked on the soldier again.

Major Headrick laughed and stepped back. He squatted in front of the young man as his eyes twinkled.

"Sister, huh? And just when I thought I knew the whole family." He put out his hand to Owen and said seriously, "I'm Major Noble Headrick and I'd like to marry your sister. Think that would be all right?"

Owen folded his arms across his chest and frowned as he studied the soldier.

"I reckon I'll have to think on that." He looked over at Huck. "Huck an' me can talk it over."

Noble grinned. He stood and took off his hat before he stretched his hand out to the grinning Huck.

"Good to see you, Huck. You too, Lucy." He glanced at her hand and laughed when he saw a ring on her third finger.

"I guess Huck finally wore you down. Where are you two headed?"

Huck pulled Lucy closer as she smiled. He grinned and shrugged.

"Don't rightly know but Owen here is our grandson—an' since he's Ava's little brother, we're a goin' wherever she goes." His grin became bigger as he added, "Ya take one, ya take all." He pointed at Noble's uniform. "Good thing ya got yoreself a promotion. You's a goin' to need plenty of room fer yore whole family!"

Noble stared from one to the other and then at Ava in surprise. She blushed.

"Yes, my family has grown." Her chin came up and she added, "Of course, if you have changed your mind, we can keep traveling west."

Major Headrick threw back his head and laughed.

"Nothing has changed for me unless Owen here won't give his permission." His eyes twinkled and he leaned over to whisper to Owen, "You know, if I marry your sister, you will be living on a military base. I might even let you train with the soldiers."

Owen tried to keep his face still, but he couldn't do it. He began to jump up and down as he hollered, "Marry 'im, Sis! Marry 'im. I wanna be a soldier an' fight wild Injuns!"

Ava put her arm around Owen and laughed. Her smile slowly faded as she looked out the window. She asked, "What—who are you looking for? Why was the train stopped?"

Major Headrick smiled and put his arms around her.

"There you go asking questions again that I probably shouldn't answer. I guess this one isn't so secret though.

"We are looking for Sergeant Nielson. Slug and Mitchell were hung several days ago, and we just received word that Nielson might be on this train.

"He is wanted for three murders at Fort Leavenworth and possibly more up this way." He squeezed Ava's arms and kissed her cheek as he added softly, "He's wanted for the murder of your family too."

Ava looked up and caught her breath as a tear pooled in her eye.

"He's dead. One of Badger McCune's mules killed him. I was there."

Major Headrick stared at Ava for a moment. He dropped her arms and wheeled around. He opened a window and shouted at a soldier giving orders nearby.

"Lieutenant Lampkin, I have a woman here who witnessed Sergeant Nielson's death. Take the men back to Fort Leavenworth. I am going to ride with her to document her story."

Lampkin peered at Captain Headrick and the people around him before he pulled his horse around. He raced alongside the train as he shouted orders.

The soldiers quickly dropped off the train. They mounted and brought their horses into formation. One of the men was leading Major Headrick's horse.

Corporal Blake joined Lieutenant Lampkin in front of the long column of soldiers. He frowned.

"That was mighty sudden. Think one of us should stay back and make sure everything is all right?"

Lieutenant Lampkin laughed and pointed at the train. They could barely see their major, but they could see that he had a small woman wrapped tightly in his arms.

"Nope, I think the major has everything under control." Lampkin's blue eyes sparkled, and he waved his arm.

"Give the order to fall in, Corporal Blake. We are goin' to take this ride slow. I think Major Headrick's interrogation is goin' to take a long time." Lieutenant Lampkin's grin became wider and he chuckled.

"Mebbie even the rest of his life."

9 781958 227473